CHRISTMAS STORIES
FROM MANY LANDS

BOOKS BY HERBERT H. WERNECKE
Published by The Westminster Press

Christmas Stories from Many Lands
Christmas Customs Around the World
Christmas Songs and Their Stories

CHRISTMAS
STORIES
from
MANY
LANDS

Edited by
Herbert H. Wernecke

THE WESTMINSTER PRESS
Philadelphia

Contents

Contents

Contents

Contents

Foreword

CHRISTMAS has become more than a Christian festival; but we hope that, basically, it may always be that. People of other faiths and of no religious faith join in the observance of this season of " good will toward men." While we rightly lament the overcommercialization of Christmas that crowds out its original meaning and its present religious significance, we can rejoice and be thankful that its spirit has pervaded the lives of people around the globe, causing non-Christian nations and peoples to adopt many of its forms of observance. Thus they have manifested its irresistible power even to the extent of arranging temporary armistices on battlefields when war has raged in the Christmas season. The Christmas spirit pervades not only the church but also the public school, the market place, and homes that do not profess Christianity or even any other religion.

It is in this broader sense of the observance of Christmas that this volume of Christmas stories has been gathered, and it is the author's hope that the collection secured from many lands may serve to bind together the peoples and the nations of the earth more closely in the bond of love that issues in sympathetic understanding and cordial co-operation.

H. H. W.

Acknowledgments

IN COLLECTING MATERIAL used in this book, every effort has been made to locate the copyright owners. If any errors have crept in, please notify the editor, and proper corrections will be made. Special acknowledgment is made to the following, who have granted permission for reprinting copyrighted material from books and periodicals:

Augsburg Publishing House, for the following material reprinted from *Christmas: An American Annual of Christmas Literature and Art:* "The Keeper of the Stable," by Henry Booth, copyright © 1936; "To Grandfather's House," by Melva Rorem, copyright © 1948; "Marusia's Christmas Eve," by Irene T. Granovsky, copyright © 1953. Used by permission.

E. P. Dutton & Co., Inc., for "A Star for Hansi," by Marguerite Vance. Copyright, 1936, by Marguerite Vance. Reprinted in its entirety by permission of E. P. Dutton & Co., Inc.

Friendship Press, for "Sara, An Arab Refugee," by Gertrude Rinden from *The World Upside Down*, by Margaret Greene; and "The Old Story in a New Land."

Princess Ileana of Romania and Dr. Stefan Issarescu, for "A Christmas Tale," by Queen Marie of Romania.

Acknowledgments

Macrae-Smith Co., for "Christmas in Belgium" and "A Roman Christmas," by Elizabeth Hough Sechrist from *Christmas Everywhere*, edited by Elizabeth Hough Sechrist.

Etta Austin McDonald, for "Karen's and Gerda's Yuletide Joys," by Etta Blaisdell McDonald and Julia Dalrymple from *Gerda in Sweden*.

Marguerita Rudolph, for "Yolka, A Little Fir Tree."

Larry Sternig, for "Of Oranges and Lebkuchen," by Lisl auf der Heide.

The United Christian Missionary Society, Disciples of Christ, Department of World Outreach Education, for "The Congo Wise Man," by Carol Hart Sayre from *Junior World*, copyright © by Bethany Press.

The Viking Press, Inc., for "Dobry's Christmas" from *Dobry*, by Monica Shannon. Copyright © 1934 by Monica Shannon. Reprinted by permission of The Viking Press, Inc. "The Shepherds" and "The Wee Christmas Cabin of Carn-na-ween" from *The Long Christmas*, by Ruth Sawyer. Copyright © 1941 by Ruth Sawyer. Reprinted by permission of The Viking Press, Inc.

A. Watkins, Inc., for "Little Hunchback Zia," by Frances Hodgson Burnett. Copyright © 1916 Frances Hodgson Burnett.

Franklin Watts, Inc., for "Three Young Kings," by George Sumner Albee.

Whiteside, Inc., and William Morrow & Company, Inc., for the following selections from *So Gracious Is the Time*, by Annie B. Kerr: "Grandmother Siranoosh Goes to Church," "Saint Nicholas and Mary Jane," "The Almond in the Pudding," "The Yule Log Travels Far," and "When They Saw the Star."

THE ARCTIC OCEAN

Yolka, A Little Fir Tree

MARGUERITA RUDOLPH

THIS IS A STORY of the farthest north, the Arctic Ocean. It is a true story, and you may read about it in Russian books. What is more, you may see the proof of it in the Leningrad Arctic Museum.

In the year 1937, three well-manned Russian ships went on a polar expedition and were forced to spend the winter in the Arctic Ocean. The ships were frozen into the ice, and the men were not able to sail them back to land. Thick strong heaps of ice surrounded the ships and held them fast. The temperature dipped as low as it could be measured, and everybody aboard the ships knew that it wouldn't warm up for many months, for it was only the end of December. There was complete darkness all around day and night, for in the Arctic the sun doesn't appear in the sky at all during the winter months. But the men were not downhearted. Most of them had sailed in the Arctic before, and they were prepared to endure the winter. Besides, all the scientists were too busy to fear or worry; they continued to make important observations of ice and wind and atmosphere; they attended to their instruments and made complicated calculations. After work there was time for rest and even for fun aboard; there were radio programs, books, and games.

The writer in the crew, Konstantin Badigin, wrote long articles about life in the Arctic. Usually the articles were too

13

long and the radio engineer, Nikolai Bekasov, kept complaining.

"I beg you, Badigin, not to write so much! Remember, I have to relay all you write by radio!" But Badigin kept writing long articles.

By the end of December the men aboard one of the ships, *The Sadko*, began to talk about the holiday preparations going on in people's homes on land.

"I imagine," said Badigin wistfully, "that people at home must be getting Christmas trees and decorating them with bright-colored lights and toys while we are aboard ship, a thousand kilometers from the nearest forest of fir trees."

"That is nothing to worry about," answered Nikolai Bekasov, the radio engineer. "Use your imagination, Badigin. Pretend there is a fresh green fir tree aboard and you won't need to write an article about it."

"Don't make fun of me," said Badigin. "What sort of celebration could we have without a real tree?" Then neither of them said anything more.

The next day a rumor spread aboard that there would be a tree.

"A tree?" questioned Pavel, the ship's cook. "Here, in the icy ocean?" He pushed his cook's hat back and scratched his head thoughtfully. Badigin, the writer, was specially curious.

"How could it have come to the Arctic?" he asked, trying to be practical. "Where could it have grown?"

"I don't know anything about it," answered Bekasov indifferently.

"But, who does know?" asked Yefremov, the captain's assistant. "And do you suppose Grandpa Frost will come around with presents for us too? My, my, what surprises!"

"Yefremov, you greedy pig!" criticized Bekasov, and he shook his head and pointed his finger.

On the eve of the holiday, New Year's Eve, the doors of the ship's wardroom were flung wide open. The wardroom was the finest cabin on the ship and was used for eating and resting and meetings and entertainment. When the sailors came into the wardroom they noticed that the tables were set for a supper with unusual care, a savory odor of cooking was in the air, and in the middle of the room there was — unmistakably, a Christmas tree!

"Yolka!" Badigin shouted in surprise, and everyone stared in astonishment at the gorgeous sight of the green tree. It was covered with hanging sparkles, and little toys and charming frills, and it was lighted brightly with electric lights. The Yolka's branches were laden with glass cotton, light as puffs of snow, and on the tip of the tree was a brilliant star. Just as it should be!

"We have a Yolka!" Yefremov shrieked with delight.

"Yolka!" cried the sailors.

The tree was so beautiful, so bright, so real, that it seemed a miracle. The sailors danced vigorously around it, singing their song of the Yolka that grew in the deep, green forest of Russia:

> "What merriment, what merriment,
> We're here in happy throng.
> We greet you, Yolka, gleefully
> With season's gayest song."

Pavel, the cook, stood by the table with a proud grin, noticing how everyone sniffed and looked expectantly. Badigin had written in his latest article that the cook had worked several days on the preparation of the holiday supper. And what a supper it was! There were plenty of meat and fish dishes, and a platter of baked goodies was placed attractively in the middle of the table. The ship's dogs, Jerry and Icicle, sniffed excitedly all during the meal. The dogs had always had enough to eat, but on that New Year's Eve they were simply stuffed.

After supper, the dogs relaxed in the warm wardroom and sprawled under the table and dozed peacefully. Suddenly both of them jumped, bristled up, and, barking loudly, dashed toward the door. Everyone in the cabin looked instantly toward the door. . . . And there, smiling most genially, was Grandpa Frost himself. He walked slowly into the cabin, swinging heavily from side to side. He had a jolly red nose and a long white beard. He was dressed properly in a long fur coat, and a big fat bag was slung across his shoulders. A real, honest-to-goodness Grandpa Frost such as can be seen in the pictures!

"Look at that!" cried Yefremov, pointing his finger at the large bag.

Grandpa Frost walked over calmly to the little Yolka and said, in a peculiarly familiar voice:

"Please, gentlemen, accept my gifts." He bowed ceremoniously and dug into his bag. Out came, first of all, an enormous pencil, the size of a flute. "This is for you, Konstantin Badigin, so that you can write longer articles for the papers." There was unmistakable sarcasm in the word "longer," and everyone laughed.

Other presents followed. Yefremov, to his great delight, received the biggest package of all. When he untied the ribbon and unwrapped the newspaper, he found a box. Inside the box was another package wrapped in newspaper and tied with ribbon. When he untied and unwrapped that, he found another box. Everyone crowded around to see what was in that box. There was a third smaller package, and inside that a third, smaller box. Then came a fourth and a fifth box! Everyone roared with laughter as Yefremov continued unwrapping one box after another, each one smaller than the one before, of course. Finally, in the tenth box there was the present. It was a very tiny baby doll. Yefremov held it in his big strong hands and passed it around to all his laughing comrades.

Pavel, the cook, received half a dozen pairs of dark glasses, which protect the eyes from the blinding sparkle of snow when the sun shines. They were, of course, useless in the Arctic winter when there was no sun at all!

Fourteen times Grandpa Frost dipped his hand into the bag full of presents. When he put his hand in for the fifteenth time, he announced curiously, "And this is for me!" There was nothing there! Then he pulled off his beard, took off his fur coat, yanked off the red nose that had been pasted onto his face, and became transformed into the radio engineer Nikolai Bekasov.

"So you are Grandpa Frost! Bekasov, you rascal!" shouted Badigin. They shook hands vigorously, in a true Russian fashion, and Badigin bumped into the Yolka. As he touched the tree, somehow it didn't feel like a fir tree. "Look, comrades!" he shouted, inspecting the tree. "Look where our Yolka came from!" Everybody looked and touched the little green Yolka and gasped and laughed merrily at the discovery. For the beautiful Yolka proved to be homemade, not forest grown.

Nikolai Bekasov, with the help of several sailors, had thought up the trick of taking a stick and attaching to it twigs from the deck broom. This make-believe tree was colored and covered and became the homemade Yolka, perfectly fitting for the New Year's celebration in the Arctic.

To this day, the homemade broom-twig Yolka is in the Leningrad Arctic Museum, and all the men who had enjoyed it aboard a ship are celebrating the season with a beautiful Yolka, a lovely green fir tree from the deep forests of Russia.

ARMENIA

(As Reflected in the United States)

Grandmother Siranoosh Goes to Church

ANNIE B. KERR

G RANDMOTHER SIRANOOSH was obviously ill. But of course she wouldn't admit it. Perhaps it was because she had insisted on cleaning every nook and corner of the little apartment, that it might become a fit dwelling place for the Son of God. Perhaps because of the fasting, which she had rigidly observed during this week which preceded the day of his manifestation. Perhaps it was because of the flu germ, which was afflicting so many people just now (only, Grandmother Siranoosh didn't believe in germs). More likely it was a combination of all three.

Her son, Dikran, and her granddaughter, Araxie, had a hard time keeping her in bed on Saturday, the day before the Christmas service in the Armenian Apostolic Church. She was worrying for fear Araxie would use butter instead of oil when she fried the fish for the Christmas Eve supper or would forget that they must have lettuce as well as spinach for that very special meal. She also feared that if she did not show them how fine she felt, by being up and helping with the Christmas preparations, they would keep her home from church tomorrow — a possibility terrible to contemplate. However, when she tried to get up, the effort was so exhausting that she had to acknowledge to herself that bed was a very comfortable place. Araxie promised to do everything her grandmother wished and even agreed to stay in the bedroom all evening and let her grandmother and her father instruct her in the history of the Armenian Church. For Araxie went to the Presbyterian church which was just a few blocks from home. It was only because the Christmas celebration in that church was long over and past that she was free to go to the Apostolic church tomorrow. The Armenian observance should have taken place on the sixth of January, but here in America it was too difficult to spend a weekday in church and so the service was held on the Sunday following.

Her son and granddaughter were very kind to Grandmother Siranoosh. They never forgot how terribly she had suffered in Armenia, and how lonely were her days when they were both away — one at work, the other at school. The church which she loved was a long ride on the subway, an impossible trip for one who could neither speak nor read English. But Dikran was always ready to go with her, for it was his church also, and for days they had looked forward to the wonderful Christmas service, with its beautiful ritual and music and the celebration of the Epiphany at the end.

After the Christmas Eve supper, which Grandmother Siranoosh confessed was as good as if she herself had cooked it, Araxie went to the kitchen to see that everything for tomorrow's feast was as nearly ready as was possible so far ahead. There would be lamb, and *dolma* (grape leaves stuffed with meat and rice, tomatoes and peppers). She had ground the wheat for the *pilav*, and the tomatoes and butter were all ready to cook with it. Pastry and fruit for dessert, and small cups of Turkish coffee. Her grandmother called to her from her bedroom, which opened off the kitchen.

"We can finish after church tomorrow. And we must be sure to bring someone home with us."

"But not when you are sick in bed, Grandmother," remonstrated Araxie, ignoring the implication that Grandmother was going to church.

"A guest is a gift of God," Grandmother reminded her and did not press the point of going to church. But she smiled the little mysterious smile that always meant that she was thinking thoughts which no one else could share.

Then Araxie and her father drew their chairs to the old

woman's bedside and she began the story which Araxie had
heard many times before.

"You do not understand about the greatness of the church,
Araxie, because you were born in America, and America knows
naught of suffering and sorrow. And yet" — she paused a moment, recalling the old proverb, "and yet, 'Until you see trouble you will never know joy.'"

"I think we've seen a good deal of trouble, here in America,
Grandmother."

Grandmother Siranoosh sat up in bed and her old eyes
flashed and her old voice shook. "*What!* You call it trouble because your father had no work for a few years and you must go
without some of the things you would like to have? And you
have food and shelter and peace and safety. Trouble, for the
Armenians, is fear and terror and massacres and loss of home
and husband and children. Ask your father — ask *me!*"

Araxie shrank back and her father pushed the trembling old
woman down on her pillows. "There, there, Mother," he said,
"we agreed never to speak of the past. You must not make
yourself ill. Tell Araxie about Christmas in Armenia."

"Ah, yes — Christmas in Armenia." She closed her eyes and
they waited.

"It is very early in the morning and we are still asleep, for
the night before we have been to Mass and we have gone home
from church and had our Christmas Eve dinner. And while it
is still dark, we hear a voice singing through the streets: 'Christ
is born and manifested today. Congratulations — God has come
down into the world.' And there is a knock on each door in the
village and the choirboys sing: 'Praise be to God, O Christian.
Rise and come to holy church.' And so we rise and congratulate
each other that we are Armenians and ours is the first Christian
national church in all the world. And for hundreds and hundreds of years we have had God's Word and God's Truth to
guide us."

A fit of coughing seized her, and her son again tried to soothe
her and to persuade her to rest.

"You tell her, Dikran. And then I can sleep and be ready for
tomorrow."

And so her father turned to Araxie and went on with the tale.

" I can remember when I was just a little boy, feeling the wonder of that voice wakening me from sleep. We would get out of bed, all shivering, and dress for church. On the road the people were gathering, carrying lanterns and candles. Snow was everywhere, white and glistening, and in the sky the stars were shining, and so we walked to church. And there are lights and music and incense. And we know that Christ is born and we are redeemed from sin and nothing else matters. And then when the service is over, we walk to the banks of the river."

" Yes, the River Arax," said Araxie breathlessly.

" No, to the River Euphrates, which to us is as the River Jordan," corrected her father. " And the priest blesses the waters, and the Epiphany hymns are sung. As we walk home, the daylight is coming and we are filled with the thought of Christ's birth and then his baptism.

" At home we read the Gospels, and keep holiday for many days. The priest comes to bless our home and the men call on the neighbors, and there are other services at church. And so through all her suffering, Armenia is sustained by the church, Araxie, the church founded in the year 301 by Saint Gregory the Illuminator."

Araxie nodded. " Yes, I know, Father. I know more than you think I do. How all the culture and education of the Armenians was centered in their church. I love my people, Father. *You* understand why I like to go to the Presbyterian church. I wish Grandmother could understand too."

" I do understand, Araxie." Grandmother's eyes opened wide and she looked lovingly at her granddaughter. " The American missionaries in Armenia have done a great work. Do I not owe my life to them? Shall I ever forget that they saved and kept me after the last great massacre and sent me to America? Go to their church with the other American-born Armenians. But do not forget the mother church. For the church *is* Armenia. And now I shall sleep."

They put out the light and left her, but she did not sleep. Her efforts to impart to Araxie the greatness and significance of

Armenia always exhausted her. The Armenian Apostolic Church was for Grandmother Siranoosh her very life. And to keep alive in the heart of her granddaughter its spirit and its meaning was her greatest desire. For, as she had said, America knew nothing of suffering, and Armenia had known nothing else. But for Grandmother Siranoosh and for her son, Dikran, the massacres during the World War were the most terrible, for her husband had been killed, her grandsons had died, her daughter had disappeared never to be found again, and she herself had hidden in the mountains until found by the American missionaries. Dikran had fled to America with his young wife, sure that his mother had also been killed. And then the wife died when Araxie was born, and Grandmother Siranoosh had come all the long way to America, to be cared for lovingly and tenderly. She had agreed not to talk of those terrible times. But Araxie must not be allowed to think that her life was hard. She drew her hand from beneath the quilt and felt of the rug which lay on the floor beside her bed. It was the one thing saved from the ruin of her home in Armenia. It had been wrapped around her on the mountains and had kept her from freezing, and she had brought it to America, the most precious thing left to her in all the world — except, of course, her church, her son, and her granddaughter.

She was restless all night. But when in the morning she heard the old familiar words, spoken by her son and granddaughter, "*Shnorhahvor dzenoont,*" "Congratulations, He is manifested today," she sat up in bed and asked Araxie to help her prepare for church.

"Wait till after breakfast, Grandmother." Araxie smoothed her hair and straightened the rumpled bedclothes. Grandmother Siranoosh was willing to wait, for she was very, very tired.

After breakfast they told her she could not go to church. It would not be safe in her condition. They would leave her comfortable in bed, and if she was feeling much better when they returned, perhaps she could come to the table for the Christmas feast. "It's too bad, dear," said Araxie. "I understand just how you feel — how disappointed you are. But we can't let you get real sick, and the subway is so drafty and the church so crowded."

Grandmother Siranoosh did not protest this wise decision of her granddaughter. What use for eighty to dispute the wisdom of eighteen? She only smiled her mysterious little smile. Already she knew what she would do. For just such an emergency as this she had prepared long ago.

Araxie and her father left the house very early. It was a long service and Dikran wished to be there for the first of the three sections and to stay until the end.

When they had gone, Grandmother Siranoosh got carefully out of bed and prepared for her first venture alone in the subway, her first deliberate deceit since she was a little girl and had stolen a plate of pastries from her mother's pantry.

Slowly and painfully she put on the clean clothing which had been waiting for this Christmas morning. When she was fully dressed she sat down to rest, though every moment was precious. She was very tired and a little dizzy. Soon she felt better. Perhaps the excitement of her adventure upheld her. She put on her coat and the little felt hat which Araxie had given her for a New Year's present to wear on this occasion. Then she tied a heavy veil over the hat, nodded pleasantly to the old woman reflected in the mirror, and opened the front door. She made sure once more of the two nickels for carfare and several dimes for church, changed the latch on the door, and crept painfully down the long flights of stairs to the street.

It was not difficult to find the subway, but to be sure of the right train was another matter. However, long ago Grandmother Siranoosh had foreseen this great adventure. She had painstakingly memorized the number of words on the train they took for church and the number of letters in each word. To her delight the very first train bore an inscription which corresponded to the picture in her mind. Then she counted the stations, and got off confidently and bravely at the right stop.

She entered the church and took her place in the crowd at the rear on the opposite side from where she usually sat. The first part of the service was over, but she did not mind missing the reading of the Gospels and the prayers. The High Mass,

the sermon — these she could not miss. For the third part
— the baptism of Christ — she would stay as long as she dared.

She crossed herself and prayed, and the old Christmas chants
swept over her and brought healing to body as well as spirit.
" Light of Lights " —

> " We bless thee, O God of our fathers,
> Joyfully we celebrate thy holy birth,
> Thou Light of Lights, who hast revealed thyself to us,
> And filled the universe with thy light.
> We bless thee, O God of our fathers."

And " Shepherds, Sing with the Angels " and " Morning Star
of the Sun of Righteousness " followed.

For Grandmother Siranoosh, suffering and tragedy and old
age and the weakness of the flesh were swept away. She was conscious only of the chanting choir assuring her that God had
come in the flesh, had been manifested today.

He would forgive her sins and restore to her in his own good
time her husband, her daughter lost these many years, and all
the other members of her family. And however dimmed the
light of the Apostolic Church in Armenia today, it would blaze
forth again at some future time. Sometime Armenia itself
would be delivered. The words of the chant, " Give peace to the
world, thy healing power to the sick, thy Kingdom to the dead,
and liberty to our nation," echoed to the very rafters of the
church, and Grandmother Siranoosh knew that the church
which had been founded in apostolic times would never cease to
be. For had it not kept the faith through all the dark ages of
history, of persecution and massacre — the very heart of Armenia?

She stayed through the singing of the baptismal hymn:

> " O wonderful mystery revealed today,
> Behold the Creator of men hath descended
>   into the Jordan.
> The Jordan is awed, has taken flight,
>   and is rushing away with its waves.
> O river, be not afraid. I, Christ, am thy creator.
> I have come to be baptized and wash away sin
>   in thy waters."

Grandmother Siranoosh was lying in her bed with her eyes shut when her son and her granddaughter returned from church with their guest. But she knew that they were there and she said quietly to Araxie, who was bending over her anxiously:

" I think I shall rest a little longer."

" Grandmother, you are not worse, are you? "

" Not worse — much better."

" Then we were right to keep you in bed."

" Yes, Araxie, quite right. But I am still tired, so I shall rest a little longer." Grandmother Siranoosh smiled her little secret smile and went peacefully to sleep.

AUSTRIA

Of Oranges and Lebkuchen

LISL AUF DER HEIDE

IT WAS CHRISTMAS EVE. Mitzi stood by the open window. The gentle wind billowed the curtains and her flowered nightgown. Through her tears she stared at the tree laden with oranges, the same tree she had joyfully and unbelievingly touched only two weeks ago. Oranges growing in your very front yard, imagine! In a nearby flower bed a camellia bush turned its first pink blooms toward the moon, and a few early narcissus buds nodded on their tall stems. How different, how very different, was this night from the other Christmases she had known!

She closed her eyes tightly and tried to imagine what it would be like in Vienna now.

There would be snow, of course. In the streets it might be slushy and gray, unless the snow was fresh, and then it would be falling. If you stretched out your mittened hand, you could watch the lovely snowflake stars, each designed separately and more exquisitely than its brothers. Icicles would hang on sills and roofs. The paper vendors would be wearing high boots and huge scarves, and their breath would be visible in puffs of steam as they slapped their hands across their chests. Every few blocks the glowing stove of a chestnut vendor would be surrounded. There you could exchange your coin for a paper cone filled with hot roasted chestnuts.

Near the church would be the last of the Christmas trees, but the piney fragrance would drift for blocks. The children would be busy picking up little branches to decorate packages and to stick behind pictures and around mirrors at home. Then, as it grew dark, the streets would empty, and windows would light up. Mitzi and her sister Resi, back from their walk, would be getting dressed, talking eagerly about the gifts they might receive, and lining up the little packages they were giving each other and the family. Anna, the maid, would take time out from her cooking to inspect them, to make sure their hair was combed neatly, their hands were clean, and their shoes shiny. Then they would sit, careful not to get their dresses wrinkled, and wait.

In the next room, the one that had been locked all week because the Christ-child was working in it, they could hear whispering and moving. Of course Mother had to help the Christ-child. Soon now the little bell would ring, and they would be able to go in. In the meantime Aunt Maria and Uncle Karl would arrive. They weren't a real true aunt and uncle, but they were lonely people, and Mother always said no one must be allowed to be lonely on Christmas. They would sit quietly together in the dim room, while the excitement grew.

At last, at the tinkle of the little bell, the doors would fly open, and there would be the tree, glittering and shining with lights, spreading the incomparable aroma of pine, candlewax, and fresh Lebkuchen. Then Mother would sit at the piano, and they would all sing " Silent Night " together, even Anna, who always wept so much she couldn't carry the tune. Then each of the children would say " Merry Christmas, " and they would all hug and kiss each other. After they had opened their gifts and ah'd and oh'd, they would look for the old familiar things — the little manger under the tree, the three-legged cow, the wooden puppet that always hung against the trunk of the tree, the bright red-and-green parakeet Uncle Fritz had sent from America.

The little candles would burn down, one by one, and sometimes the Lebkuchen Santas and stars and rings would have specks of wax on them, but they would still be delicious. Everyone would eat too much, and stay up too late, and love each other a great deal. Even the children would be allowed to wait for the midnight bells. All over the city, church bells would ring, deep booms and higher dingdongs, and together they would melt into a wonderful melody, joyfully announcing the birth of the Christ-child, Christkindl, who had been so good to them all.

That's how it had been last year. That was before the sickness. Resi got it first. Just a cold, Mother had said. But it didn't get better. Everybody was having colds or the flu. Mitzi had it too, but she was soon well again. At first they told her she would be at the orphanage only till Mother and Resi were better, but after a while they told her that she would never see them again. It grew to be summer and fall and at last winter again before they told her that she was going to America. A young couple in California, friends of Uncle Fritz, was adopting her. She would have a mother and daddy too, and she would live where it was never cold, and where oranges grew in people's yards. They had taken X-rays and given her shots, and then they had put a sign on her and put her on a big airplane. The next morning she was in America.

Now she was in California, where flowers bloomed at Christmas time, but where there was no sign of the Christ-child. Perhaps he doesn't know it's Christmas; perhaps he thinks it's still summer, Mitzi thought. But people did think of Christmas here, for there were decorations in the store windows; there were trees in vacant lots, though some of them were pink and some even purple, and there were Santa Clauses on every street, ringing little bells. Only, they were the wrong bells.

Her new mother and daddy were very nice. They tried so hard to talk to her. She had already learned quite a few words, but when they explained to her why she should hang her socks on the mantel, she could not understand, hard as she tried. They pointed to the chimney; they said " Santa Claus "; they seemed very excited and happy and wanted her to be happy too. But all she could see were the slacks her new mother was wearing, and that her hair was in curlers, and she knew they would never receive the Christ-child like that. So that could only mean he wasn't coming. Still, to the last possible moment she kept hoping. Maybe in America he comes after supper, she thought. But after supper she could see they wanted her to go to bed, even though it was earlier than usual.

She had sent back one last, puzzled glance at the mantel from which dangled her little socks, Father Barker's big ones, and Mother Barker's medium-sized ones. It certainly couldn't be to keep them from freezing, for it wasn't cold. Not at all like Vienna, where in December the laundry would often come off the line in the attic as stiff as boards, and where the water was sometimes frozen in the washbasin. But tonight the tall, tile stoves would be warm, and perhaps pine branches would be burning in them just so it would smell like Christmas. There were nice smells here too. Mother Barker had been baking cookies and even allowed Mitzi to help in the lovely, bright kitchen. But they had merely put the crisp, spicy cookies in jars instead of tying strings to them, ready for the tree. Oh, there was a tree, but it had been here for a week, right in the open, covered with strings of light bulbs and shiny glass bubbles, so it wasn't a real Christmas tree.

Mitzi tiptoed back to bed. She couldn't sleep. Mother and Father Barker were still up; she could hear them moving around in the next room, and it was almost midnight. She would wait for midnight. Maybe that was what everyone was waiting for. She watched the luminous hands of the clock move slowly, ever so slowly, toward the top. She had so hoped for a doll — a little doll with clothes and real hair, perhaps even one that walked. She had never before seen dolls such as those on display in every store window here. And not only dolls, but other toys, bicycles, and beautiful clothes. She had gasped when she saw the pink dress with all the ruffles and the little flower at the waist. Surely only a princess would ever wear anything like that. But Mother Barker had walked into the store with her and had asked the saleslady for Mitzi's size and motioned for her to try it on. Mother Barker and the saleslady had smiled and talked fast in English. Then they put the dress back, and she and Mother Barker had left. But of course, Mitzi was not a princess; it was lovely of them to allow her to try on the dress even for a moment.

At last the hands of the clock met. The clock in the tower downtown chimed twelve times; then there was silence. Mitzi strained her ears; she sat up and shook the clock; she ran to the window and leaned out. But all was still.

Mitzi fell across her bed and pulled the pillow around her head to stifle her sobbing. She cried long and hard, and at last fell asleep crosswise against the damp sheet.

It seemed that she had only just closed her eyes when she felt someone touch her. It was Mother Barker, her hair all curly, wearing her best robe, and smiling. Then Father Barker came, smelling of lotion and with his hair combed smooth. They both talked to her, saying "Santa Claus" and lots of other things she couldn't understand, and helped her into her robe and slippers. They watched her as she washed, and brushed her hair, and they seemed almost as eager as she and Resi used to be on Christmas Eve. The thought of it brought a tear, but she knew she must forget now; she must be good and happy and try to please her new parents. It certainly wasn't their fault that the Christ-child didn't come to California.

At last she was ready. They each took one of her hands and led her into the living room. She stopped dead-still. There were her socks, bulging and overflowing with oranges and apples and candy. And under the tree, glimmering with its many-colored lights, lay the pink dress and the doll, and a big, red bicycle near the wall. Mother Barker had tears in her eyes, but Father Barker pretended he didn't. She stared at them and at the gifts for a moment, as they motioned her to them and spoke to her. She forgot then and talked excitedly in German, hugging the doll and holding up the dress, too beautiful to be true. She laughed at the bulgy socks, and munched cookies and nuts and dates. Later her new grandmother came, and the new aunts and uncles, everyone talking, laughing, and loving each other very much. From the radio came the strains of "Silent Night." Mitzi suddenly realized that the words were English, but that didn't matter at all.

BELGIUM

Christmas in Belgium

ELIZABETH HOUGH SECHRIST

PIETER WAS EXCITED. He had some very pleasant news to tell to his friend Jeanne today, and he was so eager to tell it he could scarcely wait another moment. He held his hand up to his eyes and looked far down the street to see if she were coming.

Pieter was a happy-looking little boy with shining blue eyes. Today he was dressed in a bright jacket, wide baggy trousers, black stockings, and wooden shoes, or *kloefen*, as they are called in Belgium. He wore a small black hat on his curly head. He stood outside his home, a tall red-tiled house on a funny little crooked street in Antwerp. Pieter loved his father's house and all the other houses on the street. He thought Antwerp quite the nicest city in the whole world, with its sturdy old houses and beautiful churches, museums and art galleries. Best of all, he loved the Antwerp cathedral, which was not far from his home.

Pieter knew that the cathedral was the largest in all of Belgium. His father had told him that it was five hundred years old. He liked to stand off from the cathedral and look up at its tall and delicately carved spire, four hundred and two feet high! But the part that Pieter loved best of all was the chime of ninety-nine bells. What marvelous bells they were! He had been told that the largest of them required the strength of four men to ring it. Pieter, as he listened to the chimes ringing out

31

over the city to call people to church, often wished that he might help to ring them.

On the walls of the cathedral are some of the world's most famous pictures. When Pieter strolled into the quiet church of a weekday, as he often did, there were two of these pictures that he always gazed at for a long time. And, small as he was, the beauty and sadness of these two paintings made him happy and sad at the same time. They were *The Elevation of the Cross* and *Descent from the Cross*, painted by Rubens. After he had looked at these pictures, he would walk softly along the cool, wide aisles of the great church and ponder over many things. He would stand entranced before the figures of the Christ-child, of the Holy Mother, and of John the Baptist. Of the three figures, the last was the one before which he had gone that very morning and stood a long, long time. And we shall soon see why he was so interested in John the Baptist.

At last Pieter's waiting was rewarded when his friend Jeanne came into sight. Jeanne was the little girl who delivered milk in Pieter's neighborhood. Her father was a dairyman, and Jeanne, with her cart and dogs, delivered the milk to his customers. Her milk cart clattered gaily over the rough stones of the street. Today the dogs which pulled the bright little cart were coming with what seemed to be more than their usual speed. They were running! And the milk cart was lurching from side to side, with Jeanne running and trying to keep up with it. Ah, now Pieter could see the cause of the dogs' excitement. A cat was running before them, and the dogs had forgotten about their mistress, the milk cans which were bouncing up and down in the cart, and everything else. They were good dogs; but after all, what dog will not run in hot pursuit when a cat crosses its path? When the cat dashed up to where Pieter was standing, he made a dive and caught it.

" Why! " — and Pieter held the cat at arm's length for a moment, then burst into laughter. Then he turned around, opened the front door of his home, and thrust the animal inside, saying, " That is my pussy your dogs are chasing, Jeanne."

But at that moment there was a real catastrophe. The dogs had wheeled about so suddenly that the cart turned over, upset-

ting milk cans and straw all over the street. Pieter made haste
to set the cart upright, and he and Jeanne arranged the cans of
milk carefully on their beds of straw. Jeanne scolded her dogs
severely, and they hung their heads in shame.

And now Pieter could keep his good news no longer.

"Jeanne, what do you think? At last the church officials have
decided upon the boy who is to take the part of John the Baptist in the Christmas Procession. And it is I, Jeanne! Just think
of it. Last year I was too small. But this year I have grown so
tall that they have chosen me! "

Pieter's eyes sparkled with joy and excitement as he and
Jeanne talked about the coming Christmas Procession. Jeanne
was very glad for her little friend. As they talked of it, it seemed
to them both that they could not possibly wait for Christmas
Eve to come — three whole weeks off!

But there were only a few days to wait for the day when Saint
Nicholas would come. For in Belgium he comes on December
6, which is the feast day of the good saint, and rides through the
cities and towns on a white pony. It is then, and not on Christmas, that he distributes toys and candy to the children who
have been good. On that day Pieter was walking the boulevards
with his mother when he saw Jeanne. She was dressed in her
best clothes and clasped a doll in her arms. The boulevards and
streets were overflowing with people. Pieter left his mother for
a moment to stop and speak to Jeanne and show her the fine
drum Saint Nicholas had left for him.

"He must have thought I was a good boy," Pieter explained
to Jeanne, "because he took the vegetables which I left for his
pony and filled the basket under the chimney with all kinds of
candy and toys. And one of my gifts was hidden in a cabbage,
Jeanne! What do you think of that? It was not a real cabbage,
but I certainly thought it was until I looked very closely. It was
just an imitation, but it looks so very real it would fool anyone.
And inside, when I opened it, I found a penknife from Saint
Nicholas."

It seemed to Pieter as if the days between December 6 and
Christmas Day would never pass. But they did, of course, and
Christmas Eve found Pieter all ready and waiting impatiently

to join the Procession. As he waited for his mother to finish dressing, he was wondering if Jeanne would be proud of him when she saw him marching in the Procession.

As for Jeanne, she stood anxiously waiting for the Procession to pass, and little chills of anticipation ran down her spine. She had stood a long time because she wanted to be very sure of having an advantageous position on the sidewalk. She wanted to see everything. The bells all over the city were ringing, and loudest of them all were the grand old bells of the cathedral calling the people to Mass. The streets were crowded with people. With such a crowd as this to watch the Procession one wonders if there will be any people left to march!

But, ah, yes! Look at them! Here they come at last. There are hundreds of children in the Procession, from the tiniest ones, who can sing just a wee bit with their soft voices, to the larger girls, who are really young ladies. The young girls are in groups. Some of them are clad in white, some in lilac, others in blue or pink. Each group bears an emblem, and each girl grasps hold of a bright ribbon streamer. These streamers are attached to the central figure of the group — a shrine, a crucifix, or an image of some saint.

The streets are strewn with flowers and bright-colored fragments of paper, making a carpet for the Procession. Groups of children, singing to the music of the bands, and chanting priests, all pass on their way to the great cathedral. After the priests come the chariots, dazzling the eyes of the beholders with their splendid cloths of gold and silver. Each chariot carries some image or crucifix.

And now Jeanne is excited indeed, for here comes little Pieter! The men are baring their heads and all stand in silence as John the Baptist passes! In one hand he carries a cross, and with the other he leads a white lamb by a blue ribbon. Pieter, his face shining bright and smiling, sees Jeanne among the spectators, and his eyes sparkle with joy. " What a happy face has our little John the Baptist! " exclaim some of the people nearby. " Yes, a sweet face; happy, and yet serious too."

Jeanne almost dances because she is so happy over Pieter's success that she can hardly stand still. She is thinking that she will tell him, after it is all over, that he is the finest John the Baptist who has ever marched in the Procession!

And now the Procession nears the end. Last of all comes the Cardinal! He is gorgeous in gold embroidery, rare old lace, and jewels. He walks sedately under a gold and purple baldachin, which is held over him by four men, and is surrounded by acolytes in their white robes and scarlet hats.

They have all marched on; the Procession is over. The people throng in masses to the church.

After the Mass is over, the people will return to their homes. Christmas candles will be lighted for the Christ-child. Families will gather together and sing Christmas hymns. And then, after it is all over, our little " John the Baptist " will be tired enough to go to bed.

His day is over; his part has been played; he has marched in the Grand Procession! And as he closes his eyes, they are filled with visions of the bright lights of the church, and his ears still ring with the sound of the thousands of voices which sang in the cathedral that night:

" *Adeste, fidēlēs, laetī triumphantēs!* "

BULGARIA

Dobry's Christmas

MONICA SHANNON

Dobry is a boy who lives on a farm in Bulgaria. Dobry loves to sculpt, but his mother, Roda, and his grandfather would like him to become a farmer. Neda, who admires Dobry's art work, is a daughter of neighbor Hristu. It is very cold in Bulgaria in winter. So it was the particular twenty-fourth of December in our story.

The intense cold changed to a thaw and the villagers were able to open their snow tunnels into roads before Christmas. Then a quick freeze left the snow dry with a hard icy crust.

Because she was motherless, Neda and her shoemaker father always spent Christmas Eve at Dobry's home. Roda, being maternal enough for two peasant women, had years ago made Neda's coming a habit.

Their supper on Christmas Eve was eaten earlier than usual. At twilight they sat down to the simplest meal imaginable, because the forty-day fast in preparation for the Christmas feast was never broken until after midnight Mass. A suckling pig roasted under hot ashes in the *jamal* [A fireplace. In Bulgaria these are big affairs, made of tiles of various gay colors. The fireplace at Dobry's farm was green, yellow, and blue]; Christmas breads were browning in the kitchen oven; the whole house smelled of temptation — yet supper tonight was only boiled-up fruits the family had harvested and dried. Fruit soup,

36

they called it, and ate this Christmas Eve soup with bread, torn from a special loaf Roda had baked with a very old silver coin in the middle, the Christ-child's gift to the finder — a benediction.

Hristu crumbled up piece after piece of bread, impatient for the good-luck piece, but Dobry, eating a hunk of the bread, bit on the lucky old coin. " I nearly swallowed my good luck and my blessing! " he cried. He polished his luck on his blouse, showed it to Neda as if the world had no other coin like this one, and put the lucky blessing away in his sash.

Dark came long before they had done talking and laughing at table. " Time to go out to the animals," Dobry said, getting up and lighting a candle for each one to take along. For on Christmas Eve, between night and morning, every Bulgarian peasant takes up a lighted candle, goes out, wakes up each family animal, and says to him or her:

" The Child is born and blesses you tonight."

The head of the family takes with him a small earthen pot of incense, holds it under the nose of cow, pig, buffalo, ox, and lets each animal have a sniff. Dobry had often climbed the tallest pine in his mother's forest on Christmas Eve and watched candles all over the village going to and back from the barns and pens. But tonight his mind and spirit were both too absorbed in the dream he had mentioned to Neda — a dream alive in him but not yet sculptured.

After Sari and Pernik, the family pig and chickens, had been awakened and told, Neda left with her father to wake up Peter and the buffaloes, let them know that it was Christmas Eve, stroke them, thank them, and give them their blessing and sniff of incense.

" I'll come and get you for midnight Mass. I'll come early," Dobry told Neda before she left.

And because anticipation breeds impatience, they set off too early for midnight Mass, each carrying a lighted candle.

Their village church topped a hill, and on the way up Dobry stopped climbing and said to Neda: " I like to be outside when the chimes ring, don't you? Bells sound dull, don't mean anything much once you're in the church."

Above them, windows of the big low church lighted up, candle by candle, as altar boys hurried about inside. When all its candles burned, the village church became a symbol of light, a star at the top of a hill. And below Dobry and Neda, the village bobbed with candles, because every peasant was on his way to midnight Mass.

Chimes rang out and Grandfather, Roda, and Hristu climbed the hill and pushed on with the crowd of people roaring out greetings to each other before they stamped into church. Only Dobry and Neda waited outside until the bells stopped ringing.

Everybody stood through the long Byzantine ritual, but not stiffly. To these peasants their church was the hearth of God and they made themselves at home, moved about, nodded, spoke quietly to each other, or called out Christmas greetings with their eyes and their wide smiles.

Husky male voices sang the Christmas canon of Saint John Damascene, greatest poet of the Eastern Church. Without an instrument of any kind, peasants stood at each side of the sanctuary's front and chanted in answer to each other, every man expressing his quickened feelings, his childlike wonder.

And to Dobry it all seemed as old, as mysterious, as the night outside did with its symbols of God. He said no prayers in words, but his mind and his heart seemed to be on fire. Longing to do perfectly what he hoped to do grew into a desire strong enough to shake him and set his blood pounding. The priest, in golden vestments and tall black hat, altar boys, their white banded by Mary's blue, seemed to Dobry like people in a dream, and his own dream seemed real and urgent.

Dobry came home alone in the fresh snowstorm. The night was quiet — a hush of wonder possessed it, and the locust trees were in blossom now with snow. Dobry was the only one to come home covered with snow. His sheepskin cap, coat, boots of sheepskin, had fleece again — all of them completely woolly with snow.

After midnight Mass they broke their forty-day fast lightly. Nothing could be touched until little dried sparrows, soaked and broiled, were eaten. These were sparrows from the wheat fields that had known the growing of wheat and how the earth

and its peasants worked together to produce a loaf of bread.
The birds had been killed weeks before and hung to dry under
the eaves of all village houses in readiness for Christmas Eve.

" Now we eat our sparrows," Grandfather cried.

They all sat under the *jamal's* hood, warmed as much by
excitement as by the fire, because a sparrow eaten on Christmas
Eve is supposed to put music in the soul of a peasant and make
him feel that he has wings.

Grandfather finished his sparrow. " There — I knew it," he
shouted. " The music is coming up in me already! " And he
began to sing before he could get the flute out from his sash.
But when the others sang, Grandfather contented himself with
playing the flute while he thought, " It's better to keep quiet
and feel the spirit moving in me."

Roda and Dobry and Neda and Hristu sang the Byzantine
chants heard everywhere in the village on Christmas Eve and
repeated their favorite Christmas song:

> " The Daystar of the Daystar!
> And we on earth who lay
> In death shade and in darkness
> Have found a world of light,
> For, soothly, of a virgin
> Is born the Lord of Light."

The village rose very late on Christmas morning, a clear
sharp morning with new snow on top of the old. Only Dobry
got up with the tardy winter sun. He went noiselessly, crept
down the rickety outside stairway.

He massed and packed all the snow he could in a corner of
the courtyard, until it piled high above his head, a small mountain of snow, immaculate, glittering with crystals of ice. Standing on a short ladder, he cut out an open stable and with great
slow tenderness made the manger and the Holy Child, Mary
and Joseph.

His Mary, his Joseph and Holy Child were peasants, Joseph
a kindly, humorous peasant resembling Dobry's grandfather.
Mary was Neda, not a beautiful Mary, but a girl strong and
luminous with youth. And the child might have been any

village baby looking for the abundant breasts of his peasant mother.

For the two oxen of Bethlehem, Dobry modeled his own everyday Sari and Pernik. He intended to make the ass next. . . . But instead he found himself modeling Neda's little goat, and wondered at the completed figure — Peter, holy now with simplicity and quietness.

Dobry told himself as an excuse for Peter's being there and nearest to the manger: "The Child would love an animal, small like Peter, scraggly and with new horns. He would love it!"

When it was all done, Dobry looked at it and called it good. It was a dream he alone had dreamed and brought to life. The dream he had carried for months in his mind and heart had been born, and born alive.

Dobry knelt in the snow but prayed for nothing. He had already emptied his mind and heart. And now without a thought to disturb him, he felt completely one with morning and snow — at peace. Without making any noise, he went upstairs again, and tired out from his work and his feeling, threw himself on the bed in all his clothes and slept.

Grandfather went out, expecting to feed the animals and chickens, and forgot even to question how the work had been done. He took off his sheepskin cap and knelt down before the Nativity. Too forgetful of himself for prayers of asking, he knelt there, aware only of the Holy Child who had come to their home.

Roda called to him from the kitchen: "We need water. More water! Will you haul some right away?" But Grandfather never answered her. He felt that he was drinking wine.

Roda came out to hurry him, but instead of speaking, fell on her knees beside him. They stayed there together, in complete silence, forgetful of time. The Child had come to their home. And neither of them ever before had seen a Nativity like this one. The Greek Orthodox Church has paintings but no sculpture. The Child, Mary, Joseph, and the good animals blessed by the Child had been born of their snow, snow from the village sky, the water that would help create their bread and their wine.

Roda reached out her hand to touch Grandfather. She said: " You are right about Dobry. You are right. God made Dobry an artist, and who am I to set my heart against it."

Tidings of the Child spread abroad, and not only every peasant in the village came to visit with the Holy Family, but peasants from villages miles away hitched up their buffaloes to sleds and came to pray in the snow. All day long they crowded in, and on Christmas night the courtyard was lighted by their candles and loud with their songs.

CANADA

The Old Story in a New Land

GRACE W. McGAVRAN

FATHER ANTOINE shivered slightly, even in the shelter of the log hut. He was cold with the bitter chill of the Canadian northland. But he was colder with loneliness and longing for home. Home, to Father Antoine, was the ordered peace of his monastery, back on the sunny slopes of the southern French hills. Home was the sweet ringing of the chapel bell, the solemn songs of the deep-voiced choir, the conversation about high and holy things.

Father Antoine raised homesick eyes to his surroundings. Outside were the huge pine trees hung with gleaming snow; the dead stillness of the forest; the snowshoes piled beside the low door of the nearby hunter's lodge. Around and about moved the tall forms of Indians, members of an unfriendly tribe camped nearby for a few days. Their presence made Father Antoine feel that he was indeed a stranger in a foreign land. For it was Christmas Eve! Christmas Eve, and not a soul but faithful Pierre the fur trapper, his guide and companion, to join with him in the Christmas service tomorrow.

Yes, it was Christmas Eve, and all about him were the people of this unfriendly tribe. He had not expected to find them here, near the lonely hut of Pierre, where he had come to rest for a few days. Yet for the sake of just such people he had left the peace and order of the monastery and braved danger and hardship in an unfriendly, new world. Now was his chance to help.

As the thought took hold of his mind, Father Antoine's heart began to glow once more. Christmas Eve, and here were those who had never heard the most glorious story of all the world. Christmas Eve, and here was he, knowing their language and able, though haltingly, to tell them of that story. The loneliness and cold vanished from the heart of Father Antoine. The wintry woods at which he had shivered not so many minutes ago seemed to sparkle with light and joy.

Father Antoine went hurrying into the woods, filled with the delight of a new idea. He would cut boughs of pine and hemlock and the graceful balsam. He would deck the cabin door and window. Pierre would bring logs and build a mighty fire before the door. They would invite the Indians to come and listen to the Christmas story. As he worked busily to get the greens, Father Antoine began to repeat to himself the story of the angels and the shepherds and the Wise Men. In what words should he tell the story to these Indians?

Father Antoine came to a sudden pause as he worked. He remembered that he did not know the Indian word for " sheep "; nor for " shepherd "; nor for " camels," as far as that went. I must ask Pierre, he thought. Then he laughed aloud in the still forest. There would be no such words in the language of the people of the far north woods. They had never seen any sheep. Nor any shepherds! And most certainly no camels!

Father Antoine went slowly on with his work. His mind was busy planning the story in a way which could be understood by the Indians. " Perhaps it is not needful for these forest folk to hear of the beasts that live in Palestine," he said to himself. " I think not. For it is about the wonder and beauty of that first Christmas night that I want to tell them."

Pierre was delighted when he heard Father Antoine's plan. He carried the invitation to the Indian camp. He helped to deck the lodge with pine and spruce and balsam and dark hemlock. He heaped high a pile of logs near the door. Then, when the hour had come, he carried embers from the fire within and lighted the Christmas logs.

It was a strange sight that firelight showed — the keen, bronzed faces, the lean and hardy forms of chiefs and braves, the slender figures and the deep dark eyes of squaws and maidens. Among them were the children, eager to know the news this pale-faced man might bring.

Father Antoine stood upon the threshold of the lodge. He raised his hand. Then in words that sometimes faltered, but with voice strong and clear, he told the Christmas story. And in these words he spoke it.

" It was a night like this," said Father Antoine. " The woods were dark and full of snow. The moon shone bright upon the hills and valleys. Through the woods, traveling to join a gathering of their tribes, there came a man and woman, worn with cold, weary of the trail.

" Night had fallen before they reached the camp. The place was already full. There was no room for them within the wig-wams of their friends. No room in any lodge! But she, the squaw, had bitter need of shelter. So at length a place was found, beneath the spreading branches of a mighty pine. There had been heaped the poles on which the wigwam coverings were dragged in travel. There, a sort of shelter was devised where she might rest."

The Indian folk leaned forward to hear better. They knew well how weary one could be from winter travel.

Father Antoine went on. " 'Twas on that very night, within that shelter, that her child was born. There was no bed in which to lay the babe. They placed him on a deerskin, soft as moss, laid in a cradle of soft evergreen. Her brave kept a fire blazing in the open place between the trees. He dared not have the flaming logs beneath the pine tree. But he carried hot coals so as to bring their warmth to the mother and to the child."

Father Antoine paused. This next part of the story was not easy to make clear to those who listened.

" Out on the forest trails," he said, " the hunters of the tribe followed the deer in search of food for their people. When the hunt was over and they had started home, their feet came to a sudden stop upon the trail. They listened. From somewhere there came sounds such as they had never in their lives heard before. It was the music of sweet voices singing. Sweeter than the voice of wind among the treetops; fairer than the sound of rain upon parched forest; softer than the sound of waves lapping upon the lake shore, came the music. Suddenly, before them on the trail, in garments whiter than the snow itself, with great white wings that reached as high as the tallest pine tree, stood a messenger with arms outstretched. The hunters feared not man nor beast, but now they were filled with fearsome wonder. As they stood in awe, the messenger spoke and said: ' In a forest shelter near, a child is just now born. That child is sent by the Great Spirit, for your people's good. Beneath a pine tree, cradled in a deerskin, you will find him.'

" His message given, with quivering wings the messenger floated out of sight. Suddenly all the sky was filled with brightness. Praise to the Great Spirit filled the air."

Father Antoine's very voice was full of wonder as he pictured the scene. He went on with the story. " When the song was finished, and the forest once again lay silent, the hunters hurried to their camp. Beneath the ancient tree they found the child, as the messenger had said, all wrapped in deerskin. Such a tiny babe! So deep and cold the snow! The youngest hunter stripped away the wolfskin he was wearing and wrapped it around the child."

Listening carefully to the story, the squaws nodded their heads. They knew how warm a wolfskin was. The baby in the story would lie snug that night, they knew.

Father Antoine continued. " In those days, three chiefs appeared, striding along the forest trails as if in search of something. They were unarmed and carried gifts. The hunters of the tribe met them along the trails and took them before their leader. All the braves of the tribe gathered to hear what strange errand brought them here.

" The strangers had a curious tale to tell. ' Listen to how the voice of the Great Spirit came to us, in our distant hunting fields,' they said. ' It spoke to us from a glorious star whose light outshone the moon. It told us to seek a child newborn, who later would be the mightiest chief the world will ever know! '

" There were many little Indian babies in the winter camp.

How could the strangers know which one was the child they had come to see? They waited for their star. When darkness fell, the waning moon had not yet risen to give light. But a great star's brightness shone in the sky. It seemed to move, then came to quiet rest above the topmost branches of the tree beneath which lay the newborn child.

" Softly through the snow the strangers strode. They came beneath the sheltering branches of the ancient tree. They looked and saw the child. One by one, in silence, each brought out his gift and laid it before the cradleboard on which the child was bound. Rich pelts of beaver were the gift of one. The second brought long strings of wampum. But the third laid by the cradleboard an eagle feather.

" So," said Father Antoine, " was full welcome given to the Son of the Great Spirit who should save his people and the people of the world. When that child became a man, he taught his people of the Great Spirit and how to live in his ways. These ways I have come to teach to you that you also may know."

Father Antoine paused as he finished his story. Then he lifted high his arms above the listening folk. " Great Spirit, Father, God," he prayed, " be here, within this forest and among these folk. Enter their hearts that they may then come to know thy love which sent thy Son to us to teach us of thee."

When the Indians had gone, old Pierre smiled. " Father, I had forgotten it could be Christmas in such a wilderness. But as you talked I felt the same springing joy I used to know at home."

" Christmas is in the heart, Pierre," said Father Antoine. " And I pray that the good God may someday have the love of these wild children of the forest. May their hearts someday be full of Christmas love and of the love of God."

The embers of the fire cooled and blackened. Within the close-barred lodge, Father Antoine and old Pierre wrapped themselves in their skins of wolf and otter and lay down to sleep. Their loneliness was gone. They were happy in the memory of the Christmas story spread.

CONGO

The Congo Wise Man

Carol Hart Sayre

Kasuka flopped down exhausted under a palm tree for a few moments. After trudging all day under the fierce Congo sun, he had reached his destination at last — the mission school. Eagerly he looked around. That long, low building with flowers in front and a red roof must be the home of Bwana Evans, the missionary.

He went over to it and stood timidly outside the screened-in porch. He coughed once, twice, to announce his arrival. He shifted his small bundle of clothing to his other hand.

A step sounded on the porch, and Bwana Evans stood before him, his friendly smile reassuring the tired boy. "*Wako, wako,*" the missionary greeted him, clapping his hands in native fashion.

Wako must be a word from the Kiluba dialect. Kasuka was from the Chokwe tribe, but he knew a little of the trade language, Swahili. He would try that.

"Bwana, *hayambo,*" he returned the missionary's greeting. "I have come to enter school."

"The primary school?" asked Mr. Evans, noticing the boy's small size.

Kasuka drew himself up proudly. "*Hapana* — No, Bwana," he replied emphatically. "I finished primary school in my native village — five years of it. I am now twelve years old. I wish to enter the Institute."

"Good," said Bwana Evans. "We will let you try. Come. Our house boy will show you to the dormitory."

The dormitory proved to be a squat building of sun-dried brick with a grass roof. In a small room at one end Kasuka met his new roommate, Masitak, who was about the same age as the newcomer but almost a head taller.

"Fifty years ago, a Chokwe like you who came anywhere near a member of our Lunda tribe would have been killed," he remarked cheerfully. "Lucky for us both that we're Christians." Then, pointing to a corner of the room, he added, "Put your sleeping mat down there."

Other boys drifted in and out. Three or four different tribes were represented, but the fact that Kasuka was the only Chokwe seemed to make no difference.

One thing bothered Kasuka, though — his lack of height. Back home no one had thought anything about it. Most of his friends had been small too. But here, everyone was larger. He saw one of the boys nudge his neighbor, whispering, "*Muloko* — Shorty."

Then suddenly everyone disappeared, and Masitak informed him: "It's suppertime. Come on!"

His roommate led him to the hut of one of the married students, where a pleasant-faced wife was serving the steaming cassava mush. My, how good it tasted with onion-flavored meat soup! Dessert was large yellow bananas — all they could eat.

After they had chatted around the campfire a little while, Masitak suggested bed. "School starts tomorrow morning," he explained, "and that tom-tom will be beating before we know it."

Next morning Kasuka went to chapel, which was held in the large central building that served as both church and school. Breakfast followed — cold cassava mush left from the night before.

The tom-tom beat again. School was about to start. "I'll race you," dared Kasuka. For a few moments his flying feet kept up with the larger boy, but Masitak soon pulled away and beat him. As they panted into the building, his roommate said, "You are a good runner — for a *Muloko* — Shorty."

Muloko again. Why did everyone call him that? He might be small, but he'd soon show them that he had as many brains as anyone else. He'd show them.

Mangala, the geography teacher, gave him a seat in the front row. " Since this is the first day of school," he announced to the class, " we'll have a little review to see how much you remember. Let's name the capitals of some of the countries. We'll start with our own Belgian Congo."

" Léopoldville," flashed back the first boy.

The next one was England. After a moment's hesitation a boy answered, " London."

" France." It was Kasuka's turn. He knew that " Paris " was the answer, but to say it was another matter. Whenever he became nervous, he stuttered.

The teacher smiled encouragingly. " Do you know the capital of France? "

Kasuka nodded. " Puh-puh-puh," he began, then stopped. The word just wouldn't come out.

A snicker ran around the class. " He sounds like Bwana's motorcycle," came a whisper behind him. That made the boys laugh outright.

Mangala said: " Kasuka knows the answer. But we'll skip him this time and go on to the next boy."

Poyo, the oversized boy next to Kasuka, smirked and quickly answered, " Paris." And so they went on around the class.

When the alarm clock jangled at the end of the period Mangala put his hand on Kasuka's shoulder. " Just take your time, and try not to get excited," he advised kindly.

" *Wa-wa-wa-wafwako*, thank you, I'll try," came the hesitating reply.

The next class, arithmetic, made him feel a little better. The teacher sent them to the blackboard to do problems, and Kasuka was the first one through. His answer was correct too. The teacher's word of praise seemed to add fully an inch to his height.

But he fell down again in music. Back home, everyone sang the melody; they had never tried singing in parts. But here the boys were divided into first and second tenor, and first and second bass. After a look at his small size, Mamma Harris, the teacher, assigned him to first tenor. But to the great disgust of the other boys, Kasuka's voice kept wandering from the tune.

"Let's try second tenor," suggested the teacher. But then the basses kept getting him mixed up.

When Mamma Harris noticed the angry looks the other boys were giving him, she spoke up again. "Perhaps you'd better just listen this time."

For the rest of the class period, Kasuka huddled in the corner, embarrassed and miserable. His black mood persisted through the other classes. Several times when he was called on, he shook his head, though he knew the answers perfectly well.

Walking back to the dormitory after school, he summed up the day. The fellows had accepted him in spite of his being from another tribe. But they called him Shorty. And they almost rolled in the aisles when he stuttered and tried to sing. What a beginning!

The weeks that followed brought no improvement in Kasuka's standing among the other boys. He studied desperately hard. When the first report cards came out, his name ranked highest in the class, but even that didn't make him feel any better. The boys still called him Shorty and teased him unmercifully about his stuttering.

His singing hadn't improved much, either. Mamma Harris had worked with him over at the portable organ, but he still wandered dismally from the tune. He was that most unusual person, an African who couldn't sing.

Head in hands, he was gloomily pondering his unhappy fate one evening after supper. What could he do to win the respect of the other boys? Or at least to make them stop laughing at him and accept him as one of the crowd?

At this moment, his roommate, Masitak, came in and said, "*Hayambo, Muloko* — Shorty."

"*Hayambo sana*, Masitak," Kasuka returned glumly.

Masitak gave his roommate a slap on the back. "What's the matter? You look as though a witch doctor had cast a spell on you."

The joking remark gave Kasuka an idea. The witch doctor

— why not? That was the solution. He would consult the witch doctor!

The boy stared at Masitak a moment before replying. He must not let him suspect anything. " I've got a headache," he said slowly.

" Too bad," returned Masitak. " Why don't you come out for a ball game? You can be scorekeeper!"

Scorekeeper indeed! Kasuka shook his head. " Maybe later. I think I'll take a walk now."

Before he returned, he had mapped out a plan of action. The next day was Saturday. He would go to see Jimba the witch doctor, who lived in a village only five miles away. Of course, Christians were not supposed to consult witch doctors. But this was a desperate situation, and he must try a desperate remedy.

The next morning Kasuka walked to the village of Jimba the witch doctor. It was an untidy collection of dirty mud huts, each fronted by one or more tiny grass shells — spirit houses. In front of one of the larger shacks a tall man was standing with his back to Kasuka. Hoping for further directions, the boy greeted him. " *Hayambo.*"

The man spun around. " *Hayambo sana,*" he replied after a moment's hesitation. " What do you want? "

" I — I am looking for Jimba the witch doctor."

" I am Jimba the witch doctor."

" M-my name is Kasuka," the boy faltered after a moment. " I need your help."

" What! You a Christian from the mission seek help from a witch doctor? Why? "

" Because I am in great trouble," Kasuka answered.

" I do not help people from the mission," snapped Jimba.

" But, Great One, I beg you — " Kasuka drew from inside his shirt the precious hoard of francs that he had been saving for new clothes. Jimba's eyes gleamed greedily. " Maybe I can do something for you after all," he said.

After he had heard the boy's story, the witch doctor said craftily: " I can give you a powerful charm. But you must pay me first."

Kasuka poured out the money. There were ninety-eight francs. "H'm-m," grunted Jimba, "not much, but it will have to do. Now I will prepare the charm."

He prepared a slimy mess from banana tree pith, a little palm oil, and pemba powder. He poured a little into a goat's horn and handed it to Kasuka. "This will make you seem taller in the eyes of your friends," he told the boy. "Rub a little into your hair each night. And to cure the stuttering and bad singing, I will give you this charm." He drew out an anklet of curiously twisted vines. "Wear this on your left leg under your sock. Let no one see it."

"Thank you, Great One, thank you," Kasuka beamed. Now all his troubles would soon be over.

He arrived home safely. That night as soon as Masitak was asleep, Kasuka got up and rubbed some of the "medicine" on his hair. The anklet he slipped on his ankle.

He awoke before his roommate the next morning and hastily pulled on his socks and sneakers. As he was donning his shorts, Masitak sat up and sniffed.

"Whew! What a stink! I wonder if a dog or chicken strayed in here during the night."

With a start, Kasuka realized that it was his hair that was giving off the disgusting odor. He went outside and doused his head with water.

Still half asleep, Masitak appeared in the doorway. "Don't smell it now," he announced. "Maybe I was mistaken."

Well, although the first "medicine" had failed, Kasuka still had the magic anklet to cure his stuttering and singing. In geography class that morning he waved his hand frantically in answer to a question.

"Do you want to name the countries of Africa?" asked the teacher.

Kasuka nodded and sprang to his feet. "Liberia, Nigeria, Egypt, Ethiopia," he rattled off. This was easy. He'd show them. Let's see, what was next? Why, Angola, and his own Belgian Congo, of course. Then he heard a whisper behind him, "Muloko is going to imitate Bwana's-motorcycle next."

That did it. "Angola," he began bravely. "B-b-b — " He

could get no farther but slumped into his seat, his fists clenched, his spirit filled with bitterness.

One more chance remained. He would try the chorus. He marched up to Mamma Harris. " May I try second tenor once more? " he begged.

" If you like," she smiled at him. " Sit down there in the front row and listen to the rest a few minutes before you try your part."

The music today was a Negro spiritual with terrific swing. Kasuka hummed along with the rest until they came to the chorus. Then he opened his mouth and let loose a blast that was 'way off tune.

The boys on all sides stopped singing and plugged their ears with their fingers. " Muloko sings like a hyena," hooted Poyo.

" Never mind, Kasuka," Mamma Harris started to say. But the boy had had enough. Jumping up, he raced from the room and back to the dormitory. He was tearing his charm to pieces when steps sounded outside, and someone entered the room. It was Bwana Evans.

" I saw you racing home in the middle of school, and I came to see if you were sick."

Kasuka shook his head.

" Won't you tell me what's the trouble? "

After considerable urging, Kasuka poured out the whole story, even his visit to the witch doctor.

" I think I understand," said the missionary at last. " You did wrong in visiting the witch doctor, but you were desperate. Things aren't so bad as they look, though. Let's talk about your size first."

" *Muloko* — Shorty — that's what they call me. Everyone calls me *Muloko*," blurted out Kasuka.

" I know, I know," nodded the man. " But what of it? Many great men have been ' shorties.' Smallness of size is no handicap unless you let it be one," concluded Bwana Evans. " Now about your stuttering. You don't stutter very much, do you? "

" Only when I'm n-nervous."

" You can overcome that if you try. You speak too fast. Try talking very slowly whenever you recite in class."

Kasuka looked a little more hopeful. " I'll try."

" About the singing," Bwana went on, " just keep practicing, that's all, but better do it by yourself or with Masitak. He'll help you, I'm sure."

" All right, Bwana."

" Will you do me a favor? " asked the man.

Imagine Bwana Evans asking a favor of him! The boy's self-confidence began to return. " If I can, Bwana."

" I would like to see a Christmas play presented this year that is related in some way to Africa or the Congo. Maybe you can get an idea and write it out for me. I hear you do very well in written work."

Kasuka's eyes shone. " I'll try, Bwana," he said.

That evening he finished his homework quickly. He had an idea that might work — making a play from a story called " The Other Wise Man," which he had heard in chapel the other day. He rushed to Bwana Evans' home to tell him.

" The very thing," approved the missionary. " Now you work out the details."

Never had Kasuka worked so hard. His interest in the new project made him overlook the snubs and nicknames. Now he just grinned back and answered, " *Hayambo.*" His nervousness was disappearing fast too. By speaking very slowly, he was gradually overcoming the stutter. As for singing, although Masitak practiced with him faithfully every day, so far there was no marked improvement. The matter seemed to have lost its importance, however.

In time, the play was finished and approved by Bwana Evans. The missionary called together the actors for the first rehearsal.

The missionary explained the play to the group. " Now," he announced, " I want to introduce to you our director and narrator — Kasuka."

The boy seemed to have gained a full inch in height as he stood before the actors. They looked up to him with new respect as he put them through the first rehearsal.

Christmas came, the big day of the play. The church overflowed with students, wives, children, and even nursing babies. A neighboring chief arrived and took his place of honor in the

front row. Then a small figure walked to the center of the
stage. Kasuka raised his hand for silence and his play, "The
Congo Wise Man," was on.

In a slow but unhesitating voice, Kasuka explained that the
first scene would take place in the village of a Congo king,
Chief Pande. Already from the side entrance came the carriers' song: "We follow thee, we will follow thee, Mulopwe
Pande. With loving hearts, with loving hearts, we will follow
thee."

Behind them swept the chief, one of the older students,
wearing a gilt paper crown. Around his neck swung three
strings of colored wooden beads. The procession climbed the
platform, and the chief seated himself on his throne. A tired
messenger burst into his presence. Bowing low, he clapped his
hands and spoke.

"Great One," he announced, "the Wise Men of the East
invite you to travel with them to find the king who will be
born soon, as is shown by a great new star in the sky."

"*Biyampe* — good," replied the chief. "Tell them I will
join them as soon as I have found suitable gifts for the new
king."

"Take an elephant's tusk," suggested one adviser. "With
ivory you can wish him the strength of the elephant."

"Take a lion's skin," said a second adviser. "It would wish
him the courage of the king of beasts."

The third adviser scratched his head and counseled: "Take
a diamond. It would be easy to carry and would wish him
beauty and wealth."

The chief was well pleased with their advice. Striking the
floor with his spear to show that he was giving a command,
he said: "Let such gifts be found. Prepare for a long journey."
All the people clapped their hands loudly as a sign of obedience
and moved off the platform.

Then Kasuka announced that the next scene would show
Chief Pande on his way to meet the three Wise Men.

A long line of carriers marched across the platform, singing
their song and keeping time with rattles. One carried the ivory,
the second the lion's skin, and a third the diamond. The others

were loaded with food. At the end of the line rode the chief in his chair, with four soldiers following.

All at once the chief raised his hand to halt the procession.

" Listen," he commanded. " I think I hear a man groaning."

Everybody listened, and, sure enough, groans were heard. One adviser warned: " It may be a trap. Robbers may be planning to seize our food and gifts. It's getting late. We should hurry on."

" Are my soldiers afraid of robbers? Go and see what the moaning means." At a sign from the chief, the four soldiers darted away and came back carrying a man who had been beaten by robbers.

Pande looked at the man with kindness and ordered the people to be called from a nearby village. When the villagers arrived and saw the wounded man, they refused to care for him.

" He is a stranger. He is not one of us," they objected.

" Someday you may need help from strangers," the chief scolded. " You should nurse him out of kindness! "

" We will not care for him," declared the villagers.

" Will you look after him until he is strong if I pay you with this elephant tusk? " asked the chief.

" To that we agree, O Chief," the villagers said all together.

The ivory that was intended for the great king was handed to the villagers. Some villagers helped the sick man away while others lifted the tusk which would bring them much wealth, and took it toward their village. The chief gave a signal, and he and his carriers moved forward on their journey.

Next Kasuka explained that the chief, who now had only two presents left, failed to reach the meeting place in time. So he sent his carriers and soldiers back home and went on alone.

Meanwhile the three Wise Men had departed, leaving a message for him to follow them to Bethlehem. The third scene showed their arrival there.

Bathrobes, sashes, and bits of old curtains made the costumes of the boys who took the parts, but the boys had the dignity of real Wise Men. Each one sang a verse of " We Three Kings of Orient Are " as he went forward to lay his gift before the baby

Jesus. Then all eyes fastened on Mary and Joseph as they sang a lullaby in Kiluba, " *Lala Jesu* " — " Sleep, My Jesus."

At the end of this scene it was Kasuka's turn to explain that Mary and Joseph, having been warned of danger, fled into Egypt. When the Congo Wise Man arrived in Bethlehem a short time later, they had already left.

As the weary Pande walked along the street, he heard terrible sounds of crying. He said to one weeping woman: " Excuse my question, but I'm a stranger here. Will you tell me why the people are crying? "

" King Herod's soldiers are seeking our babies," she sobbed. " We are afraid and can't help crying. Any minute they may come to our street, and nobody is able to help us."

" Perhaps I could," Pande offered. " I am a chief — a person of high authority. I would be glad to speak to King Herod for you."

" Thank you, sir, but it's too late. My baby is in this house." She pointed down the street and gave a scream. " Here come the soldiers now! "

" Go inside quickly, and be sure the little one makes no cry," he ordered her. " Trust me to take care of them."

A sergeant and four soldiers marched up to the chief in the doorway and gruffly said, " Stand aside! "

Pande put his hands on his hips and filled the whole doorway. " Who tells the Congo chief to stand aside? " he asked angrily.

Very much surprised, the sergeant said: " I am acting in the name of King Herod. I must search this and every house for babies. Now please stand aside." He sounded somewhat respectful.

The chief did not budge but shouted one of his fierce orders. " In the name of the Congo chief, leave this house alone! " All the time he kept looking straight into the sergeant's eyes.

The sergeant felt uncomfortable but was afraid not to obey King Herod, so he said, " Wait here until I ask my captain what to do."

Glaring at the sergeant, Pande took from his shoulders the lion's skin he was wearing and placed it across the soldier's chest. "Suppose I should give you this beautiful skin, would the sergeant find enough courage to obey the Congo chief and go on his way?"

Delighted at the gift, the sergeant saluted smartly and called to his soldiers: "Consider this house searched. Move on."

And now the Congo chief had only one gift left for the Christ-child.

Kasuka then announced that thirty-three years had passed before the final scene in Jerusalem, and that all this time the Congo Wise Man had been searching for Jesus. The last scene showed the Congo chief, looking old and tired, seated beside a road. He stared at the ground without moving, until a voice screamed, "Chief, save me!"

He looked up to see two men approaching, dragging between them a struggling girl. He saw at once that she was from the Congo, a girl of his own tribe, now a slave.

"Release that girl!" he called, trying to sound as fierce and commanding as he had in earlier years.

"Shut up, old man!" replied one of the men rudely. "We bought her legally. She is ours."

"Will you also sell her legally?"

"Certainly," answered the rude one. "Have you money to buy her?"

"No money, but such a diamond as you never saw. Trade me the girl's freedom for the jewel."

The men looked at the diamond carefully and saw that it was worth a great deal.

"It's a bargain," they declared. "Take the girl!" Off they went, laughing at their good luck.

The chief sank down on the ground again, worn out with disappointment. The girl sat beside him. After a silence she shook his arm and asked, "Where are we going?"

"I don't know," he replied in a tired voice. "I've been everywhere looking for the great king, but I have never found him. I carried three lovely gifts for him, but now I have lost them all."

"If you were looking for the king called Jesus, I know about him."

Turning to her, he said in an eager voice, "Tell me where the king is now."

Sadly she told him in a soft voice: "This morning they put him to death on Calvary. No friend nor disciple went with him — only soldiers and enemies."

"If only I had known!" groaned the chief. "If I still had had my gifts, perhaps I could have saved him. Now it's too late — everything is lost. I have failed! I dare not go home disgraced. I will die here. And may it be soon."

The old man's last words sounded without hope. He was startled when a voice called him by name.

"Pande! Pande!"

"I see nobody, but a voice calls my name. Do you hear anything, my daughter?" asked the chief anxiously.

"I hear, my Chief. I think I know the voice. I have heard it before. Answer him quickly."

"Speak, friend," said the chief, looking upward with wonder. "I am the Congo chief, Pande."

The comforting voice seemed close beside him as it said: "Do not think your gifts are lost. Do not believe that your search has failed. 'As you did it to one of the least of these my brethren, you did it to me.'"

Comforted by these words, the chief took the girl's hand in his, and together they walked away with a light step. The play was over.

Outside, Kasuka nearly bumped into Bwana Evans. "Kasuka, that was wonderful!" the missionary exclaimed, thumping him on the back.

But the real measure of Kasuka's success came the next morning on the way to chapel when he ran into Poyo, the boy who had made so much fun of him. Kasuka braced himself, expecting to hear the familiar nickname *Muloko*.

Instead, Poyo drew back and let Kasuka enter the doorway first. There was real respect and friendship in his tone as he greeted the smaller boy, "Hullo."

CUBA

Three Young Kings

GEORGE SUMNER ALBEE

THE TOWN OF CÁRDENAS, a hundred miles to the east of
Havana on the north coast of Cuba, is an old dog — a
small, taffy-colored dog that is learning new tricks. Three times
a week, nowadays, a ferry from Key West brings Cárdenas a
boatload of American tourists, and these Americans, all of
whom have such white faces that they appear to have been
sick, seem strange and wondrous to the people of the town.
Small boys follow them on the sidewalks and, when they speak,
race around in front in order to watch their lips form the mysterious, incomprehensible foreign words.

As for the small girls, they clap their hands over their mouths
and giggle, for the American women often wear hats, and, as
everybody knows, a hat is a garment worn solely by men. But
the little girls' mothers shriek at them and snatch them indoors, for the Americans are bringing money into Cárdenas and
so they must be treated with the courtesy money deserves.

But this is the story of something that took place in Cárdenas in the days before there were tourists or a ferry. At that
time the young men sat all day on the iron rocking chairs in the
park under the royal palms, talking excitedly about the day
when they would go to work and make vast fortunes and buy
fast automobiles. The shopkeepers opened at ten in the morning, strolled home at noon for heavy dinners of rice and black
beans, took two-hour siestas and returned to their stores to

play dominoes until suppertime, setting their prices sky-high so that would-be customers would not interrupt them. The women mopped their white tile floors, cooked, gossiped and, at dusk, locked themselves into the houses behind their heavy hardwood doors. And the children, when they had fathers who could pay the tuition, went to school. The boys, in white shirts and neckties of the soft blue that is the Virgin's own color, attended the Escuela Pia. The girls, in blue pinafores with white stripes around the hems of the skirts, went to the Escuela de las Madres Escolapias.

Which brings us to three boys of the Escuela Pia: Eduardo, Ramoncito, and Lazaro.

Eduardo was sixteen, while Ramoncito and Lazaro were a few months younger. They were the oldest boys at the *colegio*, and the biggest. In fact, Eduardo amounted to a giant in Cuba, where the horses are the size of large dogs and the dogs are not much larger than rabbits; his nickname was Elephant. He had a flat, snub-nosed face and a cubical skull on which his hair looked like a coat of glossy black lacquer because he soaked it daily in scented brilliantine. Ramoncito was finely made, with a headful of tight little curls and eyelashes half an inch long over eyes the color of clear green sea water. Lazaro was the shortest of the three, but that did not keep him from being the heaviest. He was so fat that he exploded his clothes two and three times a day, popping shirt buttons and the seams of his knickerbockers or the buckles that fastened them at his plump knock-knees. Lazaro ate three huge meals a day, treated himself to custard éclairs on the way to school and fresh coconut macaroons on the way home, and devoted the recess periods to eating candy. Ramoncito's nickname was Monkey. Lazaro's was Macaroon.

The fact that they happened to be the three oldest students laid quite a few responsibilities on Eduardo, Ramoncito, and Lazaro. When the school's forty-seven boys scrambled into the bus for the annual picnic at St. Michael of the Baths it was Eduardo, Ramoncito, and Lazaro who served as monitors — umpiring ball games, arbitrating quarrels, seeing to it that appearances and decorum were maintained in general. And at Christmas time, because they were the oldest, it was their duty to play the parts of the Three Kings of Orient.

Jesus' birthday in Cuba is a day to go to church, not a day for gifts. Gifts are distributed later, on the sixth of January, not by Santa Claus but by the Three Kings who carried gifts to the newborn Christ-child in the manger at Bethlehem. On the second of January, therefore, Father Miguel called Eduardo, Ramoncito, and Lazaro into his office.

"Seat yourselves," he directed them.

Father Miguel, who was eighty-two, was so frail that his white linen cassock appeared more often than not to be unoccupied. There was very little of him still in residence on earth. He had a small, poetically modeled head and a voice, and that was about all. His voice, after all the years away from home, still had the lisp of his native Asturian mountains, and it too was fragile — a faint, musical buzz, like that made by a small but energetic fly in the schoolroom on a hot afternoon.

"Children," he said, for he was so aged that he could no longer perceive the difference between sixteen and six, "I have done this many times, but it is new to you, so I must explain the procedure of the Three Kings. All the gifts your schoolmates will receive from their families and friends are upstairs in the janitor's room. The gifts for the girls are here as well; Mother Superior brought them over to me from Madres Escolapias. I want you here two hours before dusk on Day Five to load the mules, saddle the horses, and disguise yourselves in your robes and turbans. The robes will fit; they always do. Do you ride well?"

"Yes, Father," murmured the boys. All Cuban boys ride well, using neither saddle nor bridle but only a length of rope looped at one end around the horse's muzzle.

"*Bueno*; you will be handsomely mounted. Don Alfredo de la Torre is sending me three cream-colored mares from his farm, with silver-mounted Mexican saddles and packsaddles for the mules. You will set out at dusk. It will take you three hours or so to deliver the presents; then you will return here and hand back the animals to Don Alfredo's foreman and hang away your robes. Understood?"

"Understood, Father," replied Eduardo when neither Ramoncito nor Lazaro spoke. He did not ask for leadership. It annoyed him, actually. But it was always thrust on him.

"Now go along to your homes," concluded the old priest, "and do not reveal to anyone that you are the Three Kings. We would not wish to sadden the hearts of any of the little ones."

During the next couple of days, as they discussed the roles they were to play, Ramoncito grew somewhat bitter about the "little ones." "What do we care if they find out the Kings aren't real?" he exclaimed resentfully. "We found out."

"That's no way to talk," replied Eduardo brusquely in his deep voice. "Before we knew the Kings did not exist, we thought they were marvels. We nearly went out of our heads waiting for them to come to our houses and bang the knockers. True?"

Fat little Lazaro offered no opinion one way or the other. Instead, he made a street map and planned the route they would take, so that they would be able to visit the houses on their list with the least possible amount of backtracking. Lazaro was efficient. Either that or he was lazy. Or it may be that efficiency and laziness are merely different names for the same thing.

With the school empty for the holidays, the playground seemed strange to the boys when they met there late on the afternoon of the fifth, a lonely square of red, grainy earth over which dry leaves skated. Land crabs had dug comfortable homes for themselves in the basketball court.

They loaded the four pack mules one at a time, with Eduardo carrying out the heavier toys — the tricycles and the miniature automobiles — because he was the strongest, Lazaro arranging the boxes and parcels in accordance with his map, and Ramoncito, who was a passionate fisherman and good at tying knots, filling the large burlap sacks that would serve as their saddlebags and lashing them to the mahogany packsaddles. The mules, more intelligent than the horses, understood at once that they were being invited to join in some kind of game. They behaved well, neither balking nor biting. With the mules loaded, the boys saddled the three small, beautiful mares, who would have looked to an American as if they had pranced right off a merry-go-round. Then the boys put on their costumes.

The school had had the costumes for so many years that nobody remembered any longer who had made them originally — somebody's mother, probably. Whoever she was, she had used the same rich materials she would have used in embroidering an altar cloth for the church. Eduardo's robe was of turquoise satin belted with a gold cord, and on his head he wore a multicolored turban. Lazaro's robe was of heavy silver brocade, and his turban was of purple velvet. Ramoncito wore a mandarinlike coat of blue silk, ornately embroidered, and a wine-colored turban. They wore their ordinary shoes, because the belled Mexican stirrups would hide them when they were on horseback and the long robes would cover them when they got down to enter the houses. Last of all, they attached their long white beards with liquid adhesive, and, using an eyebrow pencil, drew the wrinkles of old age on their brown young faces.

Then, the horses ready, the mules waiting eagerly in single file on their lead ropes, the boys watched the sun go down behind the palm groves to the west. It sank, a giant illuminated peach sending up a spray of golden searchlights through the massed clouds. After it was below the horizon, the sky was filled with dazzling lime-green light, and then, with no interval, it was dusk. It had been a fruit punch of a sunset, complete with maraschino cherries and lemon sherbet, but the boys had seen it every night of their lives, and they supposed that the sun behaved as extravagantly in all countries. To them it was merely a signal that the time had come for them to start.

"Mount," ordered Eduardo, and they swung themselves into the high-backed, embossed saddles. The lead mule brayed gaily in a spirit of adventure. Off they trotted.

"The top end of Princess Street," directed Lazaro. "The Montoros live there at Number 17."

"I believe thee," replied Ramoncito, whose secret intention it was one day to marry the middle Montoro girl, Gladys.

The houses of Cárdenas, like the houses in most Latin cities, are invisible. That is, you see nothing of them from the street except the front wall, which joins the front walls of the residences on either side and is plastered over with the same golden stucco. Inside the wall, from front to back, each house is divided into two long, narrow strips, side by side. One of these strips, which has no roof over it, is a tiled garden with a fountain, stone flower boxes, lime and mango and papaya trees, and an array of outdoor furniture. Here the family lives three hundred days in the year. The long strip on the other side, roofed over with faded vermillion tiles, contains the formal living room with its crystal chandelier and cumbersome mahogany furniture; the bedrooms, each of which has its own door opening into the garden; the dining room, with another chandelier and a big electric refrigerator from the United States standing in a corner; and the kitchen, where the food is cooked over square, cast-iron baskets of fragrant, glowing charcoal. Behind the kitchen live the servants and all their relatives who are able to think up convincing hard-luck stories.

But there is something about the houses of Cárdenas that is stranger still, and this is that the richest man in the block may live next door to the poorest. There are poor neighborhoods and rich neighborhoods, but often a banker lives in the poor one and a shrimp peddler in the rich one. For this reason, as the boys dismounted at the Montoro house they could not help seeing the nine barefoot children of Emilio, the shoemaker, dressed in ragged shirts and nothing else, who stared at them hopefully as they took down the saddlebag containing the Montoro youngsters' gifts. Eduardo, whose voice was already so much deeper than many a man's, thudded on the door with the brass knocker and bellowed, "Do the good young ones of the Señores Montoro live here?"

Señor Montoro swung open the tall door, elegant in his starched white jacket of pleated linen. "Yes, sir, we have good young ones in this house," he replied. "May I ask who you are, gentlemen?"

"We are the Three Kings of Orient," boomed Eduardo.

"Enter, then. This is thy house."

The Montoro children, jabbering with excitement, accepted the presents that had their names on them as Eduardo and Ramoncito took them from the opened burlap sack. Hasty good-bys were said, the Kings explaining that they had a great distance to travel before morning, and they mounted and rode on.

"The shoemaker's kids are all crying," said Lazaro over the clip-clop of the hoofs. "I can hear them. They thought we'd leave something for them when we came out of the Montoros'."

"Maybe Jaime Montoro will give them his express wagon after he smashes it," said Ramoncito. "I'll bet there won't be a wheel left by noon tomorrow."

At the Cabrera house on Shell Street they delivered a fifty-dollar French doll to Myriam Cabrera, along with a dozen other packages. Mounting again, they turned into Anglona Street. By now it was dark, the only light on the street falling from unshaded bulbs at the intersections. They were conscious, as they rode along, of people, grownups as well as children, watching them from the sidewalks. Everybody was out for an evening stroll in the cool bay breeze. Now and again somebody called out, "Look, the Three Kings!" and each time the voice was thrilled and reverent. There was mystery in the night. The mules felt it, pricking up their ears, and the horses, catching the murmurs of admiration, tossed their manes and lifted their forefeet higher than they really needed to, showing off. A group of men around the white pushcart of a *tamalero* cheered and waved. One of them, a farmer in high-laced boots with his sugar-cane knife at his belt, ran into the street and tried to feed his tamale to Eduardo's horse.

On Saint John of God Street the horses shied at the peanut seller who was chanting, "Peanuts a little hot, peanuts a little hot," and again there were watchers in the darkness under the rustling palms. Distinctly the boys heard a little girl ask in a trembling voice, "Mamma, will they come to us?" And they heard the mother's patient, desperate answer: "Who knows, soul of my soul? But if they do not come tonight, you must be valiant, for surely they will come next year."

On the lead mare, Eduardo, who knew a number of words
which did not meet with Father Miguel's approval, muttered
a particularly bad one.

"Now she's crying," exclaimed Lazaro, "because we've
passed her house."

"If you think this is bad," said Ramoncito, "wait till we
get down by the market. My brother Pepe told me when he
was a King he rode through four blocks of bawling beggar
kids there."

"The poor are always with us," replied Eduardo gruffly.
"Jesus says so in the Bible."

"He means they are always with us to remind us to do something about them, Elephant," said Lazaro. "That's what he
means."

"What do you want?" Eduardo shouted back. "Am I to
blame because there are families that can't earn a living? The
cane crop is poor this year."

Eduardo's anger was something to be quenched promptly;
it was well known. "No, Elephant, dear, you are not to
blame," said Ramoncito. "We don't say you are."

"Then shut up, the two of you!"

"I just think," said Lazaro in the clear, sweet voice that permitted him, at fifteen, still to sing in the choir, "it's a shame
to take gifts to rich kids like us when it's the poor kids that
need them."

"Me too. My father is giving me a bicycle," added Ramoncito. "What do I want with a domino set and a silly card
game that's supposed to teach me how to spell?"

"Father Miguel told us what to do," said Eduardo grimly,
"and we're going to do it."

But not a hundred yards farther on a small boy of seven or
eight, in a shirt made of secondhand cheesecloth washed white
for the holiday, ran hysterically into the street crying: "Oh,
Kings, Kings! We live here, señores, at Number 22!"

Eduardo reined in so sharply that he hurt his mare's dainty
mouth. Leaning down from his saddle, he bellowed in a voice
that frightened the boy nearly out of his senses. "What's your
name? Is there light in your house, so we can see? Then take

us there. Monkey, gallop back and get that girl that was howling!"

In the one-room house at Number 22, where an entire family
slept on the clay floor and the only light was that from the
candle blinking in its ruby cup at the feet of the Virgin, they
handed out half a dozen packages, Eduardo glowering, Ramoncito scared but resolute, and Lazaro struggling to control
the giggle that always assailed him at the wrong moment. The
gratitude of the little boy and girl embarrassed them so terribly
that they got away quickly, shutting the rickety door behind
them with a slam. They gathered around the horses.

"Well, anyhow," said Eduardo, "those two won't bawl all
night. But now what? You know we ought to obey the father."

"*Tú eres jefe,*" answered Ramoncito with a shrug. "You're
the boss."

"I'm not the boss," roared Eduardo. "You always make me
the boss, and then I get into trouble. Do you realize the scandal
it will be if we go down to the market and give all this stuff
to the beggar kids?"

"Clearly it will be a scandal," responded Ramoncito. "It
has never been done."

"We're wearing eleven-yard shirts now," protested Eduardo
as we might say, "We're in hot water now." He turned to
Lazaro. "What do you say, Macaroon?"

When a person of Spanish blood does not know what other
answer to give, he answers with a proverb. "That which does
not kill us," quoted Lazaro, "will make us fat." The saying
did not fit the situation especially well, but it conveyed his
meaning.

"All right," said Eduardo, "but you're both in this with me.
Don't you forget it, either!"

"For an elephant," said Ramoncito, "you do a lot of talking."

Dramatically Lazaro crumpled his map and flung it into the
gutter. They turned the horses' heads and trotted toward the
market. In the street approaching it, Colonel Hangman Street,
with its reek of fish heads and rotten cabbage, they drew rein.
Somebody had smashed the street light with a cabbage or a

pebble from a slingshot, but there was light enough from the stars to see by; the stars hung just over the rooftops like green and red Christmas-tree ornaments lowered from heaven on wires. Eduardo stood erect in his stirrups. " Hear me," he shouted. " Is this the town of Cárdenas, in Cuba? " That was a fine imaginative touch. " Are there good young ones on this street who have behaved well this year? If there are, come you all to the market! "

The market, a maze of heavy stone archways, was brilliantly lighted. Curious, laughing butchers and vegetable sellers at once gathered around the Three Kings as they entered, dragging their bulky saddlebags. Even as the crowd formed a ring, dirty, barefoot children with uncombed hair and noses that badly needed wiping were pushing and wriggling and, where it was necessary, kicking their way to its center. Recklessly Eduardo, Ramoncito, and Lazaro tore away tissue paper and ribbons, so that they could see what the gifts were, and passed them out. Arguments broke out in the crowd, but not among the children. They snatched their dolls and painting sets, their toy fire engines and scooters, and raced away shrieking, carrying the greatest news of their lives to brothers, sisters, and deserving friends.

In twenty minutes the saddlebags were empty. Not an all-day sucker was left. Even Ramoncito's white beard was gone, for it had fallen to the concrete floor and a youngster had snatched it in the belief that it was a toy. Streaming perspiration, and as hoarse as crows, the three boys thrust their way through the chattering, mystified, admiring crowd that jammed the sidewalk for a block, mounted and trotted back to the school under the late moon. The moon could not manage anything quite as spectacular as the sun, but it was doing its best. It turned the massed clouds over the sea into great clusters of white camellias, wrapping each cluster in shining aluminum foil.

Scientists say nothing travels more swiftly than light. This is not true; in a small town good news, bad news, any kind of news at all, travels faster. By the time the boys had hung up their costumes and turned over the animals to Don Alfredo's foreman, furious, gesticulating parents were already haranguing the boys' fathers. And by morning the anger had solidified into a demand that all three of them be expelled at once from school. The movement was headed by Triunfo Anilina, who had made a large fortune out of a small drugstore by selling medicines for much more than they were worth to people too sick to argue over price.

The druggist, sending around notes to everybody's house by messenger, demanded that all parents of boys attending the *colegio* meet there and put the matter to a vote at four o'clock.

At four that afternoon the outraged parents were at the school — not two hours late, nor even one hour late, as was the custom, but on the dot. Plump fathers with cigars, plump mothers with small, exquisite feet in high-heeled, patent-leather shoes, they followed Triunfo Anilina into the large, cool room in which arithmetic was taught. There they squeezed themselves into the seats behind the students' small desks while the burly druggist arrogantly pre-empted the mathematics teacher's desk on the dais. As for the boys themselves, without anybody's ordering them to do so, Eduardo, Ramoncito, and Lazaro ranged themselves before the blackboard, standing with their backs to it. In their own minds they were guilty, convicted and ready for the firing squad.

"We are here," stated Triunfo Anilina curtly. "Let us begin."

He presented a detailed account of the crime that had been committed, using a number of large and impressive words he had picked up from his brother, a lawyer. It took him half an hour.

After this the fathers of the culprits spoke for the defense, Eduardo's father offering to repay the cost of all the gifts, Ramoncito's father pleading that boys would be boys, and Lazaro's father volunteering to pitch Triunfo and all the other male members of the Anilina family, to whom he referred as cockroaches, through the window.

But Triunfo Anilina shouted down the defense, pounding the desk with his hairy fist and upsetting the inkwell.

" The thieves must be punished! " he cried.

" Then the truth of the matter," said Eduardo's handsome father, getting once more to his feet, " is that nothing will satisfy you — not honorable apology, not repayment, nothing. What you want is revenge."

" Yes, revenge! " gasped Triunfo Anilina, his linen jacket dark with perspiration. " What a scandal! It is the first time in the history of our *colegio* that this thing has happened! "

" Ah, Anilina," came a faint, musical buzz of a voice from the rear of the room, " you have a point there."

Every head turned as Father Miguel, pausing several times to gather strength along the way, came up the aisle in his long, tallow-colored gown. All the mothers and fathers had forgotten him.

Triunfo Anilina scrambled clumsily to his feet. " Take my seat, Father," he said.

" It is not your seat," replied Father Miguel. Standing on the dais, steadying himself with one small, dry hand on the edge of the desk, his bald skull reflecting the white light from the windows, he faced the parents. " Dear friends," he whispered, " it is so. For fifty years I have sent into the town, on the eve of Three Kings' Day, the three oldest boys of the school. And always they have distributed the gifts as I bade them, because they were good boys. Not until last night have they ever disobeyed me."

Behind the desk Triunfo Anilina jerked his head sharply in agreement.

" But these three boys are good boys also, since all boys are good boys," continued Father Miguel, " so, in fairness to them, we must examine their misdeed very closely. Exactly what, we must ask ourselves, did they do? They took rich gifts, provided by the bounty of our beloved island, and carried them to babes who sleep on straw pallets, if they are lucky enough to find any straw in the streets around the market. Does the straw remind you of anything, *señores* and *señoras?* It reminds me of another Babe, swaddled in coarse cloth, who slept on straw in a manger because there was no room for him in an inn. And with this in mind it becomes clear beyond doubt that these are not good boys. No, they are something more than ordinary good boys. In the generosity of their hearts, the sweetness of their spirit, the courage of their will they are, indeed, Three Young Kings."

At the blackboard, arms stiff at his sides, Eduardo spoke out of the corner of his mouth to fat little Lazaro. "Giggle one time," he said, "and I advise thee that it will be thy last giggle."

In the schoolroom there was silence. Then Ramoncito's mother began to cry and Lazaro's father burst into boisterous laughter.

Father Miguel raised a hand.

"Now," he said, "if you will kindly help me to my house next door, a delegation from the neighborhood of the market is waiting. They wish to thank you for your sympathy and kindliness, which have so deeply touched them. They wish also to know the identities of the Three Noble Kings, in order that they may kiss their hands."

CZECHOSLOVAKIA

Saint Nicholas and Mary Jane

ANNIE B. KERR

P AVLA sat near the green-tiled stove and waited for Saint
Nicholas. On top of the warm oven next to the stove,
Macek, the cat, carefully washed her face, as though she too
would make ready for the coming of the Bishop Saint.

Takl, the dog, was fast asleep, but the pet goose was wide
awake and noisy, as usual.

Mother sat at one end of the long table, writing a letter to
her sister in America. Ludmilla, who was sixteen, was watching the door through long lashes, which only partly concealed
the eagerness in her blue eyes.

Tomorrow was Pavla's birthday and also the birthday of the
children's friend, Saint Nicholas. But Pavla would be eight,
and the good Bishop Saint, hundreds and hundreds of years
old. On the eve of his birthday he came down to earth and
visited the children in their homes.

Pavla was filled with joyful expectation, yet she was worried.
Sometime ago she had written a letter to Saint Nicholas, which
was an unusual thing for a Czechoslovak child to do. But
Aunt Pavla had suggested it. Aunt Pavla lived in Brooklyn,
New York, and that was the city where the lovely wife of
President Masaryk was born and brought up. Aunt Pavla some-
times attended the church where Mrs. Masaryk and her sisters
were baptized, and had even met the minister. For Aunt

73

Pavla was a social worker and met a great many fine Americans in her efforts to help poor people who couldn't speak English.

She had written to her little namesake in Czechoslovakia:

" Here in America the children write letters to Saint Nicholas and tell him what they would like to have for Christmas. He is called Santa Claus here and he brings his gifts to the children on Christmas Eve, instead of on the evening before his birthday, December 6. If you will write a letter to him and tell him what you most want, maybe he will bring it for your birthday."

So little Pavla wrote that she would like very much to have a new doll from America. " Because Milenka, the doll you brought me when I was a little girl, is very old and broken. I would like one with real hair and eyes that go to sleep. I have been a good girl all year, so please do not bring me a switch."

She addressed the envelope to " Saint Bishop Nicholas, Heaven," and gave it to her mother, as she did not know where to post it, nor what kind of stamp to use for heavenly mail.

Aunt Pavla had written that in America, Santa Claus comes in a sleigh drawn by reindeer and filled with goodies which he puts in the children's stockings as they hang from a shelf in the best room. She had enclosed a picture of the funny saint with a fat face and stomach, red cheeks, and white hair and whiskers — not at all like the tall, stately bishop who in Czechoslovakia comes straight down from heaven on his golden cord and finds the children's stockings hanging from the window sill in the kitchen.

Pavla was thinking of all of this as she waited for the knock on the door. She picked up the old doll from the floor by her side and set her on the window sill, where branches of cherry trees were arranged in jars of water. Ludmilla had brought in the cherry branches from the yard just a few days ago, on Saint Barbara's day, and would tend them carefully so that they would bloom by Christmas. Milenka was a forlorn-looking doll, even though her clothes had been freshly washed and ironed, her red wig reglued, and a little color rubbed on her pale

cheeks. She was still Pavla's " darling," for that is the meaning
of her name.

Pavla was growing restless and wondered what she would do
next. Her gaze roved around the quiet room. Even her pet
goose had decided it was time for a nap. It was a very cheerful
room, with a pattern in bright colors stenciled on the plastered
walls around the doors and windows. The red cupboard was
filled with gay pottery dishes, the chairs and benches had
carved backs, and in one corner stood a fine old painted chest
of drawers. In one of those drawers were the beautiful peasant
costumes which the family wore on very festive occasions and
always when the Sokols were having their great exhibitions in
Praha. Beside the costumes, in a carved box, were the falcon
feathers which they wore in their caps at the Sokols.

In the other room were two big beds with feather mattresses
and pillows and embroidered spreads, a carved dresser and
chairs, and a tile stove not quite so large as the one in the
kitchen. On a table just big enough to hold it was an old and
very precious Bible, and on the walls pictures of the President
of Czechoslovakia, and of Jan Hus and Comenius. Over the
President's picture were draped the American and Czechoslovak
flags. There was a loft over the kitchen, where brother Bedik
had his bed. In the graveyard at the end of the village, Father
and two little brothers were sleeping.

The clatter of chains and the knock at the door came so
suddenly that Pavla ran across the room and stood close to her
mother's side. Ludmilla hurried to admit the long-expected
saint, who strode majestically into the room, followed by his
two attendants. One was all in white, as beautiful as an angel;
the other, a black imp carrying a whip and an iron chain.

The face of Saint Nicholas was quite hidden by his beard
and his bishop's hat. His long robes swept the floor. He came
straight over to Pavla, who was still a little frightened in spite
of herself.

" And so you think you have been a good girl all year? "
How much his voice resembled that of the schoolmaster!
thought Pavla.

"Yes, sir," she answered in a polite little voice. The black imp raised his whip menacingly.

"How about the time you stayed on the pond till after dark and frightened your mother?"

Pavla shrank back in alarm, even though she knew the black imp was brother Bedik, who had played this part many times before.

"And the times you didn't wash the dishes clean?" he continued. "And the time you pulled Macek's tail?"

Pavla hung her head. These things were true, as who should know better than her brother.

But the angel came forward and put the package she was carrying into the hand of Saint Nicholas.

"Don't listen to him," she begged. "Pavla *is* a good girl. She says her prayers every night and helps her mother, and takes care of the geese, and plucks the feathers for market, and — "

"Enough," said Saint Nicholas. "Here, my child: open your package." (His voice *was* like the voice of the schoolmaster!) He filled with dried fruit and apples and nuts the stockings hanging from the window sill.

Then they all watched Pavla as she drew from its wrappings a beautiful doll with golden hair and eyes that opened and closed. She wore a blue silk dress and little blue socks and white slippers. On her shoulder was pinned a note which read: "This is Mary Jane from America. She is looking for a mother."

"Me!" cried Pavla and hugged her close.

"And who is that?" asked Saint Nicholas suddenly, pointing to the other doll sitting among the cherry branches.

"That is Milenka."

"I would like Milenka to go to Vlasta, who has never had a doll in all her life. You do not need two babies." His voice was kind but firm, just like the schoolmaster's.

"Oh, but *please!*" stammered Pavla — "not — not *yet.*"

"On Christmas Eve then; don't forget." Saint Nicholas bowed to each one in turn, and his eyes looked long into those of Ludmilla as he swept past her and out the door, followed by his attendants.

The days until Christmas were busy ones indeed. First of all, there were many kinds of cookies and cakes to be mixed and baked and stored away in a safe place. And preserves and sauces to be brought to just the right consistency and kept cold and ready for the two great feasts.

On Christmas Day delicious roast pig would be the great dish, and on the evening before, carp would be served as a very special treat. Even now the fish was splashing around in a big pail of water and there would be quite a ceremony when it was killed and prepared for the feast.

There were nuts to crack and nutshells to gild for the Christmas tree, which Bedik would bring in from the woods a day or two before Christmas. Other decorations must also be made for the tree — flowers and long chains fashioned from paper; dried fruit tied up in gay wrappings.

But most exciting of all was the making of the *Jeslicky* — the manger or Bethlehem scene. Long ago Pavla's father had made the stable and the little figures — Mary and Joseph and the baby Jesus, the shepherds and the Wise Men. But since he had gone to sleep in the graveyard with the little brothers who died long ago, mother liked to make additional figures out of dough — animals, children, old men and women. When the dough had hardened they would all take a hand at painting them in very bright colors. Mother was very sad sometimes and she had to work very hard to take care of the farm and to feed and clothe them all. But at Christmas time she was wonderful, preparing the goodies and the *Jeslicky*, helping to trim the tree, even playing the Christmas games.

The figures of the Wise Men were not brought out until the Three Kings' Day — January 6. On that day three boys representing the kings would come to the door, one wearing a gold crown (made of paper, of course), one wearing a silver crown, and the other one made quite black and ugly. The boys would put three crosses on the door, and the initials of the three Wise Men — K for Kaspar, M for Melchior, and B for Balthasar — and then they would sing the *Koleda*. Mother would give the boys apples and cookies, and a few pennies if she had any to spare.

Vlasta and her brothers always looked for the Golden Pig which was supposed to run across the wall sometime during the Christmas season and bring much luck to those who saw him. They all declared they had seen him, but Bedik showed Pavla how he could throw a light around the room with a small mirror, and declared that *that* was what the children had seen. Pavla promised not to tell, but she felt very sorry that Vlasta had been so deceived.

In spite of the many interesting occupations and the joyful anticipation of the days ahead, Pavla had a little ache in her heart, because on Christmas Eve she must be parted from Milenka. She agreed that she had no right to have two dolls when just down the road lived her best friend who had none. She wanted to share her treasures with Vlasta, but she knew that it would be very hard to give up her first child. Mary Jane was so beautiful that Pavla tried to pay special attention to Milenka. Both dolls were undressed and rocked to sleep each night, and sat on the table at mealtime.

Mother helped Pavla pack a box of goodies also for Vlasta and her brothers. In Vlasta's house the two rooms were very small and the boys were careless and tracked mud all around. Pavla strongly disapproved of Vlasta's untidy brothers; still, they could not be neglected at the Christmas season.

Christmas Eve came at last. The schoolmaster, who was their guest, arrived early and was warmly greeted.

"*Stedry Vanoce!*" they cried in a chorus as he opened the door. And "*Stedry Vanoce!*" he replied.

The long table was spread with a very special and beautiful cloth and set with the best dishes. Bright red ribbons adorned the necks of Takl, the dog, the cat, Macek, and even the pet goose. The dinner was just ready to be put on the table after the first star had appeared in the sky, when there came a tramping of feet outside the door and then the "Son of the Shepherds" sung by boyish voices:

> "Wake, ye shepherds; rise, ye shepherds,
>   Ye who keep the nightly vigil,
>   We will go to Bethlehem, now forth to Bethlehem.

And we will bring every good thing,
Even a lamb to please thee,
Dear little Jesus, to please thee."

Ludmilla opened the door and handed eggs and cookies to the singers. These boys mended cracked pots by wrapping them skillfully with wire. Some of them had loops of wire over their shoulders even now, on Christmas Eve. The others carried a little *Jeslicky*, which they themselves had made in their mountain homes. The figures were beautifully carved, and the Virgin was dressed in a robe of red with blue cape over her shoulders.

The family sat down to their interrupted supper. They talked about tomorrow and the Christmas service at church and the dinner to follow. The schoolmaster, whose own home was far away, was dining with a family in another part of the village. He looked as though he wished he might come again to Pavla's home, and she wished so too.

After dinner came the lighting of the tree and the opening of gifts, mostly useful things from Aunt Pavla. Then they stood around the *Jeslicky* and sang the lovely old Czech *Koledy*, or carols, " Christ the Lord Is Born, Let Us Rejoice " and

" We bring you glad tidings, listen, give heed,
From distant Bethlehem listen indeed.
Hear diligently, listen intently, now give ye heed.

" Out of great love to us Thou didst descend,
Flower of Paradise, us to befriend.
Noble and loving, tender and loving, Thou didst descend."

Many other carols they sang. After a while Ludmilla filled a pan with water and they all sat about it to try their fortunes. Little candles fastened in walnut shells were lighted and set afloat. Pavla's boat sailed straight to the center of the pan.

" A *journey* — a journey for you, Pavla! " shouted Bedik. Pavla was thrilled but not surprised. Had not Aunt Pavla promised to send her a ticket to America, just as soon as she could save the money for it?

Ludmilla's boat and the schoolmaster's went bobbing around

together and everybody laughed. But Pavla did not notice. Her mind was on her trip to America and on Aunt Pavla celebrating Christmas so far away.

Mother cleared off the table and placed a dish of apples on one end. Ludmilla and the schoolmaster cut theirs in two in such a way that the core and the seeds formed a star — the star of Bethlehem. Then each peeled an apple — round and round, without breaking the skin. With their right hands they threw the parings over their left shoulders, then stooped down to see what letters they formed. Ludmilla gathered hers up in a hurry because, she said, no letter was formed. So did the schoolmaster, but he declared that *his* parings did form a letter, the letter L.

Pavla watched them sleepily. What a wonderful time Christmas is! she thought. The little Jesus in the manger, the lovely songs, the tree, the food, the gifts.

Suddenly she was wide awake. She went over to the window sill and picked up the two dolls and held them very close in her arms.

Bedik had gone out to give the animals their share of the Christmas feast. Ludmilla and Mother were putting the room in order. Takl and Macek were asleep as usual on top of the oven.

The schoolmaster came over to where Pavla stood with the two dolls clasped in her arms.

" How about it, Paulinka? " he asked, and his voice was very kind, like the voice of Saint Nicholas. " Shall we take Milenka to Vlasta's house? "

Pavla nodded bravely, but the slow tears gathered in her eyes. He turned away and began to put on his hat and coat. Then he looked at Ludmilla. " Come with us, the walk will do you good," he said.

" I'd like to." She nodded and helped her small sister on with her wraps. Pavla laid Mary Jane on the table and put Milenka back with the cherry branches.

" Look! " she exclaimed suddenly, pointing to a twig covered with pink buds. " The cherry tree has bloomed! "

Ludmilla went swiftly to the blossoming branch and picked

a spray, and the schoolmaster came and took it from her hand.

Pavla looked at them with surprise. Why, she thought, the cherry blossom is for the one you love best! But the schoolmaster had hidden the blossoms in his pocket and was speaking to the little girl.

"Haven't you got the dollies mixed?" he asked.

"No," said Pavla. "I am taking *Mary Jane* to Vlasta."

"You are giving away your *best* doll? How pleased Saint Nicholas will be!"

"How sweet of you!" cried Ludmilla.

"How unselfish!" said Mother, but she seemed a little worried and perplexed.

They looked at one another and smiled and did not see that Pavla had tucked a little spray of cherry blossom in the sash of poor old battered Milenka. Then the three, with Mary Jane, went out into the starlit night and down the road toward the little house with the thatched roof and a light in the window.

"Stars and dolls and two little girls. And Christmas Eve and a blossoming cherry tree," mused the schoolmaster, looking up into the sky. His voice was very kind, like the voice of good Saint Nicholas.

DENMARK

The Last Dream of the Old Oak Tree

IN THE FOREST, high up on the steep shore, hard by the open
sea coast, stood a very old oak tree. It was exactly three hundred and sixty-five years old, but that long time was not more
for the tree than just as many days would be to us men. We
wake by day and sleep through the night, and then we have our
dreams: it is different with the tree, which keeps awake through
three seasons of the year, and does not get its sleep till winter
comes. Winter is its time for rest, its night after the long day
which is called spring, summer, and autumn.

On many a warm summer day the Ephemera, the fly that
lives but for a day, had danced around his crown — had lived,
enjoyed, and felt happy; and then rested for a moment in quiet
bliss, the tiny creature, on one of the great fresh oak leaves; and
then the tree always said:

"Poor little thing! Your whole life is but a single day! How
very short! It's quite melancholy!"

"Melancholy! Why do you say that?" the Ephemera would
then always reply. "It is wonderfully bright, warm, and beautiful all around me, and that makes me rejoice!"

"But only one day, and then it's all done!"

"Done!" repeated the Ephemera. "What's the meaning of
'done'? Are you 'done' too?"

"No, I shall perhaps live for thousands of your days, and my
day is whole seasons long! It's something so long that you can't

at all manage to reckon it out."

" No? then I don't understand you. You say you have thousands of my days; but I have thousands of moments in which I can be merry and happy. Does all the beauty of this world cease when you die? "

" No," replied the tree; " it will certainly last much longer — far longer than I can possibly think."

" Well, then, we have the same time, only that we reckon differently."

And the Ephemera danced and floated in the air, and rejoiced in its delicate wings of gauze and velvet, and rejoiced in the balmy breezes laden with the fragrance of meadows and of wild roses and elder flowers, of the garden hedges, wild thyme, and mint, and daisies; the scent of these was all so strong that the Ephemera was almost intoxicated. The day was long and beautiful, full of joy and of sweet feeling, and when the sun sank low the little fly felt very agreeably tired of all its happiness and enjoyment. The delicate wings would not carry it any more, and quietly and slowly it glided down upon the soft grass-blade, nodded its head as well as it could nod, and went quietly to sleep — and was dead.

" Poor little Ephemera! " said the Oak. " That was a terribly short life! "

And on every summer day the same dance was repeated, the same question and answer, and the same sleep. The same thing was repeated through whole generations of ephemera; all of them felt equally merry and equally happy.

The Oak stood there awake through the spring morning, the noon of summer, and the evening of autumn; and its time of rest, its night, was coming on apace. Winter was approaching.

Already the storms were singing their "good night, good night! " Here fell a leaf and there fell a leaf.

" We'll rock you and dandle you! Go to sleep; go to sleep! We sing you to sleep, we shake you to sleep; but it does you good in your old twigs, does it not? They seem to crack for very joy! Sleep sweetly; sleep sweetly! It's your three hundred and sixty-fifth night. Properly speaking, you're only a stripling as yet! Sleep sweetly! The clouds strew down snow; there will be quite a coverlet, warm and protecting, around your feet. Sweet sleep to you, and pleasant dreams! "

And the Oak tree stood there, denuded of all its leaves, to sleep through the long winter, and to dream many a dream, always about something that had happened to it — just as in the dreams of men.

The great Oak had once been small — indeed, an acorn had been its cradle. According to human computation, it was now in its fourth century. It was the greatest and best tree in the forest; its crown towered far above all the other trees and could be descried from afar across the sea, so that it served as a landmark to the sailors; the tree had no idea how many eyes were in the habit of seeking it. High up in its green summit the wood pigeon built her nest, and the cuckoo sat in its boughs and sang his song; and in autumn when the leaves looked like thin plates of copper, the birds of passage came and rested there, before they flew away across the sea; but now it was winter, and the tree stood there leafless, so that everyone could see how gnarled and crooked the branches were that shot forth from its trunk. Crows and rooks came and took their seat by turns in the boughs and spoke of the hard times which were beginning, and of the difficulty of getting a living in winter.

It was just at the holy Christmas time, when the tree dreamed its most glorious dream.

The tree had a distinct feeling of the festive time, and fancied he heard the bells ringing from the churches all around; and yet it seemed as if it were a fine summer's day, mild and warm. Fresh and green he spread out his mighty crown; the sunbeams played among the twigs and the leaves; the air was full of the fragrance of herbs and blossoms; gay butterflies chased each other to and fro. The ephemeral insects danced as if all the world were created merely for them to dance and be merry in. All that the tree had experienced for years and years, and that had happened around him, seemed to pass by him again, as in a festive pageant. He saw the knights of ancient days ride by with their noble dames on gallant steeds, with plumes waving in their bonnets and falcons on their wrists. The hunting horn sounded, and the dogs barked. He saw hostile warriors in colored jerkins and with shining weapons, with spear and halbert, pitching their tents and striking them again. The watch fires flamed up anew, and men sang and slept under the branches of the tree. He saw loving couples meeting near his trunk, happily, in the moonshine; and they cut the initials of their names in the gray-green bark of his stem. Once — but long years had rolled by since then — citherns and aeolian harps had been hung up on his boughs by merry wanderers; and now they hung there again, and once again they sounded in tones of marvelous sweetness. The wood pigeons cooed, as if they were telling what the tree felt in all this, and the cuckoo called out to tell him how many summer days he had yet to live.

Then it appeared to him as if new life were rippling down into the remotest fiber of his root and mounting up into his highest branches, to the tops of the leaves. The tree felt that he was stretching and spreading himself, and through his roots he felt that there was life and motion even in the ground itself. He felt his strength increase, he grew higher, his stem shot up unceasingly, and he grew more and more; his crown became fuller, and spread out; and in proportion as the tree grew, he felt his happiness increase, and his joyous hope that he should reach even higher — quite up to the warm, brilliant sun.

Already had he grown high above the clouds, which floated past beneath his crown like dark troops of passage birds or like great white swans. And every leaf of the tree had the gift of sight, as if it had eyes wherewith to see; the stars became visible in broad daylight, great and sparkling; each of them sparkled like a pair of eyes, mild and clear. They recalled to his memory well-known gentle eyes, eyes of children, eyes of lovers who had met beneath his boughs.

It was a marvelous spectacle, and one full of happiness and joy! And yet amidst all this happiness the tree felt a longing, a yearning desire that all other trees of the wood beneath him, and all the bushes and herbs and flowers might be able to rise with him, that they too might see this splendor and experience this joy. The great majestic Oak was not quite happy in his happiness, while he had not them all, great and little, about him; and this feeling of yearning trembled through his every twig, through his every leaf, warmly and fervently as through a human heart.

The crown of the tree waved to and fro, as if he sought something in his silent longing, and he looked down. Then he felt the fragrance of thyme, and soon afterward the more powerful scent of honeysuckle and violets; and he fancied he heard the cuckoo answering him.

Yes, through the clouds the green summits of the forest came peering up, and under himself the Oak saw the other trees, as they grew and raised themselves aloft. Bushes and herbs shot up high, and some tore themselves up bodily by the roots to rise the quicker. The birch was the quickest of all. Like a white streak of lightning, its slender stem shot upward in a zigzag line, and the branches spread around it like green gauze and like banners; the whole woodland natives, even to the brown-plumed rushes, grew up with the rest, and the birds came too, and sang; and on the grass blade that fluttered aloft like a long silken ribbon into the air, sat the grasshopper cleaning his wings with his leg; the May beetles hummed, and the bees murmured, and every bird sang in his appointed manner; all was song and sound of gladness up into the high heaven.

" But the little blue flower by the waterside, where is that? " said the Oak; " and the purple bellflower and the daisy? " for you see, the old Oak tree wanted to have them all about him.

" We are here — we are here! " was shouted and sung in reply.

" But the beautiful thyme of last summer — and in the last year there was certainly a place here covered with lilies of the valley! and the wild apple tree that blossomed so splendidly! and all the glory of the wood that came year by year — if that had only just been born, it might have been here now! "

" We are here; we are here! " replied voices still higher in the air. It seemed as if they had flown on before.

" Why, that is beautiful, indescribably beautiful! " exclaimed the old Oak tree rejoicingly. " I have them all around me, great and small; not one has been forgotten! How can so much happiness be imagined? How can it be possible? "

" In heaven, in the better land, it can be imagined, and it is possible! " the reply sounded through the air.

And the old tree, who grew on and on, felt how his roots were tearing themselves free from the ground.

"That's right, that's better than all!" said the tree. "Now no fetters hold me! I can fly up now, to the very highest, in glory and in light! And all my beloved ones are with me, great and small — all of them, all!"

That was the dream of the old Oak tree; and while he dreamed thus, a mighty storm came rushing over land and sea — at the holy Christmastide. The sea rolled great billows toward the shore; there was a cracking and crashing in the tree — his root was torn out of the ground in the very moment while he was dreaming that his root freed itself from the earth. He fell. His three hundred and sixty-five years were now as the single day of the Ephemera.

On the morning of the Christmas festival, when the sun rose, the storm had subsided. From all the churches sounded the festive bells, and from every hearth, even from the smallest hut, arose the smoke in blue clouds, like the smoke from the altars of the Druids of old at the feast of thank offerings. The sea became gradually calm, and on board a great ship in the offing, which had fought successfully with the tempest, all the flags were displayed, as a token of joy suitable to the festive day.

"The tree is down — the old Oak tree, our landmark on the coast!" said the sailors. "It fell in the storm of last night. Who can replace it? No one can."

This was the funeral oration, short but well meant, that was given to the tree, which lay stretched on the snowy covering on the seashore; and over its prostrate form sounded the notes of a song from the ship, a carol of the joys of Christmas, and of the redemption of the soul by His blood, and of eternal life.

> "Sing, sing aloud, this blessed morn —
> It is fulfilled — and He is born;
> Oh, joy without compare!
> Hallelujah, Hallelujah!"

Thus sounded the old psalm tune, and everyone on board the ship felt lifted up in his own way, through the song and the prayer, just as the old tree had felt lifted up in its last, its most beauteous dream in the Christmas night.

ENGLAND

The Thieves Who Couldn't Help Sneezing

THOMAS HARDY

MANY YEARS AGO, when oak trees now past their prime were about as large as elderly gentlemen's walking sticks, there lived in Wessex a yeoman's son, whose name was Hubert. He was about fourteen years of age and was as remarkable for his candor and lightness of heart as for his physical courage, of which, indeed, he was a little vain.

One cold Christmas Eve his father, having no other help at hand, sent him on an important errand to a small town several miles from home. He traveled on horseback and was detained by the business till a late hour of the evening. At last, however, it was completed; he returned to the inn, the horse was saddled, and he started on his way. His journey homeward lay through the Vale of Blackmore, a fertile but somewhat lonely district, with heavy clay roads and crooked lanes. In those days, too, a great part of it was thickly wooded.

It must have been about nine o'clock when, riding along amidst the overhanging trees upon his stout-legged cob, Jerry, and singing a Christmas carol, to be in harmony with the season, Hubert fancied that he heard a noise among the boughs. This recalled to his mind that the spot he was traversing bore an evil name. Men had been waylaid there. He looked at Jerry and wished he had been of any other color than light gray; for on this account the docile animal's form was visible even here in the dense shade. "What do I care?" he said aloud, after a

88

few minutes of reflection. " Jerry's legs are too nimble to allow any highwayman to come near me."

" Ha! ha! indeed," was said in a deep voice; and the next moment a man darted from the thicket on his right hand, another man from the thicket on his left hand, and another from a tree trunk a few yards ahead. Hubert's bridle was seized, he was pulled from his horse, and although he struck out with all his might, as a brave boy would naturally do, he was overpowered. His arms were tied behind him, his legs bound tightly together, and he was thrown into the ditch. The robbers, whose faces he could now dimly perceive to be artificially blackened, at once departed, leading off the horse.

As soon as Hubert had a little recovered himself, he found that by great exertion he was able to extricate his legs from the cord; but, in spite of every endeavor, his arms remained bound as fast as before. All, therefore, that he could do was to rise to his feet and proceed on his way with his arms behind him, and trust to chance for getting them unfastened. He knew that it would be impossible to reach home on foot that night, and in such a condition; but he walked on. Owing to the confusion which this attack caused in his brain, he lost his way, and would have been inclined to lie down and rest till morning among the dead leaves had he not known the danger of sleeping without wrappers in a frost so severe. So he wandered farther onward, his arms wrung and numbed by the cord which pinioned him, and his heart aching for the loss of poor Jerry, who never had been known to kick or bite or show a single vicious habit. He was not a little glad when he discerned through the trees a distant light. Toward this he made his way, and presently found himself in front of a large mansion with flanking wings, gables, and towers, the battlements and chimneys showing their shapes against the stars.

All was silent; but the door stood wide open, it being from this door that the light shone which had attracted him. On entering, he found himself in a vast apartment arranged as a dining hall, and brilliantly illuminated. The walls were covered with a great deal of dark wainscoting, formed into molded panels, carvings, closet doors, and the usual fittings of a house of that kind. But what drew his attention most was the large table in the midst of the hall, upon which was spread a sumptuous supper, as yet untouched. Chairs were placed around, and it appeared as if something had occurred to interrupt the meal just at the time when all were ready to begin.

Even had Hubert been so inclined, he could not have eaten in his helpless state, unless by dipping his mouth into the dishes, like a pig or cow. He wished first to obtain assistance and was about to penetrate farther into the house for that purpose when he heard hasty footsteps in the porch and the words, " Be quick! " uttered in the deep voice which had reached him when he was dragged from the horse. There was only just time for him to dart under the table before three men entered the dining hall. Peeping from beneath the hanging edges of the tablecloth, he perceived that their faces, too, were blackened, which at once removed any remaining doubts he may have felt that these were the same thieves.

" Now, then," said the first — the man with the deep voice — " let us hide ourselves. They will all be back again in a minute. That was a good trick to get them out of the house — eh? "

" Yes. You well imitated the cries of a man in distress," said the second.

" Excellently," said the third.

" But they will soon find out that it was a false alarm. Come, where shall we hide? It must be someplace we can stay in for two or three hours, till all are in bed and asleep. Ah! I have it. Come this way! I have learned that the further closet is not opened once in a twelvemonth; it will serve our purpose exactly."

The speaker advanced into a corridor which led from the hall. Creeping a little farther forward, Hubert could discern that the closet stood at the end, facing the dining hall. The thieves entered it, and closed the door. Hardly breathing, Hubert glided forward, to learn a little more of their intention, if possible; and, coming close, he could hear the robbers whispering about the different rooms where the jewels, plate, and other valuables of the house were kept, which they plainly meant to steal.

They had not been long in hiding when a gay chattering of

ladies and gentlemen was audible on the terrace without. Hubert felt that it would not do to be caught prowling about the house, unless he wished to be taken for a robber himself; and he slipped softly back to the hall, out at the door, and stood in a dark corner of the porch, where he could see everything without being himself seen. In a moment or two a whole troop of personages came gliding past him into the house. There were an elderly gentleman and lady, eight or nine young ladies, as many young men, besides half a dozen menservants and maids. The mansion had apparently been quite emptied of its occupants.

" Now, children and young people, we will resume our meal," said the old gentleman. " What the noise could have been I cannot understand. I never felt so certain in my life that there was a person being murdered outside my door."

Then the ladies began saying how frightened they had been, and how they had expected an adventure, and how it had ended in nothing after all.

" Wait a while," said Hubert to himself. " You'll have adventure enough by and by, ladies."

It appeared that the young men and women were married sons and daughters of the old couple, who had come that day to spend Christmas with their parents.

The door was then closed, Hubert being left outside in the porch. He thought this a proper moment for asking their assistance; and, since he was unable to knock with his hands, began boldly to kick the door.

" Hullo! What disturbance are you making here? " said a footman who opened it, and, seizing Hubert by the shoulder, he pulled him into the dining hall. " Here's a strange boy I have found making a noise in the porch, Sir Simon."

Everybody turned.

" Bring him forward," said Sir Simon, the old gentleman before mentioned. " What were you doing there, my boy? "

" Why, his arms are tied! " said one of the ladies.

" Poor fellow! " said another.

Hubert at once began to explain that he had been waylaid on his journey home, robbed of his horse, and mercilessly left in this condition by the thieves.

"Only to think of it!" exclaimed Sir Simon.

"That's a likely story," said one of the gentlemen guests incredulously.

"Doubtful, hey?" asked Sir Simon.

"Perhaps he's a robber himself," suggested a lady.

"There is a curiously wild, wicked look about him, certainly, now that I examine him closely," said the old mother.

Hubert blushed with shame; and, instead of continuing his story, and relating that robbers were concealed in the house, he doggedly held his tongue, and half resolved to let them find out their danger for themselves.

"Well, untie him," said Sir Simon. "Come, since it is Christmas Eve, we'll treat him well. Here, my lad; sit down in that empty seat at the bottom of the table and make as good a meal as you can. When you have had your fill we will listen to more particulars of your story."

The feast then proceeded; and Hubert, now at liberty, was not at all sorry to join in. The more they ate and drank, the merrier did the company become; the wine flowed freely, the logs flared up the chimney, the ladies laughed at the gentlemen's stories; in short, all went as noisily and as happily as a Christmas gathering in old times possibly could do.

Hubert, in spite of his hurt feelings at their doubts of his honesty, could not help being warmed both in mind and in body by the good cheer, the scene, and the example of hilarity set by his neighbors. At last he laughed as heartily at their stories and repartees as the old baronet, Sir Simon, himself. When the meal was almost over one of the sons, who had drunk a little too much wine, after the manner of men in that century, said to Hubert, "Well, my boy, how are you? Can you take a pinch of snuff?" He held out one of the snuffboxes which were then becoming common among young and old throughout the country.

"Thank you," said Hubert, accepting a pinch.

"Tell the ladies who you are, what you are made of, and what you can do," the young man continued, slapping Hubert upon the shoulder.

" Certainly," said our hero, drawing himself up, and thinking it best to put a bold face on the matter. " I am a traveling magician."

" Indeed! "

" What shall we hear next? "

" Can you call up spirits from the vasty deep, young wizard? "

" I can conjure up a tempest in a cupboard," Hubert replied.

" Ha ha! " said the old baronet, pleasantly rubbing his hands. "We must see this performance. Girls, don't go away: here's something to be seen."

" Not dangerous, I hope? " said the old lady.

Hubert rose from the table. "Hand me your snuffbox, please," he said to the young man who had made free with him. " And now," he continued, " without the least noise, follow me. If any of you speak, it will break the spell."

They promised obedience. He entered the corridor, and, taking off his shoes, went on tiptoe to the closet door, the guests advancing in a silent group at a little distance behind him. Hubert next placed a stool in front of the door, and, by standing upon it, was tall enough to reach to the top. He then, just as noiselessly, poured all the snuff from the box along the upper edge of the door, and, with a few short puffs of breath, blew the snuff through the chink into the interior of the closet. He held up his finger to the assembly, that they might be silent.

" Dear me, what's that? " said the old lady, after a minute or two had elapsed.

A suppressed sneeze had come from inside the closet.

Hubert held up his finger again.

" How very singular," whispered Sir Simon. " This is most interesting."

Hubert took advantage of the moment to gently slide the bolt of the closet door into its place. " More snuff," he said calmly.

"More snuff," said Sir Simon. Two or three gentlemen passed their boxes, and the contents were blown in at the top of the closet. Another sneeze, not quite so well suppressed as the first, was heard; then another, which seemed to say that it would not be suppressed under any circumstances whatever. At length there arose a perfect storm of sneezes.

" Excellent, excellent for one so young! " said Sir Simon. " I am much interested in this trick of throwing the voice — called, I believe, ventriloquism."

" More snuff," said Hubert.

" More snuff," said Sir Simon. Sir Simon's man brought a large jar of the best scented Scotch.

Hubert once more charged the upper chink of the closet, and blew the snuff into the interior, as before. Again he charged, and again, emptying the whole contents of the jar. The tumult of sneezes became really extraordinary to listen to — there was no cessation. It was like wind, rain, and sea battling in a hurricane.

" I believe there are men inside, and that it is no trick at all! " exclaimed Sir Simon, the truth flashing on him.

" There are," said Hubert. " They are come to rob the house; and they are the same who stole my horse."

The sneezes changed to spasmodic groans. One of the thieves, hearing Hubert's voice, cried, " Oh! mercy! mercy! let us out of this! "

" Where's my horse? " said Hubert.

" Tied to the tree in the hollow behind Short's Gibbet. Mercy! mercy! let us out, or we shall die of suffocation! "

All the Christmas guests now perceived that this was no longer sport but serious earnest. Guns and cudgels were procured; all the men servants were called in, and arranged in position outside the closet. At a signal Hubert withdrew the bolt, and stood on the defensive. But the three robbers, far from attacking them, were found crouching in the corner, gasping for breath. They made no resistance; and, being pinioned, were placed in an outbuilding till the morning.

Hubert now gave the remainder of his story to the assembled company, and was profusely thanked for the services he had rendered. Sir Simon pressed him to stay over the night and accept the use of the best bedroom the house afforded, which had been occupied by Queen Elizabeth and King Charles successively when on their visits to this part of the country. But Hubert declined, being anxious to find his horse Jerry, and to test the truth of the robbers' statements concerning him.

Several of the guests accompanied Hubert to the spot behind the gibbet alluded to by the thieves as where Jerry was hidden. When they reached the knoll and looked over, behold! there the horse stood, uninjured, and quite unconcerned. At sight of Hubert he neighed joyfully, and nothing could exceed Hubert's gladness at finding him. He mounted, wished his friends " Good night! " and cantered off in the direction they pointed out as his nearest way, reaching home safely about four o'clock in the morning.

FINLAND

(As Reflected in the United States)

The Almond in the Pudding

ANNIE B. KERR

HILJA SAT UP with a start and snapped on the light by her
bed. Six o'clock. She hadn't heard the alarm, yet she was
suddenly awake. Then she remembered and sank down again
on the hard bed, her blue eyes wide open, her mouth curved in
a happy smile. She had planned to sleep late on this the first
morning of her holiday. But why waste time in sleep? she
thought. Better than sleep were the anticipations of the days
ahead. In her English class at the Settlement they had been
reading about Italian Pippa and her one free day out of the
whole year. She, Hilja, would have two days, and those two
days were the day before Christmas and Christmas Day. And
this was the morning of the first day.

Sounds like the Bible, she thought, and then she remembered
that she had been praying when she dropped to sleep last night.
And she blushed when she recalled her prayer:

"O God, please let me find the almond in the Christmas
pudding, so that Olli will know that I am to be his wife."

Whatever would God think of her for such a prayer? And yet
she would really have to do something to help Olli overcome
his slowness and bashfulness. Here it was almost two weeks
since he had kissed her in the snow, out in front of the Settlement House. And she had seen him twice since then, when they
rehearsed in the choir at Imatra Hall. He had never said a word
to her about marriage and she must be a very bold girl to be

96

thinking so much about it and even praying about it!

But Olli had invited her to the home of his uncle and aunt for the Christmas celebration. Surely *that* showed how much he thought of her. So if only she could find the almond in the Christmas pudding — but perhaps they wouldn't have the rice pudding with the almond in it. Hilja had heard that Mrs. Honkkonen was a wonderful cook, but she had lived in America twenty-five years, so perhaps it wouldn't be a Finnish dinner after all. In a panic she prayed fervently, " O God, please make it a Finnish dinner with rice pudding and the almond inside." She didn't quite dare add, as she had last night, " and let me find the almond." She didn't want God to think too badly of her.

The clock in the living room struck seven and Hilja got up leisurely, drew on her stockings and shoes, slipped her heavy coat over her nightdress and went into the kitchen. Three cups of strong coffee and some toast would help to start the day right.

How grand it was to be alone, with no insistent voice to say: " Hilja, hurry and scrub the kitchen. Hilja, give the bathroom a good cleaning. Hilja, polish the silver." Well, she would do none of these things. She would press her silk dress and darn her one pair of silk stockings and curl her hair. *Perhaps* she would turn on the radio, even though it was forbidden! And this afternoon she'd go to the bathhouse and then, promptly at seven o'clock, to Olli's aunt's apartment.

She climbed up on the high stool and ate from the top of the laundry tub as usual. But she ate slowly and deliberately, trying to prolong the delicious sense of unhurried leisure.

When the invitation from Mrs. Honkkonen had been given to her by Olli last week she had replied hopelessly: " Oh, I'm so sorry, but I know I cannot come. Last year I vorked for days before Christmas. And all day long on Christmas Day. Mrs. Taylor vill not let me off, even for a few hours."

When Mrs. Taylor told her several days ago that she and Mr. Taylor were going to spend Christmas at her sister's home in Cleveland, and that she — Hilja — could have two whole days for herself, Hilja could only stammer, " It iss kind — tank you "; when actually her heart was almost bursting for joy.

She put the dishes in the sink and went back to her bare little room to finish dressing. Her one best dress hung on the wall, beside her Finnish costume with its striped skirt, which she wore when she danced folk dances at Imatra Hall. Hilja pressed the blue silk carefully and spread it out on the bed. She took her worn stockings into the living room and sat down luxuriously in Mr. Taylor's big armchair and began to darn. The radio lured her, but she shook her head resolutely. " No, I vill not," she said aloud. Cheerio, the canary, sang gaily, hopping about from one perch to the other, and Hilja ran to the kitchen for fresh water and a piece of crisp lettuce.

" If you vass little vild bird in Finland, I put out rye for you, and Christmas food for odder little animals."

Cheerio chirped his thanks and Hilja began a vigorous dusting of the living room.

" Just this much vork," she apologized to herself. " Can't let the house be too dirty."

On the living room table was a little box with her name on it. Hilja opened it wonderingly and drew out — of all things! — a pair of silk stockings, a dollar bill, and a card of greeting from Mrs. Taylor.

" Oh," she choked, " I *do* tank you. Now I tink I clean bathroom."

She sang as she worked — Finnish folk songs and Christmas carols. She gave the bathtub an extra scouring, just because she was never allowed to bathe in it. She tried to forget that she had thought she might take her bath here — no one would ever know — instead of taking the long trip to the bathhouse.

She put fresh linen on the beds, cleaned the rugs, polished the floors. Her strong young arms seemed tireless and her singing drowned out the canary. At last she returned to the kitchen for more coffee and bread.

Might as vell do the silver too, she thought, and set to work, polishing vigorously and smiling back at the funny face reflected in the round sugar bowl.

Then she packed the silk dress carefully in a box, with her

clean underwear and the new stockings, and started forth to the bathhouse.

None of Hilja's friends were at the bathhouse that afternoon. She missed their chatter and the chance to tell them that she was on her way to Olli's. Stretched on the narrow bench, with the steam enveloping her, she thought again of her own good fortune and pitied the other girls who had to work so hard on Christmas.

Then she stepped out into the street, shining with cleanliness and clad in her very best, and walked slowly toward the big co-operative apartment house where Olli's aunt and uncle lived.

Finntown was gay with Christmas lights and decorations. The store windows were filled with tempting articles, and Hilja paused at one window and gazed longingly at the neckties, handkerchiefs, and other items of apparel. She *wished* she could take a present to Olli — but that would *never* do! However, she could buy something for Mrs. Honkkonen — why hadn't she thought of it before?

She went inside, selected a handkerchief elaborately trimmed with lace and with the letter *H* embroidered in the corner, saw it wrapped in a Christmas box, handed the clerk her precious dollar, and started once more down the street.

Past the church where she would be attending service early tomorrow morning, past the co-operative store where Mr. Honkkonen had his office, for he was the president, went Hilja — slowly, for it was not yet seven o'clock, and hesitatingly, for now the thought of the evening ahead frightened her.

Twice before she had been in the Honkkonen apartment, when Mrs. Honkkonen had lent her beautiful rugs and carved pictures to the Settlement for its Finnish exhibition. Now she was going as a guest, and it was Olli's home. Tall, fair Olli, who sang in the Finnish choir and danced folk dances and did beautiful wood carving, yet lived in a world apart, with his books and his degree from the University of Helsinki and his fine friends. She was to be with Olli tonight, Olli who had looked at her so strangely and who had kissed her out in the snow in front of the Settlement House. And she was just Hilja Saarinen, who worked for Mrs. Taylor on Henry Street.

At last she was inside the house, where the Christmas festivities had already begun. Mrs. Honkkonen was very kind and tried to make her feel at home, but there were other guests and Olli was too busy to pay any special attention to Hilja.

They were all Finnish, but they spoke in English because many of the young people had never learned their native tongue. The wood carvings and the woven rugs which she had helped to arrange at the Settlement House not long ago made Hilja feel at home. When they went into the dining room she was happy to find herself seated opposite the Kalevala rug, which she and Olli had almost lost and which would always be connected with one of the happiest experiences of her life.

The guests sat quietly about the table while Mr. Honkkonen read aloud the Christmas story.

" 'And there were shepherds in the same country abiding in the field and keeping watch by night over their flocks. And an angel of the Lord stood by them and the glory of the Lord shone round about them and they were sore afraid.

" 'And the angel said unto them, Be not afraid, for behold I bring you good tidings of great joy which shall be to all the people: for there is born to you this day in the city of David a Savior, who is Christ the Lord. And this is the sign unto you: Ye shall find the babe wrapped in swaddling clothes and lying in a manger. And suddenly there was with the angel a multitude of the heavenly hosts, praising God and saying, Glory to God in the highest, and on earth, peace among men in whom he is well pleased.' "

He closed the book, and while he prayed, Hilja tried to keep her thoughts from wandering and her eyes from peeping through her clasped fingers at Olli's bowed head just opposite. Even before the hearty " Amen " made it possible for her to lift her head she knew that the Christmas food of Finland was ready to be brought in from the kitchen. Gratefully she sniffed the rice pudding and *almost* said aloud, " Please, God — the almond! "

When they had all eaten heartily of fish and ham, of rye bread with caraway seeds, of white bread and vegetables, of plum cake and strong black coffee, then came the pudding and the moment of silence while the guests searched in their plates for the almond which would bring a wedding to the unmarried and good luck to anyone before the year's end.

With a little gasp of surprise and joy Hilja discovered the almond on her plate and held it up in her spoon for everyone to see. She dared not lift her eyes to Olli, though his own were gazing straight at her, and her face was crimson as she waited for the outburst of applause and congratulations to die down.

It was Mr. Honkkonen himself who came to her rescue and drew her into the other room, saying:

"Come sit with me and tell me about yourself while the others light the Christmas tree."

So she told him of her childhood on her father's farm in Finland; of her brothers, who were sailors and went home only at Christmas time; of her little sister, who longed to come to America; and of the church school which she had attended, and the old devoted pastor who had taught her all she knew and even prepared her for the university. But she had come to America instead and worked for Mrs. Taylor, sending her wages home each month, studing English at the Settlement House. And when he asked her quite suddenly and abruptly, "Like Olli, do you?" she answered simply and bravely, "Yes, I do."

Olli's Uncle Honkkonen took her hand and led her to the tree, which was blazing with candles and trimmed with toys made of paper and wood fashioned by Olli's skillful fingers and gingerbread men baked by Mrs. Honkkonen, with raisins for eyes, and gilded walnuts and cornucopias filled with candies, such as Hilja herself had made many a time on the farm at home. The tree would be kept till January 13, Canute's Day, when the neighborhood children would come in and plunder it.

At home, in faraway Finland, Hilja could imagine her own family gathered around a similar tree. Early tomorrow morning they would start for church in sleighs drawn by strong Finnish ponies, guided by the light from many candles placed in windows along the road. The rest of the day would be spent in feasting and visiting friends. She must write them a long letter tomorrow.

She had placed her gift for Mrs. Honkkonen underneath the tree, with the other gifts sent by Old Man Christmas. When the time came to open the gifts she found her own name on a beautiful blue and white silk scarf. She looked her thanks at Olli, who was distributing the gifts, but he shook his head and pointed to his aunt, who sat on the divan, her lap filled with presents. Hilja ran to her and impulsively kissed her forehead.

" Tank you, dear Mrs. Honkkonen," she whispered. " Wiss all my heart I tank you. The scarf, it iss so beautiful! "

" *Hauskaa Joulna* — happy Christmas " — they all cried as the clock struck midnight.

At five o'clock the next morning, Hilja walked through the silent streets to the early church service. Olli was waiting for her, but not until they were kneeling side by side did he have a chance to whisper, " Oh, Hilja, I was so happy when you found the almond, for then I knew — "

" Yes — Olli — vhat you knew? "

" I knew you'd marry me. Will you, Hilja? "

" Yes, Olli, but — "

" But *what?* "

" I *prayed* I'd find the almond," she confessed.

" Hilja! " He reached for her hand. " *So did I!* "

FRANCE

Salvette and Bernadou

FROM THE FRENCH OF ALPHONSE DAUDET

I

IT IS THE EVE OF CHRISTMAS in a large village of Bavaria. Along the snow-whitened streets, amidst the confusion of the fog and noise of carriages and bells, the crowd presses joyously about cook shops, wine booths, and busy stores. Rustling with a light sweep of sound against the flower-twined and berib-boned stalls, branches of green holly, or whole saplings, graced with pendants and shading the heads below like boughs of the Thuringian forest, go by in happy arms: a remembrance of nature in the torpid life of winter.

Day dies out. Far away, behind the gardens of the Résidence, lingers a glimmer of the departing sun, red in the fog; and in the town is such gaiety, such hurry of preparation for the holiday, that each jet of light which springs up in the many windows seems to hang from some vast Christmas tree.

This is, in truth, no ordinary Christmas. It is the year of grace eighteen hundred and seventy, and the holy day is only a pre-text the more to drink to the illustrious Von der Than and cel-ebrate the triumph of the Bavarian troops.

" Noel, Noel! " The very Jews of the old town join in the mirth. Behold the aged Augustus Cahn, who turns the corner by the "Blue Grapes"! Truly, his eyes have never shined be-fore as they do tonight; nor has his little wicker satchel ever jingled so lightly. Across his sleeve, worn by the cords of sacks,

103

is passed an honest little hamper, full to the top and covered with a cold napkin, from under which stick out the neck of a bottle and a twig of holly.

What on earth can the old miser want with all this? Can it be possible that he means to celebrate Christmas himself? Does he mean to have a family reunion and drink to the German fatherland? Impossible! Everybody knows old Cahn has no country. His fatherland is his strongbox. And, moreover, he has neither family nor friends — nothing but debtors. His sons and his associates are gone away long ago with the army. They traffic in the rear among the wagons, vending the water of life, buying watches, and, on nights of battle, emptying the pockets of the dead, or rifling the baggage tumbled in the ditches of the route.

Too old to follow his children, Father Cahn has remained in Bavaria, where he has made magnificent profits from the French prisoners of war. He is always prowling about the barracks to buy watches, shoulder knots, medals, post orders. You may see him glide through the hospitals, beside the ambulances. He approaches the beds of the wounded and demands, in a low, hideous growl —

" Haf you anyting to sell? "

And, hold! At this same moment, the reason he trots so gaily with his basket under his arm is solely that the military hospital closes at five o'clock, and that there are two Frenchmen who await him high up in that tall black building with straight, iron-barred windows, where Christmas finds nothing to welcome her approach save the pale lights which guard the pillows of the dying.

II

These two Frenchmen are named Salvette and Bernadou. They are infantrymen from the same village of Provence, enrolled in the same battalion, and wounded by the same shell. But Salvette had the stronger frame, and already he begins to grow convalescent, to take a few steps from his bed toward the window.

Bernadou, though, will never be cured. Through the pale curtains of the hospital bed, his figure looks more meager, more languished day by day; and when he speaks of his home, of return thither, it is with that sad smile of the sick wherein there is more of resignation than of hope.

Today, now, he is a little animated by the thought of the cheerful Christmas time, which, in our country of Provence, is like a grand bonfire of joy lighted in the midst of winter; by remembrance of the departure for Mass at midnight; the church bedecked and luminous; the dark streets of the village full of people; then the long watch around the table; the three traditional flambeaux; the ceremony of the yule log; then the grand promenade around the house, and the sparkle of the burning wine.

" Ah, my poor Salvette, what a sad Christmas we are going to have this year! If only we had money to buy a little loaf of white bread and a flask of claret wine! What a pleasure it would be before passing away forever to sprinkle once again the yule log, with thee! "

And, in speaking of white bread and claret wine, the eyes of the sick youth glistened with pleasure.

But what to do? They had nothing, neither money nor watches. Salvette still held hidden in the seam of his mantle a post order for forty francs. But that was for the day when they should be free and the first halt they should make in a cabaret of France. That was sacred; not to be touched!

But poor Bernadou is so sick. Who knows whether he will ever be able to return? And, then, it is Christmas, and they are together, perhaps, for the last time. Would it not be better to use it, after all?

Then, without a word to his comrade, Salvette loosens his tunic to take out the post order, and when old Cahn comes, as he does every morning to make his tour of the aisles, after long debates and discussions under the breath, he thrusts into the Jew's hands the slip of paper, worn and yellow, smelling of powder and dashed with blood.

III

This solemn midnight, which sounds from all the bells of the town, falls sadly into the pale night of the sick. The hospital is silent, lighted only by the night lamps suspended from the ceiling. Great running shadows flit over the beds and bare walls in a perpetual balancing, which seems to image the heavy respiration of all the sufferers lying there.

At times, dreamers talk high in their feverish sleep or groan in the clutches of nightmares; while from the street there mounts up a vague rumor of feet and voices, mingled in the cold and sonorous nightlike sounds made under a cathedral porch.

Salvette feels the gathering haste, the mystery of a religious feast crossing the hours of sleep, the hanging forth in the dark village of the blind light of lanterns and the illumination of the windows of the church.

" Are you asleep, Bernadou? "

Softly, on the little table next his comrade's bed, Salvette has placed a bottle of vin de Lunel and a loaf of bread, a pretty Christmas loaf, where the twig of holly is planted straight in the center.

Bernadou opens his eyes encircled with fever. By the indistinct glow of the night lamps and under the white reflection of the great roofs where the moonlight lies dazzlingly on the snow, this improvised Christmas feast seems but a fantastic dream.

" Come, arouse thee, comrade! It shall not be said that two sons of Provence have let this midnight pass without sprinkling a drop of claret! " And Salvette lifts him up with the tenderness of a mother. He fills the goblets, cuts the bread, and then they drink and talk of Provence.

Little by little Bernadou grows animated and moved by the occasion — the red wine, the remembrances! With that childlike manner which the sick find in the depths of their feebleness he asks Salvette to sing a Provençal noel. His comrade asks which: " The Host," or " The Three Kings," or " Saint Joseph Has Told Me "?

"No, I like the ' Shepherds ' best. We chant that always at home."

" Then, here's for the ' Shepherds.' "

And in a low voice, his head between the curtains, Salvette began to sing.

All at once, at the last couplet, when the shepherds, coming to see Jesus in his stable, have placed in the manger their offerings of fresh eggs and cheeses, and when, bowing with an affable air,

> " Joseph says, ' Go! be very sage:
> Return, and make you good voyage,
> Shepherds,
> Take your leave! ' "

— all at once poor Bernadou slipped and fell heavily on the pillow. His comrade thought he had fallen asleep and called him, shook him. But the wounded boy rested immovable, and the little twig of holly lying across the rigid cloth seemed already the green palm they place upon the pillows of the dead.

Salvette understood at last. Then, in tears, a little weakened by the feast and by his grief, he raised in full voice, through the silence of the room, the joyous refrain of Provence —

> " Shepherds,
> Take your leave! "

GERMANY

A Star for Hansi

MARGUERITE VANCE

S OPHIE IS A FRIENDLY NAME. You cannot think that a little
girl to whom it belonged would sulk, or refuse to answer to
" How do you do? " or take the largest currant muffin.

Sophie Ebbert, who lived in the large, lemon-colored house
behind the very high green hedge, was just the little girl to be
called by a friendly name. Her eyes were gray, and a dimple near
the corner of the left one gave to her face when she smiled what
Grossmutter called her " twinkly look." When Sophie smiled —
and she did very often — you thought of hidden fairy lights shining from those merry twinkly eyes. Sophie's cheeks were red and
round as snow apples, and her brown hair, in two neat, short pig-
tails, bobbed across her shoulders.

Sometimes they were tied with blue ribbons, and sometimes
with red, but on important days, or when there were guests,
plaid ribbons, red and blue and gold all together, finished the
ends of the fat brown braids.

One of the things that always made Sophie happy was that
her birthday — and this time it had been her eighth — came just
a week before Christmas when one was growing a little impatient for the great day itself to come. A birthday, though not so
important, did a great deal to make a pleasant break in the time
of waiting.

Today, however, was one of the very rare times when the

"twinkly look" was gone and even the brave plaid bows on her braids drooped.

It was Sunday afternoon. Snow drifted softly down on the garden. The bushes looked like huge white frosted cakes, the pine trees like the sugar trees in the candy shops, which would stand on Christmas dinner tables next week. Inside, the lamps had not been lighted, but from the hearth a pink warm light stole out to touch the edges of things. Sophie watched the white snowflakes lose themselves in the gray twilight, and sighed. Grossmutter closed her book and lighted the lamp — the one with the pink china shade. Then she came and stood beside Sophie.

"What is it, Liebchen?" she asked. "You are quiet today and just now you sighed much too deeply for a little girl just halfway between her birthday party and Christmas. What is it?"

"Nothing —" began Sophie, and then, before she could stop them, big tears were sliding down her cheeks and Grossmutter was wiping them with her handkerchief, which smelled of lavender and spice.

"Come, come, tell me what is troubling you, little child. Maybe I can help. Here on my lap — come."

She drew Sophie onto her lap and listened while the little story was told.

"I had saved my allowance to buy Mother and Father, and you and Peter, Christmas gifts," she began. "I got Peter's boat, and Father's pencil, and — and your gift. The man in the perfume shop has a little bottle shaped like a green lantern. It is filled with the cologne Mother likes. He is saving it for me. I had enough money to buy it, and Father was going to take me to town tomorrow afternoon to get it — and now —" Sophie's voice trailed off and stopped.

"And now what?"

"Well — you see, when Karen came for my party last week we went to the village and — I — I spent all I had left for gingerbread men, and now —" Again the big tears began to slip down Sophie's cheeks.

Grossmutter looked grave, even with the pink lamp and the firelight making everything so warm and friendly.

" So you spent all your money on gingerbread men," she said. " Ach, that is bad, little Sophie, very bad. Now, now, don't cry so! " for now the tears were coming faster and faster. " See, I shall tell you the story of the applewood box. Would you like that? "

Sophie nodded.

" What did it look like? " she asked.

" It was round — round as a chestnut, and just that color. Now listen well.

" Once long ago there stood on the edge of the great Black Forest a beautiful castle. Around it spread its parks where deer and antelope walked softly through the speckled shadows. Beyond the park was the hamlet where lived the people who served the baron of the castle. In their little cottages they lived — woodcutters, shepherds, farmers, the blacksmith, shopkeepers, the schoolteacher, the pastor, the bürgermeister.

" In the little house of the bürgermeister, besides himself there lived his wife and their three children, Tomas, little Hans, and a little girl about your age. And what do you suppose her name was? "

Sophie shook her head, and almost the dimple peeped out.

" I don't know. What was it? "

" Sophie."

" Sophie — like me? "

" Yes, Liebchen, very much like you. I think that other Sophie looked just a little like you too. Tomas was two years older than his sister and four years older than little Hans.

" In all the Black Forest region there was no child just like little Hans. His hair was like pale sunshine caught and rolled into soft curls all over his head. His dark eyes seemed to see faraway places; and when little Hans laughed Tomas put down his whittling and Sophie stopped her knitting the better to listen to so sweet a sound. Little Hans did not play their games, nor did he go with them to tend geese in the swamp. He sat and played quietly in a sunny spot where his chair was placed. Sometimes his father carried him into the woods and he called to the birds in his high sweet voice, by little names he made up for them.

" Sophie and Tomas and their parents all loved one another

dearly, but their love for little Hans was quite different. It was as though there must be enough love for Hansi to remember forever and ever.

" Now, though the bürgermeister had his snug cottage, and though his family was clothed and fed, still he was not a rich man, and his children earned whatever they could to buy the little extra things that girls and boys like. Tomas helped the woodcutter gather the lighter branches as they fell under his ax and saw, and tied them in neat, tight bundles. On baking days, when his mother's loaves were ready to be carried to the village oven for baking, he stopped at the cottage of the blacksmith, the tailor, and the doctor, and carried the loaves their wives had set too, and later returned each golden loaf, crusty and hot from the oven, to its owner.

" Sophie crocheted fine lace for the linen pillowcases in the castle and knitted worsted caps and mufflers for the children of the baron. Each morning when she drove her mother's geese to the swamp, she drove the geese of the miller and of the storekeeper too.

" For these little tasks the children received a few coppers. That is how Tomas came to own his jackknife for whittling, and how Sophie had the white knitting needles with tiny roses and violets painted on them.

" One day in early autumn the schoolteacher called Sophie to him and said:

" ' I have something here for you, Sophie, which I hope you will always treasure. Look, it was given me by my teacher when I was your age.'

" He put into Sophie's hands a small round box."

" Was it the applewood box, Grossmutter? "

" Yes, exactly, and this is what he said: ' This little box is only for a careful child, and I believe you are that. There is a coin in it now. See that there is at least one coin, however small, in it at all times. There is only one exception to this rule. When your heart quite plainly says, " Now, now is the time to spend the last coin," then spend it gladly. Otherwise, remember, always keep at least one coin in the box. It will call in others. When you have grown to be an old lady, search well for another careful child and pass the box on to him or her with this same advice.'

" So he gave the applewood box to the happy little girl, and — "

" And did it have a coin in it? "

" Yes, a pfennig; and Sophie promised that she would never let the little box be empty unless her heart quite plainly said, ' Now, now is the time to spend the last coin.'

" She was so proud of her new prize that she ran home through the woods and burst in on her mother, who was spinning beside the fire."

" What did Tomas and little Hans say? "

" Tomas was away in the woods with the woodcutter, but little Hans held the box against his cheek and laughed softly and said, ' It is smooth and cool like the moon.'

" The days flew and Sophie worked very diligently at all the tasks at home, at school, and at those other tasks which brought coins to the little box.

" One day a peddler came to the village with strange and beautiful toys from across the Russian border — little carved squirrels that climbed a string, small tops of many colors, music boxes that played wild, sweet tunes that seemed to come from faraway lovely places behind the snowy sunset. Tomas selected a set of tops, spent his last coin, and grieved when evening came and his tops were broken. Sophie knew that little Hans would have loved a music box, but as he had not seen ANY of the toys, she carried the prettiest brown squirrel home to him instead and shared his fun as he watched it run up and down the string. In the applewood box there was still the last coin to begin fresh saving for other useful and amusing things.

" Again, when the family all went to the fair in the early winter, Sophie was tempted. There was the man selling cardamon cakes, another selling chocolate and herb tea delicately spiced. In one tent a big black bear danced and boxed with his trainer; in another a troupe of dwarfs tumbled and did amusing tricks. Tomas spent his last coin, poor lad, yet saw only half that he wanted. Sophie chose a cardamon cake and saw the dancing bear, and went home happy, with a cake for little Hans, and a

coin still rattling in the applewood box. More lace to be crocheted, more cold mornings helping with the geese and chickens, and soon there would be more coins to make a gay tinkling
in the box.

" Soon it was time for the lovely Christmas festival. Mother
baked pfeffernüsse and springerle until the little cottage was
sweet with spicy fragrance. Father brought in fresh wood and
laid pine cones between the kindling to make a more snapping
Christmas fire while he told the children stories of other Christmases in the Black Forest.

" One evening he told the story of the first Christmas and
how a great, beautiful, silver star had led the way to the baby
Jesus. Little Hans was in his arms, listening to the story. His
sunny hair made a great splash of gold against his father's coat.

" ' Did they find him, Father? ' he asked.

" ' Of course,' Father answered; ' they just followed where
the star led, and there at last they found the Child, and he held
out his little arms to them.'

" The other children did not say anything, but little Hans
smiled.

" ' That was nice,' he said, ' nice.'

" The next day was Christmas Eve, so Sophie and Tomas took
their coins and went to the village, and what fun they had! A
bit of beeswax for Mother's ironingboard, a new goose quill for
Father's writing pad, a jumping jack and a stick of candy for
little Hans. For each other they chose a collection of small
things which, of course, they would not show until the tree was
lighted after sunset. Hugging their packages, they ran home
through the twilight, hoping Mother had not finished trimming
the tree and placing the little manger beneath it."

" But, was it really, truly, a manger, Grossmutter? "

" Yes, a tiny stable, and just inside, a manger filled with real
hay for the child Jesus to lie upon. And then grouped all around
were the figures of Mary and Joseph and the Wise Men and
shepherds — all made of wax.

" Tomas ran to hide his packages and Sophie threw off her
hood and cape and went to little Hans. He was not in his chair
by the window this evening, but in his little bed, for he was

tired. So Sophie put the lumpy jumping jack in its brown wrapping on the bed beside him.

" ' Guess what Sophie brought for you, Hansi,' she said, and waited while his fingers moved over the stiff paper. Never, never would he guess!

" ' Is it — Sophie, is it — a star? ' he whispered at last, and his own dark eyes were like stars.

" Sophie's heart sank. A jumping jack! and he had wanted a star! For a few pfennigs a beautiful star, all shimmering and silvery white, could be had in a shop at the other end of the village! But she had spent all her money — all but — ! Suddenly Sophie straightened up. There was that last coin which must never be touched unless quite plainly her heart said, ' Now, now is the time to spend the last coin,' and now her heart spoke.

" She smiled down at little Hans, and he smiled happily back.

" ' Is it — is it truly a star? ' he asked again; very softly.

" Sophie kissed his fingers resting on the package.

" ' Just you wait, Hansi, until Sophie comes back,' she whispered, and taking the jumping jack, she ran to the woodshed, where Tomas was helping Father with the little tree for which Mother was clearing a space on the table.

" ' Hide this with your other things, Tomas,' she said. ' I'm going to run back to the village. I'll not be gone long — I'll hurry.'

" She threw on her cape, and holding the applewood box tightly, ran through the woods to the village, thinking she never had heard anything more comforting than the sound of the coin rattling away merrily in the little box as she ran. The shopkeeper smiled at her serious face.

" ' A star for little Hansi, eh? ' he exclaimed. Together they looked over the rows of beautiful white-and-silver stars hanging like a sparkling girdle around the shop walls, and at last the shopkeeper took down the shiniest one he had and held it out to her.

" ' There,' he said, ' there is the brightest star in the shop, and little Hans is just the child it was meant to shine for. Be sure to wish him a good Christmas for me, eh? '

" Sophie gave him her last coin happily, and holding the star carefully under her cape, sped back over the snow to the cottage at the edge of the wood.

" Now the sun had set and from the windows of the bürgermeister's little house a warm welcoming light streamed out, making a gay pattern on the snow.

" 'The whole house seems to glow,' thought Sophie, hurrying toward it, ' as though it were full of lovely stars! '

" Softly she opened the door, and softly — not knowing why — hurried through the passage. At the door of the family room she stopped. There was a hush in the room — as when a bird stops singing or a bubbling fountain ceases to play.

" The little tree standing on the table shone quietly in the soft white light of its candles. Before it, all together, was the family — Mother, Father, Tomas, and in Father's arms little Hans. Mother knelt beside Father's chair, with her cheek against Hansi's curls, and Sophie could see that she had forgotten Father and Tomas and even Christmas — everything but little Hans. Father was telling the Christmas story again, very slowly, very carefully, so that even if one were tired and drowsy, still one could hear and understand.

" 'They followed where the star led,' Father said, ' and there at last — '

" Little Hans opened his eyes. He saw Sophie. He smiled all over his little face.

" 'Look, Hansi,' she whispered, and slid to her knees before Father's chair and held up the great quivering silver star.

" 'For me! For me! ' the little boy said softly, and held out his hands and laughed; and looking at his Christmas star, he fell asleep there before the baby Christ in the manger, who held out his little arms to him. And Sophie knew she had done well to take the last coin from the applewood box. And that is the end of the story, Liebchen."

Sophie stirred.

" Tell some more," she begged. " Did little Hans wake up after awhile and see his star again? and did Sophie grow up? and what did she do with the box? "

Grossmutter smiled gently.

"Little Hans woke up — yes, and never was tired any more. Sophie grew up, and what do you suppose she did with the applewood box? Jump down, dear; I am going to show you something."

Grossmutter went to her room, and in a moment she was back, carrying a small object in her hands.

"This is from one Sophie to another," she said, smiling — "to you."

Sophie could not believe her eyes, for there in her hands was a small, round, dark box of polished wood!

"Is it — oh, Grossmutter, IS IT THE APPLEWOOD BOX?" Sophie's dimple was back and so was the "twinkly look."

Grossmutter nodded.

"Then are you — were you — that Sophie?"

Again Grossmutter nodded, or tried to, because Sophie's arms were around her neck in a bear hug, and her flushed round cheek pressed so tightly to Grossmutter's that she scarcely could move.

"Oh, it was the loveliest, LOVELIEST story, Grossmutter!" she said, "and I'll be so proud of my box!"

"Then see, child; let us open it."

Carefully Sophie took off the polished lid. The box was quite filled with coins.

"Now then," Grossmutter asked, "how much shall we need to buy the lantern filled with cologne?"

Sophie's dimple disappeared.

"Fifty cents," she answered, and just saying it made it sound twice as much.

Grossmutter emptied the coins on the table and together they counted them.

"Just exactly fifty pennies!" Grossmutter beamed. Sophie shrieked with glee.

"Goody! Goody!" she cried. "Now in the morning the first thing Father and I can go to town and buy the lantern! Fifty cents is exactly what I needed and now I have it! I'm so happy! So happy!" She danced around the room. Then suddenly she noticed that Grossmutter was looking at her a little strangely, a little sadly.

" I am afraid," she said, " that my little Sophie does not remember the most important part of all in the story of the box. What about the last coin? "

Sophie stopped short in her dance.

" Oh — I forgot," she said. " I forgot."

" When does Father give you your next allowance? "

" Tomorrow. Peter and I get it every Monday morning."

" Well, then — ? "

" Oh, I see! " The dimple came twinkling out again. " I see! Look, Grossmutter, I'll leave five pennies instead of only one in the box. That will leave forty-five pennies I can keep out. Then tomorrow I'll add five pennies from my allowance, and that will give me enough to buy the lantern and still leave coins in the box to ' call in others,' as the schoolteacher said when he gave the box to So — I mean to you."

Grossmutter patted her cheek.

" That is my little Sophie," she said. " That is being a ' careful child,' a worthy owner of the applewood box."

So on Christmas Eve, tucked in her snug bed, Sophie thought happily of Mother's cologne lantern hanging bravely on the tree downstairs. Above, the Christmas stars shone softly down, and one larger, brighter than the others, she thought must look very like the one the other Sophie had brought to little Hans on that long-ago Christmas Eve in the Black Forest. As she drifted into happy Christmas dreams she made a solemn promise always to guard her last coin carefully, but to spend it gladly, thankfully, when her heart quite plainly said, " Now, now is the time."

HOLLAND

Christmas Among the Animals

AN OLD DUTCH CHRISTMAS TALE

MARY HELD HER NEWBORN BABY in her arms. She was happy, but troubled too. It was cold in the stable, and there was a nasty draft. She pressed her little son against her heart and wished that her love for him could warm his cold little body.

Worried, she glanced at the big holes in the roof. Through the largest of these a beautiful flickering star looked down, the star which later was to show the way to the shepherds and the Three Magi. But Mary did not know about this yet. She was a mother, worried about her little baby, and waiting for Joseph, who had gone out to borrow some fire.

Tenderly cradling her little son in her arms, she looked around at the animals whose home she shared: an ox, a mule, a horse, and a goat. It was obvious that the animals regarded her as an intruder, except perhaps for the ox: he looked kind of friendly, sometimes glancing behind him to a corner where his sister, the cow, was giving birth to a little calf.

Mary was looking for a tiny place in which to put her son to sleep, but all she saw was the hard, rough ground, the heavy beams and dark corners full of spider webs. Maybe she could use the animals' manger. She filled it with some hay and laid her baby down. Then she tore off part of her dress to cover him and sat down quietly beside him, now and then reaching for his little feet, to see if they were still warm.

The animals had been watching this for some time and the

118

goat was working herself into a rage. Loudly bleating, she tried to set the others against the human beings. Such manners! Intruding upon their privacy, and taking their manger and their food too! Pretty soon the horse and the mule began to agree with the goat; they pounded the floor with their hoofs and cast malicious glances at the little group of humans. Mary noticed it and felt the animals were justified. She got up and began to gather the hay which lay all over the stable floor. It was a difficult task but she felt that it was her duty, and finally she had assembled a whole lot of it.

But the big hungry horse thought that it wasn't enough. Full of contempt, he stamped his hoofs on the heap of hay, snorted indignantly, and tossed his mane and tail in anger. What he wanted was that delicious bit of hay right under the little boy in the manger. He pushed the mule out of his way and began to nibble greedily.

Poor Mary was desperate. She took her baby in her arms again and began to pray. Suddenly she heard a sound on the roof, and when she looked up — lo! —there was a beautiful angel looking down at her through the biggest hole in the roof. He addressed the horse: " You greedy and intolerant animal! Henceforth you and your offspring shall serve and carry human beings. You are larger and more powerful than they are, but you will be their humble servant." And so it came to pass.

Meanwhile the ox felt sorry for Mary and her infant, and he also wanted to make up for what his friend had done. With his heavy hoofs he scraped some hay together for a bed and blew his warm breath comfortingly over the cold little body. He whispered in Mary's ear that his sister, the cow, wished to give her little calf to her son for a playmate.

Oh, how grateful was Mary! She looked up and — lo! — there was the angel again, this time peering at the ox through the biggest hole in the roof. " Henceforth," he said, "you and your sister shall eat in peace, and even digest your food four times. And your sister shall have a calf each year and always have plenty of milk." And so it came to pass.

The mule had listened to all these prophecies but didn't really know whether to believe them or not. It was all rather silly, he thought. He had his own opinion, and very bad manners. Suddenly he began to bray stupidly. When Mary was thanking the ox for his kindness, he snatched the hay away from under the baby and began to eat rapidly, while moving his long ears up and down.

But before Mary could do anything to prevent him — lo! — there was the angel shaking a menacing finger at the mule through the biggest hole in the roof. " Mule," he said, " just for this you and your kind will never have any babies as from this day." And so it came to pass.

One would think that by this time the goat might have learned her lesson and behaved herself. But no, she was stupid and brazen. Still bleating loudly, she rushed through the stable, kicking up her heels and generally making a fool of herself. The little boy began to cry, and Mary didn't know what to do next. And when she looked up at the star shining through the roof — lo! — there was the angel sticking his head through the biggest hole. To this day the goat and her offspring have kept their silly laugh, and their milk has lost its good flavor, so that people don't like to drink it. And so it came to pass.

At long last, peace returned to the stable — wonderful, comforting peace. Joseph returned and brought some fire, the animals stood in awe, and a great and heavenly light shone through the biggest hole in the roof. The little infant fell into an untroubled sleep, and Mary folded her hands in prayer.

This is what happened during the holy night — at least, many people believe it, or at least that is what people in Holland tell one another.

HOLLAND

The Three Skaters

ANONYMOUS

IT WAS A COLD, BARREN WINTER that year. The harvest had
been poor; the barns were only half filled. The farmers wondered how they would be able to pull through the winter, how
they were to feed their hungry families and their cattle, how to
heat their homes.

A stillness hung over the wide, cold Dutch land, a tense stillness. Low gray clouds hung heavy over the snowy white fields.
Along the canals, stretching straight and frozen till they faded
out in the distant horizon, the gnarled willows stood in ragged
rows like awkward onlookers.

A farmer skated home over the frozen canal. He had been to
market that day, and all he had been able to get for his few
pennies was a bagful of red apples, which he carried over his
shoulder. He hunched his back against the icy wind and hurried
along with long, steady strokes, thinking all the while how disappointed his wife and the children would be with the meager
results of his marketing.

He stopped for a moment to refasten his curved wooden
skates. As he stood there catching his breath, he thought he
heard a soft, swishing sound in the distance. Looking up and
peering through the mist, he saw his neighbor the old miller appear through the falling dusk. His back was bent under a load
of bread which he had gotten from the baker in exchange for
his flour. The two men greeted each other without a word, and

they went on through the silent evening, each sunk in his own thoughts, each knowing that the other man's thoughts were similar to his own.

They halted at a little drawbridge, too low to pass under. With uncertain, clumsy feet on skates they stepped on land to cross to the other side of the bridge. Just as they found themselves back on the canal they were joined by another neighbor, a pig farmer who carried a side of bacon which no one had been willing to buy from him.

The three silent men hurried on, the strong, regular strokes of their skates the only sounds in the wide, wintry landscape. There should be a moon somewhere; at least the heavy clouds looked strangely lit as if by an inner light. It had become even colder now, and the men huddled deeper into their woolen mufflers. The old miller lagged somewhat behind. He felt tired, and he shifted the heavy sack from his left to his right shoulder. As he looked up he saw that the moon had appeared from behind the clouds. One cold, stark beam pointed straight down on an old barn across the snow-covered field on the left.

Suddenly a sound came from that lonely barn, a sound as if from a baby crying. " Hey! " the miller called his companions. " Hey, there — stop! Come over here! "

The other two men braked to a halt and turned around slowly, annoyed at the old man. It was cold and late, and they wanted to go home.

"Listen," said the miller, pointing his finger to the old barn. There was no mistake — they heard it too. There was a baby crying in that barn.

"But there ain't nobody living there," said the farmer. "That barn's been empty for years, ever since the old man built himself a new one next to his house."

"He keeps his sheep there," said the pig farmer, "but that sound comes from no sheep."

For a moment the three men looked at each other. Then all three removed their skates and stepped on land to find out.

As they neared the moonlit barn the crying became quieter, a mere whimper now, while a gentle woman's voice began softly to hum a little tune. The three neighbors shook their heads, completely baffled. They hesitated for just a second; then the miller moved forward and opened the barn door. All three stepped inside.

They had to become accustomed to the darkness at first, away from the clear shaft of moonlight. But as their eyes adjusted themselves to the dim glow of the lantern inside, they saw that their ears had not deceived them. As if by common impulse, all three took off their caps.

A young woman, whom they had never seen before, sat there on the cold barn floor. In her arms she held a newly born baby, which she rocked gently to and fro. She had wrapped her coat around the little boy, who was now sleeping peacefully. An older man was raking some hay together in a corner near where the sheep stood, and the mother laid down her baby tenderly on that one little heap of softness in the cold, rough barn.

" We come from far away," the old man began to explain, as if to answer unspoken questions, " and we shall have far to go. When it was time for my wife to have the baby, we tried very hard to find shelter, and we are grateful that we could get this barn. But we can't stay long, for we have no food and no firewood. We shall have to move on tomorrow. . . ."

The three men just stood there, not speaking, turning their caps in their hands. Then, driven as by a single force, each of them lowered the sack from his shoulder and emptied it before the young mother. The apples, the bread, and the bacon gleamed curiously in the flickering lantern light. Her eyes looked at them with such quiet peace and acceptance that they felt a strange sense of well-being, which made them almost uneasy at the same time. One by one they took a look at the sleeping little boy, then turned around and left, gently closing the barn door behind them.

It had become still colder now, but the clouds had disappeared and the moon shone brightly over the snow-covered landscape. The men put their caps back on, knotted the mufflers tightly around their necks, and flung their empty bags across their shoulders. Back at the canal, they fastened their skates and started on the last stretch home, each thinking about the little scene they had just witnessed.

One — two, one — two, went the skates over the frozen waterway. It was strange, but none of them seemed to feel worried about coming home empty-handed. Somehow life seemed to hold so much in store for them. They felt almost lighthearted, skating there in the clear frosty night. Yet it was as if the empty sacks they carried were getting heavier and heavier, as if somebody dropped a stone into them with every stroke they made. By the time they had reached their village and had removed their skates, they were pretty near bent double under the load they carried. They could not explain it, but somehow they knew that it was good.

At the church the three men parted; the farmer, the miller, and the pig farmer each went his own way, back to his family. The last few steps seemed almost unbearable, so heavy was the weight on their shoulders. As each opened his back door and entered his home, he dumped the sack on the floor and looked at the expectant faces around the fireplace with its blue and white tiles.

Loud cheers went up. " Father! " " Here is Father! " " Father is home! " All the youngsters jumped up and began to pull at the strings of the bags, pushing each other, laughing, romping, as if this were a new kind of game.

Oh, the wonder of it all! When the bags were finally opened and turned out over the kitchen floors, an abundance of food rolled over the neatly scrubbed tiles. And there weren't merely everyday things. There was candy for the children, Dutch honey cake for the mothers, and also tobacco for the fathers. What a feast there was in the three homes!

When all was quiet again each of the three men sat down by his fireplace, contentedly puffing his pipe. But in spirit the three were far away. . . . Their thoughts hovered around a moonlit barn, around a simple little lantern-lit scene where a miracle had come to pass.

HUNGARY

Which of the Nine?

MAURUS JÓKAI

ONCE UPON A TIME in the city of Budapest there lived a
poor shoemaker who simply couldn't make ends meet. Not
because people had suddenly decided to give up wearing boots,
nor because the city council had passed an ordinance directing
that shoes be sold at half price, nor even because his work was
not satisfactory. Indeed, the good man did such excellent work
that his customers actually complained that they couldn't wear
out anything he had once sewed together. He had plenty of
customers who paid him promptly and well enough; not one
of them had run away without settling his bill. And yet Cobbler John couldn't make both ends meet.

The reason was that the good Lord had blessed him all too
plentifully with nine children, all of them as healthy as acorns.

Then, one day, as if Cobbler John hadn't already had trouble enough, his wife died. Cobbler John was left alone in this
world with nine children. Two or three of them were going to
school; one or two were being tutored; one had to be carried
round; gruel had to be cooked for the next; another had to be
fed, the next one dressed, yet another washed. And on top of
all this, he had to earn a living for all of them. Verily, brethren,
this was a big job — just try it, in case you doubt it!

When shoes were made for them, nine had to be made all at
once; when bread was sliced, nine slices had to be cut all at
one time. When beds were made ready, the entire room be-

125

tween window and door became one single bed, full of little and
big blond and brunet heads.

" Oh, my dear Lord God, how thou hast blessed me," the
good artisan often sighed while even after midnight he still
worked and hammered away at his lasts in order to feed the
bodies of so many souls, stopping occasionally to chide now
one, now another, tossing restlessly in a dream. Nine they were
— a round number nine. But thanks be to the Lord, there was
still no cause for complaint, because all nine were healthy, obedient, beautiful, and well-behaved, blessed with sound bodies
and stomachs. And rather should there be nine pieces of bread
than one bottle of medicine; rather nine side by side than cof-
fins between them. But none of Cobbler John's children had
the slightest intention of dying. It was already fated that all
nine of them should fight their way through life and not yield
their places to anybody. Neither rain nor snow nor dry bread
would ever hurt them.

On Christmas Eve, Cobbler John returned late from his
many errands. He had delivered all sorts of finished work and
had collected a little money which he had to use to buy supplies
and to pay for their daily needs. Hurrying homeward, he saw
stands on every street corner, loaded with gold and silver lambs
and candy dolls which pushcart women were selling as gifts for
well-behaved children. Cobbler John stopped before one or two
of the carts. . . . Maybe he ought to buy something. . . .
What? For all nine? That would cost too much. Then for just
one? And make the others envious? No, he'd give them another
kind of Christmas present: a beautiful and good one, one that
would neither break nor wear out, and which all could enjoy together and not take away from each other.

" Well, children! One, two, three, four . . . are you all
here? " he said when he arrived home within the circle of his
family of nine. " Do you know that this is Christmas Eve? A
holiday, a very gay holiday. Tonight we do no work, we just
rejoice! "

The children were so happy to hear that they were supposed to rejoice that they almost tore down the house.

" Wait now! Let's see if I can't teach you that beautiful song

I know. It's a very beautiful song. I have saved it to give it to you all as a Christmas present."

The little ones crawled noisily into their father's lap and up on his shoulders, and waited eagerly to hear the lovely song.

" Now what did I tell you? If you are good children — just stand nicely in line! — there, the bigger ones over here and the smaller ones next to them." He stood them in a row like organ pipes, letting the two smallest ones stay on his lap.

" And now — silence! First I'll sing it through, then you join in." Taking off his green cap and assuming a serious, pious expression, Cobbler John began to sing the beautiful melody: " On the blessed birth of our Lord Jesus Christ. . ."

The bigger boys and girls learned it after one rendition, though the smaller ones found it a bit more difficult. They were always off key and out of rhythm. But after a while they all knew it. And there could be no more joyous sound than when all the nine thin little voices sang together that glorious song of the angels on that memorable night. Perhaps the angels were still singing it when the melodious voices of nine innocent souls prayed for an echo from above. For surely there is gladness in heaven over the song of children.

But there was less gladness immediately above them. There, a bachelor was living all by himself in nine rooms. In one he sat, in the other one he slept, in the third one he smoked his pipe, in the fourth he dined, and who knows what he did in all the others? This man had neither wife nor children, but more money than he could count. Sitting in room number eight that night, this rich man was wondering why life had lost its taste. Why did his soft spring bed give him no peaceful dreams? Then, from Cobbler John's room below, at first faintly but with ever-increasing strength, came the strains of a certain joy-inspiring song. At first he tried not to listen, thinking they would soon stop. But when they started all over for the tenth time, he could stand it no longer. Crushing out his expensive cigar, he went down in his dressing gown to the shoemaker's flat.

They had just come to the end of the verse when he walked in. Cobbler John respectfully got up from his three-legged stool and greeted the great gentleman.

"You are John, the cobbler, aren't you?" the rich man asked.

"That I am, and at your service, Your Excellency. Do you wish to order a pair of patent-leather boots?"

"That isn't why I came. How very many children you have!"

"Indeed, I have, Your Excellency — little ones and big ones. Quite a few mouths to feed!"

"And many more mouths when they sing! Look here, Master John — I'd like to do you a favor. Give me one of your children. I'll adopt him, educate him as my own son, take him traveling abroad with me, and make him into a gentleman. One day he'll be able to help the rest of you."

Cobbler John stared wide-eyed when he heard this. These were big words — to have one of his children made into a gentleman! Who wouldn't be taken by such an idea? Why, of course, he'd let him have one! What great good fortune! How could he refuse?

"Well, then, pick out one of them quickly, and let's get it over with," said the gentleman. Cobbler John started to choose.

"This one here is Alex. No, him I couldn't let go. He is a good student and I want him to become a priest. The next one? That's a girl, and of course Your Excellency doesn't want a girl. Little Ferenc? He already helps me with my work. I couldn't do without him. Johnny? There, there — he is named after me. I couldn't very well give him away! Joseph? He is the image of his mother — it's as if I saw her every time I look at him. This place wouldn't be the same without him. And the next is another girl — she wouldn't do. Then comes little Paul: he was his mother's favorite. Oh, my poor darling would turn in her grave if I gave him away. And the last two are too small — they'd be too much trouble for Your Excellency. . . ."

He had reached the end of the line without being able to choose. Now he started all over, this time beginning with the youngest and ending with the oldest. But the result was still the same: he couldn't decide which one to give away because one was as dear to him as the other and he would miss them all.

"Come, my little ones — you do the choosing," he finally said. "Which one of you wants to go away to become a gentleman and travel in style? Come now, speak up! Who wants to go? "

The poor shoemaker was on the verge of tears as he asked them. But while he was encouraging them, the children slowly slipped behind their father's back, each taking hold of him, his hand, his leg, his coat, his leather apron, all hanging on to him, and hiding from the great gentleman. Finally Cobbler John couldn't control himself any longer. He knelt down, gathered them all into his arms and let his tears fall on their heads as they cried with him.

" It can't be done, Your Excellency! It can't be done. Ask of me anything in the world, but I can't give you a single one of my children so long as the Lord God has given them to me."

The rich gentleman said that he understood, but that the shoemaker should do at least one thing for him: Would he and his children please not sing any more? And for this sacrifice he asked Cobbler John to accept one thousand florins.

Master John had never even heard the words " one thousand florins " spoken, never in all his life. Now he felt the money being pressed into his hand.

His Excellency went back to his room and his boredom. And Cobbler John stood staring incredulously at the oddly shaped bank note. Then he fearfully locked it away in the wooden chest, put the key into his pocket, and was silent. The little ones were silent too. Singing was forbidden. The older children slumped moodily in their chairs, quieting the smaller ones by telling them they weren't allowed to sing any more because it disturbed the fine gentleman upstairs. Cobbler John himself was silently walking up and down. Impatiently he pushed aside little Paul, the one who had been his wife's favorite, when the boy asked that he be taught again that beautiful song because he had already forgotten how it went.

" We aren't allowed to sing any more! "

Then he sat down angrily at his bench and bent intently over his work. He cut and hammered and sewed until suddenly he caught himself humming: " On the blessed birth of our Lord Jesus Christ. . . ." He clapped his hand over his mouth. But then all at once he was very angry. He banged the hammer down on the workbench, kicked his stool from under him, opened the chest, took out the thousand-florin bill, and ran up the stairs to His Excellency's apartment.

"Good, kind Excellency, I am your most humble servant. Please take back your money! Let it not be mine, but let us sing whenever we please, because to me and my children that is worth much more than a thousand florins."

With that he put the bill down on the table and rushed breathlessly back to his waiting family. He kissed them one after the other; and lining them up in a row just like organ pipes, he sat himself down on his low stool, and together they began to sing again with heart and soul: "On the blessed birth of our Lord Jesus Christ. . . ." They couldn't have been happier if they had owned the whole of the great big house.

But the one who owned the house was pacing through his nine rooms, asking himself how it was that those people down below could be so happy and full of joy in such a tiresome, boring world as this!

INDIA

The Return of the Magi

J. DANIEL

THIS IS A FANTASY — a web of dreams, veiling a hidden light. Lift up the veil gently with reverent hands. You may then behold a light gleaming from behind — a glowing light that bids pilgrims to Christ.

"And being warned of God in a dream that they should not return to Herod, they departed into their own country another way." This is all that is said of the Wise Men about their return. We do not hear of them again. Is this emptiness the inglorious end of all their glorious vision? It seems impossible to believe. Fancy tries to weave many possible sequels, and here is one such attempt woven round a traditional belief. Tradition holds that the three Wise Men were kings — Melchior, the king of China (the land of royal splendor), Balthasar, from India (the land of devotion), and Kaspar, from Africa (the land of sacrifice). You may not agree with this belief; but it matters little, for in following the trail of these earthly monarchs our eyes will be set on three men who follow the gleam of a distant light that leads on a sacred pilgrimage to Christ.

The Return of Melchior After His Visit

Great was the joy in China when the people heard of the return of their saintly king. They welcomed him with a flourish of trumpets. But soon enough they noted that a strange change

131

had come over him. One great thought, and only that, seemed to obsess him — the desire to build a mighty palace worthy of the newborn King of kings — a royal mansion the like of which the world had never yet seen. Was there a more fitting place where such a King could be enthroned than China — the home of splendor? Thus thought Melchior, whose heart glowed with delight at the prospect of building the dream palace that would befit the King of kings. The best of artists, architects, and craftsmen were pressed into service. But how slow the progress seemed! The king spent all his time and thought and money on the task. His other duties lay neglected. The coffers in his treasury seemed to melt away; but the building was still far from nearing completion. The people grew weary of long waiting. Some of them began to grumble. Grumbling soon gave way to groans, bitter complaints, and angry clamorings, culminating at last in an open revolt against the king. The unhappy king had to flee for his life. Imagine the shock of it! But with it came the revelation too. The rude shock had opened his eyes. He had missed something. He had to learn something yet! But what was it? That question disturbed him day in and day out. It seemed to challenge him; for there rose again a vision of the radiant Child in the manger, beckoning to him with a smile of heavenly glory. A sense of awe stole into his heart, and he bowed his head in silent submission. He would go once more to Palestine to learn what he had missed, at the feet of the King of kings. So Melchior turned his footsteps once more toward Palestine to worship the King again.

Balthasar's Return

The celestial Babe of Bethlehem had captured Balthasar's heart. He bowed in adoration before the vivid memory of the Babe crowned with the radiant halo. And on his return home from Palestine, he sprang a surprise on his ministers by announcing his decision to retire to the forest for meditation and yoga. Though the ministers were at first unwilling, they had at last to yield to his wish and reluctantly chose his son to rule in his place. The king retired to the forest and spent his days and nights in lonely contemplation of the beatific face of the heavenly Babe. The light of heaven seemed to illumine his soul, and joy filled his heart.

Years passed by with swiftest feet, and the sage's face began to glow with the light of supreme bliss. Forgetting the shadows and gloom of this dark and dreary world, he lived in a world of ecstasy, till, on a certain day, he dreamed a dream that shook him to his depths. He saw before him the yawning mouth of a deep abyss, from the depths of which thousands of men and women were wailing aloud in agony. Three times the same vision appeared and clouded his mind, stirring his heart to its depths. His ananda was dispelled in a moment. His peace was broken. When he closed his eyes again in a vain attempt to get back the lost bliss, the infant Christ, in swaddling clothes, appeared before him, raising his hands toward him as if in mute appeal. It was an unmistakable call, and he could not resist it. He had to go and learn again at the feet of the King of kings. From whom else could he learn its significance, except from him whom he had worshiped as a heavenly Babe at Bethlehem? The urge was irresistible! Leaving the verdant forests of India, he therefore wended his way to Palestine, the home of the Infant, born to be the Light of the world.

Kaspar, Back in Africa

What of Kaspar — the African king? While kneeling beside the cradle of the newborn King, he had seen something that the others had missed — the vision of a faint blood-red cross standing at the head of the cradle. To him had been vouchsafed that unique experience! True, it was only a momentary vision, but he had seen it clearly enough to bear its deep impress. The others had missed it, but he could never forget it. All the way back to his native soil, the cross haunted his memory and disturbed his peace. The cross and royalty seemed incompatible with each other; yet that emblem of suffering seemed to flash out a message urging him to dedicate his life for those who were suffering. Was it a call? Perhaps it was. That was what he felt, and the meaning of the vision burned itself so deeply into

his soul that as soon as he arrived at home he set about to re-
lieve the woes of suffering humanity. He built asylums for the
orphans and the waifs, charity homes for the poor and the destitute, and hospitals for the sick and the ailing, and all his efforts
were turned toward the uplift of the socially downtrodden.

Years passed. The zealous king had done much during those
years. Yet, when the king looked around him and surveyed what
he had done, his heart was not glad; for sickness and suffering
still had their sway. He could still hear the murmurs of the poor
and the destitute. The slum dwellers had carried with them to
their new tenements their vile thoughts and habits, and soon
enough had infected even their new surroundings with foulness
and misery. Kaspar's heart was troubled. But the vision of the
blood-red cross seemed to glow with still more brilliance, chal-
lenging him anew. A silent whisper within quickened his heart
to long for a true revelation of the meaning of the cross. Who
else but the King of kings could interpret the vision aright?
Should he not go back to him? The call was strong and clear.
He could not resist it. Obedient to the inner urge, he walked on
toward Palestine, the land of his hope.

The Kings' Second Visit to Palestine

The three kings had each taken his own path, but they
reached Jerusalem about the same time. Thirty years had gone
by since their last visit. But they had never expected to meet the
exciting scenes that faced them as they entered the city. A
motley crowd was surging toward Mt. Calvary, the scene of the
crucifixion of Jesus — that selfsame king whom the royal visitors
had come to meet and worship again. What an irony of fate!
The swaying mass carried them in its whirl onward, nearer and
nearer the scene of the cross. It was a staggering sight — a gruesome sight. Nailed on the cross hung the King of kings, crowned
with a crown of thorns. The men stood dazed at the awful spectacle of Love crucified on the cross, when from his lips came
the immortal words of love: " Father, forgive them, for they
know not what they do." There was a moment of breathless silence as these deathless words floated above the noisy din of the

scoffing crowds. God had spoken. A hush fell upon the crowd as they listened to the words of love that made them tremble.

Kaspar looked on with tears in his eyes, his mind awakened to a fuller realization of the meaning of the cross. Balthasar lifted up his hands in reverent devotion to the One whom he now perceived to be really the Son of God, Incarnate Love. Melchior bowed his head and wept in secret. They began to learn the meaning of love. The King of kings had been crucified. Love's supreme gift had been offered. Love had flowed out the drops of blood. This was the new message they caught from the cross, wonderful in depth, immense in significance.

The sun sets only to rise again. The darkness of Calvary was soon dispelled by the light of resurrection. The three kings, now no longer resplendent in their royal robes, met in a humble inn and did not know each other till their kindred spirits drew them strangely together in a sacred fellowship of devotion to the King of kings. Knit to oneness of spirit through a common adoration, they bowed their heads in reverent prayer and surrendered their all to their Lord who was Incarnate Love.

Melchior's Return Home a Second Time

When Melchior returned to China again, no one noticed him. He found a home in the slums of China. What a descent from the palace of splendor to the filthy gutters! But that was the way of love. Obedient to the heavenly vision, he labored day and night among those whom the rest of humanity abhorred and despised.

The wrecks of humanity, the fallen, the drunkards, the disgraced — these were the ones whom he loved to serve, ever pleading with them in love and prayer to worship the Lord — Love Incarnate. Houses of bad repute, taverns of vice and drunkenness, slums of filth and shame — these were the constant field of his labor. He strove to bring Christ into these homes and struggled from morn till night and from night till morn to bring back the God of light and love into the dens of vice and sin. But the forces of Satan were mighty, and they set their hearts against the Lord. They spat on the servant of God.

They slandered him, vilified him, and strove to kill him. What else could be expected?

One night, tired and weary, he was pleading hard with a drunkard, clinging to his feet with the humility of love. But to the drunken man, he seemed but a ball to be kicked away. Gnashing his teeth, this wretched man contemptuously kicked the loving servant of Christ so hard that his head was knocked against a pillar. He fell dying. But what was it that Melchior's faltering lips were mumbling? It was the selfsame prayer of love he had learned from his Lord! " Father, forgive them, for they know not what they do." Blood drops streamed down his wan face. But there were no tears in his eyes, and his lips were parted in a sweet smile. No one knew that he was Melchior, once their king. The king of China had given his life in following the King of kings. He had shed his martyr blood! And the blood cried out to the man who had kicked him down. His wayward feet turned toward the Sun of Righteousness, and great was the joy in heaven over this one sinner that had repented. A light had been lighted to light other lights! The land soon began to glow with the new light set burning by men and women who had turned their hearts toward the Light.

Balthasar's New Message

Balthasar brought back to his native land the new evangel of full light and life through the Light of the world, Jesus Christ. But who would accept it in the holy land of the many avatars? Who would turn his heart away from the gods of his forefathers? Who would give up his first love? Who would raise his hands in worship of an alien deity? Who could forget the dazzling manifestations and the many glorious miracles wrought by their powerful gods, and turn to the pale Galilean, nailed to the cross? It seemed too much to expect such a transformation. As Balthasar went about sowing the seed, he felt as if he were sowing on hard rocks. There seemed no hope. Who would accept this in the land where the gods of their ancestors had held unchallenged sway?

Years went by, and still no fruit! Balthasar therefore turned to the children and spoke to them of the Lord. He told them of how He went about doing good, healing the sick, comforting the poor and blessing little children and sweetening their lives. He spoke also of those who hated Him and of how He was crucified. The children loved this new story. They came in little groups and listened to him with rapt attention and, like little angels, carried this message of Christ's love to their homes.

It had its effect, and ere long one of these children brought his father with him. The father went half in curiosity, half in defiance. But when he saw the simple Christian saint, his heart strangely stirred within him, and he sat at his feet quietly to learn the great new message of the gospel story. For a long time he sat there, like one enthralled. But he could not understand why this good saint should think of Christ as the Savior of the human race, and why he spoke of Christ as the only way to God. He could not suppress the question that kept on coming. " There may be many ways to God," he said, " but why do you think that Christ is the only way? Our own gods supply all our needs. Why should we turn to a stranger god? " The question was in earnest and it came from the depths of the inquirer's heart. Balthasar looked into his eyes lovingly, and answered: " Yes, my brother, there may be many paths to a temple, but there is only one standpoint that gives us a full view of the face of the god in the temple. So is it with our way of approach to God. There is only one view that shows us the heart of God." " But," interrupted the inquirer, " what about the many who lived and died before your Christ came into the world? Are they doomed to damnation? Has not God revealed himself to them also? "

" Yes, my brother," answered Balthasar, " this question goes deeper still. God has been revealing himself to all men at all times in innumerable ways. Through nature, through the lives of saints, through human experiences and through supernatural events, he has always been revealing himself."

" Why, then," asked the inquirer, " should you talk of Christ as the one perfect revelation? " Balthasar's eyes glowed as he answered with quiet assurance: " But the fullness of God's light, though ever shining in full glory, has not been known in its full resplendence by his revelations through nature and through man; for even as the light of the sun gets dispersed into its component colors while passing through a prism, so the limitations of the prisms of the media of revelation have been splitting the Eternal Light into its components."

"Do you therefore mean to imply," interposed the questioner, "that only one or some of these components separately have been revealed to humanity till now?"

There was a softness in Balthasar's eyes as he went on: "Yes, my brother, you have grasped the truth. The essence of Godhood is Love. Mankind has for long been groping in eager search after Him. It has felt many of His qualities — power, justice, truth, holiness, beauty, and bliss; but could not touch the heart of God. Through Christ, the revelation of God as identical with Love, which includes and transforms as the rest, a love that is ready to pay the cost, has been brought home to the mind of man. The picture of Christ is the only possible climax of man's vision of God."

When he heard this answer of Balthasar, a new light seemed to dawn in the inquirer's mind. He spoke of it to his own priests, who found in Balthasar a dangerous enemy, to be done away with. They therefore joined together and charged him before the king as a seducer of men's thoughts and as an iconoclast and revolutionary. The trial was a sacred scene. The man who had once been king stood in solemn dignity to answer false charges, before another king, his own son. But his eyes sparkled with the delight of conquest, and love suffused his glowing face, though he was condemned to imprisonment. Long were the days of darkness in which he was confined. But the end came. When the jailer opened the cell to remove the dead body, he read there the words which the saint had inscribed in bold letters — "Except a grain of wheat fall into the earth and die, it abideth by itself alone; but if it die, it beareth much fruit."

Underneath the text was the royal signature of Balthasar, the king who had doffed his royal robes to bring the love of Jesus to his people. Had he failed? The generations of the Christians in India answer "No."

Kaspar's Second Home-Coming

Kaspar returned to his native land, only to face a scene of great turmoil and confusion. Fierce forces of revolt had reared their ugly heads against the oppressive yoke of a tyrant ruler. Kaspar's heart writhed in agony on learning that the new monarch was none other than his own prime minister, who had usurped the throne by ruthlessly murdering his son. The father's heart in him wept in deep anguish. But, as a servant of the Lord of Love, he had a sacred message to deliver. It was the message of love — love to the uttermost — love that pleaded for those that nailed Him to the cross. How, then, could he harbor hatred and bitterness? He looked up to the cross for help, and the insurge of the overflowing love of Christ swept off the rising hatred, till his heart was attuned to the Spirit of Christ, to forgive as he forgives. With this newborn Spirit of love he set his mind on making peace between the enraged mob and the hardhearted tyrant. It was of such that Jesus spoke: " Blessed are the peacemakers, for they shall be called sons of God."

Undeterred by the fires or hatred around, he strove to quench the flames of fury by the breath of love, such love as Jesus showed on the cross. He spoke of the new message that his Lord had brought to the world — " Resist not evil." " Love your enemies, do good to them that hate you, bless them that curse you, pray for them that despitefully use you." His words stirred them, but they hardened their hearts and spurned his words as those of a mad dreamer.

In the midst of the din and strife of revolt, the new message had no place. The mob wildly roared, " Should we allow our homes and hearts to be raped? " and Kaspar answered: " The soul of a man or a home cannot be lost except through want of love. The soul lives when love lives. It dies when love dies." This new message, however, was too much for the mob.

He could not reach them nor touch them. The word " Failure " seemed to be writ large on all his efforts. But the saint of God would not stop with this. He took the earliest chance to meet the king and made a pathetic appeal, beseeching him to think of his subjects as his children. The occasion of their meeting was a sublime moment. Love faced malice. Something made the tyrant tremble. Did he recognize the old king? Something increased tenfold the fires of hatred within him, and in violent anger he had Kaspar soundly horsewhipped on a charge of inciting the people to rebellion. But there broke out only a smile on his face and a blessing from his lips when the lashes lacerated his flesh and squeezed out blood from his skin. The man is stark mad, thought the king, and forgot all about him the next moment.

But to everything there is an end. Even to tyranny there is an end. The wild fires of anger shot up again. The king's every act of autocracy only fanned the flames the more. Mob violence began to rage in all its blind fury. In the midst of these hellish fires of hatred Kaspar moved about, counseling patience and the way of love. But the waters of love could not at that moment quench those burning fires. In the name of freedom, the brazen bulls of Satan were let loose, bellowing and breathing out wild fires, ever keeping alive the flames of fury. The frenzied mob that had hitherto treated Kaspar with venomous scorn could no longer endure even the sight of this angel of mercy, whose very presence excited them to greater violence. They mistook him for a seducer of faithful patriots. In one of their orgies of violence they fell upon this messenger of love and tore him to pieces, lynching him in triumphant but rapid frenzy. But the last words even in his dying agony were the words of the Lord on the cross: " Father, forgive them, for they know not what they do." No one realized that they had killed a saint and devotee of the Lord of lords and King of kings. No one knew that he had once been their own king. It seemed for a time that love had been killed forever.

But the message of victory is a live message. Crucify love; it will rise again.

So it was too in that dark land of forests and deserts. The spiritual ancestry of the thousands of devoted Christian men and women of the present day in that land dates back to the day when the blood of Kaspar flowed over the black land of Africa — the blood of sacrifice crying out with an undying voice to all the witnesses of that gruesome death. The scene haunted them like a ghastly specter. It would not let them go. The monarch had fled from the angry mob, and the mob, balked of its prey, turned away from the palace only to see the glazed eyes of the corpse of the lynched saint looking upon them with pathetic appeal. One of the mob, noting a glittering thing lying nearby, stooped to pick it up. It was a medallion. On it was engraved the royal signature of Kaspar, whom they had killed. The curtain fell on a scene of sorrow and darkness. With royal robes and honors they buried him. With blinding tears and agonized hearts they left him in his tomb. But their souls turned toward the new light — the Light of the world, Incarnate Love, whom this saint of God had come to reveal.

Yes, this is a fantasy. . . . But does not the Babe who lay in a manger, the Son that hung on a cross, work thus in the hearts of men?

IRELAND

The Wee Christmas Cabin of Carn-na-ween

RUTH SAWYER

A HUNDRED YEARS AGO AND MORE, on a stretch of road that runs from the town of Donegal to Killybegs and the sea, a drove of tinkers went their way of mending pots and thieving lambs. Having a child too many for the caravan, they left it, newborn, upon a cabin doorsill in Carn-na-ween.

The cabin belonged to Bridget and Conal Hegarty. Now these two had little wish for another child, having childher aplenty of their own; but they could not leave the wee thing to die at their door, nor had they a mind to throw it into the turf pit. So Bridget suckled it with her own wean; she divided the cradle between them. And in time she came to love it as her own and fought its battles when the neighbors would have cursed it for a tinker's child.

I am forgetting to tell you that the child was a girl and Bridget named her Oona. She grew into the prettiest, the gentlest-mannered lass in all the county. Bridget did her best to get the lads to court her, forever pointing out how clever she was with her needle, how sweet her voice when she lilted an air, the sure way she had of making bannock, broth, or jam.

But the lads would have none of her. Marry a tinker's child? Never! Their feet might be itching to take her to a crossroad's dance, their arms hungering to be holding her, but they kept the width of a cabin or the road always between her and them. Aye, there was never a chance came to Oona to marry and

142

have childher of her own, or a cabin she could call hers.

All of Bridget and Conal's lasses married; but Oona stayed on to mind the house for them, to care for them through their sicknesses, to help them gently into their graves. I think from the beginning Oona had a dream — a dream that, having cared lovingly for the old, someone would be leaving her, at long last, a cabin for her own keeping. Bridget, before she died, broke the dream at its beginning. " The cabin goes to Michael," she said. " He and his young wife will not be wanting ye, I'm thinking. Go to the chest and take your share of the linen. Who knows but some man, losing his wife, will be glad to take ye for his second. I'd not have ye going empty-handed to him."

Oona held fast to the dream; she let neither years nor heartaches shatter it. There was always a cabin waiting to welcome her as soon as another had finished with her. From the time when Oona left the Hegarty cabin, a bonny lass still, with strength to her body and laughter in her eyes, to the time when she was put out of the MacManuses', old and with little work left in her, the tale runs thin as gossamer. But if you are knowing Ireland and the people of Donegal, it is not hard to follow the tinker's child through that running of years.

From cabin to cabin, wherever trouble or need abided, there went Oona. In a cabin where the mother was young, ailing, with her first-born, there you would find Oona caring for the child as it had been her own. In a cabin where the childher had grown and gone dandering off to Belfast, Dublin, or America and left the old ones behind, there she tended them as she would have tended her own had she ever known them. In a cabin where a man had lost his wife and was ill-fitted to mind the house and the weans alone — aye, here she was the happiest. She would be after taking over the brood as a mother would, gentling the hurt that death had left behind, and for herself building afresh the dream.

But her birth betrayed her at every turn of the road. No man trusted her to be his first or second wife. Not one of the many she served and loved guessed of the hunger that grew with the years for a cabin she could call hers. All blessed her name while she lived; and for the hundred years since she has been gone from Carn-na-ween the tales about her have been kept green with loving memory. Those she served saw that she never went empty-handed away. So to Bridget Hegarty's linen was added a griddle, pans, kettles, crocks, creels, and dishes.

Each thing she chose from the cabin she was leaving was something needed to make the home she dreamed of gay and hold comfort. As the years went by, the bundle of her possessions grew, even as she dwindled. Men, women, and childher who passed her on the road at such times as she might be changing cabins would stop to blather with her. Pointing to the size of her bundle, they would say: " 'Tis twice your size, the now. Ye'll have to be asking for oxen and a cart to fetch it away from the next cabin." And they would laugh. Or they would say: " Ye might be asking the marquis to build ye a castle next his own. Ye'll be needing a fair-sized place to keep all ye've been gathering these many years."

Always she would blather back at them. For all her dream was dimming, she was never one to get down-daunted. " Ye can never be telling," she would say, " I may yet be having a wee cabin of my own someday. I'm not saying how and I'm not saying when." And she would nod her head in a wise, knowledgeable way, as if she could look down the nose of the future and see what was there.

She was in the cabin of the MacManuses when the great famine came. The corn in the fields blighted; the potatoes rotted in the ground. There was neither food for man nor fodder for beast. Babies starved at their mothers' breasts, strong men grew weak as childher, dragging themselves into the fields to gnaw at the blistered grass and die under a cruel, drouthing sun. Everywhere could be heard the crying of childher and the keening for the dead. At the beginning, neighbor shared with neighbor until death stalked them. Then it was every cabin for itself, and many a man sat all night, fowling piece across his knee, to keep guard over a last cow in the byre or the last measure of meal in the bin.

So old had Oona grown by famine time that the neighbors had lost all count of her years. She moved slowly on unsteady feet. Her eyes were dulled; her speech was seldom coming now. But for all that, she was worth the sheltering and the scanty food she ate. She milked; she churned; she helped the oldest lad carry the creel to the bog; she helped at the cutting of the turf. So long as there was food enough for them, the MacManuses kept her and blessed the Virgin for another pair of hands to work.

But famine can put stones in the place of human hearts, and hunger can make tongues bitter. As the winter drew in, Oona for all her dullness saw the childher watching every morsel of food she put to her lips. She heard the mother's tongue sharpen as she counted out the spoonfuls of stirabout that went into the bowls. Harvest had come and gone, and there was no harvest. The cold, cruel winds of December rattled at their doors and windows. Of one thing only was there enough: there was always turf in the bog to cut, to dry, to keep the hearth warm.

The childher in the cabin cried from cockcrow till candle time. Oona wished her ears had been as dulled as her eyes. But for all that, she closed her heart to the crying, telling herself she had earned what little food she took and the good heat for her old body. But a night came when she could stand the crying no longer, when the spoon scraped the bottom of the meal bin, when the last of the prateys had been eaten, their skins with them.

Saying never a word, she got up at last from the creepie, where she had been thawing her bones, and started to put together again her things into her bundle. The MacManuses watched her, and never a word said they. The corners of the great cloth were tied at last. Over her bent shoulders Oona laid her shawl. The cabin was quiet the now, the childher having cried themselves asleep with hunger. Oona dragged her bundle to the door; as she lifted the latch she spoke: " Ye can fend for yourselves. Ye'll not want me the now."

" Aye, 'tis God's truth." It was the wife who said it.

Timothy MacManus reached for her hand. " Hush, are ye not remembering what night it is? "

"'Aye, 'tis Christmas Eve. What matter? There be's not sense enough left in the old one's mind to know it. And in

times such as these there is naught to put one night ahead
of another."

" 'Twill be a curse on us, the same, if we let her go."

" 'Twill be a curse on her if she stays."

" God and Mary stay with ye this night," Oona called, going
out the door.

" God and Mary go with ye," the two mumbled back to her.

Outside Oona lifted the bundle to her back. How she had
strength for this I cannot be telling you. It often comes, a
strange and great strength, to those who have borne much
and have need to bear more. Oona took the road leading to
Killybegs and the sea. A light snow was falling and the wind
had dropped to a low whispering. As she went down the village
street she stopped to glimpse each cabin and the lighted room
within. Hardly a cabin but she had lived in; hardly a face but
she had read long and deeply over many years. Her lips made
a blessing and a farewell for every door she passed.

All cabins were left behind as the road grew steeper. She
climbed with a prayer on her lips — what prayer I do not know,
but it lightened the load she carried on her back and in her
heart, it smoothed the roughness of her going. She came at
last to the bogland. It stretched on and on beyond the reach of
eye, even in the daylight. In the dark she sensed only a leveling
off, where feet could rest. She stumbled from the road and
found shelter under a blackthorn which grew on the fringe of
the bog.

" I like it here," she said as she eased the bundle from her
back. " Always, I have liked it here. Many's the time I have
said: Some day I will take the whole of it and climb the hill and
sit under this very thorn, the way I'll be feeling the wind from
the sea and watching the sun set on it, and the stars lighting it;
and, mayhap, hearing the sound of fairy pipes. I never came; I
never had the day whole."

She said it in a kind of wonder. She was safe here from the
reach of neighbors. It was in her heart that she could never
again bear to have man or woman offer her food needed for
young mouths. Too many times she had folded tired hands;
too many times she had shut weary eyes, not to know what a

gentle companioning death could give the old at the end. " 'Tis a friend, he is, that I have known long. 'Tis as a friend he will be coming, calling softly, wishfully, ' Come, Oona! ' "

After that her head grew light. She lost all count of time; she lost all track of space. She felt no cold, no tiredness. She could gather years into her mind as cards into the hand, shuffle them about and draw out the ones she liked best. She remembered suddenly that one of the reasons for wanting to climb the hill was to find the fairy rath that lay somewhere along the bog. Conall of a Thousand Songs had slept a Midsummer Night with his head to this rath and had wakened in the morning with it filled full of fairy music — music of enchantment. Wully Donoghue had crossed the rath late one May eve and caught the fairy host riding abroad. Many a time, herself, she had put a piggin of milk with a bowl of stirabout on the back steps of those cabins she had lived in, remembering how well the Gentle People liked milk and stirabout. Aye, the Gentle People, the Good People! She hoped famine had not touched them. It would be a sorry thing to have the fairy folk starved off the earth.

She slept a little, woke, and slept again. Above the sleeping her mind moved on a slow current. Snow had covered her, warm. This was Christmas Eve, the time of the year when no one should go hungry, no one cold. It would be a white Christmas on the morrow, and the people of Donegal had a saying that when a white Christmas came the Gentle People left their raths and trooped abroad to see the wonder of it. Aye, that was a good saying. They would make good company for a lonely old woman.

Her legs were cramping under her. She strove to move them, and as she did so, she had a strange feeling that she had knocked something over. Her old eyes peered into the darkness, her hand groped for whatever it was she had upset. To her amazement, when she held her hand under her eyes there was a fairy man, not a hand high. His wee face was puckered with worry. " Don't ye be afeard, wee man," she clucked to him. " I didn't know ye were after being where ye were. Was there anything at all ye were wanting? "

" Aye, we were wanting ye."

" Me! "

" None else. Look! "

And then she saw the ground about her covered with hundreds upon hundreds of Gentle People, their faces no bigger round than buttons, all raised to hers, all laughing.

" What might ye be laughing at? " she asked. " Tell me, for it be's a lee long time since I had laughter on my own lips."

" We are laughing at ye, tinker's child. Living a lifetime in other folks' cabins, serving and nursing and mothering and loving, and never a cabin or kin ye could call your own."

" Aye," she sighed, " aye, 'tis the truth."

" 'Tis no longer the truth. Bide where ye be, Oona Hegarty, and sleep the while."

She did as she was bidden, but sleep was as thin as the snow which covered her, breaking through in this place and that, so that she might see through it what was going on about her. Hither and yon the Good People were hurrying. They brought stones; they brought turf. They laid a roof tree and thatched it. They built a chimney and put in windows. They hung a door at the front and a door at the back. As they worked they sang, and the song they made drifted into Oona's sleep and stayed with her;

> " 'Tis a snug Christmas cabin we're building the night,
>   That we're building the night.
> The stones make the walls and the turf chinks it tight,
>   Aye, the turf chinks it tight.
> There'll be thatch for the roof to keep wind out and rain,
>   To keep wind out and rain.
> And a fire on the hearth to burn out all pain,
>   Aye, burn out all pain.
> The meal in the chest will stand up to your chin,
>   Well up to your chin;
> There'll be Christmas without, and Christmas within,
>   Always Christmas within.
> There'll be plenty of currants, and sugar, and tea,
>   Aye, plenty of tea;
> With the chintz at the windows as gay as can be,
>   All as gay as can be."

There was more to the song. It went on and on, and Oona could not tell where the song ended and the dream began, so closely woven were the two together. She felt of a sudden a small, tweaking hand on her skirt and heard a shrill voice piping, " Wake up — wake up, Oona Hegarty! "

" 'Tis awake I am, entirely," said Oona, sitting up and rubbing her eyes. " Awake and dreaming at the same time, just."

" We'll be after fetching in your bundle, then; and all things shall find their rightful places at last."

Ten hundred fairy men lifted the bundle and bore it inside, with Oona following. She drew her breath through puckered lips; she let it out again in sighs of wonderment. " Is everything to your liking, ma'am? " inquired the fairy man she had knocked over.

She made the answer as she looked about her: " The bed's where it should be. The chintz now — I had a mind to have it green, with a touch of the sun and a touch of the flaming turf in it. The dresser is convenient high. Wait till I have my bundle undone and the treasures of a lifetime put away."

The Gentle People scuttled about helping her, putting the linen in the fine oak chest, the dishes on the dresser. The kettle was hung above the hearth, the creepie put beside it. The rug spread along the bedside and the griddle left standing by the fire, ready. All things in their right places, as the tinker's child had dreamed them.

" Is it all to your liking? " shouted the Gentle People together.

" Aye, 'tis that and more. Crocks and creels where they do belong. The fine, strong spoon to be hanging there, ready to stir the griddle bread. The knife with the sharp edge to it, to be cutting it." She turned and looked down at the floor, at the hundreds of wee men crowding her feet. " I'm not asking why ye have done this thing for me this night. But I ask one thing more. On every white Christmas let you be bringing folk to my door — old ones not needed longer by others, children crying for their mother, a lad or a lass for whom life has gone amiss. Fetch them, that I may warm them by the hearth and comfort them."

"We will do that, tinker's child; we will do that!" The voices of the Gentle People drifted away from her like a wind dying over the bog: it was there — it was gone. A great sleep took Oona Hegarty, so that her eyes could stay open no longer. She put herself down on the outshot bed. She pulled the warm blanket over her and drew the chintz curtains.

The next night — Christmas — hunger drove Maggie, the middle child of the MacManuses, out of their cabin. She went like a wee, wild thing, knowing only the hunger pain she bore and the need of staying it. Blindly she climbed the hill to the bogland. Weak and stumbling she was, whimpering like a poor, hurt creature. She stumbled off the road; she stumbled over the sudden rise on the bog, which nearly laid her flat. Rubbing her eyes, she looked up at a wee cabin standing where no cabin had ever been. Through the windows came a welcoming light. In wonderment she lifted the latch and went in.

"Come in, Maggie. I've been looking for ye, the lee long day." It was Oona's voice that spoke to her; aye, but what a changed Oona! She knelt by the hearth turning the griddle bread, her eyes as blue as fairy thimbles, her hair the color of ripened corn. There were prateys boiling in the kettle, tea making on the hearth. Enough to eat and to spare. But that was not what filled the child's eyes with wonder. It was Oona herself, grown young, with the look of a young bride on her. "Take the creepie." Her voice had the low, soft calling of a throstle to its young. "Ye'll be after eating your fill, Maggie, and not knowing hunger again for many a day."

And it's the truth I am telling. Maggie went back and told; but although half of Carn-na-ween hunted the cabin throughout the year, none found it. Not until a white Christmas again came round. Then old Seumus MacIntyre the cobbler died, leaving his widow Molly poor and none to keep her. They were coming to fetch her to the workhouse that Christmas Eve when she took the road climbing to Killybegs and the sea, and was never seen again.

And so the tales run. There are enough to be filling a book, but why should I go on with them? You can be after telling them to yourselves. This I know: given a white Christmas this year, the wee fairy cabin of Carn-na-ween will be having its latch lifted through the night by the lone and the lost and the heartbroken. Aye, Oona Hegarty, the tinker's child, will be keeping the griddle hot, the kettle full, and her arms wide to the childher of half the world this night — if it be's a white Christmas.

ITALY

A Roman Christmas

ELIZABETH HOUGH SECHRIST

T HE CHRISTMAS SEASON was the happiest time of the whole
year for Nello. The school children in the city of Rome,
where he lived, had only four or five days vacation at Christmas;
but Nello had three weeks; from the beginning of the novena
until after Twelfth-night, or the Feast of the Epiphany. And
those three weeks were always one round of good and beautiful
times for Nello. His tutor, Signor Alessandro, worked almost as
hard to make Nello happy during that vacation as he did to
teach him from books all the rest of the year.

You see, Nello was a little crippled boy. He had been lame
from birth and had always walked on crutches. It made Nello's
parents sad to see the difference between their son and the other
sturdy boys of Italy. But Nello was gifted with a happy heart
and a cheerful smile. With such attributes he won many friends
and was well loved.

However, in his crippled condition it was impossible for him
to get about as the other boys of his age did. And when vacation
times came round, and Signor was ready and willing to take
Nello on a series of shopping expeditions and excursions of all
sorts, it certainly made the lad very happy indeed. It was little
wonder that Nello looked upon Christmas as the best time of
the year.

Nello and his tutor were determined to make this year the
nicest Christmas of all. So they set about it by taking the car-

152

riage into town every single day, and the good-natured coachman waited patiently in his seat outside every attractive shop in Rome.

In Rome the people usually begin to do Christmas shopping as early as the first of November, while the flowers are still blooming! The stores from that time until after the New Year hold a steady stream of people. The shops are made as attractive as possible, with flowers being used everywhere for decoration.

Nello and the Signor made their way carefully through the crowds, buying gifts here and there and looking at everything. There were many foreigners among the shoppers. Nello could distinguish the tongues of English, German, French, and Scandinavian visitors among the quick chatter of his own talkative race. That made the shopping expeditions more interesting to him. Here and there he picked up a phrase or two of English, which, when repeated by him with his imitation of the accent, made the Signor laugh aloud.

Every day they bought cakes while they were out — delicious cakes for which Rome is famous — and ate them on the way home in the carriage.

As Christmas drew nearer the shops became more and more crowded, and they were obliged to keep more to the highways. On the streets they saw many different groups of children reciting Christmas poems and receiving coins from the people who gathered round to hear. What a scramble there was when Nello would toss money to them from the carriage!

One of the things which Nello enjoyed immensely was when Signor took him to the moving-picture theaters. In fact, they both enjoyed it so much that for a while they attended a different one every afternoon. This form of entertainment did not tire Nello so much as the trips through the shops.

At last, Christmas approached. The day before Christmas was a fast day. From sunset of the twenty-third of December until sunset of the twenty-fourth the people fasted. This was really the beginning of the celebration of Christmas, for in Italy, Christmas is a solemn religious observance. On that day Nello and his tutor ceased their merrymaking. After attending early Mass, they spent the remainder of the day very quietly indoors.

But at two o'clock that afternoon the yule log, or *ceppo*, was lighted in the fireplace and the family gathered around it. It was in this room also that the *presepio* was placed.

The *presepio!* It was very dear to the heart of every member of the family. From year to year they had saved it, carefully putting it away, then bringing it out again to serve for another Christmas. And it seemed dearer to them each year — more a part of them. Nello could hardly wait until the family ceremony around the *presepio* should begin.

Presepio is the Italian word for stable or manger. But gradually it has come to be known as the word for a miniature Bethlehem, or place of Nativity. It represents the birthplace of Christ. There are tiny figures of the Virgin Mary and Joseph, the shepherds, Wise Men, and angels, and also tiny animals, all cut skillfully from wood. Nello loved each figure in their little Bethlehem.

At twilight the candles around the *presepio* were lighted, and prayers were said. The tiny manger was empty until Nello's mother, while they all watched, put the last figure of all in its place. This was the figure of the *Bambino*, the baby Christ. Everyone in the room crossed himself, more prayers were said, and then Nello, leaning upon his crutch, stood beside the miniature Holy City and recited some beautiful poems of the Nativity.

After the ceremony of the *presepio*, the twenty-four-hour fast was broken by a wonderful banquet! And such things as there were to eat! Characteristic of the Italian Christmas were the delicately prepared dishes of eels and larks which Nello's family never failed to feast upon at this banquet on Christmas Eve.

Evergreens are not used in Italy as a Christmas decoration. But Nello's home was filled with flowers. They were everywhere — lovely chrysanthemums, violets, and bright holly berries! And, besides, there was music. Yes, music played from odd-looking bagpipes by young men who were dressed as shepherds.

After the banquet, and while the shepherds played upon their bagpipes, came Nello's happiest moment! For it was then that the Urn of Fate was brought forth. The whole family, including Nello's older brothers and their wives and children, the parents, the Signor, and even the servants, were there to draw gifts from the Urn of Fate. It was a very large crock which held one gift for each member of the family. It was Nello's mother who began the drawing. And it pleased Nello very much when the package she unwrapped proved to be the scarf he had bought for her. Such fun as they had drawing their gifts and examining them! To be sure, almost everyone drew a blank before actually receiving his own gift, but that only served to create more merriment.

After the excitement had somewhat subsided, the small children were put to bed. Even Nello was bidden to take a rest. The church services of Christmas Eve would be very long, and Nello was not so strong as the others.

But he would not have missed the Christmas Eve services for anything. When the rest of the family climbed into the carriage at ten o'clock to be taken to the church, Nello and Signor were with them.

The streets were filled with merry crowds of people, many of whom carried torches. Bright lanterns hung in all the shops, and music and flowers were everywhere.

At church there were more music and flowers! Here, the music was very beautiful. There were crowds of people. But it was very restful to Nello, who sat in his place listening to the well-trained voices of the choirboys. It made him think that to sit in a lovely church and listen to beautiful music was the nicest thing in the world.

Just before midnight there was a grand procession of the officials of the church, in all the splendor of their colorful vestments. With them they carried the figure of the *Bambino;* people all over the church, as it passed, knelt before it, and touched or kissed its robe. As the bells tolled midnight the procession ended, and the *Bambino* was placed in the manger at the front of the church where all would see it. At the same instant the beautiful voices of the choir began singing the Magnificat.

At two o'clock the "Shepherd's Hymn" was chanted, and soon after, Nello and his family left the church to go home. Poor Nello was glad for the support of the Signor's strong arm, for the boy was nearly asleep.

It was the custom of Nello's family to go to the services at St. Peter's Cathedral on every Christmas Day. So Christmas afternoon found them once more approaching the church door. But this time it was to the largest church in the world they were going. For St. Peter's Cathedral of Rome has the distinction of being the largest cathedral in the whole world. Nello had passed it many times and had attended services there once every year on Christmas. But it never failed to impress him with its beauty and magnificence.

The many steps approaching the cathedral made it quite a task for the brave little boy to mount them. But he was happy to climb those broad steps, knowing what awaited him at the top. They went slowly, his mother at his one side, his father at the other, and the good tutor carrying the lad's crutches. As they walked slowly up the great steps they passed many people, people from all walks of life. Many of them, of course, were from Rome. But there were countless visitors also, and it seemed to Nello that everyone in the world must have come to this greatest of all churches to celebrate Christmas. It was very probable that most of the nations of the world were represented there that day. The peasants of Italy were there in great numbers, many of them having come from their farms and villages to Rome and to the cathedral on a sort of pilgrimage, to worship and to receive the blessing of the pope.

As they made their way to the huge entrance, Nello and his family were stopped a great many times by men and boys who were selling picture post cards and cheap jewelry. "Buy, buy!" they entreated with eager voices. Many of them were crippled. Nello stopped to buy from each one of them, and by the time they had reached the entrance doors their hands were full of cards and trinkets.

Once inside the church they made their way as quickly as possible to the great church room so that Nello could be seated. On the way in, Nello passed under the magnificent dome, four

hundred feet high, which, his father told him, was the work-
manship of Michelangelo. And, too, they saw the huge bronze
statue of Saint Peter. Nello looked at it with reverence and awe.
He knew that it was ancient — that no one knew what its age
was exactly. He knew a part of Saint Peter's foot had been worn
away by the constant kissing it had received by the millions of
visitors to the cathedral. To visit the cathedral was to visit the
statue of the saint. Even now there were streams of people waiting their turn to kneel before Saint Peter and pray.

The crowds in the great church today were so large that the
service lacked some of the beauty and reverence of the Christmas Eve services which they had attended the night before.
People were coming in by the hundreds. Signor, who was seated
beside Nello, whispered to him that the cathedral was said to
be able to hold more than forty thousand people. Nello sat
thinking about this and listening to the music of a beautiful
organ. He thought: Forty thousand people! That is more than
there are in some whole cities.

The entrance of the pope was an impressive part of this
Christmas service. When the procession started which preceded
his arrival Nello became so excited that he could feel his face
getting hot and his hands getting cold. To him, the pope was
the grandest and most important figure in the whole world.

It was a wonderfully impressive entrance. In the procession
there were bishops, cardinals, and other dignitaries of the
church. Then there came the pope's guard of honor, and about
sixty noblemen of the city of Rome. The pope sat upon a scarlet chair, supported by several men who were dressed in robes
of violet. The pope himself was attired in rich robes hung heavily with precious jewels, and his head was crowned with a jeweled tiara.

As he passed between the rows of soldiers, he held up his
hand, two fingers extended, in blessing.

At last he was seated upon a raised throne at the head of the
church; the choir sang the Psalm of Entrance, and the service
had begun.

From Christmas Eve until the Eve of Epiphany, or the day
before " Old Christmas," the observance of the Yuletide in

Italy is of a religious nature. But on the Eve of Epiphany it is different. Nello had adopted the more modern custom of hanging up his stocking. When his brothers were small, they had always placed their shoes on the hearth. But Nello, along with many other boys and girls of Rome, hung up his stocking. And it was on this night that La Befana was supposed to come.

Nello had probably heard of Santa Claus. But I doubt whether he had ever thought of comparing him to La Befana, although she is the only one figuring in an Italian Christmas who could be compared to Santa Claus.

La Befana was supposed to be a woman, and not " a right jolly old elf," either. She was said to possess a stern nature and a rather forbidding appearance. On Twelfth-night, or the Eve of Epiphany, as it is known in Italy, she entered through the chimney and into the room where the stockings were hung. She carried a cane in one hand and a bell in the other. With the bell she announced her arrival. Thus it was that many little children in Italy would hear a bell ringing on the Eve of Epiphany and would be told to " hurry off to sleep before Befana comes! "

In the stockings of the good little boys and girls she would put gifts that satisfied their hearts' desires. But in the stockings of the bad children she would leave only bags of ashes! A hurried scramble early on the morning of Epiphany proved to the children whether their conduct had been approved or disapproved by the all-wise Befana.

When Nello found a bulging stocking at his bedside, with many gifts besides that would not fit into it, I am sure he felt glad that he had pleased La Befana. But when his mother came into the room while he was opening the gifts, it was she who received " many thanks " from the little boy, and a big hug and kiss. Was it possible that La Befana was merely a legend? It really did not matter at all to Nello. He saw the work of loving hands in those gifts, and his suspicions were many as to whose hands they might have been.

In spite of the fact that her little son was a cripple, and had very few of the advantages and good times of other boys, his mother on that morning of Epiphany read real joy and happiness in his eyes. And she thanked God then for the finest gift her son possessed, a happy heart.

As for Nello, his Christmas season is almost over. He will soon be speaking of it as "last Christmas," and dating happenings with "That happened just before Epiphany." He will be thinking already of next Christmas. And during those long months in between he will have many happy memories of this one — shopping expeditions with his tutor, merry crowds of people on the streets; gifts, music, and flowers; and, perhaps most vivid of all, impressive church services where he had come face to face with the true meaning of Christmas, the birthday of the Infanta.

ITALY

How Saint Francis Told the Christmas Story

SAINT FRANCIS OF ASSISI

THE ITALIAN SUNSHINE was warm and bright as Saint Francis walked in the woods near the village of Greccio (GRAY-chee-oh). The year was 1223 and the month December.

Saint Francis moved slowly, head bowed. " It's almost here, Il Natale (Eel Nah-TAH-le), the birth of Jesus, the season of good will. But the people here in Greccio seem to have forgotten Jesus. They constantly hurt each other by their cruel and selfish ways. If only I could help them think about that first Christmas night and about the baby Jesus, who, when he became a man, 'went about doing good.'"

Saint Francis continued to ponder as he walked. Then he stopped suddenly, a light glowing in his eyes. " I know! I know what I can do! "

With that he quickened his steps until he reached the home of his friend, Giovanni (Joh-VAHN-nee), to whom he unfolded his plan. Giovanni was enthusiastic too.

If you had been in the Greccio Woods the next afternoon, you would have seen a procession of Giovanni's servants making their way to the big cave. Some carried boughs of pine and cypress, others lumber and a bale of straw. Two more brought from Giovanni's stable a manger filled with hay. A neighboring farmer arrived with three white cows, sheep, and lambs.

Meanwhile, word had spread around the village that Saint Francis was inviting everyone to come to the cave that night.

160

When it grew dark, men, women, and children approached the cave, bearing torches and candles. Upon entering, they stood transfixed with awe and wonder. There, before their very eyes they *saw* the Christmas story — the stable spread with clean straw and the walls covered with sweet-smelling greens. The white cows chewed their cud and a little gray donkey looked quietly into the hay-filled manger, while sheep and lambs crouched close.

At the appointed time, a young father and mother came forward and gently laid their sleeping baby in the manger. When the picture was thus completed, Saint Francis stepped from the shadowed corner where he had been standing.

Looking into the faces of the hushed and reverent worshipers, he told the Bethlehem story of Mary and Joseph, of the shepherds and the Wise Men. He spoke not only of the baby Jesus, but also of Jesus, the man, and implored his listeners to follow Jesus' way of loving-kindness.

Later that evening when the villagers left the cave to return to their homes the winter stars were shining brightly in the dark sky.

" See! " exclaimed a child, pointing to one star which was especially large and bright. " It's the star of Bethlehem! "

Saint Francis heard it and his heart sang with joy. He knew that Christmas — the real Christmas — had come that night to the village of Greccio, Italy.

JAPAN

Old Dolls Make
a Happy Christmas

IRENE WEBSTER SMITH

S EVERAL LITTLE JAPANESE GIRLS were seated on gay-colored
cushions. In their pretty frocks, called kimonos, they looked
like a bed of flowers. They were warming their hands at the
charcoal fire burning in the *hibachi* — a big brass bowl — in the
center of the room. The little girls were telling each other what
they hoped to have for Christmas.

" Perhaps there will be no dolls from England or America,"
suggested someone.

"Oh! yes," answered another, " I *know* there will be. I saw
them in Sensei's (sounded like sen-say) big cupboard one day
when I was in her room; she slid the door back a little too far,
and I really and truly saw them! "

" Oh! I do want a new doll for Christmas; mine is getting so
old." " I *really* need a new one, because my doll's eyes have fallen back inside her head! "

" I'd like a doll with fair curly hair."

" I want one in baby clothes," chimed in a fourth little voice,
" with a lovely, long, white robe like babies have in England."

As the little girls were chatting, in came their dear Sensei,
and a space was made for her on a nice big *zabuton*, or cushion.

" Now, children, I have something to tell you! Not far away
is a village where there are some poor little children, and some
missionaries are going to visit that village for the very first time,
to tell them about the Lord Jesus and his love.

162

" These poor little children will have no Christmas presents, no Christmas tree, no Christmas dinner, and no Christmas stockings, because, you see, they are not Christians. They have never heard that Christmas Day is the birthday of the Lord Jesus, and they know nothing about the good tidings which the angels came to tell the shepherds long ago."

Sensei continued: "Now, would you like to help those children? How would you like to send them some of your old toys and dolls? Of course you will all be getting some new ones. Will you think about it and talk it over? " And then Sensei left them for a while.

The children agreed they would like to send their dolls to help those other children who knew nothing of the joy of Christmas. To the astonishment of all, Hanako (Flower child) said, "No, I will *not* give my old doll."

There was a chorus: " O Hana! you won't give your old doll? " " You are mean! " " Hana, how can you be so selfish? "

Hanako quietly replied: "Well, you see, our giving to these poor children is like giving to Jesus. I don't want to give my old doll; I would rather give him my new one."

The little girls who had spoken so quickly hung their heads, feeling quite ashamed. One after another, they said, " So will I."

When Sensei returned to hear their decision, they told her all that they had said, and that now they wanted to give their new dolls.

" Then you will have no dolls for Christmas," Sensei reminded them. " Would you be quite happy with your old ones? "

" I know what we will do," said one of the children, fairly dancing at the thought. " We'll give you our old dolls to give us on Christmas Day, and we'll pretend they are new."

On Christmas morning it was a happy thing to see the little girls receiving their old dolls with broken arms and legs carefully mended, all dressed in lovely new dresses which the older girls had made. The grown-up people watching the children declared that it was a very happy Christmas.

Now, what about the children in the village? They gazed with wide-open eyes at the dolls. Indeed, they were speechless with surprise and wonder, and also their parents, especially when they heard that the Sunrise Home girls had given their own new dolls!

When the meeting began, the people listened intently to what the missionaries had to say about the first Christmas story, that "God so loved the world, that he gave his only begotten Son, that whosoever believeth in him should not perish, but have everlasting life."

Many fathers and mothers, and children too, believed on the Lord Jesus Christ, and were willing to throw away their idols.

So the Sunrise Home children were used to send the glad tidings to that dark, heathen village, not in word but in action. Truly, it was a very happy Christmas for them all.

JAPAN

Why the Christmas Church Was Built

E. A. TAYLOR

THE LADY LOTUS YAMAMOTU threw down her fountain pen with a movement of weary disgust. What was the use of writing letters to relatives you had no real interest in? What was the use of life anyhow, when everything bored you? She rose with an impatient gesture and looked at herself in a long mirror, for the large beautiful room was furnished with every Western convenience, carefully blended with Eastern art. The picture she saw in the glass was altogether Eastern: a girl with the exquisitely refined loveliness of a hundred generations of Japanese aristocracy. Her dress was Japanese in every detail, for though modern education had robbed Lotus of all faith in the beliefs of her fathers, and she had set herself against " Western religion " as she scornfully called it, leaving her only creed an unfortunate nationalism — unfortunate because instead of love for her country and a striving to serve it, she rather spent her patriotic energies in hating other lands which had in real or imagined ways injured or insulted her own. So she wore her national dress with a certain defiance: the way her hair was arranged showing any Japanese that she was a young widow. Her Western education made her resent the marriage settled by her family, and her short married life had not been happy, but when her young husband's death had left her with wealth and freedom she regretted him; honestly, intelligently, Lotus told herself that the clashes

165

in her wedded life were largely her own fault. " If he had lived, we might have become good friends, and I would not have found life so unutterably empty."

Restlessly she went to one of the windows. The house, a beautiful bit of old Japanese architecture, had when built deserved its name of Bashoam (Banana Hermitage), being embowered in deep gardens and banana groves, away from the city; but modern business had brought the city almost to its doors. On three sides it still was secluded in its grounds, but on the fourth a street had encroached, where rattling electric cars and motor buses rushed, and the corner of a huge electric laundry pushed into the view of this one of Lotus' windows. The laundry was hers, adding much to her income, and she sometimes watched the workers coming and going, idly interested in those little blue-clad men and women who hurried to be in their places when work began at five in the morning, and worked through their long fifteen-hour day, stopping at eight in the evening, all this for a wage so small that husbands and wives both had to work. Lotus would watch the couples hurrying in together, and often the woman had a tiny baby, which she was allowed to bring with her, and tend at stated intervals.

As Lotus glanced at the laundry she could hear the thud, thud, of the electric washers, and see the little men trotting in and out with soiled linen for the washers, or clean to take home. Just for two days a month the laundry closed down, to give its workers a rest! " What a life! " thought Lotus. " Work, soul-deadening, monotonous work, just to drop down to sleep when the machines stop. Our workers are far worse off than in the old times when there was no merciless machinery for them to be chained to. But we must have all the Western inventions, or this greedy Christian civilization would swallow us alive. We must keep pace with it in preparedness for war and in our industrial life."

She was quoting half unconsciously from a magazine she had been reading, one of a heap of English and French periodicals, as well as Japanese, that were piled on her table. Yet though Lotus so resented all things Western, even Christianity, yet she thought of the workers. Her grandmother would have regarded their condition as too much a matter of course to be thought about.

Lotus picked up a magazine which opened at an advertisement page showing in flaring colors Santa Claus with a bulging sack of toys, and down below, a cloud of children's faces looking eagerly upward. " How vulgar! " thought Lotus. " What a gross materializing of that Christmas story, which, if I remember rightly, is rather pretty, with its Baby in a manger; but to personify Christmas as a huge man with a red face and fiery nose! " She thought contemptuously of her visit to the shopping districts one Christmas when she was in New York, the blatant show of the store windows, the greedy rush and push of the crowd! She smiled in her sense of scornful superiority, and then suddenly the feeling that there was something in all that noisy Christmas-keeping flashed upon her. A hundred Santa Clauses could not hide the light of the Star of Bethlehem, the spirit of giving, which, though in some cases a mere selfish exchange of gifts, in many others was a longing to help those who could give no return.

She went to the telephone and called up the city college, and then Sotan Tanaka. Soon her young brother's voice answered her, promising to be over that evening, and certainly to help her in whatever it was that she was so suddenly interested in. He came, a clever-looking young fellow, very much under the influence of the sister whom he greatly admired.

He listened to her plan, then exclaimed: " Give the laundry workers a Christmas treat! But Christmas is so emphatically Christian, and we have taken a quiet stand against these Western religions and modes of thought; what our fathers believed is enough for Japan."

He was quoting from some of their favorite periodicals, but Lotus only said: " Christmas legends and decorations are too picturesque to be ignored. This idea of gift-giving to children and poor people is charming, and we can easily cut out the religious part and have our Christmas without Christ. We have a month to get ready in, and you must help me, Sotan."

Of course, he promised, and Lotus suddenly found life interesting. She was not supposed ever to interfere with the manage-

ment of the laundry, but she found her business manager politely ready to hear her, and after a little talk he consented to
give the laundry an extra day of rest in December. " Many of
our business concerns, Lady Yamamotu," he said, " are adopting the Western six-day week for their workers, and, really, our
fourteen-day week of fifteen hours a day is too long."

So Lotus sent out her orders, and soon boxes and bales arrived, with a bundle of booklets. The ancient feudal hall of
Bashoam was dressed with palms and ferns and scarlet flowers.
Lotus kept to the Christmas colors of green and red, but would
use only plants native to her country. A huge tinsel star hung
over the platform, on one side of which stood a small Christmas
tree laden with fruit and decoration, with tiny paper lanterns
in place of candles. This would go later to the hospital. In the
other side was a tublike Japanese manger half filled with hay,
on which reposed a beautifully carved ivory Buddha, one of the
art treasures of the house. By it stood a huge stone cow carried
in from the garden, and some of the servants were to be dressed
as Japanese shepherds of ancient days. With them was to stand
an old retainer in the un-Japanese costume of Santa Claus,
Lotus having seen in one of her booklets that Santa Claus may
have originated in a vague legend that the rural god Pan went
with the shepherds to Bethlehem on that first Christmas night.

A copy of the New Testament had been included among the
Christmas necessaries, but at first Lotus had not intended to
read it. However, when she saw how poor and few the fairy
stories were, she decided to read the Christmas chapter from
Saint Luke. " Of course they are nothing but myths," she told
Sotan, " and I will tell the people so before I read."

On Christmas afternoon she stood in her soft silks on the
platform beneath the star, and the floor of the hall was covered
with men and women and children, seated in close rows on the
thick white mats, and all with shining eyes at the thought of a
double treat: this show and then a feast. And Lotus, standing
there with her books, did not tell them it was all a myth. They
were so heroically cheerful, these brave men and women, working so hard, always keeping themselves clean, and always smiling in apparent content. Lotus was sure no other race could

show workers so determinedly neat and happy. Of course they believed in the innumerable fairies, the kindly or otherwise spirits of woods and waters, and accepted literally the story that in past ages the soul of the sun had come to earth in the body of a woman, wedding the first great Japanese hero and leaving her son to be the beginner of the semidivine Mikados, whom the West called emperors of Japan. No, it was impossible to tell these happy trusting people that any beautiful story could be a myth.

In her clear, carefully trained voice she told them of Pan, to whom she gave the name of a Japanese rural deity, how he came one night to where the shepherds watched their flocks in a Far Eastern country called Palestine. Then she began to read from Saint Luke:

" And, lo, the angel of the Lord came upon them, and the glory of the Lord shone round about them; and they were sore afraid."

Lotus read " Supreme Being " for " Lord," and her hearers looked as if they quite understood the terror of the shepherds; they believed in a Supreme Being, throned afar, but were quite willing to let the Mikado have a monopoly of worshiping his awful majesty, for they were perfectly content to adore him, their emperor, and the pleasant little gods, who were not so far off from the common people.

" And the angel said unto them, Fear not: for, behold, I bring you good tidings of great joy, which shall be to all people. For unto you is born this day in the city of David a Savior, which is Christ the Lord."

Again she read " Supreme Being " for " Lord," and this time her hearers looked at her with astonished eyes. Was she telling them of the birth of the first Mikado, or was it the holy Buddha she was reading about? It was most strange that she should put a sacred image in a manger instead of keeping it in its place within the shrine set in the most honorable side of the wall. But the first Mikado and Lord Buddha, the laundry workers knew, were palace-born; they lay in golden cradles, served by adoring kings. Who was he of whom the herald of highest heaven said, " Ye shall find the babe wrapped in

swaddling clothes, lying in a manger," he in whose honor there
appeared " a multitude of the heavenly host praising God and
saying,

> " Glory to God in the highest,
> And on earth peace,
> Good will toward men "?

Then it was Sotan's turn to feel surprised, for his sister
ignored the manuscript he had prepared for her, elaborating
the journey of the shepherds to Bethlehem, keeping Pan-Santa
Claus well to the fore and turning attention from the Babe
in the manger to the distribution of gifts and the feast, which
would certainly satisfy everybody and make them forget the
unfinished story of the angel-heralded Babe. But the contrast
between the Christmas legends and the gospel story had struck
Lotus too forcibly; the first were pretty toys for children; this
was the truth for men! She had read the gospel before, but
carelessly and with a prejudiced mind. Now, because while she
had haughtily refused to honor his name, but at the same time
went in his spirit to help her neighbors, the Lord of Christmas
himself came to stand beneath that tinsel star, and the soul
of Lotus Yamamotu saw him and worshiped.

" The Supreme Being knew that we feared his greatness too
much to come to worship him," she said clearly, " so he sent
his Son, who was named Christ, to be born into the world
to be our Savior and friend. We keep Christmas in memory of
the day he was born in Bethlehem, and — I am a Christian."

She made a sign, and waiting servants carried hot tea and
white rice cakes through the hall, serving everyone, and giving
each three small food boxes, one holding fish and pickles, one
cooked rice, and the third sweetmeats. These were to be taken
home for the people to feast with their friends. Then Santa
Claus went round, filling the hands of astounded children with
gifts from his bulging sack, they kneeling and bumping polite
foreheads on the floor in their eagerness to do this possible
manifestation of a deity due honor.

Then with much bowing and homage the national hymn of

Japan was sung, and the first Christmas in the inland city was over.

That is all some years ago. Today Lotus Yamamotu is one of the heads of the Christian Social Service in Japan's capital, and her brother is in Parliament, a Christian statesman, trying to help his own people, and ever watching to keep and increase friendly feeling between East and West. In his home city the big laundry is closed every Sunday, and in many other ways the lot of the workers is being steadily made easier. Most of them are members of the pretty church built in the gardens of Bashoam, which are now a park, and the proud old aristocratic house has also given itself to Christ. His name is upon its front, and in it all the multitudinous social work belonging to our churches of today is carried on. The little church in the gardens has its name, of course, but that is seldom used: for the neighborhood and most of its members, it is the Christmas Church.

MEXICO

The Small One

CHARLES TAZEWELL

THE SAME WINTER SUN that dances on the northern snow sprawls indolently at ease in the thick white dust of El Camino del Norte, Old Mexico. This is the hour of siesta, and the road belongs to the dust devils and the little brown lizards, and lying here in the shade of a pepper tree, a man, and in this case, an old padre, can drowse and dream the strangest stories ever dreamed.

If only that bee would stop buzzing! Or is it a hornet?

" Estúpido! "

Oh, no! It's only a small boy berating a disreputable-looking donkey.

" A donkey! A donkey, you call yourself, Estúpido! A fine animal with a stout leg on each corner, a handsome, serviceable tail to shoo off the flies and two beautiful ears to point the way you are going, and what do you do with these things the good God has given you? Nothing at all! "

" Pablo! " called the padre.

" You are a disgrace to all the donkeys of Mexico! "

" *Pablo!* "

" *¿Sí ¡ Oh, buenos días, padre!* I did not see you, I — "

" Look, it's much too hot for all that commotion. "

" But this donkey — "

" What's he done? "

" He has done nothing, but nothing! "

172

" Nothing? "

" Nothing is all he ever wants to do! Here it is but two days before Christmas, when a load of wood could be sold in the village to buy gifts and a candle, but does he care? *No!* "

" Well, there's no use getting upset about it. A donkey's a donkey. They're all alike."

" *Sí*, ungrateful and stubborn."

" Oh, no — oh, no! You're wrong there, Pablo."

" Yes, but — "

" I know, yes, everybody says they are, and they beat them and curse them and call them stupid. The trouble is, they don't know the truth about little donkeys."

" No? And what is the truth? "

" Why, it's not stubbornness at all! No, sir! Why, it's pride that makes donkeys so — well, kind of aloof."

" Aloof? "

" That's right. Sun, rain, good luck, bad luck, what does it matter? Their pride is a shield against anything that man or the elements can do to them."

" I don't see what a donkey has to be proud of."

" Oh, he has! Yes, indeed! You see a long, long time ago, a great honor came to one of them, an honor so great that it lifted him and all the other donkeys to a place that you or I or all the world might envy."

" I do not envy this donkey."

" Well, you should. Do you know why? "

" Why? "

" Because of all animals and of all men, he's already fulfilled his destiny."

" What is destiny? "

" Well — it's the reason for people being born — or a thing created. Come on, bring your donkey over here in the shade and I'll tell you about it."

" *Sí, sí, señor*. Come on, Cupido! " Pablo tugged on the rope.

" Listen! Listen, Pablo! Do you hear that? Only a small donkey can make that sound with his hoofs on the stones of the road! Sit down, and I will tell you why that is!

" You see, Pablo, once upon a Christmas Eve there was a

small donkey. He was fourteen unhappy years old. He'd worked hard and long for at least fourteen masters."

"He was a valuable animal, *señor?*"

"Oh, no, he wasn't much to look at. He was battered and scarred, and his tail was like a piece of rope, unraveled down at the end. Yes — and one of his ears stood straight up like a cactus plant, but the other hung down like a wilted cabbage leaf. And on top of that, his off hind leg had a limp."

"What was his name?" asked Pablo.

"They just called him the Small One."

"Small One?"

"That's right. His latest master was a woodcutter who also owned four younger, and therefore stronger, donkeys."

"Was the woodcutter kind to him?"

"His son was. It was this boy who took care of Small One; made sure there was straw for his bed, and that the loads weren't too heavy for Small One's back."

"I guess the boy and the old donkey were what we call *amigos.*"

"Very close *amigos!* But one morning the woodcutter called his son to him and he said: 'Son, I want you to take this donkey, the one you call Small One, to a shop just inside the town gates. They'll give you a piece of silver in exchange for the animal.'"

"'Do you mean?' said the boy in horror — 'You don't mean — you're going to sell Small One?'"

"'He can no longer do his share of the work.'"

"'Yes, but —'"

"'Even when carrying half the load of the other donkeys, his worn-out legs tremble and his sides heave like a bellows.'"

"'But he'll be strong as the others soon,' pleaded the boy. 'Just give him a few weeks!'"

"'An old donkey is of no use! One day he'll drop dead on us up in the hills, a total loss.'"

"'Yes, but he's mine —'"

"'The shop you will take him to is the second on the left as you pass through the town gates.'"

" ' But — but the second shop is the tanner's — '

" ' His hide may be old, but it'll make good leather,' growled the father.

" ' But you can't do that to him! ' wept the boy. ' He's worked hard! He's been faithful! '

" ' Come now, no crying over a miserable, old donkey! ' ordered the father. ' Hurry now, be off with you! Yes, and take good care not to lose that piece of silver on the way home! '

" Well, that small boy and his small donkey made a pretty sorrowful picture as they traveled along the road to town. People along the way wondered why the boy was crying. You see, they couldn't know that the Small One's hoofs on the road were beating out the words,

" ' Going to the tanner's,'

" ' Going to the tanner's.'

" It was early afternoon when the small boy and the small donkey went through the great town gates. It was market day and all at once the boy remembered there was a horse market in the square! Why, if he could sell Small One to some new and kind master, the little donkey wouldn't be killed and yet his father would still have the piece of silver!

" Holding tight to Small One's rope, and with his face streaked with dust and tears, the boy hurried to the horse market and pushed his way to the platform of the sweating, shouting auctioneer.

" ' Seventy is the bid! Seventy for a mare so fine that naught but princes ever sat on her back. Strong of limb, sound of wind. Who'll make it seventy-one? Look at that proud head. See that flowing mane. Do I hear seventy-one? Seventy once, seventy twice, sold for seventy pieces of silver! A fine bargain, my friend! Now, who has the next animal? Step up, please.'

" ' Please, sir,' the boy tugged on his rope, ' would you try to sell this small donkey? '

" ' Go 'way, boy,' growled the auctioneer.

" ' He's a very fine animal,' insisted the boy, ' and not nearly as old as he looks! '

" ' I told you to go away! '

" 'He's terribly strong, and eats very little!'

" 'This is a horse market! We've no time to waste on donkeys!'

" 'But —' the boy's eyes pleaded — 'but a small donkey would take such a small time!'

" 'All right!' laughed the auctioneer, 'all right, my boy, if you insist! My friends, a great bargain I have to offer you! The proud owner terms it a donkey, but being truthful, I would call it an animated pile of shaking bones!'

" The crowd roared with laughter.

" 'No, he isn't!' cried the boy. 'He's strong!'

" 'Observe how the moths have been at the hide, and the tail — *is* it a tail? I think it's the stub of a broom, worn out from sweeping the courtyard!'

" 'Don't say those things about him!' protested the boy over the howls of the crowd.

" 'Yes, a true museum piece, my friends, moldy with age and loose in the joints!'

" 'He's not!' cried the boy over the jeering laughter, 'he's not like that at all!'

" 'Ah, but we mustn't laugh, my friends, because its owner assures me that this — animal — is fine enough to share a stall with the king's horses.'

" 'You can't make fun of him like that!' wept the boy. 'He's a fine donkey, and he does belong in a king's stable! Yes, and maybe someday, that's where he'll be!'

" 'All right, all right, boy,' said the auctioneer, 'take your donkey and move along! We've got business to attend to! And now, my friends, that we've had our fun and disposed of the king's donkey, I have another animal here —'

" The little boy and the little donkey left the market place. The afternoon was slipping by and the long shadows on the street told him that before long he'd have to start for home, and when he got there he must have the piece of silver to give to his father.

" He tried stopping people along the street. He went from door to door, but no one in all the town seemed to want to buy a small, tired donkey. The sun was going down when he got back to the great town gates. His hot tears fell on the Small One's back, and the little donkey's head drooped so low that his limp ear almost touched the ground. And then, just as the boy was leading Small One up the path to the tanner's door, a voice spoke to him.

" 'My son —'

" 'Yes? Yes, sir?' The boy turned a tear-stained face toward a poorly dressed traveler.

" 'I have a great favor to ask of you.' The man laid a hand on Small One's back. 'Are you the owner of this small donkey?'

" 'Oh, yes, sir!' said the boy anxiously.

" 'I have a long journey to make. My wife is not well. I have great need of a strong and gentle animal to carry her safely.'

" 'Oh, Small One is very strong and very trustworthy!' the boy said eagerly.

" 'I can see that,' smiled the man. 'Would you sell him to me?'

" 'Oh, yes, sir, and the price is only one piece of silver!'

" 'One piece of silver?'

" 'Is — is that too much?' the boy asked fearfully.

" 'Oh, no,' smiled the man, 'a very reasonable price for such a beautiful animal.'

" 'Well,' the boy looked at his friend, 'I — I guess he's not really beautiful, but he's *good*.'

" 'Yes, I believe you.' The man drew a very flat purse from his robe. 'I'll be kind to him, I promise you. Here's your piece of silver. Come, Small One.'

" 'Do you mind' — the boy's voice was choked with the tears of parting. 'Do you mind if I come as far as the town gate? You see, Small One and I —'

" 'Not at all. You'll want to say good-by to him, of course. Come along — you can do that while I see my wife safely on his back.' The man led the little donkey to where a woman waited in the shadow of the great town gates.

" 'Good-by, Small One,' whispered the boy. 'It isn't for-ever, you know. When I grow up and earn many pieces of silver, I'll buy you back. Won't that be wonderful, Small One?'

"'All right, my son,' said the man softly. 'Come, Small One —'

"'Wait, traveler!' called the guard of the town gate.

"'Yes, soldier?' the man and the small donkey with the woman on his back halted.

"'I must make out the record before you can pass through the town gates. Who are you?'

"'My name is Joseph.'

"'And your wife?'

"'They call her Mary.'

"'Your destination?'

"'Bethlehem.'

"'Pass, traveler.'

"'Come, Small One.' The man, the woman, and the small donkey moved onward into the gathering twilight.

"'Good-by, Small One,' called the boy. 'Be very gentle and sure of foot and carry her safely to Bethlehem.'

"And so, the Small One passed through the town gates and plodded the many weary miles to Bethlehem, and there in a stable, which became a King's stable, he saw a King born, a King of men, of centuries, of life, of death. Yes, and the Small One's tired old eyes saw the shepherds and the Wise Men, who came to pay homage to his small Master, and he heard the voices of angels rejoicing, and the notes that they sang were the very same ones his own hoofs had rung out on the stones of the road.

"And then it came to pass, that all those who had laughed at his ragged coat and his limping gait, and his drooping ear — they all envied the Small One — for he had become a part of a great miracle.

"Oh, this was a long, long time ago, but even today, all small donkeys stand and dream — especially at Christmas time — dream of the Small One — the Small One of Bethlehem!"

And so, this reiterates the ancient Christmas theme: that humble service may reap rich reward, and that in strange ways, the meek do inherit the earth.

NORWAY

To Grandfather's House

MELVA ROREM

KRISTOFER ELLERTSON knew all the satisfactions of each of his fifty years rolled into one as he clicked the catch that released the parlor doors this Christmas Eve. Slowly, with an air of ceremony, as his father had done before him, he parted them. And the air was at once electrified as an exciting tingle ran through the veins of eager spectators who heard the familiar rolling sound of sliding doors disappearing from sight. The room was just as they had known it would be. The stern order that reigned supreme during the rest of the year was modified, if not gone. Chairs that had stood in absolute rigidity against the walls, as though they had made up their minds always to stand that way, had been moved from their places, making an otherwise vast and lonely wilderness an inviting place. Grandfather's chair, with its back adjusted to a halfway-reclining position, was on one side of the tree. And Grandmother's wicker rocker with the flowered satin pillow that she had made for it "to soften the chill of the winter's evening" — the chair that would be empty this year — on the other. At the far end of the room the organ stood cornerwise. And at either side of the open songbook candles burned. They lighted the organ's ornate top which reached high. But not nearly as high as the ceiling where the shadows of the flickering light seemed very soft and very far. Only the leather davenport stood as it always had — huge, black, and unchanged against

179

the wall, its sameness matched by the red flowered carpet and by the mustiness of the closed-up room that even the boughs of spicy spruce and evergreen could not absorb.

And yet the presence of the tree cast its age-old splendor over everything. Like a sparkling dream it held eight-year-old John's eyes as the candlelight revealed its beauties. The walnuts covered with tin foil that hung from green fresh branches. Strings of popcorn and cranberries and kernels of red corn that found their way from branch to branch in artistic ripples. Bright candy canes and stars made from pieces of colored paper that Mother had managed to save throughout the year. Shining red apples hanging from sturdier branches here and there. And gracing the highest branch, the special shining star — one of its points reaching to touch the room's high ceiling.

"I forgot how nice it was here," John said quietly as he crawled into Grandfather's lap.

"Even I forgot," confided Grandfather, adjusting the footrest on his chair. His voice was low, but proud too of having forgotten. "Each year I forget. Just as I forget how green the spring is, and the blue of the larkspur, and autumn's gold. It's good to forget, isn't it, John? And then to remember again?"

John, who had not only Grandfather's name, but his sensitive understanding as well, answered by slipping his hand into Grandfather's, happy in the knowledge that this was answer enough.

Aunt Edith arranged her circular plaited skirt artfully and pushed up the deep cuffs of her velvet-trimmed suit jacket as she settled back in her chair, pleased with the reflection she saw in the handsomely nickeled parlor stove. She was *not* pleased about spending Christmas in the country. But the moment Peter had begun reading aloud his brother Kristofer's invitation to them, she had conceded their answer. November 2, 1910, the letter was dated. "Father joins me in asking you and Edith to spend Christmas with us on the farm. Father is well, and his spirits are good, but the years are having their way with him. . . ."

That ended any thought of argument or excuse making.

For although Edith Ellertson moved through life with power and dominance, firmly moving aside or passing by those things which did not please her or which stood in her way, she knew when she was face to face with something that ought neither to be moved aside nor passed by. Christmas plans at home in Long Island would have to be exchanged for a dull holiday near a sleepy little Midwestern village. This might be Grandfather's last Christmas. Peter wanted to be with him.

" It's a wonderful place to spend Christmas," Peter offered hopefully, and memories were bright in his eyes as he looked back over his shoulder momentarily at boyhood days. He saw the farm, and he felt its peace and quiet and strength that followed him still. He saw the mailbox out in front, and the house with friendly smoke coming from its chimneys, and neighbors stopping in to call. On the farm you didn't wait for them to knock at the door. You ran to meet them, or you called a greeting. . . . He saw his mother busily at work in the kitchen by the enormous range with its vast areas of black and its shining nickel. Without her it would be lonely. . . . He saw the kitchen table with the red-checked tablecloth at which he and Kris had done their homework on winter nights. He saw the hill in the distance. Was there ever another hill on another farm as high as this one? In an outburst of boyish enthusiasm he announced aloud: " I'm going to take my skates, Edith. There's a pond on our farm that has no equal. Why it's — it's as big as this whole block! "

"Of course, dear," she had smiled. For there were times when her discerning eye predicted that it was to her ultimate advantage to let Peter have his way.

Now her delicate hands fingered the stitched velvet bands that dignified her jacket with a fashionable stole effect. Then with a look of pleased satisfaction she folded them lightly in her lap as she listened to Kristofer's rich, full voice read the Christmas story. Or rather as she half listened. For at the same time she surveyed Kristofer's audience.

Here a little boy's pink chin was cupped in his hand, his elbow resting on the arm of Grandfather's chair. What could bind a small boy and an old man as John and his Grandfather so obviously were bound, she wondered. Aunt Edith's eye (or was it her heart?) missed those qualities of strength and tenderness that were native at once to child and grandfather. . . . Young John with his bright blue eyes, and red cheeks, and honey-colored hair. With his straight young form, and his tender heart, and his eager thoughts that leaped about his exciting country-world like light-footed deer. Old John with his white hair, his long beard, and the happy smiles that played in little wrinkles about his eyes and in the deeply furrowed lines of his face. With his quiet blue eyes where yet old fires burned now and again as he told of earlier days. With his gaunt but stalwart form and a rugged independence that came from a strength greater than earth. Now as the words of the story filled the room Grandfather's steady look met John's, which was equally composed, again and again. And every look revealed the sensitiveness to which their hearts were heir.

A shadow of irritation fell across Aunt Edith's face as her eyes rested on Ellen, John's mother. It was not only Ellen's outward appearance that she disliked. It was her inane satisfaction with the things that money could not buy, and her joy in simple things. It was knowing that for all the weapons of jewels and fashion that Ellen lacked, her world was somehow conquered. And the picture she made as she sat tonight in Grandmother's chair, despite her plainly styled hair and her simple dress, was one of rare contentment.

"It shouldn't be empty," Grandfather had said as he escorted her to the chair. "I think you are its rightful heir."

Ellen had hesitated. Then her gray eyes had lighted as if a bright candle flame had passed behind a curtain, for Kristofer's eye had caught hers. His look was proud. And when she took her place it seemed that she ascended a throne. Well, Edith for one would not bow down. Not though the look of admiration from Kristofer's eyes, and she jealously feared from her husband's too, had proclaimed Ellen queen. Edith had seen in that moment the same kindness in Kristofer's and Peter's eyes, and the same strength in their faces. Neither the miles between them nor the circumstances that had marked their lives had changed it.

Almost against her will, Edith noticed something else about Peter. Even the low glow of the lamp on the marble-topped table revealed too many shadows on his face. Shadows that a prosperous, city-bred look accentuated rather than hid. And her moment of rebellion against Ellen was interrupted by a tremor of uneasiness. For the shadows told that Peter's intricate business of stocks and bonds and financial pilotage was taking its toll. Well, a man must earn a living. And Peter certainly made a lot of money in spite of the fact that he had always been dissatisfied with the way he earned it. Peter would rather have been a farmer like Kris . . . rather have lived in an ugly house like this, rather have worked from dawn to dark, rather have smelled of manure and worried about the corn crop. . . . Humph! she thought, he could thank her for making him amount to something! It was only a weak notion of hers just now that he looked worn and tired and not quite happy. Actually, as she glanced at him again, he looked distinguished. The suggestion of fatigue that she had seen was merely the suave, world-weary look that a successful businessman ought to have.

Now Edith looked about the room from one young face to another. From Anna and Erik, home from the university for the Christmas holiday, to dark-haired Toby, the hired man, who sat with them on the davenport, where they leaned comfortably against brightly embroidered sofa pillows. (Nine pillows in all the room boasted, Edith noticed. Three on the davenport — the others sedately propped against the wall, the organ legs, and one against the library table that bore the legend " To Bestemor with love from Anna." Edith shuddered at the sentiment.) Toby seemed like another of Kristofer's sons, and this home was his as surely as it was Erik's. Quietly intent on the story, he was stroking Just, the dog, who had settled down beside him. Ellen had raised the question earlier as to whether Just ought to be a part of Christmas Eve in the parlor.

" But he'll be disappointed, Mother. He's been waiting for it as long as I have," John had interceded. " And besides — it's his anniversary."

That had seemed to settle the question. It *was* Just's anniversary. A year ago tonight John had been the lucky person whose Christmas Eve rice held the magic almond. Just was a special present.

" A little dog," John had said excitedly when Toby placed him in his arms. " What kind of a dog is he, Toby? What kind? "

" I'm afraid he's just dog," Toby had answered apologetically.

" Dear little Just," John had said, utterly undefeated. " You're the kind I wanted."

Kristofer's audience had been surveyed and found good. Yes, " good " was the word for these people — these self-satisfied, country bumpkins, Edith thought. Well, thank the fates, she was not like them!

Every eye was still intent on Kristofer as he told the centuries-old story whose mystery could never be exhausted. Carefully he had led them from the humble home of Mary and Joseph in the hills of Nazareth, over the weary miles and up the steep hill before the gates of Bethlehem. Through narrow streets they went, seeking rest from a long journey. They stood beside Mary. They saw Joseph's spirit rise and fall as each new expectation gave way to disappointment. They too laid hands on the donkey's bridle as Joseph led him from place to place. " We must go farther, Mary," they heard him say. They saw shepherds in the field, keeping watch. They saw the angel, and as the angel spoke a kind of glory filled the room. " Be not afraid," Kristofer's voice rang out, " for there is born to you this day in the city of David, a Savior who is Christ the Lord. . . ." And the Savior was worshiped anew as they joined hands and walked around the tree. "*Her kommer dine arme smaa,*" their voices sang out, John's clear, high soprano leading the rest. If you had sung the song as a solo at the Christmas tree program at church, you would *have* to be able to lead the rest.

Finally the moment had come for the tree to yield the mysterious packages that it had claimed until now. Sometimes it seemed that all the events of the preparation for Christmas — the baking and the planning, and the cleaning and the scheming — were beckoning hands that pointed to this hour, Ellen thought. And yet, had they not stood against the background of the story, the hour would not have been so shining. Kristofer's voice was jovial as he picked up the largest gift under the tree and read the tag that said " To John from Grandfather." There was no mistaking what the gift was. As soon as he came into the parlor Johnny had spied the runners which refused to lend themselves to complete wrapping up. But he hadn't let on. Grandfather must have the fun of surprising him! Now when the bright-red sled stood before him, he *was* surprised. He hadn't dreamed it could be so magnificent.

" Tomorrow we'll take it to the hill," he anticipated, and Just wagged his tail in complete agreement.

There were gifts for everyone, of course. Wrappings were excitedly torn off and in the twinkling of an eye the room knew the delightful disorder that every parlor ought to know on Christmas Eve. Grandfather's gift was a foot warmer. "Fill with three quarts of boiling water. It can't roll over, and it won't leak," the directions said.

" Why, it's guaranteed to keep my bed warm all night," Grandfather proudly declared. " What new convenience will these comfort seekers think of next? "

In Edith's opinion Peter had overrated almost everything about the farm. The barn was not so tremendously large. The hill was just an ordinary little hill. And the pond would have fit into a city block many times. But as they sat down to a festive Christmas Eve supper, even Edith felt that he hadn't done the kitchen justice. It was plainly the biggest and best room in the house. Grandmother had made it the heart of her home. Tonight the table was the center of the room. The red-checked tablecloth that Peter remembered still made it gay, and it was lighted — as it was every Christmas Eve — by a wooden wreath, suspended from the ceiling, that Grandfather had carved for his and Grandmother's first Christmas. It held ten candles, their light accenting the charms of the brightly painted shelves on one side of the room that held choice cups and saucers, and the coziness of the large but friendly range on the other.

" Yes," said Grandfather to his sons, " we've come a long way since your Mother and I celebrated our first Christmas Eve at this table. From heated bricks to foot warmers. . . ."

" But of course," Edith interrupted, " you folks in the country can't *see* progress the way we can. Just last month Peter and I attended the second international aviation meet in New York! "

" I'm not so sure that I'd like to see that kind of progress," Grandfather added wryly. " Our newspapers reported that more airplanes were smashed than records."

Edith caught her breath a bit. Why, that was true! Could it be that these people actually knew what was going on in the world? And then she was biting into the almond that was hidden in her rice.

" The almond is mine! " she exclaimed.

" Then I have the gift for you," Grandfather said, and he reached into his pocket and produced a small box.

" A lovely brooch! " Edith's eyes sparkled when she saw what it was.

" It was Grandmother's *sølje*. She always wore it on her Sunday dress." Grandfather's voice was tender, and the faraway look in his eyes mirrored his thoughts. Kristofer and Peter saw their Mother ready for church on Sunday morning.

Johnny wondered how there was always just the right gift for whoever got the almond. Just certainly wouldn't have been a very good present for Aunt Edith! But you could tell that she liked Grandma's *sølje*. There were some mysteries that you just could not solve, he concluded rather happily. It was nice, he thought, not knowing.

When the first rays of the Christmas morning sun crept in at the windows, Johnny and Just had already gone to the hill. Anna, Erik, and Toby were getting ready to try out their new skates. And Peter was searching for courage to join them. At home he had not felt the slightest trace of overconfidence when he told Edith that he would do some skating back at the farm. Skating is like bicycling, he told himself now. Once you knew how, you never forgot.

As he struggled to get his skates on at the edge of the pond, he wished he could believe that. Nor was his confidence braced by the deftness with which the young people, including neighbor children who had come to use the pond, slipped on their skates and with quick, even strokes skated agilely over the glassy surface. Now that his skates were on, it seemed that they had all stopped at the opposite end of the pond to watch him. Well, let them watch. He would show them. He would gather all the strength that was in him and with one powerful stroke glide the full length of the pond!

Undismayed he started out. But the high titter of a girl's laughter disarmed him completely. Through one painful, awkward contortion after another he writhed, trying not to fall, and then he collapsed in the center of the pond.

The slow, humiliating walk back to the house seemed interminable. His right foot had been severely twisted. It throbbed angrily, and although he leaned heavily on Erik and Toby, each step seemed more unbearable than the one before.

" Peter! What is it? " Edith questioned anxiously as she met them at the door.

" I'm not exactly sure," he answered through the pain that was tearing his ankle. " I — I guess I started out a bit too ambitiously."

His face drained of color, his forehead tightly knit by his struggle with pain, Peter could go no farther than the wicker rocker in the kitchen. Ellen made him as comfortable there as she could, lifting his right leg carefully so that it might rest on another chair. Anna hurried off to get the smelling salts from Grandfather's bureau. And Edith stood helplessly by.

" Toby and I will go for Dr. Bjornson," Erik offered.

" You must go right away," Ellen agreed. "A cold ride in the sleigh would not be good for Peter now."

There was no more skating on the pond this day. The neighbor children watched while Kristofer helped Erik and Toby hitch the horses to the sleigh. Then they were hurrying off to their homes. Soberly they reported to their parents. " They went for Dr. Bjornson."

Peter knew the same assurance that he had known as a small, sick boy when Dr. Bjornson walked into the house shaking freshly fallen snow from his fur coat and cap. Then with a strong, firm gentleness he was examining the foot and gently wrapping the aching muscles.

" You have a bad sprain here, Peter," he said seriously. And then he added with a twinkle in his eye: " Is this the same ankle you sprained when you fell from the cherry tree? The same one you sprained when your pony threw you? "

Peter agreed that it had a right to sprain easily the third time.

When twilight fell, Peter was moved to Grandfather's chair in the parlor, Edith sat close by, reviewing with him the day's events. In Long Island, they agreed, Peter would very likely have had to struggle to the doctor himself. But when they had thanked Dr. Bjornson for leaving his Christmas dinner to come, he had said: " Peter, you know you are one of my boys. Besides," and he tucked the box of Ellen's Christmas baking a bit tighter under his arm, " my Christmas dinner will be better because I came."

They talked of neighbors to whom the report that the doctor was needed meant that they must leave warm firesides to share the anxiety.

" We couldn't enjoy our Christmas goose anyway if we knew you were having trouble," Mrs. Anderson said as she brought half of the goose to Ellen. Then she had whispered to Peter, guarding his secret well, " After all, it was our girl who laughed."

" I know what it is to have a sprained ankle," Mrs. Norby had offered sympathetically along with a box of *fattigmand* and *sandbakkelse* such as only she could make. " I sprained mine last winter when the church steps were so icy. My heart was so bad then too, and the children all had the measles. . . . I tell you that foot hurt something awful! Why, every step I took . . ." and then her monologue of reminiscing was interrupted by another visit, and another.

Suddenly Edith knew that in this honest, simple, straightforward world the tinsel and trumpery of her life had fallen away. Behind her she saw years of selfishness and vain striving and pride. Years through which she had driven Peter ahead in her world where wealth and vanity reigned supreme and alone. She had managed him, and used him, and made his life unhappy. . . . But she did love him. That must have been the key to Peter's acquiescence. That, and his love for her.

" You were right, Peter. This is a wonderful place to spend

Christmas." It was all that she could say. But she knew that all her life with him had been a journey toward this hour. And her hand rested lightly on Grandmother's *sølje* as a sort of pledge that the rest of the journey would be different.

Peter's answering smile told her that he knew the things that her heart could not say. It was a smile that Wall Street would have recognized. For this was the greatest winning he had ever made.

Kristofer and Ellen stood together at the window at the far end of the room.

" There never was such a sled as this, Grandpa! " they heard John say as he ran his hand over the bright-red surface of the sled, his finger following the outline of his name that was painted there in bold, white letters.

Outside the night was dark and still. The wind had torn a rent in the clouds and moonlight shone on the winter darkness. Snow that had been sifting down quietly all day had settled in great feathery drifts and then piled itself gently against doors and windows. Great, tall trees were covered with ice, and the wind in their branches sang a silver song. In the distance the woods lay dark and foreboding against the far reaches of snow, but lights of country homesteads sparkled out their signals of joy.

" Christmas, everywhere," Edith heard Kristofer murmur. That was what going to Grandfather's house had meant, she mused. Christmas in the home, and in the lives of those about her, and now in her own heart.

PALESTINE
(Bethlehem Long Ago)

The Keeper of the Stable

HENRY BOOTH

HOSEA, THE KEEPER OF THE STABLE of the old inn at Bethlehem, stood in its doorway in the early morning looking out over the far-flung landscape that lay at his feet. From that great limestone ridge on which the village stands, as from an eagle's eyrie, could be seen a chaos of deep canyons and precipitous crags through which wound the white ribbon of the road to Jericho, while far below the Dead Sea, like a huge gem of lapis lazuli, lay embedded in that vast plain which stretched away to end on the eastern skyline (over which the sun had just risen) in the long mauve battlement of the distant mountains of Moab. It was a magnificent vista of gorge and plain and sea and mountain, a breath-taking view, glorious enough to stir any soul.

But Hosea looked out upon it with unseeing eyes. For before him still loomed the huge squat figure of Caleb, the evil master of the inn, and his harsh words still rang in Hosea's ears: " Lazy dog! Slothful good-for-nothing! Son of Belial! " Fresh from another night of dissipation the surly landlord had visited his unreasoning drunken anger upon the luckless head of Hosea as he had come upon him in the stable door, wrapped in a daydream. For every morning at daybreak Hosea would come to this doorway to look across the plain at the far hills of Moab and think of that fair maiden Ruth, who, like her famous namesake of long ago, had come from those mountains to Bethlehem to be-

190

come his bride. No Boaz was he, to woo her with his fields of golden grain, but he had given her the riches of a heart full of love, and for those brief years, though their home had been but a humble shepherd's croft, they had been supremely happy. But with her sudden passing the light had gone out of Hosea's life. It was on this very night, five years ago, that she had been taken from him by the angel of death. His spirit broken by grief and longing, his flock scattered, forced at last to take whatever work he could get, he had become the servant of this brutal and arrogant innkeeper, whose unmerited wrath had once more seared his soul.

With a despairing sigh he was about to turn back to his menial tasks, when with an uproar of voices and the braying of donkeys, a group of sturdy peasants drové their caravan amidst a swirl of dust into the great walled courtyard of the inn. Advancing toward Hosea, the leader cried, " Come, fellow, is there room in your stable for our beasts? " And as Hosea nodded, the weary animals were led into the dim interior of the stable to their respective stalls.

" Whence come ye? " asked Hosea.

" Galilee," the answer came. " From Caesarea Philippi."

" And why are ye here? "

The leader gazed at Hosea in astonishment. " Dost thou not know that this is the Feast of Dedication, the day that commemorates the freeing of Israel from the Syrian tyrant and the restoration of the temple on Zion? You Judeans have lost your patriotism, but we of Galilee recall with pride the heroic exploits of the Maccabees; and each year without fail we journey to the temple to pledge new loyalty to our nation and confusion to her enemies."

" Would that a new Deliverer would arise," said another voice, " to strike Rome's yoke from off our necks! "

" Nay, speak not so loudly," warned Hosea. " Rome's arm is long and her spies are everywhere. Do ye wish to die upon a cross? "

" Silence, coward! " cried a third voice, " we men of Galilee do not fear Rome. Even now Judas and his band of Zealots, pledged to undying hatred of Rome and resistance to her taxation, are gathering in the Galilean hills."

" Mayhap he will be the one to deliver us from Rome," said another.

" Nay," said the leader, " I fear his followers are too few to defy the Roman legions. Herod will summon the garrison from Caesarea and crush this as he has all our rebellions against Rome's rule in Israel. We must needs wait for the Lord to send us the Messiah to deliver us from the oppressor."

" Would that he would come soon! " cried the first speaker.

" Know ye not that we are now in the place where he is to appear? " said a tall man in the background. " For do ye not recall that Rabbi Eleazer told us in the synagogue but a few Sabbaths ago that the scribes declare that he shall be born in Bethlehem, for so the prophet Micah hath foretold. Even as David came from this village to be our king, so shall the new King come forth from Bethlehem."

" Oh, how I hate Rome! " broke in an angry voice, " for her iron hand is crushing our people in the dust with her heavy taxes, taxes on land, on oil, on grain, on cattle, on everything. And the tax collector sits at every crossroads."

" But what think ye of her latest decree," cried an excited voice, " that on this very day that we celebrate our independence under the Maccabees the Roman legate of Syria, Publius Quirinius, hath commanded that every Israelite go to his ancestral city (no matter how far be the journey) to be numbered by Rome; doubtless for some new and more crushing tax to fall upon us? "

" Aye, do ye not recall," said another, " that last night along the Way of the Sea, near En-gannim, we passed a man leading a donkey on which a woman was riding; and that we found that he was a carpenter from Nazareth and that the woman with him was far spent and ill, scarce able to ride upon the beast? And yet they must make this long and useless journey at Rome's command because their family hails from Bethlehem."

" O Rome! Rome! " cried the leader, lifting his clenched hands heavenward, " may Jehovah speedily free his people from thy yoke. For hath he not promised to send us the Deliverer, the Messiah, to break Rome's power and restore the kingdom to

Israel. Such is the word of the prophet:

" ' Behold, O Lord, thou wilt raise up to us a king
   At the time appointed that he may reign over Israel,
   And gird him with strength that he may shatter unrighteous
      rulers,
   That he may purge Jerusalem from the nation that tramples her
      down,
   With his rod of iron shall he break all her substance,
   And shall destroy the godless nation with the word of his
      wrath.' "

And with an angry roar of assent the Galileans passed out of
the stable into the courtyard to mingle with the ever-increasing
numbers, that, as the day advanced, crowded the old inn, its
courtyard, and stable to overflowing. Lying as it did off the
main highways, it was half empty save on feast days. But never
had such a multitude of men and camels and donkeys swarmed
here as today, drawn thither not only by the feast day but by the
census of Quirinius. And the old innkeeper, his rooms all occupied, the low-ceilinged dining hall filled with a carousing
group of gay spirits, joined in their noisy revelry with a glad
heart, for was not the pouch at his girdle full of jingling silver
coins?

The winter's day drew to its close. And in the early dusk, as
Hosea, weary from his hard day of toil, came to the doorway of
the stable, he saw little fires lighted all over the courtyard, with
groups about them preparing the evening meal; for, the inn
long since filled, the late-comers were encamped within the
sheltering walls of the court. And as he stood thus, there advanced through the dusk toward the stable door a tall man,
dust-covered, limping and footsore, leading a stumbling donkey,
on whose back sat a veiled woman, bent with weariness. They
stopped before Hosea and the man spoke in a deep voice,
" Thou art the keeper of the stable? "

" Aye," said Hosea. " What would ye? "

" I crave shelter for the night for myself and my Mary," was
the answer. " We have come all the long way from Nazareth,
driven hither by the command of Rome, of which you doubtless

know; and we are weary and well-nigh spent." His voice sharp-
ened with anxiety.

"Nay, I care not for myself, but Mary must have help as well
as shelter at once." And he leaned forward and whispered ear-
nestly to Hosea.

"But why do ye not seek shelter at the inn?" asked Hosea.

"We did," answered the man and his face darkened. "I told
the innkeeper all that I have told you and made my most earnest plea for our hour of desperate need, but he only leered at
me with his bloodshot eyes, for he was evidently in his cups,
then sneered and violently shook his head. And when I continued to plead with him he cried in a hoarse voice: 'Nay,
there is no room in the inn for such as you, ye accursed Naza-
rene swine. Go to the stable and mayhap ye may find lodging
with the cattle where ye belong.' And with a roar of drunken
laughter, he slammed the door in my face. So here we stand
before thee. Wilt thou help us in our dire need?"

A moment Hosea looked into the anxious face of the carpenter from Nazareth, then turned his gaze toward the woman,
who had thrown back her veil. Luminous eyes full of spiritual
beauty looked out of a white face lined with pain and weariness,
with a pleading loveliness that touched Hosea's inmost heart.
For it was like that last look that Ruth's eyes had given him ere
they closed in death.

"Come in," said Hosea, and swung wide the door; then tenderly helped to lift the half-fainting woman from the saddle and
support her faltering steps into the stable.

Swiftly Hosea led a protesting donkey from its stall, seized
the broom, swept away the litter from the stone floor, strewed
fresh straw upon it, then going to that little cubicle where he
slept, seized his own bedding and hastened to lay it upon the
straw. Setting the lantern down upon the floor he helped to
carry the moaning woman and lay her upon this improvised
bed.

"It is but a poor place I can offer thee," he said to the Naza-
rene, "but it is all I have. I go now to get help for thy Mary."
And he hurried across the courtyard and to the back door of the
inn.

Anna the portress, summoned by his insistent knocking, came to the door with a frown. But when Hosea had told his story, her plain face was suddenly alight with tenderness. " Aye, I will come," and together they made their way back to the stable and the stall.

Back to his little bedroom went Hosea, to stand for a moment above an old oaken chest. Swiftly he stooped and rummaged amidst its contents, then drew forth a little linen garment, the swaddling clothes fashioned by Ruth's hands for their longed-for child, who never came. And as he looked at the tiny garment, yellowed with age, with its exquisite embroidery upon which those dear hands had toiled, tears ran down his cheeks, as he thought of her, who five years ago, on that night that was to mark the advent of a child into this world, had herself gone on her journey to that other world from which there is no returning.

Slowly he walked to where the woman lay upon her bed, and placed the little bundle in her hands. " It was for my child who never came," he whispered, " now it is thine."

The tears sprang into her eyes as she looked into his face, and in broken words of thanks she voiced her gratitude for his tender thoughtfulness.

Carefully closing the door behind him, that none might intrude upon the woman of Nazareth, Hosea stood again looking across the plain at the far-off dark line of the hills of Moab. And his heart was full of sorrow as he remembered that hour when his eager hope and longing had been changed into unavailing grief. And again came that sudden sharp pain and weakness that had come to him so often of late. Was it the angel of death warning him of his approaching coming? If so, he would not care. For life here was so hard and barren with its round of monotonous toil, embittered by the harshness of his master; and his soul was so lonely for the presence of his beloved Ruth. Somehow she seemed more near tonight. And as his thoughts returned to that sweet-faced woman from Nazareth and her grave and gallant husband, he lifted a prayer to heaven that they might receive what had been denied to him — the joy of the coming of a son into their home.

And so he sat long by the doorway wrapped in profound meditation.

Toward midnight the door opened and Anna came out, worn and weary, but with that strange glow on her face with which womankind has always looked upon the wonder of birth. "It is a beautiful boy," she said. And within the stable Hosea heard a faint infant's cry. And as Anna went her way toward the inn, Hosea murmured to himself, "Why could not this have been my son that was born here tonight?"

And then he wrapped his old mantle about him and lay down by the doorway and presently fell asleep.

The hours passed by. It was long after midnight when there was a touch on Hosea's shoulder. Startled, he looked up into the face of Joshua the shepherd, his friend of earlier and happier days. Hosea rose to his feet, still half asleep and bewildered, and saw with Joshua three of those fellow shepherds that with him pastured their flocks near the Well of David within sight of Jerusalem and her hills.

"What is it, Joshua?" stammered Hosea.

"This night we were keeping watch over our flock. It was bitter cold and we were huddled about the fire and half asleep, when off to the north above Herod's palace on Mount Zion there appeared a strange and brilliant glow in the sky. Nearer it came, until we found ourselves enveloped in a mantle of light. Then out of the very heart of this white radiance stepped one whose face and figure were like a blinding flame of fire. As we cowered there trembling with terror a voice came to our ears, low and sweet like the south wind in the locust trees, saying unto us, 'Fear not!' While we listened and looked in awe and wonder the voice said again, 'Fear not!' And then in tones like the trumpets of the Levites in the temple, the angel cried:

"'Behold I bring you glad tidings of great joy! For there is born to you this day in the city of David, a Savior, who is Christ the Lord!'

"As we knelt there speechless and numb, like men dead, behold, the whole air was filled with the white garments and pearly wings of a great multitude of angels, like the armies of heaven, moving toward us along a great white way of living light. And suddenly there burst upon our ears, more glorious than the singing of the Great Hallel by the Passover congregation in the temple, such heavenly music as no man hath ever heard, as the whole host above us burst into song. And this is what they sang:

> " ' Glory to God in the highest,
>   And on earth peace,
>   Good will toward men.'

Strong at first, then more and more faint, came the music of the angel choir, and at last there was silence. And while we lay on our faces on the ground, in rapture and awe, the angel's voice came again to our ears as before: ' And this shall be the sign unto you. Ye shall find a babe wrapped in swaddling clothes and lying in a manger.' And when we dared to look up at last, lo, the glory and the angel were gone; and we were all alone. Didst thou hear aught of this heavenly music, Hosea, or see that heavenly light? "

" Nay," answered the wondering Hosea, " I have been asleep. But why come ye here? "

" This is the only stable in Bethlehem, Hosea," answered Joshua. " Is there a babe born here tonight? "

" Come with me," was the answer; and, lantern in hand, Joshua and the shepherds passed through the doorway, and advanced with Hosea to the nearby stall.

There on the straw, wrapped in the bedding Hosea had given her, lay the exhausted but happy mother; her eyes opening wide with surprise in the lantern light as she saw Hosea and the group of shepherds by his side. And as Hosea's eyes sought the Child, lo, in the stone manger at the side of the stall, lying in the straw, was the Babe of Bethlehem! And he was wrapped in the swaddling clothes destined for that child of his that never came, in that little garment that had been made by those busy hands that had long since been stilled in death.

Was this indeed the Christ, the promised Messiah of God, that lay here swathed in the garments he had given? And as they beheld the Babe in the manger, in adoration and awe, nothing doubting, the shepherds fell on their knees before the mother and the Babe, while phrases from the old familiar psalms were whispered by their lips. Yet no angel visitants stood by that manger cradle, no ethereal lullabies were sung by heavenly voices over that sleeping Child. Nearby the beasts stirred in their stalls, and the lantern light revealed the murky interior of the rock-cut stable, with its rude stone floor and its dark roof, draped with cobwebs. It seemed but a simple peasant mother and her babe who lay there before him.

Yet as Hosea looked again at that Babe in the manger, he seemed to see a soft glow of heavenly light enveloping that tiny form as in an aureole of glory. And he felt a strange warmth within him as he realized that this long-cherished baby garment of his might well be the mantle of the heaven-sent Messiah of God. As he stood there in the background while the shepherds knelt, his eyes met those of the mother as she saw where his gaze had been directed, and her smile of perfect understanding and heartfelt gratitude filled his soul with a perfect peace. It was as though the eyes of Ruth had smiled again into his own.

The shepherds rose at last, and in silence, with rapt faces, passed out of the stable and with a last word of farewell walked through the courtyard and vanished into the darkness of the night.

As Hosea stood by the doorway of the stable musing upon all that had taken place that night, he felt a numbing pain, a strange weakness came over him, and he sank slowly to the ground into an enveloping darkness. And then a glowing radiance dazzled his eyes and before him stood a glorious figure, clad in garments of light, and he beheld his beautiful Ruth smiling at him as of old!

Then in well-remembered accents her voice fell on his ears: "Hosea, my beloved, I am come to thee from the King of Kings, who hath seen thy kindness to the stranger and the lowly, as thou hast given shelter to this mother and her Babe. But know, my beloved, that the little one cradled in that manger and wrapped in the garment of our dreams is none other than the Christ, the hope of centuries, the Son of the Most High God. We longed and prayed for a son, and thy life has been darkened by that unfulfilled desire, but now hath God

granted our prayers. For that Child about whom thou hast
thrown the mantle of thy love is to be called by thine own
name, ' Hosea, ' or ' Jesus ' — and he is indeed the Child of our
souls' deepest longings. Through all the centuries the longing
hearts of all lonely men and women shall find fulfilled in that
Babe their dearest dreams."

And as Hosea looked up with awe and wonder into the radiant face of his beloved, he saw above her a long lane of splendor and the shining of myriad wings, and to his raptured ears
came the sound of the angels' choir, singing.

And through the heavenly music came again a tender and
thrilling voice: " Come, Hosea, my love; come, and let us go
unto Him that sent me. For thy act of love hath won thee the
favor of God. Inasmuch as ye did it unto the poor and helpless,
ye did it unto him."

And down that pathway of living light, all pain and sorrow
forever past, Hosea and his beloved went hand in hand into the
presence of the King.

PALESTINE
(Bethlehem Today)

Sara, An Arab Refugee

GERTRUDE RINDEN

"SARA! YOU! Out in such a storm!" Sara, bending forward against the wind and picking her way through the mud of the Arab refugee camp, looked up quickly to see who was calling. It was Helana, standing by the door of her tent. She was watching Sara, her mouth twisted into a cynical smile that sat strangely on her teen-age face. Sara nodded politely and started to hurry on, but suddenly Helana stood in her path.

"What important business took you to Bethlehem today?" There was irony in Helana's voice. "The day before Christmas too! Or don't you keep Christmas any more?"

"I had a small errand in Bethlehem," Sara said politely.

Helana moved nearer and lowered her voice so that those in a nearby tent wouldn't hear. "There's nothing secret in a refugee camp. Do you think we don't know why you hurried to Bethlehem this morning? The relief workers have come there for Christmas, and you went to beg them to—"

"Not beg," Sara interrupted. "I asked them if there was any way to get my one more year of school so I could start nurse's training."

"And their answer was no," said Helana quickly. "Their answer will always be no. You see how they like to keep us forever in refugee camps, hungry, in rags."

Sara pushed the dark curls back from her pretty face in shocked surprise. She knew now that Helana was one of the troublemakers in the camp, one of the group spreading propaganda against the relief workers. There seemed little good to be accomplished by explaining, but Sara felt compelled to contradict Helana's bitter statement. "You know, Helana, why they can't let me be a nurse now. It's not the relief workers' fault. It's a rule of our own government that every candidate for nurses' training must be a middle-school graduate. It's my bad luck that I was only in the eighth grade when war came."

But Helana was not easily convinced. " I know. That's just it. The war that took away our good stone houses and our olive groves snatched from you that year of school. Here the tent school goes only through grade six. You'll never get that year. Even though you work hard every day taking care of little children in the tents — especially Mariam — still they do nothing for you."

Sara was amazed that Helana knew so much about her. And it was all true. There were many sick children in camp for whom the nearby hospitals had no room, and Sara had been helping care for some in their tents. Much of her time had been given to Mariam, a five-year-old who had tuberculosis of the bone. One of Mariam's legs was bent under her, and she couldn't walk. But Sara knew how to take blankets and roll them into hard bolsters to tuck around Mariam. Then with the weight off her leg, the little girl was relieved of some of her pain. Sara went to Mariam's tent every day, and Helana must have been watching.

Gusts of rain-filled wind from the Mediterranean were gathering into a gale. Sara pulled her skimpy jacket around her and tried to move on. But again Helana stopped her.

" There is nothing for our age in this camp," she said softly but passionately. " There's a tent school for children and classes for old ones. But nothing for us."

" But they did try to help me at relief headquarters," Sara replied. " I found Moukhtar there. Since he used to be headman of our village, I still call him Moukhtar. He said our government is trying hard to keep its standards, standards like the rules about nursing."

" Standards," Helana muttered, gesturing toward the endless

mud. The morning's blanket of snow had melted, and rivulets of water were everywhere, finding their way under tents and forming pools in unwelcome places.

"Now that you can never be a nurse, what will you do? Go on living always in a cave? It's a shame to see your mother so thin. She needs more to eat. And I suppose your brother would like to have some books. If you had a job, you could help."

Like a musician plucking at the strings of an instrument to produce a certain effect, Helana plucked at Sara's pride and keenest wishes.

All her life — or so it seemed to her — Sara had wanted to be a nurse. When she was a very small girl, she had seen a nurse in a Christian hospital. That day she had hurried home to make herself a white cap out of a piece of woolen cloth she found among her mother's scraps. Sitting on the divan, she had cut and shaped and pinned the perky thing to her black curls. Then she had stood on the divan to reach for her mother's brass mirror. Because she liked what she saw in the mirror, she had run across to Rashid's terrace to show the cap to her playmate.

"Nice girls aren't nurses," Rashid had said scornfully. And because Rashid was two years older and her idol, Sara had shoved the white cap backward off her head and let it lie where it had fallen under a gray olive tree. But the dream had not gone out of her mind.

Later Rashid had gone off to a boys' boarding school. Upon his return for his first vacation, he had asked Sara, "Are you really going to be a *nurse?*" Then he added: "Girls in good families *can* be nurses. Maybe you should be a nurse."

It was soon after this that Sara's and Rashid's families had separated them. According to the custom of Arab families, they were too old to play together any longer.

By the time that Sara was thirteen and in the second year of middle school, her black ringlets had lengthened into waves of heavy hair that hung to her shoulders. A white cap would accent their shining blackness, she knew. But her thoughts about nursing had grown. She was absorbed now with the idea of becoming an Arab girl with a profession.

Even after war came and Sara and her mother and brother

Jameel had been forced to flee to the cave near the Bethlehem camp, she had cherished her dream. Rashid's family had fled too, but since his school was located in the Arab area of the divided country of Palestine, he did not have to live in the camp.

" If I were a nurse, I could buy food," Sara had reasoned. " Even when our rations run out near the end of the month, still we could eat. I would never, never again have to watch our mother put her food at Jameel's place, pretending she isn't hungry. I would buy her wool for a dress too. For Jameel, I suppose I would buy him a book. Though if he had his own schoolbook, there would be no living with his cockiness."

Today in Bethlehem all of her dreams had been shattered.

" Why don't you join us? " Helana whispered low. " Don't you want to work for the freedom of your family and all our people? "

" Freedom? "

" Come to our meeting in my tent this afternoon. Don't tell your mother. Tell her you are going to care for Mariam, but come here instead."

Just then a blast of wind struck with such fury that Helana added, " If the storm is too bad today, come tomorrow."

" I'll come," said Sara, and she hurried on half relieved and half wondering what she had done. She was glad for the piercing wind with its needles of cold to fight against.

Suddenly she remembered that her path was taking her straight past Mariam's tent. " She'll be waiting for me," she thought. " I mustn't let her see me. If I can never be a nurse, why should I take care of her any more? " Sara's bitterness rose in a sudden burst of anger, and she darted to a different row of tents. As she did so, she thought she saw behind her a dark figure that had changed its course and disappeared between tents just as she had turned. The wind whipped and beat the tents, which were sagging with wetness.

Sara had just reached the curve of the hill when she heard a cough behind her.

" Rashid," she exclaimed as she recognized her pursuer. " You — you came home for Christmas. I mean you came here for Christmas. Your good school is your home. You are lucky."

Rashid was looking very serious. " I've left school."

Sara was shocked. Everything was as topsy-turvy as the storm itself.

" I have news, Sara, but we mustn't talk here. So I will come to your home."

" My cave, you mean. But you can't come there to see me, either. My mother would not allow it."

" I can come and present myself to your brother Jameel, can't I? Is he not the head of your house? Does he not enjoy that honor? "

She laughed to think how proud Jameel would be to receive the attention of Rashid, who was older and who went to a fine boarding school.

" You will be sitting in the back of your home embroidering and pretending not to see me. But you will listen, won't you? " asked Rashid.

" Sitting there, patching rags on rags, you mean. But I will listen to you," Sara said.

" Then listen, because I have important news."

Sara was as mixed up as one of the tents with the wind beating it from every side. First Helana and her talk of freedom. Now Rashid and his mysterious news. Had he overheard her conversation with Helana? So many thoughts had been tossed together in her mind today. No wonder it was in a turmoil.

Rashid disappeared, and Sara hurried to her hillside home. For once she was glad it was a cave and not a tent. Neighbors were not so near. She raised the mat that hung at the entrance in place of a door.

" Sara! Child! " Mother breathed her relief. "Lower the mat quickly. My fire is nothing but smoke. How is Mariam today? Poor child. Is her tent leaking? "

Jameel broke in. " Our bread is going to have sesame seeds sprinkled on it for Christmas," he announced with excitement. Then with brotherly concern: " Your jacket is wet, Sara. What will you wear when we go to the Church of the Nativity tonight? Next time there is a clothing distribution, I will get you a warm coat," he added with all the importance of his ten years.

"I don't want anything from the relief committee," Sara blurted out.

Her mother looked up quickly and searchingly. Sara was ashamed of her outburst — ashamed already of her conversation with Helana. She was glad to hear Rashid's cough, announcing his arrival at the door.

If a sheik had come, Jameel could not have been more politely formal. "You have returned for the Christmas," he greeted Rashid.

"And I bring my family's greetings to yours," Rashid replied.

"Thank you. We accept and send ours. You are too kind."

Between statements, the boys made the customary gestures of greeting, and Jameel's gestures were twice as sweeping as Rashid's.

Watching out of the corner of one eye, Sara almost forgot her troubles. A smile wavered on her mother's face.

"Be seated though it is not a divan," Jameel said as he placed a reed stool for the guest.

"Your good father. Is he well?" Jameel set out upon the customary order of conversation. But suddenly Rashid broke with custom.

"Today I must be like the storm that comes and goes suddenly. I have something to tell you."

"Tell me?" Jameel asked in surprise.

Sara reached for a portion of the bread dough and began to work it vigorously.

"I have left school," Rashid went on.

"You — have — left — Oh! Of course! Your father has betrothed you, and your wedding day is drawing near," Jameel guessed.

Sara's face burned, and she turned her back completely on the two boys.

Her mother gasped, "Jameel!" Rashid filled the cave with emphatic denials.

"Then why?" Jameel asked.

"I myself chose to leave. I decided it today since coming to the refugee camp. Some of my classmates, five of them, had made up their minds before. I thought I couldn't bring my-self to make the sacrifice, but now I must."

Jameel was too surprised to speak, and Rashid went on with his explanation. " You know that hill, the one next beyond us? "

" The one all covered with rock? " Jameel asked.

" You sound like my father. He sees nothing but the rocks. He will not even listen to my plan. Nor will he look up at that hill. Rather, his face is turned toward the fields that he lost, and he cannot think of anything else. But some boys in our school, working in co-operation with the relief committee, will terrace that hill and plant olive groves."

" You! You will do the work with your own hands? " Jameel asked in amazement, knowing that Rashid had been destined for the life of a scholar.

" With our own hands," Rashid said firmly. " As soon as winter storms are over, we will begin. This very year we will plant trees. Then later we must pitch our tents up there until we can build stone houses, for we must be close to the groves." Rashid hesitated, then said, " When we are older we will take our families up there."

When Jameel asked, " Why don't you finish school first? " Rashid pounced eagerly upon that question as though its answer was what he wanted most to say.

" We can't wait. The troublemakers are increasing in our camp, Jameel. Cold and hunger fan the fire of their secret propaganda. They work hard to prevent the things the relief workers are trying to do. We must work hard too, if we don't wish always to live in tents like nomads."

While Rashid talked, Sara felt hotter waves of shame cours-ing through her. He had overheard her conversation with Helana! Would he never stop so that she could rush out and tell Helana that she would never, never join her group?

When Rashid finally rose to go, Jameel, weighed down with his position as head of the family, tried to delay him with farewells that were more flowery than his welcome. But when

he lifted the reed mat at the door, such a blast of wind swept
in that he could only gasp.

"The tents!" he cried out. "Look, look! They are blowing
over." The rain had stopped, but the wind was now a hurricane. It roared and whistled, and high above its fury there
was a ghastly and ominous whine. Rashid was gone at once.
Pulling on her wet jacket, Sara, too, rushed to the door. The
sight of the battered tents had changed her mind. She wouldn't
even bother with her message to Helana, but, if she died in the
attempt, she would try to rescue Mariam.

"It's too late, Sara. You can't go out in such a storm," her
mother protested. "You couldn't even stand up."

But Sara would not listen. "I will bring Mariam here if I
can. Her tent will blow away, and she can't even walk."

As she stumbled through the storm, fell, and got up again,
she felt twice the strength she had ever known before. Ahead
of her, the camp was a blur of the flowing garments of running
men, of flapping tents, and of toppled tents turning somer-
saults in the gale.

Soon she reached the area where tents had already blown
away. Homeless families crouched over their belongings. Sara
shouted to them to take their children to the caves, but she
herself kept on hunting for Mariam. Hot tears came to her
eyes as she fought her way through the mob of frightened
people who, battling with the wind, were trying to rescue
homes and pitiful possessions.

Mariam's tent had blown over, and, at first, Sara couldn't
find the child. Then suddenly she saw a blanket in the shape of
a small tent. Mariam was under the blanket.

"I can carry her. I want to," Sara insisted, begging Mariam's
father to tie the child and her blanket to her back. Because he
could not leave his tent, the father complied, and Sara turned
toward the caves. It was a frightful journey back. As it grew
dark, the wind itself seemed to become black. Sara struggled
on, but the unnatural strength that had sustained her first
efforts was gone. She felt weak and limp, and at last she had
to fall to her knees to rest.

She was so worn out that she didn't even hear a jeep coming, not even when it stopped close behind her. The wind's growl was all she heard until a man beside her spoke. It was Moukhtar whom she had seen this morning — an age ago — in Bethlehem. His jeep was piled high with blankets.

"Wait here," he said, "until I come back. I'll take the blankets to the caves, then come to get you and your little charge."

That night Sara's cave was full of children, each rolled in a blanket that Moukhtar had brought. Sara lay next to Mariam to see that she was kept comfortable through the long night.

Toward morning the wind, as though it had done all the damage it possibly could, stopped raging. In the strange quietness that follows a storm, the day dawned, and relief work began in earnest. Rashid and others came with load after load of clothing and blankets that had been sent by American church people.

In the late afternoon Moukhtar came again to the cave.

"We think there is going to be a way," he said to Sara, who was too busy at first to realize what he was talking about. But her understanding grew as he continued. "One of the British relief workers who came in this morning knows five other girls up and down the valley who, like you, need just one year of school," Moukhtar went on. "He is making arrangements with a mission school to take them. He has added your name to the five. You deserve it."

As his lined face broke into a warm smile, Sara felt that Christmas had indeed come again to Bethlehem.

POLAND
(As Reflected in the United States)

When They Saw the Star

ANNIE B. KERR

M ORRIS STOOD IN THE KITCHEN with his nose pressed against the windowpane. The window looked out upon a narrow shaft which supplied air and light to the back rooms of the tall tenement house where Morris and his mother lived.

Because their three rooms were on the top floor he could look up into the blue sky, where white clouds drifted past in the daytime and stars shone out at night. The stars gave him a feeling of their friendliness and protection when his mother was away working and he was left alone at night.

But it was not his patch of sky that had kept him standing by the window for so many hours on this particular Christmas Eve. It was the Christmas preparations of the Kalenski family, whose kitchen window was just opposite.

All day long Mrs. Kalenski had been busily cooking and making ready for the feast which was about to take place, right there before the fascinated gaze of the little Jewish boy.

She stood now, with her broad back to the window, attending to the food cooking on the stove. The window was open a few inches and Morris sniffed hungrily the fish soup, which was boiling merrily in one big kettle, the cabbage and mushrooms which filled another to the very top, and the fish with stewed prunes, which was to be the high point of the celebration.

Mrs. Kalenski lifted a corner of her apron and wiped the perspiration from her round, smiling face. Then she cleared off the big table and called Jadwiga and Helen to come and help her set it.

They spread smoothly the heavy linen cloth, having first arranged handfuls of yellow straw all around the edge of the table. Morris pushed back his mop of curly hair from his eyes and flattened his nose against the pane until it hurt, so surprised was he at the straw. The girls saw him standing there and ran to their own window and beckoned to him. He shook his head mournfully.

The Kalenskis were very kind, but his mother had forbidden him ever to go inside their apartment. They were Christians. They hated the Jews. In Poland, even now, the Christians killed the Jews; he must promise never to go to their house. Morris had promised, although he was sure the Kalenskis didn't hate anybody. And so he shook his head sadly when Jadwiga held up a plate of twisted pastries with gestures indicating that he was to have some.

They were such kind people, the Kalenskis. There was Mr. Kalenski, who worked in a tailor shop in the next block, and Mrs. Kalenski always ready to help a sick neighbor or a lonely little boy, and Jadwiga (named for a queen), and Helen, and Janina, and the three boys. Sometimes, when his mother was away at work and the hours from five to twelve dragged on endlessly, Morris would tap on the pane and one of them would run to the bright window opposite, and smile and wave to him. They were such comforting people, thought Morris, and it comforted Mother too, to know that they were there, ready to come to their window, whenever he tapped on his.

And yet Mother had said: " They are Christians. You must never go to their house."

Mother was a very wonderful person. Ever since Father died she had had to work very hard. Morris would not think of disobeying her, but there were many puzzling things she did not seem able to explain. For instance, Christmas.

The shop windows were filled with fascinating toys, warm sweaters, beautiful dresses, all marked " For Christmas." In the bakery windows were Christmas cakes and candies and other delicious things to eat. At school all the children sang

"Silent Night! Holy Night!" and "Tannenbaum, O Tannen-baum," and when they trooped out of the building for the last time till "next year," teacher had called, "Merry Christmas, children."

"Why don't *we* have Christmas?" Morris had asked his mother one evening over a week ago, as they ate their early supper on the white enamel table in the kitchen.

"It is not for the Jews," Rachel said, gazing proudly into the puzzled eyes of her small son.

"We have Chanukah, and we have lights and presents then. If you are a good little boy, Mother will bring you a red sweater to wear to school like the one we saw in the window this morning."

Morris gave a little gasp. The sweater cost three dollars! And Mother did not have enough money to buy the coat she greatly needed when she went out to work on cold winter nights. Then his eyes filled with sudden tears.

"It's not the sweater I want," he sobbed.

"Why, Morris! Don't cry, dear," she pleaded. "What is it you want so badly?"

He pointed across the shaft to the Kalenskis' lighted kitchen. Mrs. Kalenski was, as usual, busily preparing supper for Mr. Kalenski and Jadwiga and Helen and Janina and the three boys. Her movements were somewhat hampered by the fact that Stanislas, aged two, was draped across her shoulder, fast asleep.

"I want a baby brother," said Morris.

"Darling!" cried Rachel, and ran around to his chair and gathered him up in her arms.

"Or else," pondered Morris, snuggling his dark head against his mother's neck, "or else the baby Jesus to play with when you are away at night."

"Don't, Morris." His mother unclasped his arms from around her neck, and went back to her chair.

"But the baby Jesus was a Jew, Mother."

"When you are older, Morris, you will understand about Christmas and the little Jesus. And next month, when they are not so busy, you may invite the Kalenski boys to come here

and play with you. But you must never go to their house.
Now remember."

"Yes, Mother," promised Morris with a little sigh.

Rachel was away all day, the day before Christmas, as well
as at night, because one of the stores in the neighborhood
needed extra help. It was a chance to earn a few more dollars
to make up for the wages she had lost those days when she
was sick. She had left crackers and milk for Morris and promised to bring something more substantial home with her at
eleven o'clock, and they would have a little feast together, if
Morris thought he could stay awake that long.

He had forgotten to eat his early supper, and the sight and
smell of the Kalenskis' feast reminded him of how hungry he
was.

The Christmas Eve feast of his Polish neighbors appeared to
be ready and the entire family was assembled. A small Christmas tree stood on a shelf in one corner of the room and two
tall candles, in gaily decorated candlesticks, gave an additional
touch of festivity to the bright, crowded kitchen.

Morris turned away from the window reluctantly. A light
snow had fallen and the flakes had made beautiful shapes and
patterns against the windowpane. He dragged his feet to the
cupboard and took out the milk and crackers. How bare and
dreary the room seemed! He would set the table for two and
then wait for his mother's return. There was a lump in his
throat, and in spite of himself he turned back to the window.

The Kalenskis were crowded against their own windowpane,
gazing up at the small patch of sky. Jadwiga opened the window
and leaned out, her blue eyes searching the heavens eagerly.

"I see it!" she cried. "The evening star! *Now* we can have
our feast!"

She saw the wistful little face at the other window and
called across to him: "Come and eat with us, Morris. We have
much to eat tonight — see?" She pushed the children aside
and pointed to the loaded table.

But he shook his head. They had invited him before and he
had always refused, as gently as possible. He could never tell
them the real reason. That would be impolite. Better let them

think he was shy and afraid, though he smiled to himself at the idea of being afraid of the kind, friendly Kalenskis.

Jadwiga brushed the snow from her fair hair and flushed face. Then before she shut the window she called once more across the darkness that separated them, " Then we'll save some supper for you and bring it when your mother comes home, before we go to church tonight."

Morris opened his own window and leaned out in a vain effort to see the star for whose appearance the Kalenskis had evidently been waiting. Tears of loneliness filled his eyes as he watched the happy family across the way. He put out the light and drew a chair close to the window. There they were, stand-ing behind their chairs. Mr. Kalenski, tall and thin with gray hair and a worried look on his face. It was the same kind of look that Mother had sometimes. Perhaps he was afraid there wouldn't be enough money to pay for all the food, thought Morris. And Mrs. Kalenski, who didn't look at all worried, was very beautiful indeed in a new silk dress with a lace collar which fell in ruffles down the front. And Jadwiga, her smooth yellow braids wound around her head, her two hands holding little Stanislas, who stood upright in his chair at her side. The other four — Josef and Ignace and Janina and Helen — watched their mother break a thin wafer in eight pieces and hand a piece to each member of the family. As they ate the wafer Mrs. Kalenski spoke to each one. Then they bowed their heads reverently while Mr. Kalenski said a long prayer. Morris bowed his head also.

The Kalenskis pulled back their chairs and broke into a merry chatter, while Mrs. Kalenski filled their plates from the big kettles on the stove. Then Morris saw that one chair was empty. Not Mrs. Kalenski's, which was at the end of the table nearest the stove, but the one between little Stanislas and Josef. He counted carefully. They were all there. W*ho* could the chair be for? Jadwiga had explained to him that the family would be alone tonight. Tomorrow there would be many guests for the big Christmas Day feast. How strange that there should be an empty chair! Morris slid down from his own chair in order to press closer against the window.

How good the supper looked, and how happy they all were! Surely his mother wouldn't mind if he accepted their invitation just this once on Christmas Eve. He was hungry and cold and lonely, and there, just around the other side of the hall, were food and warmth and friendship. But they were Christians and he was a Jew. What difference did that make, really? The Kalenskis had never been unkind to the Jews, either in Poland or in America, he was sure of that. They had tried very hard to be kind to Morris and his mother, ever since they came there to live, six months ago. His mother didn't understand. She wouldn't mind his being with them tonight if she knew them as he did. Yet he had promised her.

He looked again at the empty chair. Surely no one could come now to be their guest. Josef came to the window and looked across to where Morris was standing, but he could not see beyond the darkness. Morris opened the window a crack. A gust of wind blew the snow inside from the sill and he closed it hastily. Then he jumped up and down in excitement. The empty chair — who could it be for but himself, Morris Lewisohn? *He* was the guest they had invited — the chair was set for him. That being so, his mother could not object to his going. It would be impolite to leave it empty. He snapped on the light, washed his thin little hands at the kitchen sink, straightened his collar, smoothed down his rumpled hair, and slipped out into the dim hall. His timid knock on the Kalenskis' door was not heard because of the merriment inside. Finally Morris pushed open the door and stood blinking in the bright light of the Kalenskis' kitchen.

Then he walked quietly around the table and slipped into the empty chair.

A sudden startled silence fell upon the children. At last Ignace voiced the dismay which they were all feeling.

" He has taken the chair belonging to the Christ-child! "

" Hush." Mrs. Kalenski leaned across the end of the table and gave the unexpected guest a reassuring pat.

" We are so glad to have you come, Morris. And now I give you soup and mushrooms and fish hot from the stove."

" I thank you," said Morris politely, his eyes fixed on the

generous dishes which Mrs. Kalenski was placing in front of him. " I think my mother would like to have me come to your party." He spoke hesitatingly, trying to curb his eagerness. He had not understood Ignace and was quite unaware of the consternation he had caused.

Then his assumption of adult politeness vanished and a very hungry little boy fell upon the appetizing food with gusto.

" Let us sing," cried Mrs. Kalenski, anxious to put their guest at ease and divert attention from him. And so they sang an old Christmas carol, the last verse of which is something like this:

> " We too await thee, Lord,
> As once they did of old,
> And when thou comest,
> On our knees we'll fall before thee
> And in spirit we'll adore thee."

Morris settled back in his chair with a little sigh of satisfaction, while the girls cleared away the plates and brought pastries, various kinds of fruit and a pudding of noodles, honey, and poppy seed. His eyes gazed around the cheerful room, with its gay linoleum, its curtains and pictures. On the wall opposite hung a portrait of an interesting-looking man in uniform.

" Our great hero — Kosciusko." Mr. Kalenski, following the little boy's gaze, spoke for the first time.

" Yes," explained Jadwiga, " he helped fight in the war, here in America, long ago. He is in my history book. Once when my teacher sassed me in school and called me Polack I asked her: ' What did your old Ireland ever do for this country? But Kosciusko and Pulaski fought for it and you don't dast to call me a Polack!' "

" Jadwiga very sassy to her teacher," apologized Jadwiga's mother.

" You can't understand, Mamma," explained Jadwiga hotly. " The teacher was sassy first. And she made me call myself Julia instead of Jadwiga 'cause she don't like Polish names! "

" I think the Polish people are the most grandest in all the world," announced Morris fervently, his mouth full of crisp Polish pastry.

"God bless him!" cried Mrs. Kalenski, filling a plate with goodies for him to carry home. "Now we pull out the straw. What for do you wish, Morris?"

Morris looked around at them with a question on his face and Jadwiga explained: "We tell our fortune by the straw. We each make a wish and if it is a very long straw, or if there is any grain on it, then the wish will come true. See?" She held up a long straw. "Now I know I'll be married soon to a rich husband."

"And I," cried Morris, excitedly waving two straws over his head — "I shall have a brother — *two* brothers, like Josef and Stanislas!"

The children looked at their mother questioningly, but she shook her head.

"I tink — not, Morris." Then seeing the tears slowly gathering in his eyes, she added hastily: "But Jadwiga not tell why we have the straw. It is because the little Jesus was born in stable — where are cattle — and straw. In church we have the stable, and the — what you call?"

"Manger," said Jadwiga.

"Oh — and do you have Santa Claus — like in Dabrowski's store?"

"No," explained Mrs. Kalenski. "In Poland we have Saint Nicholas on December 6. And if all the children be good, he will send presents for Christmas."

"Yes," broke in Josef, "tomorrow we will have our presents — 'little stars,' because a beautiful lady, all dressed in white, brings them. She is the Good Star from heaven like we saw in the sky tonight."

"Oh, I love the stars!" Morris' own eyes were starry as he lifted them to Mrs. Kalenski's. "And please, may I come tomorrow?"

"God bless him!" exclaimed Mrs. Kalenski again. "If your mother say yes, we like have you come. But now it is for church we must make ready."

"But see the tree first." Janina caught her mother by the

hand and pulled her toward the corner where stood the little tree, Morris following in their wake.

" We have put on the balls and the ornaments and all the little lights, with the star on top. Oh, Mother, we must turn on the lights before Morris goes home! "

Jadwiga turned off the big center light overhead and flashed on the tiny lights of the Christmas tree. Morris stood in rapt admiration. Then he turned and looked slowly around at each one.

" I thank you, one and all," he said quaintly.

But they did not answer. They only gazed at him breathlessly. His dark, childish head blotted out the little Christmas tree, but the yellow bulbs threw a light around it which glowed softly, and just above, the star shone down upon him.

ROMANIA

A Christmas Tale

QUEEN MARIE OF ROMANIA

THIS IS A VERY STRANGE TALE I have got to tell you today. It is about a mysterious well — a deep, deep well which lay in the center of a dark forest. It is also a Christmas tale.

No one knew why that well was there, nor who had dug it, nor how old it was.

The peasants from the villages around stood in great awe of this well, because from its depth a weird sound could be heard, a sort of moan, half sob, half gurgle, and sometimes a sound as though someone were knocking against its sides, which made you think of a lost soul in distress, perhaps held captive down there and unable to get out.

The village nearest the forest was called Galea. It was a very poor little village, its cottages small and miserable, with tiny gardens in which the flowers always looked sad and anemic, for the ground was stony and unfruitful.

In the center of the village stood a little wooden church. It was ancient and rather shaky; its huge roof looked too big for it, but the passing seasons had toned it down to a rich brown with a gray shimmer, which was pleasant to the eye.

Old stunted lilac bushes clustered around it, protecting the humble graves which lay scattered about beneath their shade, like a forlorn flock of sheep.

The peasants were rather ashamed of their tiny dilapidated church and dreamed of building a fine edifice, all white with

218

a tin roof, that would shine like silver in the sun, and not let the rain or the snow through in the bad seasons, a church with stout columns in front, all decorated in bright colors, and with God's eye painted over the door.

You and I would probably have infinitely preferred the crooked little wooden church with its overlarge roof, but then you see, each community has its ambition and its pride, and does not want to stand behind other communities. Bostea, the village on the other side of the forest, had a beautiful new big church of the kind that Galea coveted. But Galea was a much, much poorer village than Bostea, and it sadly felt its inferiority.

But it was about the mysterious well I was going to tell you, was it not?

The villagers for some reason had conceived the idea that the unknown being who was held captive in that well could become a danger to the countryside if it ever managed to get out, and that the only way to keep it contented was by throwing small offerings down into its depth.

The poor often think that they must make sacrifices to God or to any power greater than themselves; it is a sort of way of keeping off ill luck from their thresholds. And yet God knows their lives are full enough of sacrifices from beginning to end.

There were certain feast days on which the villagers had the habit of taking their offerings to the dreaded well, and these were especially Saint Maria Mare and Saint Dumitru.

The moment Mass was over, before any dancing or drinking could begin, they would collect in groups and start off into the forest with their queer little offerings.

Some brought flowers or colored eggs, others flat breads sprinkled with poppy seeds; some brought bunches of corn tied with bright ribbons. Little children would sacrifice their first ripe plums, cherries, or nuts, also the precious little pebbles picked up in the river bed, which became a lovely bright pink when you licked them.

The maidens made sacrifice of beads from their girdles and little painted cards with pictures of the saints or small holy medals, or of trinkets bought at the *moshi* (fair). The young men would throw down small coins, buttons from their military tunics, or the bright-red carnation they so fondly wore stuck behind their left ear.

Even quite old women would go limping through the sunshine, distaff in hand. Quite exhausted they would sink down on the well's edge and pronounce strange wishes over the water, throwing in wisps of wool or flax, whilst they murmured prayers, watching the while with one eye what the young ones were doing, always ready to criticize or to disapprove.

But in winter the well was almost quite forsaken, for no one particularly cared to go through the forest in that season. Right on the outskirts of Galea lived a widow in a cottage so small and humble that it was really hardly more than a hut. In all the village she was known as poor Maria, and she had but one little boy, Petru, who had large gray eyes set in a pale, anxious small face.

Petru had had two little sisters, but both of them lay under the lilac bushes of the churchyard, and so poor was Maria that she had not even been able to mark the spot with crosses, and this made Petru very sad.

Petru was pious and an ardent believer. He faithfully observed all the precepts of the church; he was a conscientious faster, though verily at all times Petru had but little to eat.

He would devoutly listen to all that old Popa Toader had to say, though sometimes he did not properly understand what it meant, and certain scraps of his exhortations would remain sticking in his mind, taking undue proportions.

Amongst others, Petru had conceived an uncomfortable belief that because the church of Bostea was larger and newer than their poor little wooden church, it was, therefore, also a holier place.

This idea had come to him because, on Easter Sunday, Popa Toader had spoken about collecting money for building a new church and had held up as example the Bostea church which God would surely bless, as it had been erected by sacrifices made by every inhabitant, who each year had offered part of his hard-earned money for the honor of God.

Petru of course had no money, not even the poorest little farthing; certainly if he had, he would have gladly given it for the building of the new church.

Petru had never been to Bostea, and just because of that, he had created in his imagination a wonderful vision of its church, which must have all the beauties and qualities Galea's poor little sanctuary never possessed.

Petru was about seven years old when his mother fell very ill indeed; it was just at the beginning of winter, which that year had set in with unusual severity. Petru loved his mother beyond all things on earth, and his poor little heart was wrung with terrible grief, seeing her thus pining away, and he so utterly helpless before her suffering.

Maria was a very patient woman, she never complained; it was from her that Petru had his big gray eyes and pathetic face.

There was no real bed in Maria's hovel; she lay on a sort of wooden bench over which a few ragged rugs had been spread, and upon this miserable pallet she lay all shaken by fever, her lips blue and cracked. A large earthen oven took up part of the hut; it had all sorts of shapes so as to fit into the crooked little room. Maria lay behind this oven, which Petru tried to keep as warm as he could by going each day to fetch wood on the outskirts of the forest, whence he would wearily return carrying on his back as many dry branches as he could. Petru was small, so that the weight was almost too much for him, and would quite bend him in two until he looked like a giant porcupine crawling home through the snow.

Petru would also try to cook. A few strings of dry onions hung against the wall behind the oven, and in a wooden bowl on the floor was their meager provision of *malaiu* (meal, maize).

Probably Petru was not a very successful cook; anyhow Maria turned away with a weary sigh from the daily mess he so anxiously offered her.

This made Petru terribly unhappy and great round tears would roll down his pinched little face. He would hide away in a corner and say his prayers over and over again, all the prayers Popa Toader had ever taught him, even if they had no connection with his trouble — but they were prayers, therefore of course acceptable to God.

After that the little boy would crawl on to the wooden pallet beside his mother, nestling close up to her, hoping to keep her warm with the embrace of his skinny little arms.

Alas, God did not seem to listen to Petru's prayers, because his mother grew worse and worse instead of better, till Petru began tormenting himself, imagining that he must have displeased God in some way. Yet worry his head as he would, he could not remember a single occasion upon which he had broken the law, for Petru was an almost painfully well-behaved little boy, who never had any time to enjoy life or to be naughty, having had to work and make himself useful, ever since he had been able to stand on his feet. He had always been an anxious little soul, ever ready to carry burdens too heavy for his frail shoulders.

It was Christmas Eve, and still poor Maria lay on her pallet, sick unto death, when an idea came into Petru's head.

Petru had ideas sometimes, but they would not always work out, because no one ever had time to bother about his mind, nor to help it to expand. But this idea had grown and grown till it had become a fixture, and then, when it was quite ripe, Petru set about carrying it out, and this is what it was:

He knew that when one desires something very, very much, one must offer a taper to some blessed image, more especially to that of the mother of God. Those little lights have a wonderful way of reinforcing prayer. Now Petru had obtained one of these little tapers from the old village chanter, as recompense for small services rendered last Sunday during Mass. It was certainly a very thin, fragile-looking little taper, a thing to be treated with infinite care, but the old man had also given him a smashed old match box, in which there were still five unused matches, and if he could keep them from the damp, they certainly would light his little taper for him when he placed it before the icon of his choice.

All might have been quite simple, had not Petru been possessed with the idea that he must carry his candle to the Bostea church, for, with the other villagers, he shared the mistaken idea that their own old wooden church was not quite an entirely worthy house of God — poor dear crooked little church.

Now to get to Bostea, you had either to take a very, very
long road, or you had to take the short cut through the dark
forest where the mysterious well stood.

Even in summertime Petru dreaded the groaning, moaning
well; how much more, therefore, in winter, when the forest
was all black and when wolves might be prowling about. Yet
he dare not remain away too long from his mother's bedside,
so in spite of his fear he made up his mind that he must face
that grim path through the wood.

Petru put on his rough, well-used *suman* (cape, overcoat)
and the old *caciula* (peasant's fur cap or bonnet) which had
once been his father's, and which gave him the quaint appearance of a wandering fungus, slipped on his fingerless
gloves, which were so much darned that there was more darn
about them than glove, and having hidden the precious taper
and matches in his pocket, he was ready to start.

Before slipping outside, however, he did not forget to pile
all the reserve of dried sticks upon the fire, and to place a small
mug of water beside his mother, who lay with her face turned
to the wall, mumbling all sorts of strange things which had
no sense and which filled poor little Petru's soul with dread.

Dusk was already gathering, but Petru had not been able
to get off sooner. He felt nervous, but now that his mind was
made up he meant to carry out his plan, no matter what the
effort might cost him.

Soon he reached the edge of the forest and bravely plunged
into its shade, but his heart beat like a heavy hammer in his
breast.

Perhaps I shall be able to avoid the well, thought the boy.
I know there are two paths — one is a little longer, but it does
not go past the well. . . .

The wind was howling through the branches; in the stillness
of the forest it sounded like an angry voice. Petru shivered; it
was terribly cold. But luckily the snow was not very deep, except in places where it lay in drifts.

Hurry as he would, night seemed to be pursuing him, gain-
ing on him, catching him up. His breath came in hard gasps
which hurt him at the bottom of his throat. What a terribly big

forest, and how tall the trees were! Never had poor Petru felt so small.

"I hope, oh, I do hope I am on the right road," said the child almost aloud. "I do not want to come past that terrible old well."

And just as he said this, thump, thump, he heard an uncanny sound that made his heart jump into his mouth.

Thump — thump, and then came another sound more like a moan rising from the very bosom of the earth.

Perspiration broke out on poor Petru's forehead in spite of the cold. How dark it was getting, the trees had become walls of darkness shutting him in on all sides. . . .

Thump — thump . . . oh, dear, oh, dear, that certainly was the sound of the well.

As though hypnotized, Petru advanced. He might have turned away, have slipped through the trees avoiding the place of dread, but he somehow never thought of this but advanced steadily, fascinated by the horror of the thing!

Yes, there stood the well, a dark, sinister object that he could not avoid.

In his anxiety Petru stumbled, tried to recover his footing, but fell with a little gasp at the very edge of the well!

For a moment he lay there, his face buried in the cold snow whilst great dry sobs tore his breast. But what was that? Someone else was weeping? He was not alone in his solitude, someone besides himself was in distress, and — could he be mistaken? It seemed to be a child's voice, weeping, weeping.

Petru picked himself up. He was feeling less afraid now — why should he be afraid of a little child crying in the dark?

But then came again the sound he dreaded — thump, thump. Oh! That dreadful well! His knees shook beneath him, and yet he must look over the edge — some force stronger than himself seemed to oblige him to do so.

Petru had always hated looking down into the well, even in the daytime, when his mother had held his hand; for nights afterward he could not sleep, always imagining that he was falling down that terrible black shaft. Now he was quite alone, it was almost night, nevertheless he *must* look over the edge.

Who could be down there? What secret could be hidden in that unknown depth?

Thump — thump — was it Petru's heart beating, or did the sound really come from the well?

Then suddenly a shrill child's voice cried: " Oh, let me out! Let me out! Throw me down your little taper — I am all alone here in the dark, and so cold, so cold."

" My little taper! " gasped Petru, forgetting his astonishment, his fear, and everything else in the one desire of guarding that most precious of possessions. " Oh, I cannot throw you down my little taper, that I really cannot, cannot do."

" But I am cold down here," cried the child's voice, " I am cold and frightened. It is Christmas Eve, and I am all alone down here, and it is so dark."

" But my mother's ill; she is dying," answered Petru, now quite fearlessly leaning over the shaft. He did not pause to ponder about the extraordinary thing that was happening to him. Instinctively his one thought was to cling to that precious taper which was to buy back his mother's health. " I cannot give you my taper " — there was anguish in his voice — " I must go to Bostea to light it in front of the Virgin's image, so that Mother may get well."

" There are many tapers lighted before that image on Christmas Eve," answered the voice. " The Blessed One would not miss your poor little light, whilst down here I am cold and lost and forsaken; give me, give me your light."

" But all the other lights burning before the Queen of Heaven would not be my light," sobbed Petru, now entirely overcome by grief. " I'll never be able to get another taper; I am quite a poor little boy, and if Mother dies, I am alone upon earth, and I am too small to know how to live all alone! " and the little fellow sank to his knees, resting his forehead against the well's edge.

" In the name of the Holy Virgin's blessed Child, give me your taper," pleaded the voice. " This is the night of his birth, can any prayer be refused if asked in his name tonight? "

Still Petru wavered, soul torn in two — what was his duty? Both ways his religious convictions stood up to confront him;

he had put all his hope in the lighting of this taper in the Bostea church.

" In the name of the Holy Child," repeated the voice, which was becoming fainter. " On this night of his birth, and in the name of his mother — oh, I am so cold, so lonely, and I too am a child, a little child — oh, give me your light."

Petru was sobbing now, his soul seemed to be dissolving in the bitter grief. Grief for the captive child down there, grief for his mother, grief for himself, grief for the whole sad world where everything was sordid and miserable and poor — poor like their hut and like the little old wooden church with the overlarge roof, and as he leaned there, all bent in two by grief, a vision of the Bostea church rose before him, that church he would now never reach. An impossible glory surrounded it, the glory of things one cannot touch, for now Petru knew that he would sacrifice his little taper — had it not been asked for in the name of the Blessed One, whose birthday it was tonight?

Somehow Petru never paused to consider how his one poor little taper could save the captive down there. In the confusion of his thoughts that one small candle had taken enormous proportions, had become the one important thing upon earth.

"Here is my little taper," he sobbed, " take it. And here are the five only matches I have — be sure and catch them before the water can damp them," he added with childish anxiety, " because if they get wet they will not light." And leaning over the shaft of the hated well, little Petru made sacrifice of all he possessed.

After that he fell with his forehead against the frozen edge, his face hidden in his hands, weeping as though his heart would break.

Suddenly he raised his head. What was that? Music? Was he dreaming? A sound of harps seemed to be throbbing in the air around him, the sound of many, many harps. And whence did that light come! That wonderful golden light?

Petru stumbled to his feet, his *caciula* falling from his head as he did so. Both the light and the rapturous music were mounting out of the well, out of that dreaded dark shaft. What was it? What was happening? Why had he suddenly the feeling that his heart was filled to overflowing with joy, with infinite joy?

"Oh!" gasped Petru, and as in church, when the Holy Mystery is being fulfilled, the ragged little fellow fell to his knees.

For now a wondrous child had stepped out of the well and stood before him, a child with golden curls and a beautiful face, a child who seemed all made of light.

"Thank you," said the bright vision to Petru. "You had pity on me, delivering me from the dark, you sacrificed to me what seemed your only hope, but see what glory your one little taper can shed around," and the child held up his hand and Petru saw how his one little taper had become as a light that could light the whole world!

"Go home to your mother, she is waiting for you," said the Wonderful One. "I am going to carry your taper to the little old wooden church, for verily it is just as holy as any great church ever built."

With trembling hands Petru picked up his *caciula*, but he did not put it on his head, which he would not cover in a presence so holy, and as one walking in a dream he followed the Child of Light whose radiance filled the whole forest.

Petru felt neither cold nor fear, nor fatigue, and it was as though wings had grown on his feet.

When the village was reached, the Child of Light stood still for a moment, and with his hand pointed toward poor Maria's hut.

"She is waiting for you," he repeated, "then after you've seen her, go to the old, old church."

Of course Petru obeyed the Wondrous One's bidding, and with beating heart hurried to his mother's dwelling. Tearing open the door and bursting into the room, "Mother, Mother!" he cried.

And there stood poor Maria with a smile on her face, all trace of illness wiped from her; she seemed suddenly to have become very beautiful, even the rags she wore had become lovely, so young did she look. Her arms were wide open, those arms which were the only soft place Petru had ever known upon earth. And into those arms did Petru take refuge, hiding his face upon her bosom, too overcome for speech.

Maria did not ask what had happened, she only knew that all sickness had gone from her, that it was Christmas Eve, and that Petru, her only child, was lying against her heart.

Later Petru stole out of the hut toward the old wooden church as the Child of Light had bidden him do.

The stars were all out, but the village was fast asleep, everything was quite silent, the houses were but dark shadows on the white snow.

Generally the church was but a darker shadow amidst shadows, hardly more dignified than the peasants' dwellings, except that it possessed a small belfry. But tonight! oh! tonight, it had suddenly turned into a casket full of light!

Light streamed out through its windows, through the cracks of its beam walls, through the chinks of the great roof; the much-despised little building had become a thing of radiance, casting long rays of light toward the heavens, and long rays of light over the frozen snow.

Hands folded, with faltering step, Petru approached God's house, like a pilgrim come from afar; with bent head he stepped over the threshold and there fell on his knees, overcome by wonder and joy. The three doors of the altar screen stood wide open, and on the altar itself burned Petru's little taper; no other candle had been lighted in all the church, and yet the light of that one little taper was strong enough to turn the lowly little sanctuary into a thing of beauty, a thing of radiance, a thing of peace and joy.

Surely even the church of Bostea could not be more beautiful than Galea's church was tonight!

Petru understood that a miracle had come to pass: his mother had been healed, the old well delivered of its curse, and although the Holy Child was nowhere to be seen, the Holy Child's hand it was which had placed Petru's humble offering upon the altar of God.

But one thing Petru had not realized: that it was his love which had brought about the miracle — his love and his faith.

And this strange thing came to pass one Christmas Eve — on the birthday of Christ.

Queen Marie of Romania was born at Eastwell Park, England, on October 29, 1875. She was the daughter of Alfred, Duke of Edinburgh and Saxe-Coburg-Gotha, second son of Queen Victoria, and Marie Alexandrovna, the only daughter of the Emperor Alexander II of Russia.

In 1893, she married Ferdinand of Hohenzollern-Sigmaringen, heir to the Romanian throne. She was Queen of Romania from 1914 to 1927, and Queen Dowager from 1927 to 1938.

She was instrumental in determining the alliance of Romania with the Entente during World War I. She showed great courage and heroism working for the Red Cross and the Romanian people, winning their unequaled affection and devotion.

She was the author of several books (all in English): My Country, Ilderim, Maska, Kildine, The Stealers of Light, The Story of My Life, *etc.*

She was a Membre Correspondente de l'Academie des Beaux Arts de l'Institut de France.

RUSSIA

The Legend of Babouscka

ADAPTED FROM THE RUSSIAN

IF YOU WERE A RUSSIAN CHILD, you would not watch to see Santa Claus come down the chimney, but you would stand by the windows to catch a peep at poor Babouscka as she hurries by.

Who is Babouscka? Is she Santa Claus's wife?

No, indeed. She is only a poor little crooked wrinkled old woman, who comes at Christmas time into everybody's house, who peeps into every cradle, turns back every coverlid, drops a tear on the baby's white pillow, and goes away very sorrowful.

And not only at Christmas time, but through all the cold winter and especially in March, when the wind blows loud, and whistles and howls and dies away like a sigh, the Russian children hear the rustling step of the Babouscka. She is always in a hurry. One hears her running fast along the crowded streets and over the quiet country fields. She seems to be out of breath and tired, yet she hurries on.

Whom is she trying to overtake?

She scarcely looks at the little children as they press their rosy faces against the windowpane and whisper to each other, " Is the Babouscka looking for us? "

No, she will not stop; only on Christmas Eve will she come upstairs into the nursery and give each little one a present. You must not think she leaves handsome gifts such as Santa Claus brings for you. She does not bring bicycles to the boys

230

or French dolls to the girls. She does not come in a gay little sleigh drawn by reindeer, but hobbling along on foot, and she leans on a crutch. She has her old apron filled with candy and cheap toys, and the children all love her dearly. They watch to see her come, and when one hears a rustling, he cries, " Lo! the Babouscka! " then all others look, but one must turn one's head very quickly or she vanishes. I never saw her myself.

Best of all, she loves little babies, and often when the tired mothers sleep, she bends over their cradles, puts her brown, wrinkled face close down to the pillow and looks very sharply.

What is she looking for?

Ah, that you can't guess unless you know her sad story.

Long, long ago, a great many yesterdays ago, the Babouscka, who was even then an old woman, was busy sweeping her little hut. She lived in the coldest corner of cold Russia, and she lived alone in a lonely place where four wide roads met. These roads were at this time white with snow, for it was wintertime. In the summer, when the fields were full of flowers and the air full of sunshine and singing birds, Babouscka's home did not seem so very quiet; but in the winter, with only the snowflakes and the shy snowbirds and the loud wind for company, the little old woman felt very cheerless. But she was a busy old woman, and as it was already twilight, and her home but half swept, she felt in a great hurry to finish her work before bedtime. You must know the Babouscka was poor and could not afford to do her work by candlelight.

Presently, down the widest and the lonesomest of the white roads, there appeared a long train of people coming. They were walking slowly, and seemed to be asking each other questions as to which way they should take. As the procession came nearer, and finally stopped outside the little hut, Babouscka was frightened at the splendor. There were three kings, with crowns on their heads, and the jewels on the kings' breastplates sparkled like sunlight. Their heavy fur cloaks were white with the falling snowflakes, and the queer humpy camels on which they rode looked white as milk in the snowstorm. The harness on the camels was decorated with gold, and plates of silver adorned the saddles. The saddlecloths were of the richest

Eastern stuffs, and all the servants had the dark eyes and hair of an Eastern people.

The slaves carried heavy loads on their backs, and each of the three kings carried a present. One carried a beautiful transparent jar, and in the fading light Babouscka could see in it a golden liquid which she knew from its color must be myrrh. Another had in his hand a richly woven bag, and it seemed to be heavy, as indeed it was, for it was full of gold. The third had a stone vase in his hand, and from the rich perfume which filled the snowy air, one could guess the vase to have been filled with incense.

Babouscka was terribly frightened, so she hid herself in her hut, and let the servants knock a long time at her door before she dared open it and answer their questions as to the road they should take to a faraway town. You know she had never studied a geography lesson in her life, was old and stupid and scared. She knew the way across the fields to the nearest village, but she knew nothing else of all the wide world full of cities. The servants scolded, but the three kings spoke kindly to her, and asked her to accompany them on their journey that she might show them the way as far as she knew it. They told her, in words so simple that she could not fail to understand, that they had seen a star in the sky and were following it to a little town where a young child lay. The snow was in the sky now, and the star was lost out of sight.

" Who is the child? " asked the old woman.

" He is a King, and we go to worship him," they answered. " These presents of gold, frankincense, and myrrh are for him. When we find him we will take the crowns off our heads and lay them at his feet. Come with us, Babouscka! "

What do you suppose? Shouldn't you have thought the poor little woman would have been glad to leave her desolate home on the plains to accompany these kings on their journey?

But the foolish woman shook her head. No, the night was dark and cheerless, and her little home was warm and cozy. She looked up into the sky, and the star was nowhere to be seen. Besides, she wanted to put her hut in order — perhaps she would be ready to go tomorrow. But the three kings could not wait; so when tomorrow's sun rose they were far ahead on their journey. It seemed like a dream to poor Babouscka, for even the tracks of the camels' feet were covered by the deep white snow. Everything was the same as usual; and to make sure that the night's visitors had not been a fancy, she found her old broom hanging on a peg behind the door, where she had put it when the servants knocked.

Now that the sun was shining, and she remembered the glitter of the gold and the smell of the sweet gums and myrrh, she wished she had gone with the travelers.

And she thought a great deal about the little baby the three kings had gone to worship. She had no children of her own — nobody loved her — ah, if she had only gone! The more she brooded on the thought, the more miserable she grew, till the very sight of her home became hateful to her.

It is a dreadful feeling to realize that one has lost a chance of happiness. There is a feeling called remorse that can gnaw like a sharp little tooth. Babouscka felt this little tooth cut into her heart every time she remembered the visit of the three kings.

After a while the thought of the little child became her first thought at waking and her last at night. One day she shut the door of her house forever and set out on a long journey. She had no hope of overtaking the three kings, but she longed to find the child, that she too might love and worship him. She asked everyone she met, and some people thought her crazy, but others gave her kind answers. Have you perhaps guessed that the young child whom the three kings sought was our Lord himself?

People told Babouscka how he was born in a manger, and many other things which you children have learned long ago. These answers puzzled the old lady mightily. She had but one idea in her ignorant head. The three kings had gone to seek a baby. She would, if not too late, seek him too.

She forgot, I am sure, how many long years had gone by. She looked in vain for the Christ-child in his manger-cradle. She spent all her savings in toys and candy so as to make friends with little children, that they might not run away when she came hobbling into their nurseries.

Now you know for whom she is sadly seeking when she pushes back the bed curtains and bends down over each baby's pillow. Sometimes, when the old grandmother sits nodding by the fire, and the bigger children sleep in their beds, old Babouscka comes hobbling into the room, and whispers softly, "Is the young child here?"

Ah, no; she has come too late, too late. But the little children know her and love her. Two thousand years ago she lost the chance of finding him. Crooked, wrinkled, old, sick and sorry, she yet lives on, looking into each baby's face — always disappointed, always seeking. Will she find him at last?

SPAIN

The Shepherds

RUTH SAWYER

YOU WHO KEEP CHRISTMAS, who keep the holy tide, have
you ever thought why a child needs must be born in the
world to save it? Here is a Christmas story about God, meaning Good. It begins far back when the world was first created.

In the beginning God had two favorite archangels: one was
called Lucifer, meaning light, and one called Michael, meaning strength. They led the heavenly hosts; they stood, one
on the right hand and one on the left hand of God's throne.
They were his chosen messengers.

Now the Archangel Michael served God with his whole heart
and angelic soul. There was no task too great for him to perform, no thousand years of service too long. But the Archangel
Lucifer chafed at serving any power higher than his own. As
one thousand years swept after another thousand years — each
as a day — he became bitter in his service and jealous of God.

The appointed time came for God to create the universe. He
made the sun, the moon, the stars. He made earth and water
and separated them. He made trees and flowers and grass to
grow; he made creatures to walk the earth and eat thereof; and
he made birds for the air and fish for the waters. And when
all else was created, he made a man and called him Adam,
and a woman and called her Eve. It took him six heavenly days
to create this universe; and at the end he was tired and rested.

While the creation was coming to pass and God was occupied

most enormously, Lucifer went stealthily about heaven. He spoke with this angel and with that, whispering, whispering. He spoke with the cherubim and seraphim — to all and everyone who would give him an attending ear. And what he whispered was this: "Why should God rule supreme? Why should he be the only one to create and to say what shall be created? We are powerful. We are worthy to rule. What say you?"

He whispered throughout the six days of creation, and when God rested, Lucifer led a host of rebellious angels against God; they drew their flaming swords and laid siege to God's throne. But the Archangel Michael drew his flaming sword; he led God's true angels to defend heaven. The army of Lucifer was put to rout and his captains were taken prisoner and led before God's throne. And God said: "I cannot take life from you, for you are celestial beings. But you shall no longer be known as the hosts of light; you shall be the hosts of darkness. You, Lucifer, shall bear the name of Satan. You and those who have rebelled must seek a kingdom elsewhere. But I command you this — leave this earth, which I have but freshly made, alone. Molest not my handiwork." So spoke God.

So Lucifer was banished with his minions; and henceforth he was known as Satan. He established a kingdom under the earth and called it hell. But because God had commanded him to leave earth untouched, he straightway coveted earth for his own. He sent his spirits abroad to tempt and make evil those born upon earth. So it came to pass that the people of earth knew at last the power of evil as well as of good; they felt the long reach of darkness even while they lifted their eyes to the Face of Light.

And now the years became millions. Earth became peopled in its four corners; and God looked down upon it and sorrowed. He called Archangel Michael to him and spoke: "It has come to pass that Satan's power upon earth is great. No longer can my angels prevail. A kingdom of destruction, of greed, of hate, and of false-witnessing has been set up among my people on the earth I have created. Their hearts have grown dark with evil; their eyes no longer see the light. I must send to earth my own Spirit that evil may be conquered. He shall be one conceived of

heaven and born of earth, none less than my own beloved Son."
So spoke God.

Earth had been divided into countries, some great and powerful, some small and weak. And the strong reached out even
with their armies and took the weak. Now such a one, taken,
was called Judea. Within its rolling hills, its olive groves, its
high pastures, and twisting rivers, men had built a little city
called Bethlehem — King David's city. And to this city the
conquering Romans had ordered all of the tribe of Jesse to
come and render tribute unto Caesar.

Beyond the city, on the high pastures, many shepherds
herded their sheep. And it came to pass that God chose Bethlehem to be the place of birth for his Son and the time to be the
taxing time of the year. He chose to reveal the coming to the
shepherds, they being men of simple faith and pure hearts. And
God sent forth a star to show them the way and commanded
angels to sing to them of the glad tidings.

The night had grown late. High in the pastures the shepherds
had built fires to keep themselves warm, to frighten off stray
wolves or robbers. All slept but Esteban, the boy. He alone saw
the angel, heard the tidings; and straightway he woke the sleeping ones: " Lo, an angel has but now come among us, singing.
Wake — wake, all of you! I think this night must have great
meaning for us."

Now at this time Satan stood at the gateway of hell. Of late
he had been troubled in mind, a sense of impending doom
moved him. And as he gazed abroad upon the earth he saw the
angel appear. Then did his troubled mind grow fearful. He
summoned his hosts of hell, commanding them to make ready:
" Tonight I think again we defy God's power over the universe.
We fight, I think, for earth, to make it ours. I go to it now.
Come when I smite the ground."

Swift as his thought Satan reached the earth. He came as a
wanderer, upon his head a wide sombrero, about his shoulders
and falling to the ground a cloak, in his hand a staff. Across the
earth he traveled even as the lightning crosses the sky. He was
here — he was beyond. And so he came to the high pastures of
Judea and stood at one of the fires about which the shepherds

watched. Again the angel came, shouting God's tidings: " Fear not! For unto you is born this day in the city of David a Messiah! "

Satan covered his face and spoke, " What means that message? "

The shepherds cowered. " We know not."

" What is that Savior — that Messiah yonder apparition shouts of? "

" We know not."

Satan dropped his cloak that they might see the fire that damns and burns shining even in his eyes. " I command you to know! "

It was Benito, the oldest shepherd, who asked, " In the name of God, who are you? "

And Satan answered: " In my own name I am a wanderer. Once I had taken from me a mighty kingdom. I am here to restore it unto myself."

Could this be the Savior of whom the angels sang? The shepherds drew close — close. They looked. And to each came terror. Here truly was darkness, not light; here was nameless evil, not good. Here was one who had denied the name of God. Together they shouted, " Begone! " They drew brands from the fire and crossed them, making fiery crosses to burn between themselves and Satan.

While they had been talking among themselves Esteban, the boy, had gone far off seeking stray lambs. Now Satan sought him out. " You heard the angel sing. Where is this City of David? "

" I know not."

" Who is this Messiah? "

" You speak of Matias? " The boy was stupid with fear. " You mean my mother's brother, a shepherd, wise and faithful? But he is ill. I tend his sheep."

" Idiot! Dolt! Fool! " The voice of Satan rose like a whirlwind. " In your great stupidness you sin against me, and that is more terrible than sinning against God. For this you die! "

The boy tried to open his mouth to shriek for mercy. Before words could come, before Satan's hand could smite him, there came between them, out of the vast spaces of the universe, one who thrust a flaming sword between the devil and the boy; while through the vast dome of heaven rang a voice, " Thou shalt not take the innocent! "

It was the voice of the Archangel Michael. He stood now, all in shining armor, beside Esteban, his sword shielding him. And again he spoke, " How dare you break God's command! "

" I dare do more than that." Satan spoke with mockery. " God's earth is no longer his but mine. My minions rule it. But tonight I shall fight you for it. I shall take it from you by right of sword and mightier hosts."

He stamped the ground. It split asunder, and from its very bowels came forth rank after rank of devils, waving their double-bladed swords forged in hell's own fires. Then Michael thrust his sword aloft and behold a mighty stairway, even like Jacob's ladder, was built between earth and heaven. Down its shining way came rank on rank of the heavenly hosts. Across the sky rang the shout of " Combat! "

Then such a battle was fought between the armies of darkness and the armies of light as had not been waged since the beginning of all things. And Michael's sword pinioned Satan to the ground so that he could not rise; and Michael's hosts put Satan's to rout, so that the earth's crust broke with them and they were swallowed in belching flames. And when the earth was rid of them, Michael spoke to Satan: " You have asked of many this night who is the Savior — the Messiah. I will answer you, Defeated. He is God's Son, and man's. He is peace. He is love. He is one against whom your evil cannot prevail. For next to God he is supreme."

The face of Archangel Michael shone with the light of conquering heaven, all goodness, all strength. And Satan, crawling to his feet, looked upon it and hated it. " I am conquered now. But wait another thousand years, two thousand! "

Meanwhile the boy Esteban watched. And with the crawling of Satan back to hell, Michael commanded Esteban to lead the shepherds to Bethlehem that they might look upon the face of their Savior and worship him.

And as the boy joined the shepherds about their fires, there came the angel again, the third time; and with it was a multitude of the heavenly host, praising God and singing hallelujahs! While over all shone a star of a magnitude never seen by them before in all the heavens.

But of the many watching their flocks that night only a few heeded. These wrapped their cloaks about them and followed the boy Esteban. As they walked he pointed out the roadsides, guarded by rank on rank of angels in shining armor. But none saw them.

Yet a great joy welled up in each heart, so that every shepherd needs must raise his voice in song. Benito, the oldest, gave them words for the beginning:

> " Yonder star
>   in the skies
>   marks the manger
>   where he lies."

Then Andrés caught the air and gave them the second verse to sing:

> " Joy and laughter,
>   song and mirth
>   herald in
>   our Savior's birth."

Miguel lifted his voice in a great swelling tumult of thanksgiving:

> " Now good will
>   unto all men.
>   Shout it, brothers,
>   shout again! "

Carlos caught from him the song and threw it back to the others with gladness:

> " Peace then be
>   among us all;
>   upon great nations
>   and on small! "

It was Esteban who gave the words for the last, singing them down the end of the road, leading them to the stable opening:

" Let each shepherd
raise his voice
till the whole world
shall rejoice;
till in one voice
all shall sing —
Glory to our
Savior — King! "

The star overhead lighted the way into the stable. Within they found a young woman, very fair, and on the straw beside her a small, newborn child. Benito spoke the questions that were on the minds of all: " What is thy name, woman? "

" They call me Mary."

" And his — the child's? "

" He is called Jesus."

Benito knelt. " Nene Jesús — Baby Jesus, the angels have sent us to worship thee. We bring what poor gifts are ours. Here is a young cockerel for thee." Benito laid it on the straw beside the child, then rose and called: " Andrés, it is thy turn."

Andrés knelt. " I, Andrés, bring thee a lamb." He put it with the cockerel, rose, and said, " Miguel, give thine."

Miguel knelt. " I bring thee a basket of figs, little one. Carlos, thy turn."

Carlos knelt and held out shepherd pipes. " I have made them. Thou shalt play on them when thou art grown. Juan, what hast thou? "

Juan knelt. " Here is some cheese — good goats' cheese."

In turn they knelt, each shepherd, until all but Esteban, the boy, had given his gift. " Alas, Nene Jesús, I have little for thee. But here are the ribbons from my cap. Thou likest them, yes? And now I make a prayer: ' Bless all shepherds. Give us to teach others the love for all gentle and small things that is in our hearts. Give us to see thy star always on this, the night of thy birth. And keep our eyes lifted eternally to the far hills.' "

And having made the prayer, and all having given their gifts, the shepherds departed into the night, singing.

SWEDEN

Karen's and Gerda's Yuletide Joys

ETTA BLAISDELL McDONALD AND JULIA DALRYMPLE

IT WAS THE DAY BEFORE CHRISTMAS — such a busy day in the Ekman household. In fact, it had been a busy week in every household in Sweden, for before the tree is lighted on Christmas Eve every room must be cleaned and scrubbed and polished, so that not a speck of dirt or dust may be found anywhere.

Gerda, with a dainty cap on her hair, and a big apron covering her red dress from top to toe, was dusting the pleasant living room; and Karen, perched on a high stool at the dining-room table, was polishing the silver. The maids were flying from room to room with brooms and brushes; and in the kitchen Fru Ekman and the cook were preparing the lutfisk and making the rice pudding.

The lutfisk is a kind of smoked fish — salmon, ling, or cod — prepared in a delicious way which only a Swedish housewife understands. It is always the very finest fish to be had in the market, and before it reaches the market it is the very finest fish that swims in the sea. Every fisherman who sails from the west coast of Sweden — and there are hundreds of them — gives to his priest the two largest fish which he catches during the season. It is these fish which are salted and smoked for lutfisk, and sold in the markets for Christmas and Easter.

When Gerda ran out into the kitchen to get some water for her plants, she stopped to taste the white gravy which her mother was making for the lutfisk.

Then as she danced back through the dining room to tell Karen about the pudding she sang:

> " Away, away to the fishers' pier,
>   Many fishes we'll find there,
>   Big salmon,
>   Good salmon:
>   Seize them by the neck,
>   Stuff them in a sack,
>   And keep them till Christmas and Easter."

" Hurry and finish the silver," she added, " and then we will help Mother set the *smorgasbord* for our dinner. We never had half such delicious things for it before. There is the pickled herring your father sent us, and the smoked reindeer from Erick's father in Lapland, and Grandmother Ekman sent us strawberry jam, and raspberry preserves, and cheese, and oh, so many goodies! " Gerda clapped her hands so hard that some of the water she was carrying to her plants was spilled on the floor. " Oh, dear me! " she sighed, " there is something more for me to do. We'd never be ready for Yule if it wasn't for the Tomtar."

The Tomtar are little old men with long gray beards and tall pointed red caps, who live under the boards and in the darkest corners of the chests. They come creeping out to do their work in the middle of the night, when the house is still, and they are especially helpful at Christmas time.

The two little girls had been talking about the Tomtar for weeks. Whenever Karen found a mysterious package lying forgotten on the table, Gerda would hurry it away out of sight, saying, "Sh! Little Yule Tomten must have left it."

And one day when Gerda found a dainty bit of embroidery under a cushion, it was Karen's turn to say: " Let me have it quick! Yule Tomten left it for me." Then both little girls shrieked with laughter.

Birger said little about the Tomtar and pretended that he did not believe in them at all; but when Gerda set out a dish of sweets for the little old men, he moved it down to a low stool where they would have no trouble in finding it.

But now the Tomtar were all snugly hidden away for the day, so Gerda had to wipe up the water for herself, and then run back to her dusting; but before it was finished, Birger and his father came up the stairs — one tugging a fragrant spruce tree, the other carrying a big bundle of oats on his shoulder.

" Here's a Christmas dinner for your friends, the birds," Birger told Karen, showing her the oats.

For a moment Karen's chin quivered and her eyes filled with tears, as she thought of the pole on the barn at home where she had always fastened her own bundle of grain, but she smiled through her tears and said cheerfully, " The birds of Stockholm will have plenty to eat for one day at least, if all the bundles of grain in the markets are sold."

" That they will," replied Birger. " No one in Sweden forgets the birds on Christmas Day. You should see the big bundles of grain that they hang up in Rattvik."

" Come, Birger," called his father from the living room, " we must set up the tree so that it can be trimmed, and then we will see about the dinner for the birds."

Gerda and Karen helped decorate the tree, and such fun as it was! They brought out great boxes of ornaments and twined long ropes of gold and gleaming threads of silver tinsel in and out among the stiff green branches. They hung glittering baubles upon every sprig, and at the tip of each and every branch of evergreen they set a tiny wax candle, so that when the tree was lighted it would look as if it grew in fairyland.

But not a single Christmas gift appeared in the room until after all three children had had their luncheon and gone to their rooms to dress for the afternoon festivities. Even then, none of the packages were hung upon the tree. Lieutenant Ekman and his wife sorted them out and placed them in neat piles on the table in the center of the room, stopping now and then to laugh softly at the verses which they had written for the gifts.

" Will the daylight never end! " sighed Gerda, looking out at the red and yellow sky which told that sunset was near. Then she tied a new blue ribbon on her hair and ran to help Karen.

"The postman has just left two big packages," she whispered to her friend, "I looked over the stairs and saw him give them to the maid."

"Perhaps one is for me," replied Karen. "Mother wrote that she was sending me a box."

"Come, girls," called Birger at last; "Father says it is dark enough now to light the tree." And so it was, although it was only three o'clock, for it begins to grow dark early in Stockholm, and the winter days are very short.

All the family gathered in the hall, the doors were thrown open, and a blaze of light and color met their eyes from the sparkling, shining tree. With a shout of joy the children skipped round and round it in a merry Christmas dance.

The cook in her white apron, and the maids in their white caps, stood in the doorway adding their chorus of "ohs" and "ahs" to the general excitement; and then, after a little while, the whole family gathered around the table while Herr Ekman gave out the presents.

It took a long time, as there were so many gifts for each one, and with almost every gift there was a funny rhyme to be read aloud and laughed over. But no one was in a hurry. They wondered and guessed; they peeped into every package; they admired everything.

When the last of the gifts had been distributed, there was the dinner with the delicious lutfisk, the roast goose, and the rice pudding. But before it could be eaten, each one must first taste the dainties on the *smorgasbord* — a side table set out with a collection of relishes.

There was a tiny lump in Karen's throat when she ate a bit of her mother's cheese; but she swallowed it bravely, and was as gay as any one at the dinner table.

All the boys and girls in Sweden are sent to bed early on Christmas Eve. They must be ready to get up the next morning, long before daylight and go to church with their parents to hear the Christmas service and sing the Christmas carols. So nine o'clock found Karen and the twins gathering up their gifts and saying good night.

"Thanks, thanks for everything!" cried the two little girls, throwing their arms around Fru Ekman's neck; and Karen added rather shyly, " Thanks for such a happy Christmas, dearest Tant."

" But this is only Christmas Eve," Gerda told her, as they scampered off to bed. " For two whole weeks there will be nothing but fun and merriment. No school! No tasks! Nothing to do but make everyone joyous and happy everywhere. Yuletide is the best time of all the year! "

SWITZERLAND

The First Picture

J. C. HERR

FIFTY YEARS AGO in the old crannied house which the river passed with a loud singsong, we were three small boys: Jakob, Heinrich, and I, Emil, the youngest of them.

Christmas stood in the distance.

Then the strange news reached us that a man in town, Peter Stephan by name, could make a true-to-life picture of any man willing to stand before his camera obscura. Soon we saw a product of his art. Our sixteen- or seventeen-year-old Uncle Johannes, apprentice mechanic, had his picture taken by the photographer, and on it not even the trace of mustache which adorned his lip was missing.

Amazed at the likeness of the portrait, we boys were seized by the conceit that it would be a special joy for our parents if we placed *our* picture under the Christmas tree for them, all three of us in a group, and that father would be particularly pleased, since he frequently was away from home for long periods. Wherever he went among strangers, he could take the picture out of his pocket and say, " Here are my three boys."

Convinced as to our own importance and that of our Christmas plan, we discussed the difficult problem of where to get the money for the picture. If we wanted to keep our secret, we would have to earn it ourselves. I thought of a way.

This was the time of oil lamps as of yore when the wise and the foolish maidens of the Bible were still walking the land. In our neighborhood, the half-blind Mrs. Susanna Keller earned

247

her bread by weaving wicks for these lamps with the aid of a spool studded with four small brass nails. We made up to the old woman, who liked us well enough anyway, watched how she looped the thread over the brass nails, how she pulled the woven wick through the spool, and established ourselves as wick makers without betraying our plan to anyone. But since I didn't have the skillful hands of my brothers, we divided our work so that they manufactured while I took over the sale of the foot-long wicks. All this with the understanding that whichever one should betray our secret would be beaten to a frazzle by the other two. Our mother, who had unusually sharp eyes and ears for the activities of her boys, learned nothing about our new profession.

How much hide-and-seek we had to play toward this end! For, to be photographed in those days was still an expensive undertaking, and in order to raise the money we needed to make no less than four hundred wicks. Many of them we wove while hidden among the willow trees along the river, and others, when the weather got colder, in the hayloft of our grandparents' house; but most of them were made at night in the little room behind our kitchen. There we slept together in a bed so wide that, because of its size, it was known familiarly as " The Steamboat." Under the bedcover, which we held up with the aid of sticks, was our workshop. If Mother, after the first good night, entered the room again, the light was out in no time, the sticks kicked down under the coverlet, and the three boys slept like dormice in their nests. But a minute later work started again, work that my brothers were soon able to do in the dark. It was my task, lying between them, to tell them stories in a whisper so that they wouldn't fall asleep; but either my stories weren't very good, or else I told them badly, because soon a brother to the right or a brother to the left while sitting up would begin weaving to and fro like a pendulum. That invariably earned him a pitiless crack in the ribs and the admonition, " We've got to work, otherwise we can't order the photograph." Not until midnight did the worn-out boys stop their wick-making.

I, too, had my troubles in disposing of them, even though we had set the price as low as one rappe per piece. To my acquaintances who had theretofore known me as a happy-go-lucky youngster it seemed odd that, all of a sudden, I was out earning money. The girls from the neighborhood began calling me " Joggeli, the wicked wick maker." Our relatives, too, began to shake their heads over my industry and didn't display the eagerness to buy, on which we had counted. Those to whom we had secretly assigned as many as fifty wicks, took only twenty; those who were supposed to buy twenty, only ten or five. And the prying questions as to the purpose of such great industry! Yes, if we had betrayed our secret, it would have been more than likely that here and there an extra twenty or so might have been sold. But that would also have meant putting an end to the charm of our secret.

Finally I had exhausted our own circle of acquaintances, and we didn't even have half of the necessary sum on hand. Then I extended my excursions to parts of the village whose inhabitants I knew less well and in my eagerness never noticed the sidelong glances, only the coppers I harvested. Then a woman who had always been referred to at home with the greatest respect told me to my face what, no doubt, all the others thought: "You've probably got too much of a sweet tooth, Joggeli. If this were for something proper, your mother would surely give you the money. Nor is it very nice of you to take the bread out of the mouth of your poor neighbor Susanna Keller, who's got to live on what she makes out of her wicks. I'm sure you snitched this wick-making from her."

The poor peddler crept away from that woman as if he had been chastised with birches. What hurt most was that we brothers were actually accused of committing a theft through learning by stealth the art which our kindhearted neighbor needed to make a living. I was so ashamed that in my own village I never entered another house to offer a wick for sale. Instead, I turned to a farmer's village high up in the mountains beyond the woods. There Susanna Keller never went because of her weak legs. Nobody knew me there, and in all likelihood the farmers practically fell over when they saw our artistic wicks. I had already called at a dozen houses without much success when I came to a farmer's wife who let her eyes rest benevolently on the little peddler. She bought twenty wicks just like that, and I was nearly away when she said: " Don't you belong to Mr. Stöffi, the engineer? I think I remember the mold! "

Now I was discovered again! However, she proceeded: " Give your father my regards. He and I liked each other once upon a time and we are not to blame, either of us, that we didn't get married."

She was very nice to me, returned the wicks, much to my chagrin, without taking her money back and stuffed my pockets full of apples. I went home heartbroken. What a shame for my father that, before he married my mother, he had liked someone else! What a shame for me if this woman now thought that he, perhaps, needed this — this wick-peddling! And never, never would I give my father her regards!

However, I did make another halfhearted attempt to sell some more of my merchandise in that village, but only because I saw the woman I intended to approach standing in her doorway. She listened to my mercantile proposition most benevolently, but suddenly her husband, a heavy-set peasant, joined her and remarked grumpily, though no doubt merely in jest: " Boy, I am the mayor of this village. Have you got a peddler's license? No? Well, in that case I'll have to call the policeman to put you behind bars."

Fear of the police and terror that my father might learn that one of his sons had been jailed made me tremble in my boots. The pair had their sport with me, and the wife finally said with a smile, " Quick, now, boy — run! " pointing down toward the woods.

I accepted her invitation with alacrity, ran without even looking for a path, and returned home in the dusk with my face scratched by thorns to tell my brothers, once we were in bed, the story of my miraculous adventures. I wound up with the statement, " All my life, I swear, I'll never sell another wick."

" And we still have so many left! " Heinrich sighed.

We struck a trial balance and, lo and behold, only one franc was between us and our proposed picture.

" That's easy," I consoled my brothers. " We'll simply promise the photographer to pay the balance after New Year's. During the holidays one always gets money from someone for a Christmas present."

" And if Peter Stephan doesn't want to trust us? " Jakob objected.

" Well — all we have to do is look honest and innocent."

That ended our torture, with my brothers glad that their nightly weaving had come to an end. One difficult question still remained: How could the three of us together get to town on Sunday without Mother becoming suspicious?

In town we had only one relative, known to our entire family as " Grumpy Anneli." To us she always seemed like a man in disguise, big, rawboned, and loud-voiced. When, in the absence of our father, Mother's patience was exhausted, she often played a threatening role, " Now I'll ask Anneli to visit us and put you to right." Anneli took care of her thankless task with complete decency and never hurt a hair on our heads, but a secret dread of her heavy, coarse hands remained with us.

But suddenly a great affection for her seized us when we wanted to get to town to be photographed. We explained to Mother that, really, it wasn't nice of us at all that we never visited " Grumpy Anneli" and that, honestly, we should do so before holy Christmas. Mother laughed.

" All you rascals want to do," she said, " is look at the store windows. But since you came to me in such a sly way, you will have to pay Anneli a visit! "

In order to make a good impression on our cousin she made us wear our best suits, on which green braid had been threaded in meandering playfulness; and in order to prevent our forgetting to visit Anneli, she also gave us a letter to her.

" Run along now, boys."

The road led through a long row of poplars, and the city found our young hearts filled with both joy and terror. The doors and gates were picturesque, adorned as they were with multicolored coats of arms and scenes from past wars. The less we understood them, the more they occupied our imagination. But the most marvelous sight of all for us was, as always, the " Snake Mill." On its wall was the picture of a wild man who, clad only in a laurel wreath around his forehead and a larger one around his loins, was defending himself with a tree torn out by the roots, trampling a whole pile of hissing snakes under his mighty feet. Oh — if this wild man ever came to life, perhaps at dusk, and stepped down into the street, that would be thrilling, now, wouldn't it?

"Grumpy Anneli" was so surprised and pleased to have us finally visiting her that she spread the butter particularly thick on our bread. I wondered whether it might not be a good idea to discuss the question of the missing franc with her, rather than go without sufficient funds to the photographer, whom we didn't even know. My brothers trembled while I told our secret to this relative whom we had always looked upon with some distrust. She, however, was so touched that she not only gave us the coin but even put on her big black silk crinoline skirt to take us to the photographer. Nor could we understand any longer why this friendly cousin had ever been called "Grumpy Anneli."

At the photographer's it went as it always does. The heavy box on its three legs, hidden under a black cloth, created some misgivings; but the jolly Peter Stephan knew how to infuse three timid country bumpkins with courage. When he lined us up before a backdrop showing a city on the sea with palms in the foreground and placed a balustrade in front of us, Heinrich whispered, "By gosh, this is going to be elegant, all right."

But Jakob groaned: "Too elegant, I think. We probably won't be able to pay for all this."

Meanwhile, the photographer fumbled around excitedly with his apparatus and finally said, "Now, boys, smile!" But at this very moment it occurred to me that, no, such an important picture should be serious; and, thinking of the village mayor who had wanted to call the policeman, I forced my face to assume a most solemn expression.

"One, two, three!"

After a while Stephan smiled and said: "Now we are all finished. It's going to be a grand picture."

In an hour we were permitted to call for the masterpiece, all framed under glass. Our enthusiasm knew no end, particularly when we found out that we had money enough to pay for it.

Our fists tightened courageously as we saw our treasure safely past the wild man at the " Snake Mill," and it was agreed that each of us would be permitted to carry it alternately for a distance of three poplars. The youngest, and thus the least likely to be suspected, was assigned the honorable task of smuggling it into the house and hiding it in the attic in an apple chest under the schoolbooks of our great-grandparents. Innumerable times during the days before Christmas we got it out and studied it jubilantly, even though my brothers deplored the fact that I made such a serious face. I, however, enjoyed the conceit that this was just right because in that way I looked like the cleverest of the three.

I proved once again how clever I really was the day before Christmas. As evidence of his mechanical skill, Uncle Johannes had made a small and delicately wrought branding iron for us. He proceeded to mark every broomstick and wooden handle in the entire house with this branding iron. I thought it also might look well on the back of our picture. So I sneaked up to the attic, the hot iron in my hand. I placed the picture wrong side up on the apple chest and pressed the iron on it. Then — a crash. The glass had broken to bits! Crestfallen, I removed the shreds. My brothers found me and, in their wrath, fell upon me with their fists. In my knowledge of guilt I didn't even defend myself. They were clever enough to take the picture to the glazier at the last minute. And thus it found its way under the Christmas tree in good shape.

When we told our parents that we had earned the money for the picture by honest and long toil, making wicks, they were pleased with this likeness of their three sons and praised our Christmas idea.

But even so the picture really wasn't the biggest surprise on that Christmas Eve. That was provided by Father who had been installing spinning machines near Basel and returned home unexpectedly for the occasion. When the Christmas candles had burned down, he lighted a big kerosene lamp which he had brought along from Basel — the first one in our village. To us it seemed as if it were turning night into day, and all through the holidays neighbors came and went, even distant acquaintances who wanted to see this new, miraculous light.

But most enthusiastic of all was Johannes, who was then attending the technical academy. " Now you can at least study at night — what a difference from all this miserable oil and candlelight, and these bothersome trimming shears and snuffers! We are heading for a glorious time, boys. Why, homework will be a pleasure! Everybody will be reading at night, and a period of learning will come to all mankind. Everyone will know the laws as to what's right and what's wrong. Now they can get rid of all the judges because all accusations and crimes and trials merely stem from the stupidity of people. And not only the judges — even courts and wars — will disappear from this earth. Men will be so well educated that everything will be just fine. Yes, boys, petroleum is bringing us a new epoch! "

Thus he made his speech, and we boys listened trustingly.

My good Johannes! Neither you nor my brothers lived to see mankind become much wiser or better because of the kerosene lamp or any other invention. You died too soon for that. Nor will I, the only one left of our family, live long enough, though much has changed. From the fields of our homeland the oil-giving flax, whose blooms gilded the land, has now disappeared, and no child can solve the riddle you taught us to solve: " Who am I? In my youth I wear a crown, but in my old age, with sticks and hatchets, they beat me down." Our land has become monotonous. No longer are there boys who, for the sake of a mere photograph, would make wicks under their bedcovers for weeks at a stretch.

I, too, have changed. At that time I took upon myself the obnoxious peddler's rounds in order to be photographed; today a photographer frightens me. Thus, ideals change. True, I would like to look once more upon that picture showing the three of us; but to the discredit of Mr. Peter Stephan — whom this, fortunately, can no longer offend — I must confess that it didn't turn out to be particularly durable, but has long since faded out, my laughing brothers and my frowning self included.

Of all the marvels, nothing is left except the festive Christmas tree which conjures up youth even in oldsters, and the everyday kerosene lamp which smiles down upon my work.

SYRIA

The Little Hunchback Zia

FRANCES H. BURNETT

T HE LITTLE HUNCHBACK ZIA toiled slowly up the steep road,
keeping in the deepest shadows, even though the night
had long fallen. Sometimes he staggered with weariness or
struck his foot against a stone and smothered his involuntary
cry of pain. He was so full of terror that he was afraid to utter a
sound which might cause any traveler to glance toward him.
This he feared more than any other thing — that some man or
woman might look at him too closely. If such a one knew much
and had keen eyes, he or she might in some way guess even at
what they might not yet see.

Since he had fled from the village in which his wretched
short life had been spent he had hidden himself in thickets and
behind walls or rocks or bushes during the day, and had only
come forth at night to stagger along his way in the darkness. If
he had not managed to steal some food before he began his
journey and if he had not found in one place some beans
dropped from a camel's feeding bag, he would have starved.
For five nights he had been wandering on, but in his desperate
fear he had lost count of time. When he had left the place he
had called his home he had not known where he was going or
where he might hide himself in the end. The old woman with
whom he had lived and for whom he had begged and labored
had driven him out with a terror as great as his own.

"Begone!" she had cried in a smothered shriek. "Get you

255

gone, accursed! Even now thou mayest have brought the curse upon me also. A creature born a hunchback comes on earth with the blight of Jehovah's wrath upon him. Go far! Go as far as thy limbs will carry thee! Let no man come near enough to thee to see it! If you go far away before it is known, it will be forgotten that I have harbored you."

He had stood and looked at her in the silence of the dead, his immense, black Syrian eyes growing wider and wider with childish horror. He had always regarded her with slavish fear. What he was to her he did not know; neither did he know how he had fallen into her hands. He knew only that he was not of her blood or of her country and that he yet seemed to have always belonged to her. In his first memory of his existence, a little deformed creature rolling about on the littered floor of her uncleanly hovel, he had trembled at the sound of her voice and had obeyed it like a beaten spaniel puppy. When he had grown older he had seen that she lived upon alms and thievery and witchlike evil doings that made all decent folk avoid her. She had no kinsfolk or friends, and only such visitors as came to her in the dark hours of night and seemed to consult with her as she sat and mumbled strange incantations while she stirred a boiling pot. Zia had heard of soothsayers and dealers with evil spirits, and at such hours was either asleep on his pallet in a far corner or, if he lay awake, hid his face under his wretched covering and stopped his ears. Once when she had drawn near and found his large eyes open and staring at her in spellbound terror, she had beaten him horribly and cast him into the storm raging outside.

A strange passion in her seemed her hatred of his eyes. She could not endure that he should look at her as if he were thinking. He must not let his eyes rest on her for more than a moment when he spoke. He must keep them fixed on the ground or look away from her. From his babyhood this had been so. A hundred times she had struck him when he was too young to understand her reason. The first strange lesson he had learned was that she hated his eyes and was driven to fury when she found them resting innocently upon her. Before he was three years old he had learned this thing and had formed the habit of looking down upon the earth as he limped about. For long he thought that his eyes were as hideous as his body was distorted. In her frenzies she told him that evil spirits looked out from them and that he was possessed of devils. Without thought of rebellion or resentment he accepted with timorous humility, as part of his existence, her taunts at his twisted limbs. What use in rebellion or anger? With the fatalism of the East he resigned himself to that which was. He had been born a deformity, and even his glance carried evil. This was life. He knew no other. Of his origin he knew nothing except that from the old woman's rambling outbursts he had gathered that he was of Syrian blood and a homeless outcast.

But though he had so long trained himself to look downward that it had at last become an effort to lift his heavily lashed eyelids, there came a time when he learned that his eyes were not so hideously evil as his taskmistress had convinced him that they were. When he was only seven years old she sent him out to beg alms for her, and on the first day of his going forth she said a strange thing, the meaning of which he could not understand.

"Go not forth with thine eyes bent downward on the dust. Lift them, and look long at those from whom thou askest alms. Lift them and look as I see thee look at the sky when thou knowest not I am near thee. I have seen thee, hunchback. Gaze at the passers-by as if thou sawest their souls and asked help of them."

She said it with a fierce laugh of derision, but when in his astonishment he involuntarily lifted his gaze to hers, she struck at him, her harsh laugh broken in two.

"Not at me, hunchback! Not at me! At those who are ready to give!" she cried out.

He had gone out stunned with amazement. He wondered so greatly that when he at last sat down by the roadside under a fig tree he sat in a dream. He looked up at the blueness above him as he always did when he was alone. His eyelids did not seem heavy when he lifted them to look at the sky. The blueness and the billows of white clouds brought rest to him and made him forget what he was. The floating clouds were his only friends. There was something — yes, there was something, he did not know what. He wished he were a cloud himself and could lose himself at last in the blueness as the clouds did when they melted away. Surely the blueness was the something.

The soft, dull pad of camel's feel approached upon the road without his hearing them. He was not roused from his absorption until the camel stopped its tread so near him that he started and looked up. It was necessary that he should look up a long way. He was a deformed little child, and the camel was a tall and splendid one, with rich trappings and golden bells. The man it carried was dressed richly, and the expression of his dark face was at once restless and curious. He was bending down and staring at Zia as if he were something strange.

"What dost thou see, child?" he said at last, and he spoke almost in a breathless whisper. "What art thou waiting for?"

Zia stumbled to his feet and held out his bag, frightened, because he had never begged before and did not know how, and if he did not carry back money and food, he would be horribly beaten again.

"Alms! Alms!" he stammered. "Master — Lord — I beg for — for her who keeps me. She is poor and old. Alms, great lord, for a woman who is old!"

The man with the restless face still stared. He spoke as if unaware that he uttered words and as if he were afraid.

"The child's eyes!" he said. "I cannot pass him by! What is it? I must not be held back. But the unearthly beauty of his eyes!" He caught his breath as he spoke. And then he seemed to awaken as one struggling against a spell.

"What is thy name?" he asked.

Zia also had lost his breath. What had the man meant when he spoke of his eyes?

He told his name, but he could answer no further questions. He did not know whose son he was; he had no home; of his mistress he knew only that her name was Judith and that she lived on alms.

Even while he related these things he remembered his lesson, and, dropping his eyelids, fixed his gaze on the camel's feet.

"Why dost thou cast thine eyes downward?" the man asked

in a troubled and intense voice.

Zia could not speak, being stricken with fear and the dumb-
ness of bewilderment. He stood quite silent, and as he lifted
his eyes and let them rest on the stranger's own, they became
large with tears — big, piteous tears.

" Why? " persisted the man, anxiously. " Is it because thou
seest evil in my soul? "

" No! no! " sobbed Zia. " One taught me to look away
because I am hideous and — my eyes — are evil."

" Evil! " said the stranger. " They have lied to thee." He was
trembling as he spoke. " A man who has been pondering on sin
dare not pass their beauty by. They draw him and show him
his own soul. Having seen them, I must turn my camel's feet
backward and go no farther on this road which was to lead me
to a black deed." He bent down and dropped a purse into the
child's alms bag, still staring at him and breathing hard. " They
have the look," he muttered, " of eyes that might behold the
Messiah. Who knows? Who knows? " And he turned his
camel's head, still shuddering a little, and he rode away back
toward the place from which he had come.

There was gold in the purse he had given, and when Zia
carried it back to Judith, she snatched it from him and asked
him many questions. She made him repeat word for word all
that had passed.

After that he was sent out to beg day after day, and in time
he vaguely understood that the old woman had spoken falsely
when she had said that evil spirits looked forth hideously from
his eyes. People often said that they were beautiful and gave
him money because something in his gaze drew them near to
him. But this was not all. At times there were those who spoke
under their breath to one another of some wonder of light in
them, some strange luminousness which was not earthly.

" He surely sees that which we cannot. Perhaps when he is
a man he will be a great soothsayer and reader of the stars,"
he heard a woman whisper to a companion one day.

Those who were evil were afraid to meet his gaze and hated
it as old Judith did, though, as he was not their servant, they
dared not strike him when he lifted his soft, heavy eyelids.

But Zia could not understand what people meant when they whispered about him or turned away fiercely. A weight was lifted from his soul when he realized that he was not as revolting as he had believed. And when people spoke kindly to him he began to know something like happiness for the first time in his life. He brought home so much in his alms bag that the old woman ceased to beat him and gave him more liberty. He was allowed to go out at night and sleep under the stars. At such time he used to lie and look up at the jeweled myriads until he felt himself drawn upward and floating nearer and nearer to that unknown something which he felt also in the high blueness of the day.

When he first began to feel as if some mysterious ailment was creeping upon him he kept himself out of Judith's way as much as possible. He dared not tell her that sometimes he could scarcely crawl from one place to another. A miserable fevered weakness became his secret. As the old woman took no notice of him except when he brought back his day's earnings, it was easy to evade her. One morning, however, she fixed her eyes on him suddenly and keenly.

" Why art thou so white? " she said, and caught him by the arm, whirling him toward the light. " Art thou ailing? "

" No! no! " cried Zia.

She held him still for a few seconds, still staring.

" Thou art too white," she said. " I will have no such whiteness. It is the whiteness of — of an accursed thing. Get thee gone! "

He went away, feeling cold and shaken. He knew he was white. One or two almsgivers had spoken of it and had looked at him a little fearfully. He himself could see that the flesh of his thin body was becoming an unearthly color. Now and then he had shuddered as he looked at it because — because — There was one curse so horribly beyond all others that the strongest man would have quailed in his dread of its drawing near him. And he was a child, a twelve-year-old boy, a helpless little hunchback mendicant.

When he saw the first white-and-red spot upon his flesh he stood still and stared at it, gasping, and the sweat started out upon him and rolled down in great drops.

"Jehovah!" he whispered. "God of Israel! Thy servant is but a child!"

But there broke out upon him other spots, and every time he found a new one his flesh quaked, and he could not help looking at it in secret again and again. Every time he looked it was because he hoped it might have faded away. But no spot faded away, and the skin on the palms of his hands began to be rough and cracked and to show spots also.

In a cave on a hillside near the road where he sat and begged there lived a deathly being who, with face swathed in linen and with bandaged stumps of limbs, hobbled forth now and then, and came down to beg also, but always keeping at a distance from all human creatures, and, as he approached, the pitiful, rattled loudly his wooden clappers, wailing out: "Unclean! Unclean!"

It was the leper Berias, whose hopeless tale of awful days was almost done. Zia himself had sometimes limped up the hillside and laid some of his own poor food upon a stone near his cave so that he might find it. One day he had also taken a branch of almond blossom in full flower and had laid it by the food. And when he had gone away and stood at some distance watching to see the poor ghost come forth to take what he had given, he had seen him first clutch at the blossoming branch and fall upon his face, holding it to his breast, a white, bound, shapeless thing, sobbing, and uttering hoarse, croaking unhuman cries. No almsgiver but Zia had ever dreamed of bringing a flower to him who was forever cut off from all bloom and loveliness.

It was this white, shuddering creature that Zia remembered with the sick chill of horror when he saw the spots.

"Unclean! Unclean!" he heard the cracked voice cry to the sound of the wooden clappers. "Unclean! Unclean!"

Judith was standing at the door of her hovel one morning when Zia was going forth for the day. He had fearfully been aware that for days she had been watching him as he had never known her to watch him before. This morning she had followed him to the door, and had held him there a few moments in the light with some harsh speech, keeping her eyes fixed on him the while.

Even as they so stood, there fell upon the clear air of the morning a hollow, far-off sound — the sound of wooden clappers rattled together, and the hopeless crying of two words, " Unclean! Unclean! "

Then silence fell. Upon Zia descended a fear beyond all power of words to utter. In his quaking young torment he lifted his eyes and met the gaze of the old woman as it flamed down upon him.

" Go within! " she commanded suddenly, and pointed to the wretched room inside. He obeyed her, and she followed him, closing the door behind them.

" Tear off thy garment! " she ordered. " Strip thyself to thy skin — to thy skin! "

He shook from head to foot, his trembling hands almost refusing to obey him. She did not touch him, but stood apart, glaring. His garments fell from him and lay in a heap at his feet, and he stood among them naked.

One look, and she broke forth, shaking with fear herself, into a breathless storm of fury.

" Thou hast known this thing and hidden it! " she raved. " Leper! Leper! Accursed hunchback thing! "

As he stood in his nakedness and sobbed great, heavy, childish sobs, she did not dare to strike him, and raged the more.

If it were known that she had harbored him, the priests would be upon her, and all that she had would be taken from her and burned. She would not even let him put his clothes on in her house.

" Take thy rags and begone in thy nakedness! Clothe thyself on the hillside! Let none see thee until thou art far away! Rot as thou wilt, but dare not to name me! Begone! Begone! Begone! "

And with his rags he fled naked through the doorway, and hid himself in the little wood beyond.

Later, as he went on his way, he had hidden himself in the daytime behind bushes by the wayside or off the road; he had crouched behind rocks and boulders; he had slept in caves when he had found them; he had shrunk away from all human sight. He knew it could not be long before he would be discovered, and then he would be shut up; and afterward he would be as Berias until he died alone. Like unto Berias! To him it seemed as though surely never child had sobbed before as he sobbed, lying hidden behind his boulders, among his bushes, on the bare hill among the rocks.

For the first four nights of his wandering he had not known where he was going, but on this fifth night he discovered. He was on the way to Bethlehem — beautiful little Bethlehem curving on the crest of the Judean mountains and smiling down upon the fairness of the fairest of sweet valleys, rich with vines and figs and olives and almond trees. He dimly recalled stories he had overheard of its loveliness, and when he found that he had wandered unknowingly toward it, he was aware of a faint sense of peace. He had seen nothing of any other part of the world than the poor village outside which the hovel of his bond mistress had clung to a low hill. Since he was near it, he vaguely desired to see Bethlehem.

He had learned of its nearness as he lay hidden in the undergrowth on the mountainside that he had begun to climb the night before. Awakening from sleep, he had heard many feet passing up the climbing road — the feet of men and women and children, of camels and asses, and all had seemed to be of a procession ascending the mountainside. Lying flat upon the earth, he had parted the bushes cautiously and watched and listened to the shouts, cries, laughter, and talk of those who were near enough to be heard. So bit by bit he had heard the story of the passing throng. The great Emperor Augustus, who to the common herd seemed some strange omnipotent in his remote and sumptuous paradise of Rome, had issued a decree that all the world of his subjects should be enrolled, and every man, woman, and child must enroll himself in his own city. And to the little town of Bethlehem all these travelers were wending their way to the place of their nativity, in obedience to the great Caesar's command.

All through the day he watched them — men and women

and children who belonged to one another, who rode together on their beasts, or walked together hand in hand. Women on camels or asses held their little ones in their arms, or walked with the youngest slung on their backs. He heard boys laugh and talk with their fathers — boys of his own age, who trudged merrily along, and now and again ran forward, shouting with glee. He saw more than one strong man swing his child up to his shoulder and bear him along as if he found joy in his burden. Boy and girl companions played as they went and made holiday of their journey; young men or women who were friends, lovers, or brothers and sisters bore one another company.

"No one is alone," said Zia, twisting his thin fingers together, "no one! no one! and there are no lepers. The great Caesar would not count a leper. Perhaps, if he saw one, he would command him to be put to death."

And then he writhed upon the grass and sobbed again, his bent chest almost bursting with his efforts to make no sound. He had always been alone — always, always; but this loneliness was such as no young human thing could bear. He was no longer alive; he was no longer a human being. Unclean! Unclean! Unclean!

At last he slept, exhausted, and past his piteous, prostrate childhood and helplessness the slow procession wound its way up the mountain road toward the crescent of Bethlehem, knowing nothing of his nearness to its unburdened comfort and simple peace.

When he awakened, the night had fallen, and he opened his eyes upon a high vault of blue-velvet darkness strewn with great stars. He saw this at the first moment of his consciousness; then he realized that there was no longer to be heard the sound either of passing hoofs or treading feet. The travelers who had gone by during the day had probably reached their journey's end and gone to rest in their tents, or had found refuge in the inclosing khan that gave shelter to wayfarers and their beasts of burden.

But though there was no human creature near, and no sound of human voice or human tread, a strange change had taken place in him. His loneliness had passed away and left him lying still and calm as though it had never existed, as though the crushed and broken child who had plunged from a precipice of woe into deadly, exhausted sleep was only a vague memory of a creature in a dark past dream.

Had it been himself? Lying upon his back, seeing only the immensity of the deep blue above him and the greatness of the stars, he scarcely dared to draw breath lest he should arouse himself to new anguish. It had not been he who had so suffered; surely it had been another Zia. What had come upon him, what had come upon the world? All was so still that it was as if the earth waited — as if it waited to hear some word that would be spoken out of the great space in which it hung. He was not hungry or cold or tired. It was as if he had never staggered and stumbled up the mountain path and dropped shuddering, to hide behind the bushes before the daylight came and men could see his white face. Surely he had rested long. He had never felt like this before, and he had never seen so wonderful a night. The stars had never been so many and so large. What made them so soft and brilliant that each one was almost like a sun? And he strangely felt that each looked down at him as if it said the word, though he did not know what the word was. Why had he been so terror-stricken? Why had he been so wretched? There were no lepers; there were no hunchbacks. There was only Zia, and he was at peace and akin to the stars that looked down.

How heavenly still the waiting world was, how heavenly still! He lay and smiled and smiled; perhaps he lay so for an hour. Then high, high above he saw, or thought he saw, in the remoteness of the vault of blue a brilliant whiteness float. Was it a strange, snowy cloud or was he dreaming? It seemed to grow whiter, more brilliant. His breath came fast, and his heart beat trembling in his breast, because he had never seen clouds so strangely, purely brilliant. There was another, higher, farther distant, and yet more dazzling still. Another and another showed its radiance until at last an arch of splendor seemed to stream across the sky.

" It is like the glory of the Ark of the Covenant," he gasped,

266 Christmas Stories from Many Lands

and threw his arm across his blinded eyes, shuddering with
rapture.

He could not uncover his face, and it was as he lay quaking
with an unearthly joy that he first thought he heard sounds
of music as remotely distant as the lights.

" Is it on earth? " he panted. " Is it on earth? "

He struggled to his knees. He had heard of miracles and
wonders of old, and of the past ages when the sons of God
visited the earth.

" Glory to God in the highest! " he stammered again and
again and again. " Glory to the great Jehovah! " and he touched
his forehead seven times to the earth.

Then he beheld a singular thing. When he had gone to
sleep a flock of sheep had been lying near him on the grass.
The flock was still there, but something seemed to be happening to it. The creatures were awakening from their sleep as if
they had heard something. First one head was raised, and then
another and another and another, until every head was lifted,
and every one was turned toward a certain point as if listening.
What were they listening for? Zia could see nothing, though
he turned his own face toward the climbing road and listened
with them. The floating radiance was so increasing in the sky
that at this point of the mountainside it seemed no longer
to be night, and the faraway paeans held him breathless with
mysterious awe. Was the sound on earth? Where did it come
from? Where?

" Praised be Jehovah! " he heard his weak and shaking
young voice quaver.

Some belated travelers were coming slowly up the road. He
heard an ass's feet and low voices.

The sheep heard them also. Had they been waiting for
them? They rose one by one — the whole flock — to their feet,
and turned in a body toward the approaching sounds.

Zia stood up with them. He waited also, and it was as if at
this moment his soul so lifted itself that it almost broke away
from his body — almost.

Around the curve an ass came slowly bearing a woman, and
led by a man who walked by its side. He was a man of sober

years and walked wearily. Zia's eyes grew wide with awe and wondering as he gazed, scarce breathing.

The light upon the hillside was so softly radiant and so clear that he could see that the woman's robe was blue and that she lifted her face to the stars as she rode. It was a young face, and pale with the pallor of lilies, and her eyes were as stars of the morning. But this was not all. A radiance shone from her pure pallor, and bordering her blue robe and veil was a faint, steady glow of light. And as she passed the standing and waiting sheep, they slowly bowed themselves upon their knees before her, and so knelt until she had passed by and was out of sight. Then they returned to their places and slept as before.

When she was gone, Zia found that he also was kneeling. He did not know when his knees had bent. He was faint with ecstasy.

"She goes to Bethlehem," he heard himself say as he had heard himself speak before. "I, too; I, too."

He stood a moment listening to the sound of the ass's retreating feet as it grew fainter in the distance. His breath came quick and soft. The light had died away from the hillside, but the high-floating radiance seemed to pass to and fro in the heavens, and now and again he thought he heard the faint, far sound that was like music so distant that it was as a thing heard in a dream.

"Perhaps I behold visions," he murmured. "It may be that I shall awake."

But he found himself making his way through the bushes and setting his feet upon the road. He must follow; he must follow. Howsoever steep the hill, he must climb to Bethlehem. But as he went on his way it did not seem steep, and he did not waver or toil as he usually did when walking. He felt no weariness or ache in his limbs, and the high radiance gently lighted the path and dimly revealed that many white flowers he had never seen before seemed to have sprung up by the roadside and to wave softly to and fro, giving forth a fragrance so remote and faint, yet so clear, that it did not seem of earth. It was perhaps part of the vision.

Of the distance he climbed his thought took no cognizance. There was in this vision neither distance nor time. There was only faint radiance, far, strange sounds, and the breathing of air which made him feel an ecstasy of lightness as he moved. The other Zia had traveled painfully, had stumbled and struck his feet against wayside stones. He seemed ten thousand miles, ten thousand years away. It was not he who went to Bethlehem, led as if by some power invisible. To Bethlehem! To Bethlehem, where went the woman whose blue robe was bordered with a glow of fair luminousness and whose face, like an uplifted lily, softly shone. It was she he followed, knowing no reason but that his soul was called.

When he reached the little town and stood at last near the gateway of the khan in which the day-long procession of wayfarers had crowded to take refuge for the night, he knew that he would find no place among the multitude within its walls. Too many of the great Caesar's subjects had been born in Bethlehem and had come back for their enrollment. The khan was crowded to its utmost, and outside lingered many who had not been able to gain admission and who consulted plaintively with one another as to where they might find a place to sleep and to eat the food they carried with them.

Zia had made his way to the entrance gate only because he knew the travelers he had followed would seek shelter there and that he might chance to hear of them.

He stood a little apart from the gate and waited. Something would tell him what he must do. Almost as this thought entered his mind he heard voices speaking near him. Two women were talking together, and soon he began to hear their words.

"Joseph of Nazareth and Mary his wife," one said. " Both of the line of David. There was no room for them, even as there was no room for others not of royal lineage. To the mangers in the cave they have gone, seeing the woman had sore need of rest. She, thou knowest — "

Zia heard no more. He did not ask where the cave lay. He had not needed to ask his way to Bethlehem. That which had led him again directed his feet away from the entrance gate of the khan, past the crowded court and the long, low wall of

stone within the inclosure of which the camels and asses
browsed and slept, on at last to a pathway leading to the gray
of rising rocks. Beneath them was the cave, he knew, though
none had told him so. Only a short distance, and he saw what
drew him trembling nearer. At the open entrance, through
which he could see the rough mangers of stone, the heaps of
fodder, and the ass munching slowly in a corner, the woman
who wore the blue robe stood leaning wearily against the heavy
wooden post. And the soft light bordering her garments set
her in a frame of faint radiance and glowed in a halo about
her head.

"The light! The light!" cried Zia in a breathless whisper.
And he crossed his hands upon his breast.

Her husband surely could not see it. He moved soberly
about, unpacking the burden the ass had carried and seeming
to see naught else. He heaped straw in a corner with care and
threw his mantle upon it.

"Come," he said. "Here thou canst rest, and I can watch
by thy side. The angels of the Lord be with thee!" The woman
turned from the door and went toward him, walking with slow
steps. He gazed at her with mild, unillumined eyes.

"Does he not see the light!" panted Zia. "Does he not
see the light!"

Soon he himself no longer saw it. Joseph of Nazareth came
to the wooden doors and drew them together, and the boy
stood alone on the mountainside, trembling still, and wet with
the dew of the night; but not weary, not hungered, not athirst
or afraid, only quaking with wonder and joy — he, the little
hunchback Zia, who had known no joy before since the hour
of his birth.

He sank upon the earth slowly in an exquisite peace — a
peace that thrilled his whole being as it stole over his limbs,
deepening moment by moment. His head drooped softly upon
a cushion of moss. As his eyelids fell, he saw the splendor of
whiteness floating in the height of the purple vault above him.

The dawn was breaking, and yet the stars had not faded
away. This was his thought when his eyes first opened on a

great one, greater than any other in the sky, and of so pure a brilliance that it seemed as if even the sun would not be bright enough to put it out. It hung high in the paling blue, high as the white radiance; and as he lay and gazed, he thought it surely moved. What new star was it that in that one night had been born? He had watched the stars through so many desolate hours that he knew each great one as a friend, and this one he had never seen before.

The morning was cold, and his clothes were wet with dew, but he felt no chill. He remembered; yes, he remembered. If he had lived in a vision the day before, he was surely living in one yet. The Zia who had been starved and beaten and driven out naked into the world, who had clutched his thin breast and sobbed, writhing upon the earth, where was he? He looked down upon his hands and saw the cracked and scaling palms, and it was as though they were not. He thrust back the covering from his chest and saw the spots there. But there were no lepers, there were no hunchbacks; there were only Zia and the light. He knelt and turned himself toward the cave and prayed, and as he so knelt and prayed the man Joseph rolled open the heavy wooden door.

Then Zia, still kneeling, beat himself softly upon the breast and prayed again, not as before to Jehovah, but to that which he beheld.

The light was there, fair, radiant, wonderful. The cave was bathed in it. The woman in the blue robe sat upon the straw, and in her arms she held a newborn child. Zia touched his forehead to the earth again, again, again, unknowing that he did so. The child was the light itself!

He must rise and draw near. That which had drawn him up the mountainside drew him again. The child was the light itself! As he crept near the cave's entrance, the woman's eyes rested upon him soft and wonderful.

She spoke to him — she spoke!

" Be not afraid," she said. " Draw nigh and behold! "

Her voice was not as the voice of other women; it was like her eyes, soft and wonderful. It could not be withstood even by awe such as his. He could not remain outside, but entered trembling, and trembling drew near.

The child lying upon his mother's breast opened his eyes and smiled. Zia fell upon his knees before him. He held out his piteous hands, remembering for one moment the Zia who had sobbed on the mountainside alone.

" I am a leper! " he cried. " I may not touch him! Unclean! Unclean! "

" Draw nigh," the woman said, " and let his hand rest upon thee! "

Zia crouched upon his knees. The newborn hand fell softly upon his shoulder and rested there. Through his body, through his blood, through every limb and fleshly atom of him, he felt it steal — new life, warming, thrilling, wakening in his veins new life! As he felt it, he knelt quaking with rapture even as he had stood the night before gazing at the light. The newborn hand lay still.

He did not know how long he knelt. He did not know that the woman leaned toward him, scarce drawing breath, her wondrous eyes resting upon him as if she waited for a sign. Even as she so gazed she beheld it, and spoke, whispering as in awed prayer: " Go forth and cleanse thy flesh in running water," she said. " Go forth."

He moved, he rose, he stood upright — the hunchback Zia who had never stood upright before! His body was straight, his limbs were strong. He looked upon his hands, and there was no blemish or spot to be seen!

" I am made whole! " he cried in ecstasy so wild that his boy's voice rang and echoed in the cave's hollowed roof. " I am made whole! "

" Go forth," she said softly. " Go forth and give praise."

He turned and went into the dawning day. He stood swaying, and heard himself sob forth a rapturous cry of prayer. His flesh was fresh and pure; he stood erect and tall. He was as others whom God had not cursed. The light! the light! He stretched forth his arms to the morning sky.

Some shepherds roughly clothed in the skins of lambs and kids were climbing the hill toward the cave. They carried their crooks, and they talked eagerly as though in wonderment at some strange thing which had befallen them, looking up at the heavens, and one pointed with his crook.

" Surely it draws nearer, the star! " he said. " Look! "

As they passed a thicket where a brook flowed through the trees a fair boy came forth, cleansed, fresh, and radiant as if he had but just bathed in its clear waters. It was the boy Zia.

" Who is this one? " said the oldest shepherd.

" How beautiful he is! How the light shines on him! He looks like a king's son."

And as they passed, they made obeisance to him.

TURKEY

The Poor Nobleman and
His Three Daughters

ANONYMOUS

IN THE THIRD CENTURY A.D., during the days of Bishop
Nicholas, for many years Bishop of Demre (the ancient
Myra, which is close to and east of Patara in Turkey), there
lived in Patara an impoverished nobleman who had three
charming daughters. The little family was in deep distress.
They hardly had enough to eat. Moreover, the girls were now
of marriageable age, but there was no money to provide them
with dowries. And who would marry a maid without a dowry?
In those days it simply was not respectable.

The maidens could not bear to see their beloved father in
want and misery. So they took counsel among themselves.

" I have heard," said the oldest daughter to her sisters, " that
women have sometimes sold themselves into slavery to raise
money for those they love. I would gladly do this to aid our
beloved father. At the very first opportunity, I intend to run
away and offer myself at auction in the slave market. I should
be worth some hundreds of ducats to some master, for I have
now learned to cook and sew, and I am, if not beautiful, at
least not unpleasing to the eyes."

" No, no! " cried her two sisters. " You must not do this!
You are our father's most precious possession, and his dearest
consolation. You must not leave him now. We are the ones
who should sell ourselves as slaves. We have not your skill
in cooking nor sewing, nor are we as fair as you, but certainly
someone would buy us."

" You are but children," said the oldest sister. " You must not think of such a thing."

" We are only the least bit younger than you are," they said, " and in no time at all we shall be your age."

And so they fell to disputing which of them should be a slave, but no two of them would hear of the other's going away, and in the end they fell in each other's arms and vowed that, whatever they did for their father, they would first agree among themselves.

Of course, the noble but impoverished head of the family knew nothing of all this.

Word of the family's distress came to Nicholas. Being a good neighbor, he pondered how he might come to their aid. He could not offer them money, for they were a proud and noble family, and would never have accepted charity at anyone's hands. But Nicholas was determined to help them. He surmised what difficulties they must be in, and feared lest the daughters, who were high-spirited and lovely girls, might in their distress resort to desperate courses.

So Nicholas decided to help them in secret, as he had helped many others. He had, in fact, developed quite a technique for helping people without their knowing he was responsible.

On a still December night — just such a night as that one, some three hundred years before, when the stars shone down on Bethlehem and lighted the way to a new era for mankind — Nicholas put his little plan into execution.

As he slipped silently out of his house into the quiet of the stone-paved street, all Patara lay asleep, as Bethlehem had lain asleep on that first Christmas Eve. At one end of the street, seen through a Roman arch, lay the Mediterranean, its breeze-ruffled waters sparkling back at the studded heavens above. At the other end of the street, the mountains of Lycia stood like a rampart beyond the town. Nicholas paused for a moment to drink in the splendor of the scene.

" On such a night as this," he mused, " one hears the angels sing." They were indeed singing in Nicholas' heart. As he sped softly along on his mission of good will, he chuckled inwardly. Neither his housekeeper nor his porter, he was sure, had heard him leave the house. He had given them the slip. They would know nothing about this venture of his.

This, he felt, was the way to do a deed of kindness: silently, alone, in secret. No fanfare, no self-seeking. How odd, he thought, that so few give themselves the joy of generosity. There it is, to be had for the doing — yet the world so often passes it by, this priceless gift of giving.

What dire prophecies the wiseacres had made when, upon coming into his father's estate, he had systematically begun to distribute his income among the poor! The cynics had said he would make the people discontented, and that he himself would live or perhaps die in want. Yet none of the foretold disasters had come upon him. He had never been happier. He had never suffered want; on the contrary, it seemed his every need was met even before he became aware of it.

Pondering on these things, Nicholas had reached his destination. Here at a turning in the street stood a small *palazzo*, a thick-walled house of stone with a massive iron-studded door. An air of neglect overhung the place. A ground-floor window shutter hung loosely on one hinge. From behind the shutter came a tiny gleam of light.

Nicholas slipped up to the window and peered in. There before an empty hearth sat the nobleman. At his elbow was an earthen lamp, its wick flickering feebly for want of oil. Tears were streaming down the poor man's face.

"Alas!" sighed Nicholas, "that this good man should find himself in such straits."

Instantly he did the thing he had come to do. Drawing a well-filled purse of gold from out of his sleeve, he tossed it through the unglazed window and ran away. The thud of the purse upon the floor at his feet aroused the nobleman from his sad reverie. For a moment he glanced, unbelieving, at this strange apparition. He bent forward to touch it, then withdrew his hand.

"Come, come, my man," said he to himself. "You must not let yourself go to pieces in this way. Rouse yourself from your fantasies."

He deliberately turned his eyes away from the purse, stood

up and shook himself. Then he looked again. It was still there.

"It is not an apparition! It is a purse!" he cried. He snatched it up, undid its string. Into his hand poured a stream of golden coins. Their brightness reflected the glimmer of the lamp and lighted up the somber room.

"Oh, merciful Father in heaven," he sobbed. "Thou hast indeed heard my prayers!" And he fell upon his knees in thanksgiving.

When he had regained his composure, he called his daughters. "Children! Children! Come quickly, and see what an angel has brought us from heaven!"

The girls came running in their nightgowns. "What has happened, Father?" they asked in amazement when they saw him standing beside the lamp, fingering the golden coins as they rolled in a shining avalanche upon the table.

"A fortune, my darlings," he cried. "God in his goodness has sent us riches. It fell at my very feet but a moment ago."

He sank into his chair, and the girls clustered around him, counting the pieces of gold and weeping with joy at their good fortune.

"Now we shall have food to eat!" cried one.

"Now we shall have pretty clothes to wear!" cried another.

"Now we shall have dowries, and can be married!" cried the third.

"But wait," said the father, suddenly assailed by doubts. "Perhaps the money was not meant for us. Perhaps it has been stolen!"

"But how could it fall precisely at your feet, if it is not meant for us?" chorused the daughters. "Of course it is for us. An angel brought it. And now we shall all be rich and happy!"

"Not so fast, dear daughters," cautioned the father. "It is a princely gift, but it will not provide dowries for all of you."

"Then it shall be for our eldest sister," said the younger ones.

But she hesitated to accept the gift. "Let the money go rather," she proposed, "to the first of us to be married."

And so it was agreed that, after the family's most urgent needs were met, the remainder of the gold should be set aside as a dowry for her who should first enter the holy state of matrimony.

Nicholas, returning from his mission of good will, quietly returned to his house, went directly to bed and slept soundly. When he awoke in the morning he was aglow with the consciousness of a good deed well done. He was even more jovial than usual at breakfast; so jovial, indeed, that his housekeeper was suspicious.

"The master was up to some of his pranks last night, I suspect," she confided to the porter. "He's simply bubbling over with jollity this morning. Are you sure he didn't go out in the night?"

"Absolutely certain," said the porter. "But what if he did? Is that anything to us?"

"Indeed, so!" said the housekeeper. "You men are all children, and besides you're thick as thieves. If it weren't for us women, goodness knows what scrapes you'd be in!"

"If the master did go out last night," ventured the porter, "mind you, I'm not saying he did — but if he did, you may be sure it was for some good purpose."

"Then why should he be so stealthy about it? I'll wager he was out giving his money away, or playing some other disgraceful prank unworthy of a gentleman." And the housekeeper flounced off in disgust.

When she saw the master again at lunch time, she was not so sure she was right. Nicholas was not as gay as he had been at breakfast. On the contrary, he was very quiet and thoughtful. He had gone to his study after breakfast full of self-gratification. He could see now that it *was* self-gratification. He had been pleased with himself for having done a good deed. And what had he done to be so pleased about? He had merely taken a sum of money from the large amount at his disposal and had given it to someone who needed it. And what was so wonderful about that? Was it not merely a Christian duty? And had he not been rather stingy in his gift?

That poor nobleman had three beautiful daughters ready to be married to fine young men. Yet he, Nicholas, had given them only enough to provide for one of the three. The more Nicholas thought about it, the less he felt inclined to be proud, and the more cause he felt to be ashamed of what he had done.

" The riches of God," he pondered, " are infinite, yet I am stinted in my giving. How can a man be happy if he acts like that? "

So Nicholas resolved to do something about it. That very night he made his way back to the nobleman's house. The familiar shutter was still hanging loose on its hinge — there had not been time to fix that — but the light that shone around it was bright, not pallid. The view inside, when Nicholas tiptoed up for a peek, was very different from what it had been the night before.

A fire blazed warmly in the fireplace, and several lamps, full of oil and with fresh wicks, shed a cheery glow over the once gloomy room. There was a long table decked with fruit and flowers, and at the head of it sat the nobleman. Nicholas hardly recognized him as the same man who, only the night before, had sat dejectedly in this very spot with tears streaming down his cheeks. Now he was smiling and happy. His face positively shone as he told a jolly tale to his three daughters and several friends and neighbors who sat around the table. The girls had fresh ribbons in their hair, and their dresses looked new. They were just finishing dinner, evidently a real good one.

" And now," said the nobleman, rising with a glass of wine in his hand, " I come to the object of this joyous gathering, which God has so mercifully made possible. It is with happiness that I announce the betrothal of my eldest daughter Chloe to our good friend Jason. My son, give me your hand. May both of you be very happy."

In watching the merrymaking that followed, Nicholas almost forgot the purpose of his mission. There was nothing he enjoyed more than seeing people have a delightful time. He stood enraptured for a while, and then suddenly recalled why he was there.

At an opportune moment, he drew another purse of gold from his sleeve and tossed it straight into the nobleman's lap.

He did not wait to see the results of his act but turned and ran.

"Incomplete," murmured Nicholas to himself, as he sat in his study the next evening. "Incomplete is the word for it. God in his goodness does not deal in half measures. Why should we be content with less than the whole performance of our duty?"

A knock at the door interrupted his musings. It was the housekeeper. "I suppose you'll not be going out tonight, sir?" she inquired.

"Out? Tonight? Oh, of course not," replied Nicholas. But he had his fingers crossed.

"Very good, sir. It's quite cold. Raining too, sir."

Nicholas chuckled when she had gone. She seemed positively pleased that it was raining. She thought a little cold air and dampness could keep him indoors. Why was there always someone who wanted to keep a person from doing what he knew was right?

Nicholas had made up his mind. He was going to finish the job. He was going to make the happiness of the nobleman and his daughters complete by providing a dowry for the third and last daughter.

It was nearly midnight when he slipped out of the house and betook himself for the third time to the little *palazzo*. As before he peeked around the shutter. There was the nobleman, alone, gazing into the fire, the light of happiness in his face.

Nicholas tossed his purse of gold at the nobleman's feet and turned to run. But his sleeve caught on the hook of the shutter and his feet slipped on the wet pavement. The nobleman rushed to the window and, reaching out, grasped Nicholas' arm.

"Who are you?" he asked. "I must thank you for the kind deed you have done, for my happiness and my daughters' too."

Nicholas hid his face with his other arm. "Pray, let me go and ask no questions," he pleaded. "You have received only what you deserve. I have but one favor to ask in return for anything I may have done for you. It is that you let me go and make no effort to find out who I am."

He wrenched himself free from the nobleman's grasp, leaving a fragment of his sleeve in his hand and ran away into the night.

Nicholas had completed his mission. The three daughters were now provided for and their father could live happily ever after in the bosom of their families. Nicholas had done all that needed to be done for those he knew were in need. He was content at last.

Perhaps the nobleman suspected who the benefactor was, a fragment of whose tunic was left in his hand that chilly December night in Patara — even as you and I may suspect who it was that put a Christmas present in our stocking. But whether he ever knew or not is unimportant. The kindly deed was done, and countless millions have since been made happy by its repetition for young and old in all kinds of surroundings.

UKRAINE
(Old)

Marusia's Christmas Eve

IRENE T. GRANOVSKY

T

OMORROW WOULD BE CHRISTMAS. What a wonderful feeling it was! For weeks Marusia had been getting more and more excited, until now it seemed that she could hardly wait for the day to pass and the first star of evening to appear.

Yesterday Ivan had come home from school, and for weeks Mother had been sewing and cleaning and preparing for this very occasion. Ever since the beginning of the fast for Christmas, just thirty-nine days ago, preparations for the Feast of the Nativity had been under way. Only last week the little *khata*, as the Ukrainian house is called, had received a nice clean coat of whitewash, newly embroidered towels had been hung over the ikon in the corner, and every speck of dust had been routed out.

Out of doors, Father had been cleaning everything in the courtyard and barnyard so that all would be in order on this day. Quantities of wood had been hauled and cut too, enough to last all through the holidays, for it wasn't considered proper to cut wood during the Nativity celebration.

Last week Marusia had driven to town with Mother and Father when they had gone to buy necessary supplies for the holiday season. As they drove along, they saw other families, bound on similar errands.

" God be thanked for having granted us to live to see this

281

holiday which happens but once a year," they greeted each other.

"God grant you good crops in the year to come," was the reply as the carts met and passed on the narrow mountain roads.

While Mother bought extra-fine white flour now being made up into special Christmas bread, fish to be used for tonight's supper, and dried fruits which had been put to soak last night, Father had bought a fur coat, caps, shawls, candles, and other necessities.

Marusia knew that she would not receive gifts on Christmas Day, for among the Ukrainian people it was not the custom to give gifts freely. Only small children and old servants were remembered with some articles of clothing or small gifts of money, and Marusia was no longer a child. Indeed not, she was almost ten years old. But she was anxious for Christmas because she so vividly remembered the thrill of last year, when the deep significance of the Christmas celebration and the real meaning of many things had become clearer to her.

All through the long, hot summer months, the remembrance of that beautiful holy season had given her a happy feeling. That was why she had worked so hard in her garden all summer. Mother had told her that if the peas which she planted on Saint Dorothy's Day were as nice as they should be, Marusia could save them until Christmas time, and from them the Christmas Eve soup, called borsch, would be made. Could there be any greater incentive than that? Marusia had felt that if only she could get a nice crop from her garden, she would ask for nothing better. How carefully she had tended her garden, lugging heavy pails of water to the plants, pulling away the weeds almost before they poked their inquisitive little heads above the ground, and staking up the vines so that each pod would receive its share of the life-giving sunlight.

"Marusia, come and set your dried peas to soak for the borsch," called old Anna. Anna had been with the family as long as Marusia could remember, longer than that, for brother Ivan said she had been there as long as he could remember, and he was a man now, old enough to go to the Gymnasium to school almost a hundred miles away from home.

"How long do they have to soak?" asked Marusia as she put two cupfuls of dried peas in a dish and covered them with a quart of cold water.

"When I take the Christmas bread from the oven, then it will be time to cook the sauerkraut and other things to add to the peas for the soup," answered Anna as she deftly kneaded into shape a large braided *kalach,* or Christmas bread, and set it to rise for the last time before baking it.

"Why don't we have meat with our Christmas Eve meal?" asked Marusia as Anna began to prepare the goose for the noon meal on Christmas Day.

"Because this is a Holy Eve, and we never eat meat in any form on the holy birthday of Christ," replied Anna.

"Now, Marusia, if you like, you may help me mix the filling for the *nalysniky,*" said Mother as she came in from the storeroom, carrying a bowl of dry cottage cheese and a pitcher of sour cream, preparing to make the thin pancakes filled with cottage cheese.

While Mother beat up the eggs, Marusia stirred and stirred the cottage cheese in the deep earthenware bowl. Round and round went the wooden paddle as it broke up the curds of cheese. When it was almost as fine as kernels of rice, Mother added a little honey, a handful of white raisins, the well-beaten eggs, a little salt, and three tablespoons of sour cream to the bowl of cheese to make it taste just right. Then the bowl was covered with a clean white cloth and set aside, to be used later as the filling in paper-thin pancakes. Just as soon as Mother had made the pancakes, she would let Marusia help fill them, rolling up each one carefully and turning the edges all in. Anna would fry each one gently in a little cooking oil before they appeared, almost smothered with sour cream, on the supper table. How her mouth did water at the very thought of their good taste.

Singing old folk songs as they worked, Mother and Anna seemed fairly to fly through the work of preparing the evening meal. What fun it was for Marusia to help!

She sang with Mother and Anna over her work and once

asked, "Mother, is it true that on Christmas Eve the cattle are able to speak to each other?"

"Well," said Mother thoughtfully, "it is said that on Christmas Eve the cattle do acquire the gift of speech of Christians and are able to speak of the past, present, and future. But of course no one has ever heard them, for a man who knows the future soon dies."

Marusia thought she was never going to be able to wait until time for the evening meal. She was hungry now, and it was hours before she would be able to break her fast. All the long day before Christmas it was the custom among her native Ukrainian people to fast until the holy meal in the evening. Even the children were faithful to this tradition.

"God give you health and plenty," called Father as he came into the room carrying a great sheaf of wheat, saved from the summer harvest for this very night.

"God give you health and plenty," echoed Ivan as he followed Father into the room, carrying an armful of fragrant hay.

"Cluck, cluck, cluck. Cheep, cheep, cheep," called Marusia, as she dropped to her knees and crawled about in the hay which was being spread under the table.

"Moo, moo. Baa, baa. Neigh, neigh," said Ivan as he spread a little hay on the bare dining-room table.

"May my farming tools be saved from rust and breakage," said Father as he handed Ivan a small axhead to be put in the hay under the table.

"String, tie up the legs of the table, so that the fruit trees will not break in the wind this year," said Ivan, carefully tying each table leg with a length of string.

"Scissors, be tied together, so that Ivan will not be drafted into the army," intoned Anna as she securely knotted the cord about the blades of the shears.

Neither Mother nor Father laughed as these superstitious rituals were being followed. It had been the custom among the Hutzuls, or Ukrainian mountaineers, to perform these same rituals for centuries. Without their observance the Christmas Eve festivities would not seem complete. To them the hay, nestling on the table top, under the beautifully embroidered tablecloth, was symbolical of the lowly place where the Christ-child had first lain. The hay on the floor was put there to show their humility for the lowly place of his birth.

As soon as these ceremonies had been performed, Father stood the bundle of wheat in the corner, under the ikon. Mother brought ribbons, flowers, and a small wreath of dried basil to decorate the *Deed* or " Old Man " as the wheat was called. Wheat was the chief crop of their little farm as well as the main agricultural product of their vast country, and it was only fitting and proper on this Holy Eve to bring into the home the token of their livelihood.

Taking a basket, Mother put into it a jar of soup, a loaf of bread, salt, honey, cookies, and a bowl of jellied fish. Marusia, warmly dressed in her fur-lined coat, pulled on her heavy mittens and, taking up the basket, started out on her particular Christmas Eve errand. Ever since she had been old enough to toddle over the snow, she had taken this same basket, every Christmas Eve, to her godparents who lived just over the next hill.

How cold it was! The snow crunched and creaked under her feet as she walked along singing her favorite song:

> " Oh! I love a morn in summer,
>   Happy hours flying past.
>   Over hillside quickly running,
>   Falling down in the grass.
>   Playing house up in the treetops,
>   Climbing over the fence."

Ivan, who had been on a similar errand, met Marusia as she came along the path and together they turned into the court-yard. Just then Father came from the stables where he had given all of the animals an extra portion of fodder that they might be content on this night of miracles.

Together they watched the sky, for it was fast growing dark and they were all eager to be the first to see the first evening star appear.

" There it is! I see it! I see it! " and Marusia jumped up and down and clapped her hands in excitement. "Mother, the star! The star!"

"Come, Father," called Mother from the doorway. Father entered the house, to emerge a moment later carrying the decorated Christmas bread. It looked beautiful, its braided top glistening as though it had been varnished. In the center of the bread flickered a lighted candle, tied with blue and yellow ribbon. Followed by Marusia and Ivan, Father circled the house three times as he said prayers for the health of his family, his dear ones, and the beasts of the barnyard.

Entering the house, they found the table in readiness for the meal. Father replaced the Christmas bread on the table, and Marusia carried the pinch of salt and jar of honey, which symbolized the earthly substance of man, to the table.

Places were set for twelve. There were four for the family; a place for Anna — for before Christ on this Eve there was no distinction between servant and master; places for George and his wife who had gone to America last year, and of course had not returned for this celebration; four places for Father's and Mother's parents who had died; and a place for anyone who might this night come their way and be without food.

When all the family had taken their places, Father led the saying of prayers. He prayed for all poor lost souls, and especially entreated mercy for those who labored to free their homeland from the iron heel of Ukrainian conquerors and oppressors.

"God's blessing and health to you all, my family," said Father as he tasted the *kutyia*. This dish is the traditional first course on Christmas Eve. Symbolic of the body and soul of Christ, it is made of cooked whole wheat, ground poppy seed, nuts, and honey.

"God keep us safe and together until another Christmas comes," replied Mother, as she in turn ate of the ceremonial dish.

"May his mercy be on us all through the year," said Anna in her turn, helping herself to the traditional Christmas dish. Marusia's round little face was beaming with pleasure and excitement as she tasted the delicious *kutyia*, and the soup was placed on the table. Anxiously she watched as Father took up his spoon and tasted the borsch. Not a word did he say as he took another taste, then another.

Just when she thought she couldn't bear it if he didn't speak soon, he laid down his spoon, saying: "This is the best soup I have ever tasted. Tell me, child, are these peas from your garden?"

"Yes, Father," laughed Marusia, "I am so glad you like them."

"Indeed I do, and I hope you will raise as good ones next year as these are for our Christmas soup," said Father as he resumed his meal.

Happy, low-voiced conversation prevailed all through the twelve-course dinner. The memory of Christ's twelve disciples seemed to pervade the little room as course followed course in their honor. The pungent, tantalizing odor of the soup gave way to the savory, jellied fish course. Then came three steaming hot bowls of *vareniky*. These were stuffed noodle dough, each one with a different kind of filling. And a piquant dish of mushrooms, a bowl of *holubtzee*, or filled cabbage rolls, made especially as Father liked them, as well as a dishful of the kind Anna liked, a baked stuffed fish, the *nalysniky* which Marusia had helped roll, and a deep dish of stewed fruit and a piece of Mother's especially nice honey cake which finished the meal.

"How much I ate tonight, Mother! I think that this next year I will not be at all hungry. Thank you for the dinner," said Marusia as she left the table.

As each one rose from the table they thanked Mother for the dinner, according to the ancient custom of the Ukrainians, and then Ivan, taking up his warm coat and hat, asked to be excused so that he might join the carolers.

While Mother and Anna cleared the table, Marusia took her bowl of nuts and sat in the hay on the floor. Soon the table was cleared and the bowl of *kutyia* was replenished and set back on the dinner table with small dishes and spoons set beside it. Marusia knew that when they went to bed that night, Father would leave one of the doors unlatched, so that any departed spirit might return and share in this Christmas Eve festival. Mother and Anna also set out clean dishes and a big plate of Christmas cookies and cakes in order to have something to serve to the carolers when they came.

Soon a bell was heard at the window. Father opened the door and asked, " Who is there? "

" We have come, householder, to sing to you the story of Jesus and his birth tonight. May we have your permission? " asked the leader of the little group of carolers, who, carrying a ten-pointed star, lighted within by a candle, stood near the door. Gaily colored ribbons streamed from the staff as it held the star high over the heads of the little group.

" Please do come in and sing," responded Father.

> " New gladness befalls us,
>   On earth this night is born the Christ."

Thus sang the carolers. Marusia sat as still as a mouse. Oh, she hoped they would sing more.

Entering the house, the carolers stood behind the leader as they sang:

> " An exceeding great joy was born into the world,
>   When the Holy Virgin gave birth to a Son.
>   Let us go to greet him and bring him gifts,
>   At his feet let us lay a pure heart and true faith.
>
> God will reward us on earth and in heaven.
>   Gladly we sing from the depths of our hearts,
>   Happy we make your home and your family
>   As we wish you everything which you may want.
>
> May God in his heaven grant you your wish,
>   And for these greetings which we have just given
>   We ask you, humbly, that you give us a *Kolyada*
>   [Christmas Song],
>   A dish of *holubtzee*, a tasty cake, a loaf of bread,
>   or a green one [money]."

" Thank you, my friends," responded Father. " May we have another song? "

" ' Oh, good evening to you, master of this household,' " sang Ivan, who had a deep, deep bass voice.

" ' Rejoice ye, oh, rejoice ye. On earth Son of God is born

this night,'" responded the other carolers.

On and on they sang, through the seven verses of this traditional Christmas *Kolyada*.

After Father had given the leader a sum of money, which was to be used for the school that had lately been established in their district, the chorus sang another song — this time an ancient mountaineers' song, which told the story of how Jesus lay in his humble bed in the deep cave of the manger. It seemed to Marusia to be the most beautiful one she had ever heard.

" Please be seated, all of you. Father, you may pass the glass, and Marusia will help you with the cakes," said Mother.

After everyone had tasted and exclaimed over Mother's lovely delicacies, they bundled up again in their warm wraps, for the brilliant moonlight night was cold. Then they left to sing many more times that evening at the homes of other Ukrainian mountaineers.

Marusia, tired but happy, and scarcely believing it possible for one little girl to hold all of that happiness, prepared for bed. Soon she was snuggled down under the covers ready to sleep. Tomorrow they would all go to church together, and she had heard that this year the *Vertep*, or outdoor puppet show, which came right after the church service, was about the birth of Christ in the manger.

Dreaming of the morrow, her eyes closed in sleep as she heard Mother singing:

> " Heaven and earth rejoice,
> Great is our joy today,
> Christ the Savior is born this night,
> Gladly we welcome his birth."

UNITED STATES

The Gift of the Magi

O. HENRY

ONE DOLLAR AND EIGHTY-SEVEN CENTS. That was all. And sixty cents of it was in pennies. Pennies saved one and two at a time by bulldozing the grocer and the vegetable man and the butcher until one's cheeks burned with the silent imputation of parsimony that such close dealing implied. Three times Della counted it. One dollar and eighty-seven cents. And the next day would be Christmas.

There was clearly nothing to do but flop down on the shabby little couch and howl. So Della did it. Which instigates the moral reflection that life is made up of sobs, sniffles, and smiles, with sniffles predominating.

While the mistress of the home is gradually subsiding from the first stage to the second, take a look at the home. A furnished flat at eight dollars per week. It did not exactly beggar description, but it certainly had that word on the lookout for the mendicancy squad.

In the vestibule below was a letter box into which no letter would go, and an electric button from which no mortal finger could coax a ring. Also appertaining thereunto was a card bearing the name " Mr. James Dillingham Young."

The " Dillingham " had been flung to the breeze during a former period of prosperity when its possessor was being paid thirty dollars per week. Now, when the income was shrunk to twenty dollars, the letters of "Dillingham" looked blurred, as though they were thinking seriously of contracting to a modest and unassuming *D*. But whenever Mr. James Dillingham Young came home and reached his flat above he was called "Jim" and greatly hugged by Mrs. James Dillingham Young, already introduced to you as Della. Which is all very good.

Della finished her cry and attended to her cheeks with the powder rag. She stood by the window and looked out dully at a gray cat walking a gray fence in a gray back yard. Tomorrow would be Christmas Day, and she had only one dollar and eighty-seven cents with which to buy Jim a present. She had been saving every penny she could for months, with this result. Twenty dollars a week doesn't go far. Expenses had been greater than she had calculated. They always are. Only one dollar and eighty-seven cents to buy a present for Jim. Her Jim. Many a happy hour she had spent planning for something nice for him. Something fine and rare and sterling — something just a little bit near to being worthy of the honor of being owned by Jim.

There was a pier glass between the windows of the room. Perhaps you have seen a pier glass in an eight-dollar flat. A very thin and very agile person may, by observing his reflection in a rapid sequence of longitudinal strips, obtain a fairly accurate conception of his looks. Della, being slender, had mastered the art.

Suddenly she whirled from the window and stood before the glass. Her eyes were shining brilliantly, but her face had lost its color within twenty seconds. Rapidly she pulled down her hair and let it fall to its full length.

Now, there were two possessions of the James Dillingham Youngs in which they both took a mighty pride. One was Jim's gold watch that had been his father's and his grandfather's. The other was Della's hair. Had the Queen of Sheba lived in the flat across the air shaft, Della would have let her hair hang out the window some day to dry just to depreciate Her Majesty's jewels and gifts. Had King Solomon been the janitor, with all his treasures piled up in the basement, Jim would have pulled out his watch every time he passed, just to see him pluck at his beard from envy.

So now Della's beautiful hair fell about her, rippling and shining like a cascade of brown waters. It reached below her knee and made itself almost a garment for her. And then she did it up again nervously and quickly. Once she faltered for a minute and stood still while a tear or two splashed on the worn red carpet.

On went her old brown jacket; on went her old brown hat. With a whirl of skirts and with the brilliant sparkle still in her eyes, she fluttered out the door and down the stairs to the street.

Where she stopped the sign read: Mme. Sofronie. Hair Goods of All Kinds. One flight up Della ran, and collected herself, panting. Madame, large, too white, chilly, hardly looked the "Sofronie."

"Will you buy my hair?" asked Della.

"I buy hair," said Madame. "Take yer hat off and let's have a sight at the looks of it."

Down rippled the brown cascade.

"Twenty dollars," said Madame, lifting the mass with a practiced hand.

"Give it to me quick," said Della.

Oh, and the next two hours tripped by on rosy wings. Forget the hashed metaphor. She was ransacking the stores for Jim's present.

She found it at last. It surely had been made for Jim and no one else. There was no other like it in any of the stores, and she had turned all of them inside out. It was a platinum fob chain, simple and chaste in design, properly proclaiming its value by substance alone and not by meretricious ornamentation — as all good things should do. It was even worthy of the watch. As soon as she saw it she knew that it must be Jim's. It was like him. Quietness and value — the description applied to both. Twenty-one dollars they took from her for it, and she hurried home with the eighty-seven cents. With that chain on his watch Jim might be properly anxious about the time in any company. Grand as the watch was, he sometimes looked at it on the sly on account of the old leather strap that he used in place of a chain.

When Della reached home her intoxication gave way a little

to prudence and reason. She got out her curling irons and lighted the gas and went to work repairing the ravages made by generosity added to love. Which is always a tremendous task, dear friends — a mammoth task.

Within forty minutes her head was covered with tiny, close-lying curls that made her look wonderfully like a truant schoolboy. She looked at her reflection in the mirror long, carefully, and critically.

" If Jim doesn't kill me," she said to herself, " before he takes a second look at me, he'll say I look like a Coney Island chorus girl. But what could I do — oh! what could I do with a dollar and eighty-seven cents? "

At seven o'clock the coffee was made and the frying pan was on the back of the stove hot and ready to cook the chops.

Jim was never late. Della doubled the fob chain in her hand and sat on the corner of the table near the door that he always entered. Then she heard his step on the stair away down on the first flight, and she turned white for just a moment. She had a habit of saying little silent prayers about the simplest everyday things, and now she whispered, " Please God, make him think I am still pretty."

The door opened and Jim stepped in and closed it. He looked thin and very serious. Poor fellow, he was only twenty-two — and to be burdened with a family! He needed a new overcoat and he was without gloves.

Jim stopped inside the door, as immovable as a setter at the scent of quail. His eyes were fixed upon Della, and there was an expression in them that she could not read, and it terrified her. It was not anger, nor surprise, nor disapproval, nor horror, nor any of the sentiments that she had been prepared for. He simply stared at her fixedly with that peculiar expression on his face.

Della wriggled off the table and went for him.

" Jim, darling," she cried, " don't look at me that way. I had my hair cut off and sold it because I couldn't have lived through Christmas without giving you a present. It'll grow out again — you won't mind, will you? I just had to do it. My hair grows awfully fast. Say ' Merry Christmas! ' Jim, and let's be happy.

You don't know what a nice — what a beautiful, nice gift I've got for you."

"You've cut off your hair?" asked Jim laboriously, as if he had not arrived at that patent fact yet even after the hardest mental labor.

"Cut it off and sold it," said Della. "Don't you like me just as well, anyhow? I'm me without my hair, ain't I?"

Jim looked about the room curiously.

"You say your hair is gone?" he said, with an air almost of idiocy.

"You needn't look for it," said Della. "It's sold, I tell you — sold and gone too. It's Christmas Eve, boy. Be good to me, for it went for you. Maybe the hairs of my head were numbered," she went on with a sudden serious sweetness, "but nobody could ever count my love for you. Shall I put the chops on, Jim?"

Out of his trance Jim seemed quickly to wake. He enfolded his Della. For ten seconds let us regard with discreet scrutiny some inconsequential object in the other direction. Eight dollars a week or a million a year — what is the difference? A mathematician or a wit would give you the wrong answer. The Magi brought valuable gifts, but that was not among them. This dark assertion will be illuminated later on.

Jim drew a package from his overcoat pocket and threw it upon the table.

"Don't make any mistake, Dell," he said, "about me. I don't think there's anything in the way of a haircut or a shave or a shampoo that could make me like my girl any less. But if you'll unwrap that package you may see why you had me going a while at first."

White fingers and nimble tore at the string and paper. And then an ecstatic scream of joy; and then, alas! a quick feminine change to hysterical tears and wails, necessitating the immediate employment of all the comforting powers of the lord of the flat.

For there lay the combs — the set of combs, side and back, that Della had worshiped for long in a Broadway window. Beautiful combs, pure tortoise shell, with jeweled rims — just the shade to wear in the beautiful vanished hair. They were expensive combs, she knew, and her heart had simply craved and yearned over them without the least hope of possession. And now, they were hers, but the tresses that should have adorned the coveted adornments were gone.

But she hugged them to her bosom, and at length she was able to look up with dim eyes and a smile and say, " My hair grows so fast, Jim! "

And then Della leaped up like a little singed cat and cried, " Oh, oh! "

Jim had not yet seen his beautiful present. She held it out to him eagerly upon her open palm. The dull precious metal seemed to flash with a reflection of her bright and ardent spirit.

" Isn't it a dandy, Jim? I hunted all over town to find it. You'll have to look at the time a hundred times a day now. Give me your watch. I want to see how it looks on it."

Instead of obeying, Jim tumbled down on the couch and put his hands under the back of his head and smiled.

" Dell," said he, " let's put our Christmas presents away and keep 'em a while. They're too nice to use just at present. I sold the watch to get the money to buy your combs. And now suppose you put the chops on."

The Magi, as you know, were wise men — wonderfully wise men — who brought gifts to the babe in the manger. They invented the art of giving Christmas presents. Being wise, their gifts were no doubt wise ones, possibly bearing the privilege of exchange in case of duplication. And here I have lamely related to you the uneventful chronicle of two foolish children in a flat who most unwisely sacrificed for each other the greatest treasures of their house. But in a last word to the wise of these days let it be said that of all who give gifts these two were the wisest. Of all who give and receive gifts, such as they are wisest. Everywhere they are wisest. They are the Magi.

YUGOSLAVIA
(As Reflected in the United States)

The Yule Log Travels Far

Annie B. Kerr

THE YOUNG MAN stood in front of Kelly's china store and gazed longingly at the dishes displayed so temptingly in the window. One set of blue ware held his attention for some time. It was marked four dollars and ninety-eight cents. Then his eyes wandered to a larger set, cream colored, with a gay border. But the price was eight ninety-eight, and he hurriedly looked again at the blue ones. He was tall, with dark hair and eyes, thinly clad and obviously foreign.

A few years ago he had come from Belgrade with his young wife, Darinka, determined to master the English language and to obtain a degree from Columbia University. After that — he didn't know.

The difficulties and hardships had been many, but success was just around the corner, for in one year more the coveted degree would be his.

At first he had worked at anything he could find — dish-washing in a restaurant, waiting on table, furnace man in various apartment houses near the university. But now he had a steady position — though it didn't pay much —as night man in a Y.W.C.A. building.

Darinka did beautiful Croatian embroidery for some of the big stores on Fifth Avenue. But even so it was hard to make both ends meet.

Living was high in New York City, the expenses at Columbia were great. And then there were the old people back home dependent on their son in America for support in their old age.

Christmas was approaching, was, in fact, only a week off. He had dreaded that season of gaiety and rejoicing with a keen and secret dread.

For there was not enough money in the family pocketbook for even the customary Christmas feast. How Darinka felt he could only guess. She was too plucky to say a regretful word, but there was a homesick longing in her eyes that hurt him every time he looked at her.

He was examining the dishes because he wanted so terribly to buy them for Darinka. They were sorely needed — and so cheap — a whole set for only four ninety-eight! *Perhaps*, this very night, he could come back and get them. He could, that is, if he could conquer the fear that was gripping him and keep the appointment at which he was due just an hour from now.

Last night, in the lobby of the Y.W.C.A., a lady had stopped him and had made the most amazing request.

" Mr. Konstantin " — the Americans all called him by his first name, because his last name was so difficult to pronounce — " Mr. Konstantin, will you do something very special for the Y.W.C.A.? The speaker on our Christmas program tomorrow night is ill and cannot come. We want you to take his place. I am told that the Serbians have very elaborate and interesting Christmas customs. Will you come and tell us about them? We will put another man on night duty, and of course there is a small remuneration. And you will be helping us out of a real difficulty."

When he had stammered that he had never spoken in public in his life — that his English was inadequate — that he really *couldn't* do it, she had skillfully overcome all his objections.

His English was excellent, she said. It wouldn't be hard to speak on a topic with which he was so familiar and there would be many in the audience who knew him and who would help him by asking questions. And so he had consented, and that awful ordeal was almost upon him.

The thought sent cold shivers down his spine. Oh, *why* had he agreed? But there was the Christmas gift for Darinka — the dishes. He didn't know what the " small remuneration " would be, but surely as much as five dollars. He could get them on the way home, for the store was open until eleven o'clock. He had not told Darinka about the lecture. She would be more nervous than he was if she knew about it. He had merely said, " They are letting me off early tonight, so you'd better sit up till I come home."

It was beginning to snow and he was shaking with cold and nervousness. A cup of hot coffee would brace him up. He *couldn't* back out now — he *must* go through with it.

A little later that same evening, Konstantin, who ran the elevator at night, stepped onto the platform of the Y.W.C.A. and was introduced as the lecturer of the evening.

He looked into the upturned faces of what seemed to him a vast throng of people. For one terrible moment panic seized him. Then out of the sea of faces familiar ones emerged and smiled encouragingly. He forgot the grand opening sentence which he had so carefully composed and began simply: " It is a very great privilege to speak to you about my country, Serbia, which since the war is part of Yugoslavia. Because it is Christmas time I will now tell you how we keep Christmas in the village near Belgrade where I was born."

He paused a moment and wiped the perspiration from his forehead, then plunged in again: " In my country we celebrate Christmas on the date January seven, because the Serbians belong to the Eastern Orthodox Church. I will now tell you about one of our great customs. We are the only ones who have the *badnyak*, which you call the Yule log."

He paused, disconcerted by the fact that some listeners were shaking their heads. Then reading their thoughts, he hastened to explain. " Oh, I know there is the Yule log in England. I mean to say that of the Yugloslav countries it is only in Serbia that we have the Yule log. It has traveled far, has it not — from England to Serbia, or perhaps — who knows? — from Serbia to England?

" In my village on the day before Christmas we all go to the forest and cut a big log. There is a little ceremony that my father says, and the log falls and we carry it home. Then Mother and all the girls sing songs of rejoicing and the log is placed in the fireplace. But just the end is in the fire, so it will burn many days. Then Father throws grain and wine on the log so we shall have plenty of grain and wine all the year. On Christmas morning the neighbors come to visit us, and the first ones strike the log so the sparks fly out, and they wish for us as much cattle and horses and sheep and goats and pigs and bees as there are sparks.

" But on Christmas Eve, before we have our supper, Mother puts straw on the floor like the manger — or stable — of the Christ-child. And Father stands by the log fire and throws walnuts into four corners of the room — to send Christmas north, east, south, and west. Then the boys and girls find them and eat them. I cannot think of more to tell you about the *badnyak*, the Yule log."

There was a burst of applause, and he smiled happily at his audience, feeling their interest and approval. Then he continued. " It is now time for our Christmas Eve supper. We are all very hungry, but it is a fast time, so we can have no meat, no milk, no butter, no eggs. But first my father lights a candle and says a prayer: ' Thy birth, O Christ, brings light to our homes and hearts.' Then we take our seats at the table and greet each other — like ' Merry Christmas ' — only we say ' Christ is born ' and another answers, ' He is born indeed! '

" For supper we have soup and fish and salad. The fish is cooked in olive oil. There is one special dish — noodles covered with chestnuts and with prunes cooked in wine. In the middle of the table is a wonderful Christmas cake. It is made in a ring shape and on the edge are little birds sitting, all made of dough with black seeds for their eyes."

His vivid picture brought another burst of applause. He looked anxiously at the clock on the wall opposite. His time was half up, soon it would be over. And then home to Darinka with the dishes.

" But we do not eat the cake now — not till twelve days later on the Day of the Three Kings. And when we eat the cake on that day the birds and the chickens are given some wheat that is on the plate with the cake.

" I forgot about the candle which Father lighted in the beginning. It is kept in the middle of the cake, which you know is made in a circle. This is our first candle. At twelve o'clock on Christmas Day there is a second candle lighted, and then my father blows it out and sticks it in the place where is his grain. If much grain stays on the candle he knows he will have good crops this season. On New Year's Day there is a third candle lighted.

" Well — on Christmas Day we all go to church. And we greet our neighbors and kiss each other three times and forgive each other.

" At home a little pig has been roasting on a rod, and after church we have our great feast, for the fast is over. Chicken soup we have, and noodles, and chicken and ham. Stuffed cabbage — sour like your sauerkraut, but the whole cabbage, not all cut up. And of course, the little pig — oh, so good he is! "

His audience laughed, as he meant them to do. He was learning fast the devices of the popular lecturer.

" There is also a salad, and then the Christmas Day cake — *chesnitsa* ('the Lord's birthday') — made that morning with the first water from the village well, and with a coin inside that brings good luck to the one that gets it. My father cuts a piece for each one and an extra piece for the poor man who may come to the door."

From someone in the audience came a question, " May I ask you how many of these customs are observed here in this country? "

" Well, not so many," he replied. " It is not possible here. But we have the Christmas feast and always the cake. Of course we cannot roast the little pig, so we take goose instead. And sometimes here we throw the straw on the floor. But my wife will not like that. It is too — how do you say — mussy! "

His time was up but there was one thing more he must tell them. They were waiting expectantly. " And now for twelve days the people visit their friends and make merry and play the *tamburitza* — it is like a harp — and sing. They believe it is wrong to work in this holy season. If they do, the souls of the children who were not baptized will harm them, because these souls are free at this time till the baptism of Jesus on Epiphany.

On that day we all go to the river, where the priest blesses the waters and throws the crucifix in and the young men jump in after it. But of course that is not Christmas. And now I have finished. Thank you very much."

He found a chair at the back of the stage and sank down exhausted. That was harder than a whole month of night work, he thought. And yet it was wonderful to realize that all that applause was for him — Konstantin — who ran the night elevator.

Their questions brought him to his feet once more. " No — not so many Serbians in New York. But don't forget that Michael Pupin was a Serbian." " No, there is no Serbian Church here. But we go to the Russian Church. The language we can understand, because we use the old Slavonic in our church and that is much like the Russian."

" The Yugoslav countries? They are Serbia and Montenegro, and many provinces like Croatia and Slovenia and Dalmatia. There are many religions also, Roman Catholic and Mohammedan, some Jews and Greek Catholic as well as Greek Orthodox. But they are all South Slavs, as the name means."

It was after ten when he left the Y.W.C.A. and started for Kelly's store, an envelope containing the " small remuneration " carefully hidden in his vest pocket. His fatigue had disappeared. He walked swiftly and joyously.

" They liked it; they really liked it," he thought. " It was a success; I could do it again. Now I can buy the dishes. I should wait till Christmas, but that I cannot do. I could not hide all this from Darinka. And I want to see her face tonight when she opens the box." Not until he reached the store did he remember to examine the contents of the envelope. There were *three* five-dollar bills instead of one! He drew a long breath and ordered the dishes with the bright border.

" Where shall we send them? " the salesman asked.

" Oh, but I am taking them with me. Hurry, please! " Konstantin could hardly be polite, so anxious was he to reach home with the dishes.

" But they must be carefully packed — and it will be a big box — and very heavy."

" Never mind, I shall take them in a taxi. Hurry, I tell you! "
And then as he waited another idea came into his mind — two
in fact. Why, now we can have a Christmas goose! But two
people could never eat a whole goose. We'll invite that poor
hungry student from the West and give him a feast that he'll
remember all his life!

And so Konstantin from Serbia, poor student at Columbia
University, who ran an elevator at night, rode home in a taxi
for the first time in his life.

The realization that he had just made his debut as a lecturer
made him a bit dizzy. But the tangible proof reposed on the
seat beside him. And there, in their one-room apartment, Darinka was waiting.